The Loki Project

The Loki Project

A NOVEL

BENJAMIN KING

PELICAN PUBLISHING COMPANY
Gretna 2000

Library of Congress Cataloging-in-Publication Data

King, Benjamin, 1944-
The Loki Project : a novel / by Benjamin King.
p. cm.
ISBN 1-56554-283-5 (hc : alk. paper)
1. World War, 1939-1945—Underground movements—Fiction.
2. Hitler, Adolf, 1889-1945—Assassination attempts—Fiction.
3. Atomic bomb—Germany—History—Fiction. I. Title.
PS3561.I473L65 1999
813'.54—dc21 98-55982
CIP

Manufactured in the United States of America

Published by Pelican Publishing Company, Inc.
1000 Burmaster, Gretna, Louisiana 70053

This book is dedicated to
the memory of Glenn Stratton

Acknowledgments

The author would like to thank the following people for their assistance with the writing of *The Loki Project:*

Sandi Gelles-Cole for her superb editing of the manuscript.

Dolores Rogers-Nunis, Pierre Kirk, Joe Fortner, and Jon Rigsby for their helpful suggestions and encouragement.

Last but not least the author would like to thank his wife Loretta, who can still smile after suffering through the history of nuclear physics in the 1930s.

The Loki Project

Nazi Ranks

Reichsführer SS—Rank of Heinrich Himmler, head of the SS, Hitler's personal bodyguard, and the Gestapo, the Nazi Secret Police.

Reichsleiter—Rank of Martin Bormann, the secretary of the Nazi Party.

Gauleiter—District leader, just below the senior Nazi leadership. In 1942 there were 42 Gaue.

Kreisleiter—Circuit or county leader. Main division of the Gau.

Nazi SS and Army ranks, and U.S. equivalent.

SS Ranks	German Army Ranks	U.S. Ranks
SS Mann or Sturmmann	Soldat, Musketier, Jäger	Private
SS Rottenführer	Gefreiter	Corporal
SS Scharführer	Unteroffizier	Sergeant
SS Oberscharführer	Unterfeldwebel	Staff Sergeant
SS Hauptscharführer	Feldwebel	Platoon Sergeant
SS Sturmscharführer	Hauptfeldwebel	First Sergeant
SS Stabsscharführer	Stabsfeldwebel	Sergeant Major
SS Untersturmführer	Leutnant	2nd Lieutenant
SS Obersturmführer	Oberleutnant	1st Lieutenant
SS Hauptsturmführer	Hauptmann, Rittmeister	Captain
SS Sturmbannführer	Major	Major
SS Obersturmbannführer	Oberstleutnant	Lieutenant Colonel
SS Standartenführer	Oberst	Colonel
SS Oberführer	Generalmajor	Brigadier General
SS Brigadeführer	Generalleutnant	Major General
SS Gruppenführer	General der Infanterie	Lieutenant General
SS Obergruppenführer.	Generaloberst	General

CHAPTER 1

JEWISH PHYSICS

Berlin
December 22, 1938

THE ICY BERLIN NIGHT STUNG Dr. Maximilian Lamm's cheeks as he hurried to the Kaiser Wilhelm Institute for a lecture on physics. Despite the late hour and the chill, pedestrians clustered around shop windows filled with Christmas wares to browse. Lamm wished he could join them, because the lecture promised to be boring nonsense. As with most things in Hitler's new Reich, appearance was more important than substance, and for new Party member Lamm, presence at this lecture was essential. He was late and, to save time, he turned down a dimly lighted side street that led to the institute through one of the less prosperous districts of the capital city. A few steps away from a brightly lighted corner of the main street, Lamm froze at the sound of harsh thumps and a loud groan. Not more than ten feet away was something about which he'd heard, but never dreamed he would witness personally. Two Storm Troopers were beating someone up. Instead of turning around and escaping into the light, Assistant Professor of Physics Maximilian Lamm instinctively stepped deeper into the shadows, unable to tear his eyes from the scene before him. These were, after all, Nazi Party men doing this, but he couldn't possibly be like them. When he regained his presence of mind, he thought of going for help, but he remained rooted to the spot.

The Storm Troopers' faces were distinct in the glow of a street lamp as they pummeled their victim. One of them was a huge ape-like man with a scar across his nose, while the other was thinner and shorter, with cold, sadistic eyes. The bulk of the larger man hid their victim. The Brownshirts, engrossed in their work, took no notice of Lamm. Even if they had, they would not have stopped. No one interfered with men like these. It wasn't healthy. The smaller Storm Trooper held their victim, while the huge one smashed his fists into the man's body and face.

"Please stop," the man begged several times before he fell silent.

The big Storm Trooper kept punching until he grew tired and let his arms drop to his sides. Letting the victim slide to the ground, the small one kicked the motionless body in the torso and the head until he, too, grew tired. Exhaling a cloud of breath from his exertion, he bent over, took the victim's wallet from his coat, and removed a wad of bills. Stuffing the money into his pocket, he tossed the wallet onto the still unmoving shape.

"Hey," the big one protested. "What about my share?"

"Later," the slim one said sharply.

Lamm thought, *This isn't political action—it's robbery. It's wrong.*

The big Storm Trooper spat on the motionless form, as his partner unbuttoned his trousers, shouted, "Merry Christmas, Jew!" and urinated on him. Finished, the Storm Troopers walked away laughing.

Despite the cold, Lamm sweated as he digested what he saw. The man on the sidewalk rolled on his back and opened his eyes to stare at Lamm. He was an old man who was no match for the small Storm Trooper, much less both of them. His bearded face was battered, and blood was pouring from his open mouth to puddle on the paving stones. *I should go for help,* Lamm told himself. Taking a deep breath, he moved hesitantly to the man, whose glassy eyes were staring not at him but at some unknown place in the distance. His lips were split and his features were a barely recognizable bloody pulp. Lamm gagged at the sight of the pummeled flesh and the smell of the blood and the urine and quickly stepped back to keep from vomiting. *How could anyone do such a horrible thing?* The unmoving form lay beneath the door of a boarded-up shop. The sign on the shop read "Abraham Winkelmann, Tailor." Across the sign was painted "Don't buy from Jews!"

Lamm wondered if the motionless heap on the sidewalk was Abraham Winkelmann. He reached for the man's wallet to find out who he was and if he was still alive, but stopped. The Storm Troopers had said he was a Jew, and that meant he was an enemy of the state. Lamm was late for the lecture and needed time to think. *Enemy of the State!* How often had he heard that before? Everyone used it when they were beating up helpless victims. The Freikorps did it right after the war, and the communists did it, too. The Nazis were past masters at it. There was no way to stop it. If you tried, you became an enemy of the state and got pummeled, too. You had to accept it. This was the path the New Germany had to follow to greatness, Party officials insisted. Germany must have its freedom and Adolf Hitler was the man to lead them to it. The Führer's list of successes was already unequaled by any ruler in modern times. The remilitarization of the Rhineland, the Anschluss with Austria, and the occupation of the Sudetenland demonstrated to the world that Germany was the strongest nation on earth. If a few Jews got in the way then it was just too bad for the Jews, wasn't it? Lamm stepped around the pathetic heap on the sidewalk and resumed his rapid stride. He didn't know what caused him to look down, but he stopped, aghast at the trail of bloody footprints from his right shoe. He vigorously scraped the sole of the shoe on the paving stones until no blood was visible. *Filthy Jew,* he thought as he continued his journey.

The nagging thoughts filled his mind, and they would not go away. Lamm distrusted all governments and parties. As a youth he had watched both the Empire and the Republic fall apart while Germany remained. It was hard to believe in parties and governments when fighting other boys for lumps of coal found in the street, lumps of coal that meant the difference between a little warmth and freezing to death in a Berlin tenement. He was smaller than the other boys, and he quickly learned to use his wits rather than his muscles. He also learned the ugly lessons of betrayal. Supposed friends had turned on him to steal a few pfennigs or a loaf of stale bread he got as payment for a day of backbreaking work for a baker. He stood beyond arm's length of other boys and learned to watch their eyes and the way they stood and shifted their weight. That way he could run away as soon as they grabbed for him or threw a punch. He didn't like running, but there was no way he could hope to successfully fight bigger boys. Running was the only practical solution, and Maximilian Lamm learned very quickly to be practical.

The soup kitchens were his salvation. They all wanted something for the soup, so he passed out leaflets for the socialists and wore a placard for the Catholics. He took a little tin bucket and filled it with soup for his father, mother, and sister, who were trying to make ends meet cleaning houses and mending clothes. But the lack of food weakened them all and when the flu epidemic hit in 1919, only the fourteen-year-old Maximilian didn't get sick. Within a week, his father, mother, and sister all died, leaving him to fend for himself. After his family died, he survived because he trusted no one. He was careful to hide the food he had from prying eyes and he was smart enough to find a warm, dry place to sleep.

In the brutal experiences of youth, Lamm's boyhood patriotism transformed itself from loyalty to the government in power to a mystical belief in an indefinable Fatherland that transcended the Kaiser or the Nazis. In Lamm's mind, this mythic Germany was the one his father had fought for in the Great War, and the Germany that Maximilian Lamm chose to serve on his own terms.

Lamm was late, and had to sit in the back of the hall where he could not be seen. There was little to distinguish him from the rest of the academicians in the auditorium. At thirty-three, he was younger and thinner than most of his colleagues, and he still had a full head of light brown hair, which was cut very short. His eyes were hazel, and beneath a straight nose he sported a thin mustache. He was not very tall, but as one of the more brilliant minds at the institute, he was an imposing personality. What set him apart from his colleagues was the small Nazi Party badge on his lapel. Many of his counterparts chided him for joining, insisting the Nazis were a bunch of hooligans and would not last long. Lamm thought they had their heads in the clouds. He had held similar views until November 10, when Germany awoke to find its synagogues burned and gutted. The Jewish population had been fined and was rapidly losing their remaining civil rights. The "Kristalnacht," the night of shattered glass, clearly demonstrated the Nazis' power. Along with that power came the proscription of everything Jewish. Literature, art, music, and science by anyone who was Jewish or part Jewish was labeled degenerate and banned. If that were not enough to demonstrate the power of the new order, the demise of Abraham Winkelmann was. *The Jews,* Lamm thought. *Why was it always the Jews?* The Jews were also the primary reason for the lecture he was attending.

The speaker, Prof. Wilhelm Schiller, was reading his paper denouncing Jewish physics as proposed by the subhuman Einstein. Old and distinguished, Schiller stood at the podium slightly stooped, with a shock of gray hair hovering over his glasses and a gold Nazi Party pin on his lapel. He looked every inch the respected academician he was, but modern atomic theory had left him behind. Unable to grasp new concepts, he had become a willing representative of Nazi science and philosophy. Lamm paid cursory attention to Schiller. The man who interested him most sat on the dais behind the speaker. Erwin von Bartz was also a full professor, but it wasn't evident as he sat erect in the black dress uniform of an SS Sturmbannführer, with its red Nazi armband and a silver insignia on the collar. It was rumored that von Bartz was a personal friend of Reichsführer SS Heinrich Himmler, the third most powerful man in the Reich. Von Bartz's uniformed presence in the hall and the fact that he had been made a professor over Lamm and many others who were senior to him should have convinced Lamm's fellow academicians how powerful the Nazis were, but by and large university people were politically naive and didn't understand what was happening. Von Bartz betrayed no emotion as Schiller spoke, leaving Lamm to wonder if von Bartz agreed with the speaker. It was difficult to see how anyone could.

Schiller's quavering voice was high pitched as he tried to imitate the public speaking techniques of his Führer, Adolf Hitler. "And I must conclude," he shouted, "that we have a sacred duty to reveal the truth about Jewish physics to the world. The discovery of the true atom was made by Niels Bohr, a racial German. The atom is the building block of the Aryan universe, and we cannot have this universe polluted by degenerate theories of deviates like Einstein.

"If, as Einstein and his ilk insist, atoms are not the indivisible foundation of matter, why then has there never been evidence of one object falling through another? The answer is simple. The atom cannot be taken apart, nor will it fall apart! Jewish physics is not science. It is politics aimed at undermining the solid foundation of German thought and German society. We cannot allow these perversions to undermine truth. We who have defeated Jewish pollution in the streets must not allow it to succeed in the classroom. Heil Hitler!" Schiller's arm shot out.

"Heil Hitler!" echoed about a third of the audience, as they stood. Lamm was a little slow, but he also stood up and raised his arm. Looking around, he noticed many of his colleagues leaving in disgust, thinking that a few weeks ago he would have been among them. Soon the "Heils" subsided, and Schiller stepped down from the podium to greet the members of the audience who had gone to the dais to congratulate him on his paper. Lamm was among them.

"My heartiest congratulations on your paper, Herr Professor," Lamm told him. "Are you going to publish your notes?"

Schiller looked surprised as the two shook hands. "I hadn't thought of it," he said.

"You really should," Lamm insisted. "It was truly inspiring."

"You really think so?"

"Of course. Many of us have been misled. There are a lot of people who would benefit from something like this."

"Thank you, Doktor Lamm." Schiller smiled and turned to accept congratulations from someone else.

"I'm happy to see you here tonight, Doktor Lamm," said a voice behind Lamm.

He turned to face a smiling SS Sturmbannführer Erwin von Bartz. The two men shook hands. "Yes, it was a very interesting speech," Lamm replied, skillfully hiding his wariness. One had to be very careful of what one said these days.

Von Bartz smiled blandly. "Doktor Lamm, these are revolutionary times, and we can't let old ideas get in the way of the New Germany." He glanced in Schiller's direction.

"Of course," Lamm agreed, not really clear on what he was agreeing to.

"While traditional universities serve their purpose," von Bartz continued, "what we really need is an organization to ensure that science best serves the interests of the Third Reich. Such an organization would need brilliant and dedicated men."

Lamm nodded. "Yes, I'm sure it would." *Is von Bartz trying to tell me something?* Lamm wondered.

"When I was a doctoral candidate, I attended your lecture on absolutes in the universe. It had a great influence on me."

"It did?" Lamm smiled graciously. "I am flattered."

"It's not flattery, Herr Doktor," von Bartz said seriously. "These are difficult days, and very few can recognize those absolutes or the truth. It is up to the party to guide them. You are very good at explaining these things and the Reich has great need of people who can do that. Well, I must greet some other guests. Have a merry Christmas. Heil Hitler."

"Heil Hitler," Lamm replied, with his arm outstretched. He put his arm down and watched von Bartz mingle with the crowd. Lamm was deeply puzzled. In the lecture von Bartz referred to, Lamm had suggested that there might be universal laws and principles which scientists should look for, but never absolutely stated there were any. Was von Bartz speaking scientifically or philosophically? It was all very confusing, but von Bartz's statement that few could recognize the truth was unfortunately correct, and Lamm wondered if von Bartz really understood the implications of his own statement. The whole business of making science subordinate to political doctrine bothered Lamm. It had bothered him for some time.

The assistant professor put on his coat and headed for the door. From the front of the hall, SS Sturmbannführer Erwin von Bartz watched him leave. Von Bartz had more than a passing interest in Lamm. The Sturmbannführer intended to make himself the arbiter of all science in the Third Reich. Once he established himself, no one would be able to make an experiment or write a paper without his permission. He had taken the first step toward that goal by using Dr. Schiller to espouse the party line at the university. Party officials were pleased, but a large part of the audience had paid no attention to the old scientist. What von Bartz needed was someone young and brilliant to enhance his credibility, and Maximilian Lamm was such a man. With the assistant professor working for him, von Bartz could easily achieve his goal. Lamm was not only intelligent, but he knew which way the political wind was blowing, and that was a rare combination in an academician. The fact that Lamm was already a member of the Nazi Party made it even better. Yes, he would definitely recruit Lamm, and for that von Bartz needed to see Heinrich Himmler.

Unaware of the SS officer staring at his back, Lamm stepped into the clear night and inhaled deeply to fill his lungs with cold air. He felt much better. Not far away children were singing Christmas carols. In the nineteenth-century Gothic stone building across the way, all the windows were dark except for one, brightly lighted on the second floor. Lamm smiled wryly. On this cold evening, Prof. Otto Hahn and his assistant were writing their report. Three days before, Hahn and his team had done the impossible by splitting uranium atoms into barium and lanthanum atoms. With only simple equipment like test tubes and beakers, they had done what people in other countries had failed to do with cyclotrons. Unnoticed by the likes of Professor Schiller, the world had slipped silently into the atomic age. Lamm, one of the few who understood the significance of Hahn's discovery, gazed at the window. This was the future and he wanted . . . no . . . *needed* to be a part of it, and he wasn't about to let the likes of Schiller get in his way. He stared at the window for a few seconds wondering if von Bartz knew about and understood the significance of Hahn's discovery. Then, he turned away to continue his musings on the way to the subway station.

In his early youth, Lamm had been too busy trying to survive to worry about abstract things like physics, but shortly after his parents and sister died, he discovered he had an uncle, his mother's estranged brother, Sigmund. Lamm never learned the reason for the estrangement, because his uncle was as silent about the subject as his mother. Once he learned that Sigmund was willing to take him in, the young boy was reticent to ask about this, lest it might offend his benefactor and make him change his mind.

Sigmund, a science teacher in a high school near Dortmund, betrayed no emotion when he met the shabby boy at the train. There was no embrace, only a handshake before Uncle Sigmund took Maximilian to the small rented house on a treelined street. Lamm was shown the cubicle in which he was to sleep, and could not believe his good fortune. The room was warm and the bed had clean sheets and woolen blankets. Matter-of-factly, Uncle Sigmund explained the rules. Maximilian would clean his room and make his bed. He would wash his hands and face and put his dirty clothes in the hamper for the housekeeper. He would use good table manners, be polite to adults, and study. After this lecture, they had a lunch of chicken soup with liver dumplings, and there was plenty of bread and tea.

Young Maximilian had just entered paradise, and was not about to ruin his good fortune. He followed his uncle's instructions to the letter. The study part was difficult at first, but Uncle Sigmund, who was distant in every other way, was an excellent teacher. The young Maximilian looked upon his uncle's prosperity with awe, and decided it was a worthy goal to pursue. He turned the considerable talents for analysis he learned on the streets of Berlin to mathematics and physics. Once he mastered the rules, those subjects were simple. Maximilian Lamm's teachers had only one word for their pupil—brilliant.

The problem that faced Lamm in Hitler's Berlin was not simple. How did one reconcile the world of Otto Hahn with the world of Prof. Wilhelm Schiller and the Storm Troopers who killed and robbed Abraham Winkelmann? Where did von Bartz fit in the equation? The gnawing uneasiness in Lamm's brain became a conscious thought, and his initial reaction was that this mental reconciliation couldn't be done. *But,* Lamm thought, *I am a scientist. I exist to solve difficult problems.* Thinking furiously, he unconsciously started down the side street where the Storm Troopers had beaten up the old Jew. Stopping abruptly, he wondered if the man was still lying there in his own blood. Unwilling to find out, Lamm retraced his steps. Deep in thought, he walked a block past his subway stop. Backtracking again, he descended the steps into the station to purchase a ticket.

The train came immediately, and at this late hour there were plenty of seats. Lights flickered past as Lamm's thoughts returned to the Jews. The price of strength. Too bad for the Jews. But, was it just the Jews who would suffer? It was easy to stand on a street corner and call them degenerate subhumans, burn their books and paintings, and beat them up, but it didn't address the problem. The Jews weren't stupid beasts. They had survived culturally intact for five thousand years of recorded history. Many of them were positively brilliant. Einstein was Jewish, and the present world of atomic research was based on his theories. He was now in the United States. Lisa Meitner, another Jew, had been Otto Hahn's assistant until the Anschluss made her Austrian passport worthless. She had gone to Sweden.

Where had the others gone—the writers, the musicians, the scientists? They had gone to the United States, Britain, France, and the Soviet Union—all countries hostile to the Reich. Lamm clenched his fist tightly and crushed his ticket. There it was, if one wanted to see it—the problem. The Nazis had made the German nation whole and given it a healthy body, but in the process had sacrificed the German brain. How many of the finest minds in the world had the Nazis driven out of Germany? Dozens? Hundreds? Thousands? How many were Jews? How many had left because of sympathy for the Jews?

Maximilian Lamm left the subway and ascended the stairs to the street. Once again taking a deep breath of cold air for a stimulant, he realized how blind and stupid the Nazis were. How did they expect to keep a healthy body alive without a healthy brain? There was no clear answer. He had to do something, but what? He was an assistant professor, and in the massive Nazi Party he was a nobody. How could he change the tunnel vision of the leaders of the Nazi Party and set the Reich on a new path? Perhaps he could influence von Bartz. He had to try. It was his duty to his mystic Fatherland.

Lamm opened the door to his apartment, and the familiar rooms with their heavy furniture and drapes made him immediately forget the Nazis and the Jews and Germany. Irma, his loving wife, greeted him at the door. Blonde and nearly as tall as Lamm, she had a round face with deep blue eyes. Beneath the small button nose were smiling lips. With a hug and a kiss, Irma helped him off with his coat.

"Was it a good lecture, Liebchen?" she asked solicitously.

"Boring, utterly boring," he replied with a sigh.

"Come have supper, Max," she countered brightly. "You'll feel better."

"Where is Karl?" Lamm asked.

"Your son is in the parlor playing with those new toy soldiers and that cannon that fires those wooden bullets," Irma told him. Her voice was tinged with mild irritation. "They're all over the place."

"Let him play. He'll be back in boarding school soon enough."

"Those things aren't clogging our carpet sweeper," Irma told him.

"Yes, dear, of course." Lamm headed for the parlor.

"Don't get too involved, Max. Supper's ready."

Lamm smiled, nodded, and went into the parlor, where Karl was intently firing at some toy soldiers with the offending cannon. He pressed the trigger and a wooden plug shot across the room. It struck one of the soldiers, and the little figure tottered and fell over.

"You got him!" Lamm cried. It was only then that the little boy in the *Deutsches Jungvolk* uniform noticed his father.

"Papa!" he cried in delight, and jumped up to give his father a hug.

Lamm embraced Karl and kissed him on the cheek. After a moment, Lamm held his son by the shoulders at arm's length. *He favors his mother,* Lamm thought.

"Karl, you're getting taller every day."

"I'm nearly as tall as Mama."

Lamm kissed his forehead. "Pick up your bullets and come to supper."

"But I want to shoot the cannon some more." Karl's face screwed up in disappointment.

"Pick up the bullets and come on," his father repeated. "Your mother is waiting."

"But, Papa . . ."

"When it comes to supper your mother is the boss and you must obey her."

"You don't obey her."

Lamm laughed heartily. "Oh, yes I do. If you only knew the discussion we had about you joining the Jungvolk, you'd know better. As usual, Mama got her way. Now come, let's have supper."

Irma stood in her apron, and when Lamm and his son sat at the table, she brought a large tureen of soup to the table. Lamm watched her ladling out the soup. She was the love and foundation of his life. They had met at Heidelberg when Lamm was doing graduate work, and from the moment he saw Irma, Lamm had been in love with her. And this wasn't the infatuation of a naive young boy. He knew about women. On his fifteenth birthday, Uncle Sigmund had dutifully taken him to the local brothel to begin his education in life, and there had been others since, but the other women in his life were nothing like Irma Oberth. She was blonde and pretty and her blue eyes sparkled. She was happy and radiated a warmth the young graduate student never knew existed. Irma made him feel as no woman had before or since, and he determined to marry her as soon as he had a position at a university. In the following years he never regretted his decision.

At home Irma ruled the roost, and when she made up her mind, there was no sense arguing. He had not wanted Karl to join the *Jungvolk* but instead to concentrate on his studies, but Irma was determined that he should.

"All of his friends are joining," she had said. "Why shouldn't Karl?"

"He needs time to study."

"Max, he's a little boy who needs to be with his friends. You were never a member of a club when you were a little boy, so you don't understand."

That was true. Lamm didn't understand the need to be in a large organization. He never would. When he was growing up, large institutions such as the government, the churches, and the political parties did little to relieve the suffering of the people. The only thing they were good for was what one got out of them. The only reason he joined the Nazi Party was because through it, he might wield some influence. However, if he were going to accomplish anything, he alone would have to do it, not the docile masses of the Party.

Lamm sighed and returned to the present. "How is school, Karl?"

"If you obey orders, it's easy," Karl said with a knowing grin. "The Führer has done great things for Germany, and he will do more. One day the whole world will see his greatness."

"Never mind all that," Irma told them. "You can't do anything for the Führer without a good supper. Eat."

Lamm and Karl smiled at one another and lifted their spoons. It was a good Christmas.

February 8, 1939

When the remaining Jews at the institute were dismissed from their positions, Lamm was shocked that there were so many of them. Most he never knew were Jewish. The vacancies created were filled first by Party members, and Lamm found himself promoted to full professor. Among those dismissed was Prof. Benno Friedmann, who had been Lamm's advisor for his doctoral dissertation. Lamm went to see him on his last day at the institute. Friedmann, tall and distinguished with his shaved head and small goatee, was cleaning out his desk when Lamm arrived at what had been his office. The walls were covered with unfaded patches where diplomas and honors had hung, most of which now lay in the trash bin. Lamm knocked on the door.

"Oh, it's you," Friedmann snapped.

"May I come in, Herr Professor?"

"Why don't you just kick in the door like the rest of your Party members do?"

"Professor, I came to say I'm sorry."

"Hmmph."

"And also to warn you."

"About what? Having my life's work stolen from me? Too late."

"No, you must leave Germany."

"Doktor Lamm, of all of them, I am disappointed in you the most. I never thought you would join these hooligans." His glance at Lamm was as sharp as his tone. There was no softness in memory of their earlier relationship.

Lamm felt the blood rush to his cheeks. Here was a man who had helped him when he needed it most, and the party to which Lamm now swore allegiance had ruined the man's life.

"I came to warn you, Herr Professor." Somehow he had to tell Friedmann about Winkelmann.

"Don't worry. I'm not staying. My family and I are going to stay with my sister in New York. Do you think I'm naive, like some who think things will get better in a few months?"

Lamm made one last attempt to explain. "The Fatherland . . ."

Friedmann cut him off. "The Fatherland? There is no Fatherland. There is only Adolf Hitler and the Nazi Party and before they are through, Germany will be a wasteland."

Overwhelmed by Friedmann's bitterness, Lamm guiltily stepped aside as his former mentor stalked out of the room, giving him one last vicious look. Stepping to the trash bin, Lamm looked at the certificates and plaques that Friedmann had left behind. They were from the most prestigious scientific organizations in the country. Friedmann, an officer in many of them, had been expelled because he was a Jew.

Until the encounter with Friedmann, it had been easy for Lamm to deal with everything, including the Storm Troopers beating Winkelmann. He respected and looked up to Friedmann, and they had enjoyed a cordial relationship. The hatred Friedmann now had for him unnerved Lamm. How many "Friedmanns" were there? Despite Nazi propaganda, they were native Germans, and it wasn't wise to tear a German from his Fatherland. It leaves an emptiness in him that must be filled. But what fills the emptiness? Hatred? A desire for revenge? All those brilliant people thirsting for vengeance was a chilling thought.

Lamm forced himself to concentrate on preparing the upcoming undergraduate exam. His current assistant didn't have the draft examination on his desk on time. He rang his secretary on the intercom.

"Frau Dorfmann."

"Yes, Herr Professor."

"Tell Herr Steiber to come to my office immediately!"

"Yes, Herr Professor."

Lamm's previous assistant had been brilliant and terribly efficient, but the young man was a Jew and had also been forced to leave. *Damn it!* Lamm threw down his pencil. *The Jews!* He was sick of them. If they weren't so damned smart, you could shoot them all and forget it. Lamm ran his fingers through his hair as Bertrand Steiber cautiously opened the door.

"You wanted to see me, Herr Professor?"

"Come in," Lamm commanded.

Steiber, a pudgy, pale young man of twenty-two, hesitated before he stepped inside. "Yes, Herr Professor?"

"Where are the questions for the next undergraduate exam?" Lamm asked sharply.

Steiber put his hands together and looked down. "They aren't finished, Herr Professor."

"I know they aren't finished, Herr Steiber." Lamm raised his voice. "We wouldn't be having this conversation if they were finished. We have to give the exam in two weeks and I haven't reviewed the questions yet."

"Over the holidays I was with my fiancée in Mainz and didn't get a chance to work on it, Herr Professor," came the lame reply.

"Is your fiancée going to recommend you for your degree when the time comes?" Lamm asked, his voice growing louder.

"N . . . no, Herr Professor."

"Then you'd better get your priorities straight!" Lamm was a decibel away from shouting. "I will not tolerate this sort of incompetence. Do you understand?"

"Y . . .yes, Herr Professor." Steiber was sweating.

"Have an exam with decent questions on my desk in two days or you'll be a street sweeper instead of a physicist. Do you understand me?"

"Yes, Herr Professor." Steiber swallowed and nodded.

"Then get started!" the professor snapped.

Steiber was gone in a flash.

Lamm sat down at his desk and sighed. Steiber was a twit. Before Lamm could turn to other business, Helga Dorfmann, his secretary, knocked on the door and slowly opened it. An attractive woman in her early thirties, with a particularly nice figure, she was completely intimidated by Lamm and was terrified of bothering him after he had reprimanded one of his students.

"Excuse me for the interruption, Herr Professor . . ."

"Yes, Helga, what is it?" He made no attempt to hide his irritation.

"There is someone here to see you," she said timidly.

"Does he have an appointment?"

"No, Herr Professor." Lamm failed to notice her reluctance to dismiss the visitor on her own.

"Then send him away," Lamm said irritably. "I'm busy."

Helga made a funny face. "Er . . . he's from the SS—an officer."

Lamm knitted his brow. He didn't know anyone in the SS. "Who is he, Helga?"

"He gave me his card," the secretary said, quickly handing von Bartz's card to the professor, who stared at it.

"I wonder what he wants," Lamm mused. "Send him in."

Helga left the room to usher a smiling von Bartz into the office.

"Very good of you to see me on such short notice, Professor Lamm."

Lamm smiled in return and raised his arm. "It is good to see you again. Heil Hitler."

"Heil Hitler."

The two men shook hands, and Lamm motioned von Bartz to a comfortable chair. As Lamm moved his own chair so the desk would not be between them, he noticed that von Bartz had been promoted in the SS.

"Congratulations, Herr Obersturmbannführer," Lamm said, stressing the "ober."

Von Bartz beamed. "I see you, too, have had a well-deserved promotion, Professor Lamm."

"It was most welcome," Lamm replied. "To what do I owe the

honor of this visit, Herr Doktor? Am I speaking to Doktor von Bartz, my honored colleague in physics, or Obersturmbannführer von Bartz of the SS?"

Von Bartz smiled warmly. "Both, as a matter of fact, Herr Professor. Tell me, what is your opinion of the intellectual situation in Germany today?"

Automatically suspicious, Lamm raised an eyebrow. *There is a loaded question if ever there was one,* he thought. He looked at von Bartz, using all his analytical skills to assess the situation he was in. He knew he had to be very careful and follow the Party line. He pondered von Bartz's question a few seconds and stated, "Dangerous."

The answer surprised von Bartz, and Lamm hoped he was on the right track.

"Dangerous?" Von Bartz was obviously puzzled. "I don't understand."

Lamm paused. He would have to think quickly and play to von Bartz's prejudices. "We are in a period of transition." He moved his chair forward. "We swept the Jew from the streets, and now we have swept him from the classroom. But what do we do about the myths and ideas that remain? It might take generations to root them out. And there's quite another matter."

"Which is?" von Bartz asked, still not sure what Lamm's point was.

"How many Jews stole perfectly valid ideas from true Germans."

Von Bartz blinked as if someone had popped a flash bulb in a dark room and nodded in agreement. "Professor, I am in awe of the way you see problems so clearly. Which is why I have the greatest respect for your work." Secretly, von Bartz was relieved. Lamm was politically more astute than he thought. He would be a great asset to von Bartz's new organization.

"Thank you." Relieved he had not said anything wrong, Lamm decided to be congenial. "Would you like a cup of coffee, Herr Doktor?"

"Yes, thank you."

Lamm rose and went to the door to get some time to think. "Helga, bring us two cups of coffee, please."

"Yes, Herr Professor."

Von Bartz continued before Lamm sat down again, "As I was saying, I have always had the greatest respect for your work, and I feel your promotion was long overdue. However, that is not why I am here. I have recently been appointed to the Central Bureau for Race and Settlement, which was organized to ensure that SS marriages take place between persons of pure Aryan blood."

A knock interrupted him. "Coffee?" Helga asked.

"Ah yes, come in," Lamm told her.

As Helga served the two cups of coffee and gracefully left, von Bartz watched her with more than passing interest. He poured milk into his coffee and tasted it.

"Very good!"

"That's one of the reasons she stays," Lamm said with a sly look. "Her typing isn't that good."

Von Bartz glanced at the door and smiled knowingly. *So,* Lamm thought, looking at von Bartz's wedding ring, *he's a ladies' man. That might be useful information in the future.* Lamm found that sort of attitude distasteful. He was happily married to Irma, and was not a philanderer.

Still smiling, von Bartz continued in an expansive vein. "We have eliminated Jewish pollution from the Fatherland, we have made the streets free of Jews, and we have ensured that Jews no longer corrupt the fabric of our everyday life. But as you said, much of the poison remains behind. It has to be rooted out."

"That, Herr Doktor, will be a formidable task," Lamm replied.

"Exactly, Herr Professor." Von Bartz struck the table with his fist for emphasis and in so doing spilled coffee from his cup. He continued. "Don't think that the Reichsführer doesn't recognize the size and complexity of the task. It is only his dedication to the Führer and the ideas of racial purity that have allowed us to get this far in our struggle. However, he knows that our work has just begun. That is why he authorized the creation of the Racial Science Section under the Central Bureau. Its responsibility is to cleanse German science and teaching of Jewish influence."

Lamm looked at his guest seriously, then said, "I am indeed honored that you should discuss these things with me, Herr Obersturmbannführer. But, if you'll forgive me, why are you taking valuable time away from such important duties to see me?"

Von Bartz smiled broadly. Lamm was interested. Now was the time to proffer the bait. "Professor, you are the one man I know who sees everything clearly. As soon as I received this assignment, I remembered our discussion after Professor Schiller's speech last December. The Reichsführer told me I could select my own assistant, so naturally I thought of you."

"I?" Lamm stammered in genuine surprise. "I—I am overwhelmed that you should think of me. But I am only a professor of physics."

"Yes, and one whose brilliance should have been recognized long ago. Every time I bring up a subject, you have already thought of it. Not only that, you analyze a problem and present the solution with remarkable clarity and logic. Herr Professor, I need you, and what's more, the Reich needs you." Von Bartz paused, reached into his briefcase, and pulled out a copy of *Naturwissenschaften,* the prestigious scientific journal. A brief glance at the cover told Lamm it was the January 6, 1939 issue, in which Hahn had written an article about splitting the atom. It certainly wouldn't sit well with the likes of Schiller, but why did von Bartz have it?

"Have you seen this?" von Bartz asked.

Lamm took the magazine and leafed through it to gain some time. "Yes, I have. I presume you're referring to Dr. Hahn's article?"

"Precisely," von Bartz replied. "This article of Hahn's has raised some serious questions within the Party."

"It has?" Lamm wondered why.

"There is even talk of having the Gestapo arrest him," von Bartz continued.

"What?" It was Lamm's turn to be surprised.

"You understand the concern about Jewish physics expressed by Professor Schiller last December . . ." Von Bartz let the phrase hang.

Quickly, Lamm told himself. *Think!* "Hahn is full-blooded German, and exceedingly honest." He was also terribly naive, Lamm knew, but left that out. Lamm felt a tinge of desperation. He couldn't let them arrest one of Germany's greatest minds. "Why haven't we considered the alternative?" Lamm asked suddenly.

"Alternative?" This time it was von Bartz's turn to be puzzled. "Please explain." The Obersturmbannführer picked up his coffee cup, leaned back in his chair, and watched Lamm intently.

"The Jews are not stupid, Herr Doktor," Lamm began. "The Führer has said so, has he not?"

"Yes," von Bartz agreed.

"What if . . ." Lamm paused for effect. "What if there was as great a Jewish conspiracy in science as there is in economics and art?"

"Conspiracy?" Von Bartz knotted his brows. "I don't follow you."

"Hahn is German, and what he has done is unlock some of the secrets of nature. It is something the Jews only theorize about. The reason I suspect this is the amount of energy released during these fissions. It's millions of times more than the energy needed to begin it. So, if you have millions of fissions, you get a lot of power. Do you know what that would mean to us? Limitless energy. We wouldn't have to concern ourselves with oil from Rumania or coal from the United States."

"But what about this conspiracy?" von Bartz injected. As a long-time member of the Nazi Party, he knew his superiors were much more interested in cabals and intrigue than science.

"Ah, yes." Lamm nearly smiled. If one could tie something into the "Great Jewish Conspiracy," the Nazis were easily led. "I don't believe for a minute that all those Jews were unable to do what Hahn did. They were waiting. They were waiting for the triumph of international Zionism before they used it. Until now they have deliberately misled honest scientists throughout the world and have sent them down the wrong track. Look at us. Only now are we beginning to realize how devious they are. If it hadn't been for the Führer, who knows what would have happened to us as a nation? In science Hahn has foiled their schemes. International Jewry has cyclotrons and billions of marks in sophisticated equipment, and yet, they have been unable to do with that equipment what Doktor Hahn has done with a simple apparatus. If that is not a demonstration of Aryan genius, I don't know what is. But one thing still puzzles me."

"What's that?" Von Bartz was having difficulty following Lamm's rapid train of thought.

"There is, no doubt, a pattern, and this is a single aspect of a much greater problem." Lamm looked sternly at von Bartz. The SS Obersturmbannführer sat silently, his blue eyes blank. *My God, I've lost him,* Lamm thought. Suddenly an expression of understanding spread across von Bartz's countenance.

"Then you are saying the Jews are twisting scientific doctrine to dominate the Aryan race?"

Lamm breathed a sigh of relief. Von Bartz had caught on. "Isn't this proof?" Lamm asked. "Who knows where all this will lead? If we don't expose this, they could turn the entire world against us."

Von Bartz was now smiling broadly. Lamm was an absolute genius. Not only did he understand the scientific aspects of Hahn's discovery, but he could put it in terms that even the Gestapo found acceptable. The professor was definitely the man he wanted. Von Bartz was so delighted his voice went up nearly an octave. "That is why I want you for my assistant," he told Lamm. "You understand these things more clearly than anyone I know."

"Except you, Herr Doktor."

Von Bartz shook his finger at him. "This is no time for false modesty, Herr Professor. Germany needs you and your clarity of thought. The entire matter of the Jewish conspiracy in science is vital to us. Think what would have happened if we'd arrested Dr. Hahn. It's shocking. The foremost Aryan genius under arrest for exposing the Jews. That is devilishly clever of those bastards. But you, Professor Lamm, can stop all this. What do you say?"

Lamm was suspicious of von Bartz's motives, and his first impulse was to turn him down. Then he thought, *I want to do something and I just saved Hahn's life. If I were close to the center of power I might be able to do much more. I might even be able to experiment with atomic physics.* "When you put it that way, how can I refuse?"

"Good," von Bartz said. "In order not to upset the Reichsführer's sensibilities, you will be accepted into the SS as an Untersturmführer."

This time it was Lamm's turn not to understand. Von Bartz looked at the surprise on Lamm's face and laughed. "Oh, don't worry, Professor. You won't have to go through all that combat training. It's been arranged. There will be, of course, a few formalities, but we've already checked on your background. Your and your wife's families have been pure German for over two hundred years. You will receive pay as an Untersturmführer, plus an allowance for research. It's more money than you make now and considerably more prestige."

"The money is only secondary," Lamm insisted. What was one more lie among so many?

"Excellent," von Bartz said, extending his hand. "As soon as the paperwork is approved you will be inducted into the SS. By that time we should have a suitable office."

CHAPTER 2

THE RACIAL SCIENCE SECTION

Berlin
March 13, 1939

IT TOOK THREE WEEKS FOR Lamm's paperwork to get through SS headquarters. When he was notified that he was accepted, he began having second thoughts about joining the SS. The morning he was to be picked up and taken to Lichterfeld Barracks, he was so nervous that he needed every ounce of self-control to project an appearance of calm routine. His stomach was so knotted he was unable to concentrate on the morning paper, and his hand shook ever so slightly when he sipped his coffee. *Joining the SS was crazy,* he thought. *How could I have been so foolhardy? I know what the Brownshirts are capable of, and the SS even brought them to heel. What must they be like?* The thought made Lamm shudder. He was a teacher, not a soldier or a politician. How could he possibly belong in the SS? He was soberly aware that he was sailing in uncharted and dangerous waters where there was no safe haven. His idea of going to South America surfaced again. With its large German enclaves, it was the logical place to go. He wished there were someone with whom he could dispassionately discuss the alternative, but there was no one he could readily trust. He had always been able to discuss things with Friedmann, but the Jewish professor was no longer his friend.

It was impossible to discuss the issue with Irma on the level that he wanted to. He had tried the previous evening.

"Sweetheart," he had asked over supper, "do you think I should join the SS?"

"Of course, darling," Irma gushed. "It's a great honor. You'll be around the Führer and Himmler and all those marvelous people. And didn't you say you would be making more money? Just think, Max. We can get new drapes."

New drapes. Lamm didn't pursue the conversation further. Irma's universe was their home. She loved her husband and her son, and dutifully made their home as comfortable as possible. The outside world hardly mattered unless it impinged on those things Irma held most dear, and for most of her life it hadn't. Irma had never known privation or hardship or betrayal. She was born when her parents, Franz and Maria Oberth, were in their mid-thirties. She was their only child, and they doted on her. Her father was a music teacher at the university in Heidelberg, and her mother taught literature. Their world centered on the subjects they taught and was far removed from forces moving to destroy Europe. When the war came her father was too old to serve at the front. He was put in a military orchestra that entertained high-ranking officers close to the university, so he never strayed far from home. Irma was six when the war began, and her memories of the great struggle were her daddy in his nice uniform bringing her an occasional sweet. When the war ended, Franz Oberth still had his position at Heidelberg, so despite the depression, they were fairly comfortable. Being an academic town, Heidelberg escaped much of the violence of the Spartacists and the Freikorps, so Irma's *Weltanschauung* was that of her parents and Heidelberg.

When Lamm met Irma at Heidelberg, she represented everything the emotion-starved young man craved. When he was accepted at the Kaiser Wilhelm Institute, he proposed. The Oberths liked Lamm and approved of his intentions, but wanted to meet his family, which meant Uncle Sigmund. His uncle dutifully traveled to Heidelberg, where he got on quite well with the Oberths, who gave Lamm and Irma their blessing. When the visit was over Lamm saw his uncle to the station and thanked him. As they shook hands, Uncle Sigmund told him solemnly, "She's a nice girl, Maximilian. Her parents are twits."

Lamm married Irma after a three-month engagement, and never

regretted it. She gave his life the warmth and happiness he had never known. Her laugh was like music and their son was the most beautiful child on earth. She built an emotional cocoon around their family life that he treasured, but now he was aware of the forces that were tearing at the new Germany, and she could not see it. Lamm had not felt so isolated since his parents died. Yes, South America was the best chance. Perhaps they could go there on vacation with Karl and attempt to stay.

"Irma, what would you say to a vacation in South America?"

"Darling, we always go to Chiemsee. Why should we go all the way to South America?" Irma darted to and fro, singing little songs while she fussed over him. "Darling, you've hardly touched your breakfast. Don't you like it?"

"I'm just a little nervous."

"But why?"

"I want to make a good impression. Do you remember when I went to defend my doctoral dissertation?"

"You were shaking," she giggled. "But you did so well. You got an appointment right away thanks to that nice Professor Friedmann. Maybe you should talk about it with him."

"I can't. He's leaving the country."

"Why?"

"He is Jewish, Irma."

"Oh, he seemed so nice. Well, it's all for the best. They don't really belong here, the Jews."

Lamm sighed and retired with his paper to the parlor, to await his fate in his favorite chair. Irma was straightening the absurdly large gold-framed portrait of Hitler she had recently purchased. *I'm trapped,* he thought, *and everyone is crazy except me.*

"He's so handsome," Irma sighed.

"Who?" Lamm asked, before he realized she was talking about Hitler. He was amazed at the Germans' capacity for self-deception. It was true that Hitler was a great statesman. Since Hindenburg's death he had proven that to everyone. But a tall, blonde, Nordic god, he wasn't.

"The Führer, of course. He has done wonderful things for Germany and for us."

"He has?"

"Of course, Liebchen. After Hitler came to power you became a full professor with a raise. Now in the SS, you'll make even more money and have greater prestige because you'll be near the Führer and Reichsführer Himmler."

"You're right," Lamm agreed. From Irma's point of view, the Nazis had done a lot of good. There were many other Germans who felt the same way. Lamm wondered if he were the only one looking behind the facade of the Third Reich.

"Perhaps Karl should join the SS," Irma mused.

"I suppose it wouldn't do any harm, dear," Lamm replied absent-mindedly. "But that's years from now. He should go to the university first."

Lamm was still considering South America. *Maybe I can get a position in Argentina and send for them,* he thought. There were a lot of Germans in Argentina. They would be comfortable there. Then it suddenly occurred to him. How would he do atomic research in South America? The countries in South America were all poor and backward and none of the universities had the facilities that existed in Germany. He could never become a great physicist in Argentina. The knock on the door ended all speculation. *It is the SS,* Lamm thought. *The die is cast, and like Caesar I am crossing the Rubicon. From this point on there can be no turning back.* Irma opened the door for a serious, tall, blonde young man in the all-too-familiar black uniform.

"Heil Hitler!" the young man said, with his arm outstretched.

"Heil Hitler!" Irma replied. "Won't you come in?"

"Thank you. This is Professor Lamm's residence?" he inquired stiffly.

"Yes," Irma replied.

"I am Hauptsturmführer Dietrich Weiler. I am to escort Professor Lamm to Lichterfeld Barracks."

The professor rose from his chair and introduced himself. Weiler towered over him. "You're early. Can I offer you a cup of tea or coffee, Herr Hauptsturmführer?" Lamm asked.

Hauptsturmführer Weiler relaxed and smiled. "Yes, thank you. Tea, please."

Lamm motioned to a comfortable chair and Weiler sat down.

"Quite frankly, Professor, you're much younger than I had imagined."

"Ah, all professors are graying old men with beards."

Weiler smiled in mild embarrassment. "Quite frankly, there aren't many professors in the SS."

"How long have you been in the SS, Herr Hauptsturmführer?"

"Five years, Herr Professor. All of it in the Leibstandarte Adolf Hitler."

Lamm hoped he appeared suitably impressed.

"That's the Führer's personal bodyguard, is it not?" Irma asked.

Lamm and Weiler turned as Irma brought the tea. "Yes, Frau Lamm," Weiler said. "It is quite an honor." He took the cup. "Thank you. But it is not only serving the Führer that is so wonderful. It is being in the forefront of the New Order. I was in the Rhineland, Austria, and the Sudetenland. The people were hysterical with joy as we marched in. They threw flowers before us. You cannot imagine. They were liberated and returned to the Reich at last. We Germans are so fortunate to have Adolf Hitler as our Führer."

Lamm forced a smile.

"Do you think our Karl could get into the SS?" Irma asked seriously.

"Of course, Frau Lamm."

Lamm hid his irritation. He wanted his son to finish his studies, but Irma would have her way as usual. They made small talk until Weiler checked his watch.

"Excuse me, Herr Professor," the SS officer said. "It is time to go."

"Of course. I'll get my coat," Lamm told him. He went into his room.

"Is your family from Berlin, Herr Weiler?" Irma asked. "Oh excuse me, Hauptsturmführer."

"No, Frau Lamm. They are in Stuttgart."

"That's a long way. Our son is at boarding school, so we know how it is being away from home. Please come and visit us again."

"It would be an honor, Frau Lamm."

As they left the apartment and walked down the steps, Lamm felt the eyes of the other apartment dwellers upon him, even though none were visible. They were probably wondering if he was leaving on business or being arrested. They would ask Irma, and she would no doubt tell them that he, Maximilian Lamm, was to be the Führer's new scientific deputy.

"Your wife is a very warm person, Herr Professor," Weiler said, helping him into the car.

Lamm grinned. "You'd better watch it, Herr Hauptsturmführer," he said with mock seriousness. "Irma may adopt you whether your family likes it or not."

Weiler laughed softly. "After the combat training they put us through, I think I'd like that."

"Combat training? I thought all you did was provide protection for the Führer, like a palace guard."

"Oh, we do that, but Reichsführer Himmler also wants us prepared for war. It wouldn't be right if Germany went to war and its National Socialist soldiers stayed home. That's why we're training to be a Panzergrenadier regiment."

"I see," Lamm said, as Weiler gave instructions to the driver. "I hope they don't have me training on tanks."

Weiler laughed. "Hardly. You will be a member of Reichsführer Himmler's personal staff as a science advisor, so you will not be in the SS defense troops. You're a very important man, Professor."

Lamm smiled. "I feel like an old horse that's moving a little bit too slowly for the New Germany."

"No need to worry. Once you're near the Führer and Reichsführer Himmler, everything becomes crystal clear."

"Yes, I'm sure it will be." Lamm wondered if Schiller was Weiler's idea of crystal clear.

They spent the rest of the trip in silence. Lamm perused the scenery. The driver was a heavy-set man named Schmidt who looked more like a beast than a soldier, despite the neat black uniform. His tiny cold eyes reminded Lamm of the Storm Troopers who had beaten Abraham Winkelmann. All he lacked was the scar. On Schmidt's sleeve was the silver chevron that indicated he had been a member of the Party since before 1933. Lamm tried not to prejudge, but it was obvious that Schmidt, like the two Storm Troopers, was an unthinking, unfeeling brute, the cornerstone of the New Germany.

Lichterfeld Barracks was once the home of the Rifle Battalion of the Kaiser's Guard, and had been the scene of pomp and grandeur unknown to regiments of lesser reputation. Raised in 1813 to fight the War of Liberation against Napoleon, the Guard Rifle Battalion had fought in every German war until they were disbanded at the end of the Great War. Now once again the barracks housed the personal guard of the leader of the German nation, and many saw this as a logical progression. After all, a guard is a guard, a view few older army officers shared. The Guard Rifle Battalion had fought the

French, the Danes, and the Austrians, while the SS had won its spurs slaughtering the victims of the Röhm Putsch during the "Night of the Long Knives" in 1934. For these brave and noble acts, they were designated Schutzstaffel, or more conveniently, "SS," for Security Staff of the Führer. Adolf Hitler's personal guard was christened Leibstandarte Adolf Hitler, or Bodyguard Regiment Adolf Hitler.

The new guard announced its presence in Lichterfeld in true Nazi style. Above the main building was perched a huge golden eagle, wings outspread, grasping a swastika in its talons. Beneath the wreath-encircled swastika was printed "LEIBSTANDARTE ADOLF HITLER" in golden two-foot-high letters. As they drove through the gates and past the parade ground, Lamm watched hundreds of impressive young men in black uniforms at their drills. The car pulled up in front of the dispensary.

Weiler grinned at Lamm's puzzled expression. "It's for your physical," he reassured him.

Schmidt opened the door for Lamm, and Lamm went up the stairs. Like everyone else, the doctor and his aides wore the SS uniform. He gave the professor a thorough physical. After checking Lamm's heart and lungs, he took blood and urine samples, then washed his hands and put on a pair of rubber gloves. "Bend over and spread your cheeks," the doctor said. Lamm complied and groaned until the ordeal was over.

"All right, get dressed," the doctor finally said. "Except for the fact that you smoke too much, you're in good shape, Herr Professor. Unless the blood or urine show something, welcome to the SS."

"Heil Hitler!" Lamm said and waddled uncomfortably out of the dispensary.

"I see you have met Doktor Haufnitz," Weiler said with a grin.

Lamm just looked at him.

"It is rumored in the Leibstandarte that doctors' hands are measured before they are inducted. Those with small hands are automatically rejected. Haufnitz reputedly has the largest hands of all," Weiler said with a chuckle.

Lamm tried to smile. "I believe it. What's next?"

"Your tattoo," Weiler said matter-of-factly.

"My what?" Lamm exclaimed.

"Your tattoo. Everyone in the SS has his blood type tattooed inside his upper left arm. It's an identification mark in case of accident or injury."

"No, I refuse," Lamm said adamantly. "I am not a drunken sailor on his first shore leave."

"Herr Professor, I have my orders. Should I call Schmidt?"

And if I refuse once more, he'll beat me to a bloody pulp, Lamm mused. "All right."

The tattooist was swift and efficient and, Lamm had to admit, it didn't hurt too much. After the tattoo, Weiler took Lamm to the tailor for his uniform.

"Everything will be deducted from your pay, Herr Professor," Weiler explained, "but don't worry. They only take a little each payday. It doesn't come out all at once."

The tailor shop was unlike any Lamm had ever seen. Everything in it was SS. Lamm never dreamed that there were so many different types of uniforms. First there was the black dress uniform with its coat, tie, and leather belt. Then there was the black dress cap and the black helmet. In addition to the uniform, there were the insignia, armbands, dagger, and sword. Next there was the field uniform, and each uniform had to have its own overcoat and boots. The tailor measured the professor for everything in half an hour, with his assistant making constant notes.

"It will take an hour or two to finish, Herr Untersturmführer," the tailor told Lamm, addressing him by his SS rank. It took a moment for Lamm to realize that the tailor meant him.

"Excellent," Weiler said. "What do you say to an early lunch?"

"I suppose we are going to have hardtack and beans?" Lamm said, not knowing what to expect.

Weiler laughed good-naturedly. "No, Herr Professor, but I wish we were, just to see the expression on your face."

They walked across the parade ground to the Officer's Mess. There was, of course, a huge portrait of Adolf Hitler that seemed to stare at them wherever they were in the room. Lamm and Weiler joined a group of younger junior officers at a large table, where they all welcomed Lamm to the SS. Stewards in white jackets served an excellent lunch, which began with potato soup. The conversation was quite animated and Lamm listened intently, becoming rapidly appalled at the racial nonsense some of the officers mouthed from Rosenberg's *Myth of the Twentieth Century* and some of Richard-Walther Darré's nonsense. Not only did they attack the Jews, but also the Catholic Church. One obnoxious Sturmführer named Schach, whom Lamm thought particularly vacuous, stated emphatically that it was best to throw away the Bible, which was basically a Jewish and Asiatic document, and turn to the old Nordic myths as the true revelation of the German soul. By the time lunch was over Schach and his cronies had attacked virtually everyone in one way or another. No matter, Schach seemed to feel, the German race was superior and would triumph over all. Throughout it all, whenever someone said, "Don't you agree, Herr Professor?" Lamm would smile politely and say, "Of course."

Finally Schach asked, "Herr Professor, how long do you think it will take before the world is free of Jews?"

Lamm should have smiled again and replied with an answer equal to their ignorance. He wanted to tell Schach and his cronies how really stupid they were. The only way to do it was to use their own so-called logic against them. He put down his fork, looked from his half-finished fruit torte to the eager young face, and replied curtly, "Gentlemen, unless we rid ourselves of the attitudes you have just demonstrated, I doubt that we should ever get rid of the Jews."

The young man looked at him as if he were a five-year-old who had just said a naughty word in front of a dinner guest. Lamm continued. "Do you realize that some of the greatest minds in theoretical science are Jews? The Jews may be degenerate subhumans, but their achievements in finance and science make them particularly dangerous. You should read more of *Mein Kampf* and less of this other tripe. Adolf Hitler will tell you how clever the Jews are. When we start underestimating the Jew, we will lose the struggle." Lamm removed the napkin from his lap and put it on the table. "Excuse me." He bowed politely and stalked out.

The conversation at the table erupted into laughter at Schach's expense. "I guess he told you," one of the other SS men told the shocked young officer.

"That will teach you to match wits with a professor," quipped another.

Weiler caught up to him at the door. "Herr Professor," he said, blushing. "This is most embarrassing."

"Not for me," Lamm told him. "I am sick of hearing this gibberish from a bunch of babies who don't even understand the intellectual basis of this struggle. You think you can beat up a few Jews and break some windows and win this struggle?"

"I know," Weiler agreed. "I think we should go."

Lamm looked closely at Weiler, who was pale, and realized he had drawn blood from some sacred cow, which made him feel better. When they returned to the tailor shop and Lamm put on the complete uniform, he didn't recognize the man in the mirror. The short, studious professor in the gray suit was gone, and the reflection that stared back was that of a man of threatening presence. The cap with the skull and bones was low over his face, and the black boots made him taller. The jagged silver "SS" on his collar riveted his attention and he smiled, enjoying the effect. On his left sleeve was a light-colored cuff band with the Germanic letters "RFSS," which identified him as a member of Reichsführer SS Himmler's personal staff. Turning to Weiler and the tailor with a smile, Lamm raised his right arm stiffly and clicked his heels. "Heil Hitler!"

"Heil Hitler!" Weiler and the tailor replied.

Leaving the tailor shop, Lamm continued to marvel at how the uniform made him feel. Lamm's father had served with the local regiment in the Great War, and the professor remembered the unattractive uniform the elder Lamm wore home on leave. Those uniforms were for the trenches, not for pretty girls and politicians. Weiler took Lamm to get his new identity book, then drove with him to Wolfstrasse Number 20.

"This is the place, Herr Professor," Weiler said.

"Thank you, Hauptsturmführer," Lamm said as he got out of the car. "Call on us when you get a chance."

"Do you have a telephone?"

"No, but there is one in the building. The number is 74361."

"Thank you, Herr Professor. Heil Hitler!"

"Heil Hitler!"

As the car pulled away, Lamm turned to find workmen removing the slogans "Death to Jews" and "Jew-Traitor!" from the walls. Obviously, the building had been owned by a Jew and forfeited to the SS as part of the indemnity levied after the Kristalnacht. Inside the door a Scharführer sat at a table on which were several rosters, an entry control chart, blank passes for visitors not on the roster, and two rubber stamps. Across from the table stood a guard wearing the black SS service dress with steel helmet and armed with a Gewehr 98 rifle. He snapped to attention as Lamm entered, and the Scharführer briefly glanced up at the short man in the black uniform approaching him. He was obviously not a member of the SS defense troops. *Another cursed bureaucrat, strutting around in an SS uniform,* he thought. *Who do they think they are? I was fighting communists in the streets while they were in their nice comfortable offices. I can't stand them . . .* He looked back down at his roster as Lamm walked up.

"I am Untersturmführer Lamm. Can you tell me where the Racial Science Section is, please?"

The Scharführer opened his palm, but didn't look up. "Identity book, please," he said blandly.

Lamm handed the identity book to the Scharführer, who checked the number against the roster and then glanced at Lamm to check the photograph.

"Hmmm." The Scharführer wrote the time of Lamm's entry on his chart and handed the identity book back without extending his arm, which forced Lamm to lean over to retrieve it. "Third floor."

Lamm pocketed his identity book and glared at the Scharführer, who was paying no attention. He wondered how many times the Scharführer treated newly arrived junior SS officers with such calculated insolence and got away with it. Most well-bred people would rather overlook a situation like this than make a scene, but Lamm was angry. He wouldn't countenance inefficiency from Steiber or stupidity from Schach, so why should he tolerate insolence from this man?

"Scharführer!" Lamm shouted.

The expression on the man's face was as if Lamm had struck him.

"Stand at attention when an officer addresses you!" Lamm continued in a loud voice.

The Scharführer snapped to attention so quickly that his chair fell over.

"Is that the way you always address officers?"

"No, Herr Untersturmführer," he replied nervously.

Lamm leaned close to him and spoke softly. "If I ever see or hear of this kind of behavior again, you'll be lucky to wind up a Rottenführer. Do you understand me?"

"Yes, Herr Untersturmführer."

"Now, where is the Racial Science Section?"

"Third floor, Herr Untersturmführer. Take the elevator and walk to the end of the hall. That is Obersturmbannführer von Bartz's office."

"Aren't you forgetting something?" Lamm asked.

"Sir?"

"I've been in this building five minutes, and I haven't seen a German salute yet."

The Scharführer swallowed hard. Perspiring, he clicked his heels and thrust his arm out. "Heil Hitler!"

"Heil Hitler," Lamm said, returning the salute.

As Lamm turned to go to the elevator, the guard once again snapped to attention, and there was a bit of a smirk on his face.

"Third floor," Lamm told the elevator operator as the door closed. He felt much better. It was best to begin from a position of strength, a lesson he learned years ago in the classroom. The only thing the Nazis understood was strength, so one had to be forceful with them. "Heil Hitler, Herr Untersturmführer," the operator said as Lamm left the elevator.

"Heil Hitler," Lamm repeated, wondering how soon his voice and arm would give out from the endless Nazi salutes.

The third floor was chaos. Cartons and filing cabinets were piled everywhere, and workmen were busily carrying things from one room to another. Lamm made his way through the confusion of new desks and chairs in the hall to von Bartz's office. It, too, was in chaos, and the two workmen arranging furniture looked at Lamm with mild surprise.

"Excuse me. I'm looking for Obersturmbannführer von Bartz."

"Over there." One of the workmen nodded toward the backs of von Bartz and a visitor. At the sound of the voice they turned around. The visitor, wearing an SS uniform with leaves on his collar insignia, was obviously a person of high rank. He looked familiar, but Lamm could not place him. Not much taller than Lamm, his gray eyes peered out from behind pince-nez glasses, and he had a neatly trimmed mustache beneath a Grecian nose. He looked like a literature professor from a small university.

"Oh, Herr Professor," von Bartz said, putting his hands together in a gesture of satisfaction. "Nice to see you. The uniform makes a pleasant difference. Come here. I'd like you to meet Reichsführer Himmler."

Lamm was stunned. No wonder von Bartz's visitor looked familiar. This mousy-looking man was the third (some said second) most powerful man in the Third Reich. Lamm clicked his heels and raised his arm. "Heil Hitler."

Himmler smiled blandly at Lamm and only raised his arm halfway to return Lamm's salute, then offered his hand after the customary "Heil." The Reichsführer's handshake was as bland as his smile.

"Nice to meet you, Professor Lamm. Erwin has told me a great deal about you and the insight you have shown when discussing our problems. He also told me about this Hahn development. Most interesting. I just want you to know that I have the greatest confidence in your abilities."

"Thank you, Herr Reichsführer," Lamm said. "This is a great honor for me."

"Relax, Professor," Himmler said softly. "Here in the SS we are all part of the Aryan family. The blood of the ancient Teutonic Knights runs in our veins, and we must dedicate ourselves to the eradication of the blight of world Jewry." Himmler turned to von Bartz. "Well, Erwin, I must be leaving."

"I'll see you to the elevator, Herr Reichsführer," von Bartz said obsequiously.

Watching them go, the professor was astounded that Himmler actually believed the legends about the Teutonic Knights, and the fact made him uncomfortable.

When von Bartz returned, he was flushed with excitement. "Marvelous person, isn't he?"

"The Reichsführer? Yes," Lamm replied. "I was deeply impressed by his interest and sincerity."

"It makes you feel wonderful to know that the fate of Germany is in the hands of such remarkable men," von Bartz sighed. He looked at the door longingly for a moment. His plan to make himself the arbiter of all science in the Third Reich was progressing better than he had hoped. He turned to Lamm with a smile. "Come, let me show you around. We occupy the entire third floor. Your office is the second door on the left, the last one before the end of the hallway. You are the head of the research and experimental section."

"Research and experimental section," Lamm said, savoring the title, delighted with the prospect of having his own facility in which to carry out experiments with uranium atoms. First they would have to duplicate Hahn's experiment in splitting the atom, then they could look for practical applications for the energy given off. "Where are the laboratory facilities?"

"Alas, there aren't any," von Bartz informed him with a shrug. "Laboratories cost money, and we have a very small budget. We tried leasing facilities from the Kaiser Wilhelm Institute, but they turned us down. We're looking elsewhere, but it hardly looks promising." Von Bartz was obviously unconcerned with the lack of facilities, and Lamm wondered how they were going to check other people's work if they couldn't check their experiments. "This way."

Von Bartz continued the tour as if nothing were amiss. "The room we were in will be my office, and the small one next to it will be for my secretary. You will have your own typist and two SS clerks. Our function will be to review every scientific work in the Reich."

"Just the two of us?" Lamm asked incredulously.

Von Bartz shrugged. "We have to start somewhere, Herr Professor. Money is not readily available. We will have a much larger staff once the Führer solves this Polish business. Then I'm sure we'll get more resources. Until that time we will have to do our best to ensure that German science is not tainted with mongrel theories."

"By German science, you mean physics?" Lamm asked.

"Oh, no," von Bartz replied blithely. "We are now responsible for all German science. Biology, botany, chemistry . . . everything."

Lamm smiled weakly. He was beginning to wonder what he had gotten into. "Who are my assistants?" he asked.

"I don't know. They won't arrive until May."

"May?" Lamm exclaimed. "That's another six weeks."

"Herr Professor," von Bartz replied condescendingly, "the National Socialist Revolution is not yet complete. Many sacrifices must be made."

"Of course," Lamm hid his dismay.

Von Bartz returned to his office to supervise the arrangement of the furniture, leaving Lamm to stare at the piles of boxes. Sacrifices were one thing; intellectual anarchy was quite another. This was hardly the way he imagined he would save the German intellectual situation. With no laboratory in which to conduct experiments and no way to check data, all they could do was fill out forms and create paperwork. Lamm wondered if that was precisely what von Bartz had in mind. But perhaps he was rushing to judgment. After all, von Bartz was right. Money didn't grow on trees. Lamm sighed, then got up and began unpacking boxes. It would get better, he told himself.

At the end of his first day in the SS, Maximilian Lamm went home deflated. At this point his intellectual revolution was nothing more than another bureaucratic quagmire. He needed a good supper and a quiet evening at home with his wife. Her warm and cheerful personality could brighten the worst day. After supper he would sit and listen to the radio and think.

"Oh Max," Irma gushed as he walked in the door. "Your uniform is so . . . so elegant."

Lamm's plans for the evening changed.

Irma loved her husband deeply and had always been a dutiful wife, but seeing him in the black uniform sent goosebumps down her spine. He was so handsome. She couldn't do enough for him and as they retired for the night, she put her arms around his neck and kissed him passionately. "Oh, Max, darling, I'm so proud of you, an officer in the SS. I love you."

Lamm was taken aback for a moment, but he couldn't help but be aroused by his wife's fervent kisses and the passionate words in his ear. Later she fell asleep cuddled close to him. *Well,* he thought, *the SS is good for something.*

CHAPTER 3

GERMAN PHYSICS

The Racial Science Section
April 17, 1939

HITLER'S SPECTACULAR DIPLOMATIC VICTORIES CONTINUED as 1939 matured. On March 15 German troops rolled across the Czechoslovakian border and that hapless nation ceased to exist. Eight days later, Nazi troops occupied Memel. Hitler then demanded unlimited access to the Free City of Danzig. Poland naturally refused, but most Germans expected a repeat of the Munich Agreement of 1938. In that confrontation, Britain and France had caved in to Hitler's demands and ceded a large portion of Czechoslovakia to Germany. But there was no diplomatic triumph this time. On the last day of the month France and Great Britain guaranteed the sovereignty of Germany's eastern neighbor. Another Munich was out of the question.

These were momentous events, but they brought Lamm no satisfaction as he stood before the desk of Obersturmbannführer Erwin von Bartz on a rainy April morning.

"I don't care what your reasons were," von Bartz shouted hysterically. His face was purple with rage. "You should never have done it. Anywhere else it wouldn't have mattered, but in Lichterfeld . . . I received a note from the Reichsführer himself . . ."

Lamm stood at attention, staring at the painting of Hitler behind von Bartz while the head of the Racial Science Section yelled. Early in their association, Lamm had learned that flying off the handle was von Bartz's way of coping with unexpected situations. The elementary principle of leadership in the New Order was screaming loud and long until someone came along to solve the problem. When that failed you tried to solve the problem yourself. Unimpressed, Lamm tuned von Bartz out. Schach, his feelings hurt by the laughter of his comrades, had forwarded a note through channels to Himmler. After weeks in the bureaucratic labyrinth it had reached the Racial Science Section without the Reichsführer seeing it. Because it was routed through the Reichsführer's headquarters, von Bartz overreacted.

"And you don't go around telling the Leibstandarte Adolf Hitler that their training is not valid."

"I didn't say that—" Lamm interjected. This was another ploy. It was useless trying to explain, but if Lamm said nothing von Bartz got even more upset and the shouting lasted longer. When he pretended to defend himself, the head of the Racial Science Section could demonstrate his superiority by cutting his subordinate off in mid sentence and would calm down more quickly.

Von Bartz pounded his fist on the table and gave Lamm a vicious stare. "I don't care what you said!" He was almost screeching now. "Do you know who the Leibstandarte are? Do you?"

"They are the Führer's personal bodyguard." Lamm hoped he sounded naive.

"The Army's Leibwache is also the Führer's bodyguard. The Leibstandarte Adolf Hitler is more than just a bodyguard. It is the Führer's pet. It traces its roots back to the putsch of 1923. It was first into the Rhineland and Austria and," he emphasized, "it is the symbol of the new Germany, and of racial purity. So from now on say nothing of your ideas about the Jews. If you must say something, clear it with me first. Understood?"

"Understood, Herr Obersturmbannführer," Lamm replied, hoping he sounded suitably chastened and impressed.

"There is one other thing." Von Bartz looked directly at Lamm and lifted a sheet of paper from the desk.

"Yes, Herr Obersturmbannführer?"

"Your request for laboratory space in order to duplicate Dr. Hahn's experiment is denied, along with your incessant requisitions for filing cabinets and 'qualified' technical assistance. As I have explained time and again, we have no money. Besides, what good is it repeating Hahn's experiment? It is already done. From now on you will not submit any requisitions until I tell you it is appropriate to do so. Is that understood?"

"Yes, Herr Obersturmbannführer."

"That is all, Herr Untersturmführer," von Bartz said imperiously. "You are dismissed."

Lamm clicked his heels and raised his arm. "Heil Hitler!"

"Heil Hitler!" Von Bartz stared at Lamm's back as the professor left his office. It had been a coup recruiting someone as respected as Lamm for the Racial Science Section, but his assistant was proving more trouble than he was worth, constantly harping on the need for more assistance, better organization, and more filing cabinets. Von Bartz crumpled up the latest requisition and tossed it into the wastebasket. Who did Lamm think he was, trying to turn the Racial Science Section into a laboratory? There were plenty of those in the Reich, but none had the power that Erwin von Bartz had. One word from him and a project could be shut down immediately. That was real power, and he wasn't about to have Lamm get in the way.

Von Bartz had thought of going to the Reichsführer and having Lamm removed, but that wouldn't do. After praising Lamm to the heavens, he couldn't just ask for his dismissal. It wouldn't look good to Himmler. No, he had to find another way to get rid of Lamm, and it had to be soon, before he caused any real damage. In either case, Maximilian Lamm would find his career in the SS very short. *If I have my way, you'll end up in a concentration camp,* von Bartz thought. *That will cure your prodding.*

Down the hall, Lamm returned to his desk, looked in the direction of von Bartz's office, and shook his head, wondering how in the world he had gotten into this mess. It was now evident that von Bartz wanted nothing to do with pure science. He was content with having the power to approve or disapprove other people's scientific work rather than do original research. Didn't the fool understand that unlocking the secret of atomic energy meant real power—something that no bureaucrat could comprehend? Maximilian Lamm was angry. The Racial Science Section to which he had pinned all his hopes was a dead end.

Lamm was swamped with work as he tried to evaluate each paper honestly, agonizing over the fact that many of the papers he was tasked to comment on had little to do with physics. Von Bartz seemed to have no problem reading two or three papers a week regardless of the subject or discipline. Physics, botany or civil engineering, it made no difference, since most of the papers were passed without comment and only a small percentage returned for revision. Every now and then von Bartz denounced a paper for reasons that Lamm could only describe as fatuous. Lamm needed every ounce of self-control to mask his aggravation with his boss whose main interest, other than serving the Third Reich, was the mistress he visited every Wednesday afternoon. Lamm considered resigning, until the promised help arrived. To his surprise Scharführer Adalbert Loring, Sturmmann Friedrich Bittner, and Frau Trude Norbert were a cut above the other SS personnel who worked in the building.

Loring, of medium height, with a stocky build, was thirty-seven. He had a handsome face, with a small scar on his left cheek. On his sleeve, he wore the Old Fighter's Chevron, indicating he had been in the party for a long time. The scar and the chevron made Lamm suspect that Loring had once been a brawler. The Scharführer was intelligent, witty, and pleasant, and it was hard to imagine a man like him in the Nazi Party, until the conversation turned to Jews and other "inferior" races. Loring, who could give the listener an earful of Rosenberg, Darré, and Chamberlain, didn't just dislike Jews. The very idea that Jews, Slavs, and Negroes lived somewhere on the planet Earth was anathema to him.

Bittner, an SS Mann, was an enigma. Intelligent, he was reserved and hardly smiled or spoke. A slim man in his late twenties with dark blonde hair and a round face, he had workman's hands, and Lamm guessed he was a socialist who became a Nazi at just the right time. Bittner did have an eye for the ladies, and he liked them a little on the plump side. Trude Norbert, Lamm's new secretary, was just such a woman, pleasant, intelligent, and extremely efficient. Every day she arrived early to prepare a pot of coffee. Lamm wished she were a little less attractive, but she was married to a sergeant in the Luftwaffe and didn't play around. The term "playing around" reminded Lamm of von Bartz's secretary, Ingrid Trautner. She was slim, with a curvy figure and a beautiful face and wore very feminine light-colored dresses that accentuated her figure. Fräulein Trautner was also intelligent and efficient, but there the similarity between her and Frau Norbert ended. Fräulein Trautner collected men the way some people collected stamps. Every morning her desk was ringed with admirers until just before von Bartz arrived. Lamm doubted she ever bought her own lunch. Just her presence seemed to please von Bartz, and Lamm often wondered what went on in von Bartz's office when the good Fräulein took dictation with the door closed. One big happy family.

Lamm's musings were cut short by Frau Norbert.

"We have just received more scientific papers, Herr Professor," she said, gesturing to a pile of boxes a deliveryman was unloading from a hand truck. "Where do you want them?"

"That's a good question. We don't have a third of the filing cabinets we're supposed to. Is there any place we don't have boxes piled?"

"The back room is full," Frau Norbert reported.

"We may have some room left in the storage room in the basement," Bittner offered.

"I wanted to keep them in some kind of order," Lamm muttered more to himself than to any of them. He looked around at the boxes piled in every unused space. "Never mind. Put them where they will fit. I suppose we'll get to them eventually. What's in them?"

Bittner and Frau Norbert shrugged, so Lamm walked over to the stack of new boxes, opened the top one, and withdrew a folder. He glanced at its contents and said, "This is absurd."

"Herr Professor?" Frau Norbert asked, a little bewildered.

"Look at this. Just look at it."

Bittner and Frau Norbert looked over Lamm's shoulder at the paper. "I don't understand," Frau Norbert said.

"This is a paper written on the nature of mercury by some unknown professor of physics in 1847. Eighteen forty-seven! Why?"

Frau Norbert, intimidated by the professor in any circumstance, ventured, "Perhaps the author was Jewish?"

"If he was, he's a dead Jew, so the Reich needn't worry about him. Label the boxes with the date they arrived and get them out of my sight." He didn't want his subordinates to think he was angry at them, so he turned to them, smiled, and added, "Please."

Loring then strode into the room, grinning. "Have you heard the news?"

"No, what is it?" Bittner asked.

"That Jew-lover Roosevelt wrote a letter to the Führer a couple of weeks ago begging him to respect the sovereignty of the nations of Europe. The Führer read part of the letter to the Reichstag yesterday and they laughed. Who does Roosevelt think he is anyway? Hitler will do as he damned well pleases, and nothing will stop him. Danzig will be returned to the Reich before the end of summer. Wait and see."

May 18, 1939

Despite the Reichstag's laughter that Loring had referred to, something indefinable had changed, and diplomats scurried to and fro trying to come to grips with what was happening. In an atmosphere of crisis, no one could be bothered with the world of physics. Lamm read the article of a French experiment in the April 22 issue of *Nature* with intense interest. If it was correct, the number of neutrons released by each fissioning uranium atom was incredible, which meant a chain reaction was possible. Others in Germany noticed this article also. During a physics seminar in Göttingen, one of the participants read a paper theorizing the use of uranium in a reactor to produce energy. The Ministry of Education swiftly convened a secret meeting in Berlin, and in late April Dr. Paul Harteck and a colleague wrote a letter to the War Ministry pointing out the potential destructive power of a bomb made with uranium. The War Ministry took steps to establish a research program to see if a uranium bomb was possible. The outcome of this initial activity was very positive, as numerous organizations attempted to establish atomic research programs.

Lamm was not slow to understand the implications of these developments. Here was the chance he had been looking for. This time he prepared his case in terms von Bartz could understand, and submitted a written report before he went to see his superior.

"We in the SS should exercise central control over all the experiments concerning uranium burners or 'reactors' as they are sometimes called, as well as bombs," Lamm explained. "Not only will this allow us to control this atomic power, but it will discourage rivalries between agencies and duplications of effort that will waste valuable resources."

"Do you really think this is possible, Professor Lamm?" von Bartz asked. "I know Hahn split a few atoms in the laboratory, but that doesn't mean it can be used right away to make electricity or a bomb. It will take years of research to do that."

"That's just my point, Herr Obersturmbannführer. We must get in on the ground floor. Otherwise we will be left behind. The War Ministry has given all subjects having to do with atomic energy a secret classification and declared uranium oxide a critical material with its own code name."

"Then we shall have the Reichsführer's headquarters notify the War Ministry to send us copies of all their material on their research. That way we shall have control of all they do. You were quite right to bring this up, Professor," von Bartz declared with a smile. "This definitely falls within our charter. I will take charge of this from now on."

A painful knot formed in Lamm's stomach. Von Bartz wasn't going to do a thing. Nevertheless he forced a smile. "Thank you, Herr Obersturmbannführer. Should I start a file on this?"

"Yes, by all means, Herr Professor, by all means. Now, if you have nothing else, I have other matters to attend to."

"Of course, Herr Obersturmbannführer. Heil Hitler."

"Heil Hitler."

Lamm returned to his desk, barely able to control his anger. Von Bartz was a dunce. Here was the future of physics and all he wanted to do was deal with administrative poppycock! There had to be a way around this stupidity. First he had to learn everything he could about this new experiment.

On May 22, Germany and Italy signed a military alliance they called "The Pact of Steel." The following day, Adolf Hitler told his generals that war with Poland must come. When the pocket battleships *Deutschland* and *Graf Spee* sailed for open waters with sealed orders, Maximilian Lamm made a decision.

"Frau Norbert, I want you to start a special file on atomic physics. The file will be kept in my office."

"Yes, sir."

"Since you pick up the mail and distribute it every morning and afternoon, I want you to review every piece of unsealed mail before you give it to Fräulein Trautner to determine if it has anything to do with atomic physics. Obersturmbannführer von Bartz is not to be annoyed by any of this. He is very busy and I have promised him that he won't be bothered. I also want this office put on distribution for foreign scientific publications, especially the American magazine, *Physical Review.*"

"But how will I know what to look for?" she asked, completely dismayed.

"I will give all three of you a short course in atomic physics so that you will all know the basics."

"Excuse me, Herr Untersturmführer," Loring asked, "but why is this atomic physics so important?"

Lamm's mind searched for an answer to satisfy Loring. "Scharführer Loring, how crafty are the Jews?"

"I don't understand the question, Herr Untersturmführer," Loring said.

"Hmm," Lamm remarked. "What if I told you the Jews have accidentally discovered one of the basic secrets of the universe, and that this secret was the key to unlocking, theoretically at least, enormous power. Could you believe that?"

Loring thought for a moment and grinned. "Considering the skill they have shown in stealing from us Germans, why not?"

"Good," Lamm said. "Imagine, then, that once they discovered this power, they found that they did not have the capability to exploit it. Despite all their wealth and influence they lacked the one thing that would enable them to capitalize on this power—a nation."

Loring's eyes widened in amazement. "Then that is why they wished to subvert the Fatherland?" he asked.

"Very good! That's one of the reasons," Lamm continued. "Now, once a nation had this power under its control, it would be the strongest nation on earth."

"And Germany now has this power?" Bittner asked.

"No," Lamm told him, "unfortunately not. The Jews are crafty. Too long have we underestimated them. The Führer has said so, has he not? They realized they could not use this power immediately because they didn't have a nation. Fearing that others might discover this power, they hid it by developing plausible, but misleading, theories, which the world accepted as true. In 1938, Professor Hahn unlocked the key to the mystery and exposed the plot. Now this power will be ours as soon as we develop it. The Racial Science Section can help by monitoring everything that is published and identifying what is true and what is false."

Lamm looked at his three subordinates. Loring's eyes shone with understanding and a will to defeat the Jews. Bittner looked vaguely curious, and the expression on Frau Norbert's face indicated she wasn't sure about any of this at all.

"Getting back to the assignments," Lamm continued. "Loring and Bittner, you will go through all the files and separate anything to do with atomic physics. If either of you find anything of which you're not sure, bring it to me. I will review everything at the end of each day. Are there any more questions?" The three of them shook their heads. "Heil Hitler!" Lamm said, raising his arm.

"Heil Hitler!" they said, returning the salute.

After they left, Lamm sat down at his desk. He really didn't know what he was going to do with all the information on atomic physics. All that claptrap about Jewish Physics was fine for people like von Bartz and Loring. Since they believed that sort of nonsense it made them feel that they understood the problem. It was also a good method for Lamm to get his way. Only he understood what was really at stake—the intellectual dominance of the Fatherland. Just what part atomic physics would play, he didn't precisely know, but his instinct told him it was the key to what he wanted.

June 7—December 31, 1939

By June 7, Lamm's reorganization was in effect, and the world was breathing a sigh of relief that Germany had signed non-aggression pacts with Latvia, Estonia, and Denmark. International tension was easing, though Lamm knew with certainty that the Nazis wanted war. They were crazy. Couldn't they remember what it was like after the Great War? For the first three years of so-called peace, the nation was wracked by political upheaval and revolution that were made worse in 1922, when the French occupied the Ruhr and crippled any chance of economic recovery. In the late twenties came inflation, depression, and unrest. When Adolf Hitler came to power, he brought stability and prosperity to the weary German public. If that prosperity cost the Jews a few million Reichsmarks, who cared? It was time for Germany to enjoy its newfound wealth and power. The only reason for war was revenge, and Lamm knew that was a stupid reason.

Vengeance was important to many Germans because Germany had been forced to sign the Versailles Treaty at the end of the Great

War, a document that to the average German meant rape and humiliation. Article 231 of the treaty made Germany accept all responsibility for the war. In addition, Germany lost 15 percent of her arable land, 40 percent of her coal reserves, and 65 percent of her iron ore. Nearly all her overseas investments, including her transatlantic cables, were gone. The Reich also lost her colonies, which cut off her access to rubber and oil—except through her erstwhile enemies. Every aspect of German life was scarred by the *Diktat* of Versailles, and the German people thirsted for revenge. Many wondered what good was power and wealth if a country didn't use it? And what better way to use it than to wage war to avenge the humiliation of Versailles? So far the Führer had wielded that power with remarkable skill. Not a shot had been fired, and Germany was now larger and more powerful than she had ever been. Some thought that Hitler could accomplish the impossible and avenge the humiliation without war. Lamm doubted it.

As the summer of 1939 neared its end, it seemed likely war would be avoided once more. On August 23, 1939, the Russo-German Non-Aggression Pact was signed, and the German people and general staff rejoiced. There would be no war with Russia.

But on August 25, the British signed a mutual defense treaty with the Poles. Still, few Germans were really worried. Surely the British and French would back down again. On August 31, Poland announced its willingness to negotiate. The world went to bed thinking war had been avoided. It woke to discover that Germany's vengeance had been unleashed upon Europe.

Twenty-seven days after the commencement of hostilities, the Poles capitulated. Germany was still at war with Britain and France, but there were only a few skirmishes on the Western Front, and the War in the West was derisively called the "Sitzkrieg," or the phony war.

January 9, 1940

Had it not been for the radio in Fräulein Trautner's office, the Racial Science Section would have missed it. To Lamm, the boring task of reviewing thousands of scientific papers seemed pointless, but to von Bartz it was a dream come true. The Racial Science Section had become a unique power in the German academic world. One disapproving word from von Bartz and a professor or researcher could be ruined for life. Noted scholars and writers courted him, and scientific manuscripts arrived at the office with a request for von Bartz's personal attention. On a quiet Wednesday afternoon in January, Lamm learned why.

With von Bartz visiting his mistress and Ingrid Trautner at the dentist, Lamm had to enter the Obersturmbannführer's office to retrieve a document. Under the document was a paper protruding from an open envelope. On the paper was the word "atomic." Lamm raised an eyebrow and picked the paper up. It was a theoretical article concerning the atomic structure of metals. There was also a letter in the envelope. When Lamm lifted it out and opened it, five 100-Reichsmark notes fluttered out and landed on the desk. A bribe! Lamm nearly exploded with rage. He could tolerate stupidity, and even incompetence, but this was unconscionable! The Reich, which had just accomplished the greatest rebirth in the history of the world, was now involved in a major war to consolidate that renaissance, and von Bartz was using it as an opportunity to make a profit. Lamm picked up the phone to call the Reichsführer's office immediately.

It took the operator a few moments to answer, "Number please?"

"Get me . . . " Lamm hesitated. No matter how angry he was, he couldn't go off half-cocked. Sitting in von Bartz's chair, he read the letter carefully and found no mention of the money. It was a bribe, but he couldn't prove it. Lamm sighed. Who would believe him if he made the accusation? It would be his word against von Bartz's, and that wouldn't go very far, considering Himmler and von Bartz were personal friends. Perhaps documentary evidence was the answer, but Lamm quickly discarded that thought. There had to be another way to fix von Bartz and whatever it took, he would find it. "Never mind." He returned the receiver to its cradle.

April 1—July 31, 1940

The Blitzkrieg in the west began in April with the campaign against Norway. By the end of June, the victorious armies of the Reich had conquered Denmark, Norway, Holland, Belgium, and France.

The British Army, forced off the continent at Dunkirk, was besieged on its tiny island. The Racial Science Section, as usual, followed the greatest military campaign in history by listening to the radio. For Lamm, the campaign in the west held far more interest than the war in Poland. Germany's new victories had suddenly thrust her ahead in atomic physics. In Norway, the Norwegian hydro-electric facilities for the production of heavy water were now in German hands; in Belgium, hundreds of tons of uranium oxide had been captured; and in France, the nearly complete cyclotron was captured intact.

At the fall of France, the German people were ecstatic. The traditional enemy of the last 150 years had been brought to her knees in six short weeks. Some of the fruits of victory were promotions for Lamm and many others in the SS. As a member of Himmler's personal staff, he and Irma were invited to an endless round of parties in one elegantly appointed ministry after another. Irma gushed over everyone in a field-gray uniform, especially those of the Waffen SS, which was what the SS Defense troops were now called. French champagne flowed ceaselessly as everyone spoke of the future.

Great Britain, the only remaining enemy, was weak and isolated. There was no way she could resist the victorious Wehrmacht and Luftwaffe, so she would have to accept the generous terms the Führer was offering his gallant enemy, so everyone said—nearly everyone. The officers who were veterans of the Great War exhibited a subtle pessimism. They had a high regard for the British, and knew they wouldn't surrender. If Germany wanted England out of the war, she would have to take the island by assault.

During the endless parties, Lamm was impressed by the number of high-ranking officers and Party officials that von Bartz knew, and was relieved he had not made the phone call to Himmler. To gain some credibility, Lamm made a point to meet as many of these officials as he could. Although Goebbels was one of the most intelligent high party officials that Lamm met, he disliked the Reichsminister of Propaganda immediately. Goebbels riveted Lamm with his deep-set dark eyes, and during the course of their short conversation, the Reichsminister did all the talking. Göring, on the other hand, was an extremely likable, jolly, fat man, and it was hard to believe that he had created the Luftwaffe, Germany's primary instrument of victory in Poland and the West. No doubt, the Luftwaffe would also bludgeon England into submission in a few short weeks.

Most of the Nazis Lamm met were second-rate intellects, which didn't surprise him. They were, after all, politicians, but Martin Bormann's stupidity in particular shocked him. It was hard to believe the Reichsleiter of the Party and Hitler's secretary didn't have the intellect of a farmhand. Worse yet, Bormann was the custodian of the Adolf Hitler Fund, the Führer's primary source of income. During their discussion, Bormann asked Lamm some basic questions about physics. Lamm had drunk a little too much champagne, and out of sheer malice launched into a detailed explanation of the subject. Bormann, with an expression of bafflement, withdrew. Lamm returned to Irma, who giggled and asked for more champagne. Lamm took the empty glasses to the table where white-coated SS waiters were pouring refills.

"You have impressed our Martin, Herr Professor," someone said behind him.

Lamm turned around, stared at a necktie, and then looked up to see SS Gruppenführer Reinhard Heydrich, head of the security services of the SS. Heydrich was tall, blue-eyed, and blonde—the ideal Nazi. Lamm had met him in the receiving line and knew Heydrich's reputation as an icy man with a sharp tongue. This evening, however, Heydrich had had several glasses of champagne and was charming and sociable. He also seemed to be the only Nazi leader who had any culture, good taste, or education.

"Good evening again, Herr Gruppenführer," Lamm said with a deferential bow.

Heydrich smiled and took a full glass from the table. "You really did impress him, you know," he said.

"I beg your pardon, Herr Gruppenführer?" Lamm replied.

"Bormann. You impressed him."

"I suppose I got a bit too technical," Lamm said apologetically.

"Too technical?" Heydrich laughed. "Mashing potatoes is too technical for Bormann. Trouble is, he'll probably survive us all. You know, he's nearly as stupid as Erwin von Bartz."

Lamm's jaw dropped, and he spilled some champagne.

"I know, I know, " Heydrich said. "Von Bartz has a degree, though how he got it I'll never know. You, on the other hand, have excellent credentials, Herr Professor. How did you wind up working for him?"

Lamm explained the entire story. “I thought I’d be doing a service to the Reich by experimenting with new concepts,” he concluded, “but all I do is shuffle papers.”

“Typical,” Heydrich remarked. “You do all the work and von Bartz gets all the credit.”

Before Lamm realized what he was saying, he quipped bitterly, “And the money.”

“Money? What money?

My God, Lamm thought in a panic, *I have had too much to drink.* Frightened, Lamm stammered, “I’m sorry, Herr Gruppenführer, a slip of the tongue. I’ve had too much to drink. All I meant was that he has a much higher rank than I.” He should never have let that slip. If Heydrich pressed the matter, he was in real trouble.

“That isn’t what you mean,” the Gruppenführer said softly. “You can trust me. I’ll keep everything you tell me in confidence.”

Lamm hesitated, but he found himself wilting under Heydrich’s icy stare. Heydrich will know if I lie. *When in doubt, tell the truth,* he thought.

“Von Bartz is taking bribes to ensure scientific papers are approved.”

“You’re sure?”

“I saw the money in one of the envelopes myself. It was five hundred Reichsmarks.”

Lamm waited for a violent reaction, but it never came.

“Unfortunately, that sort of thing is more common than you expect.” Heydrich calmly sipped his champagne. After a moment he mused. “You know, Professor Lamm, I’m going to need a man of your talents in the near future. We’re going to have a tremendous problem even before the war is over.”

“What’s that, Herr Gruppenführer?”

“The Jews.”

“We’ve already eliminated the Jews from the Reich. What else is there?” Lamm asked naively.

“Disposing of them,” Heydrich said simply. “There won’t be any room for them in a German Europe. The Führer wants to send them to Madagascar, but he always did have a soft spot in his heart for dumb animals.”

"Where would you send them, Herr Gruppenführer?" Lamm asked, still not sure he understood.

"To hell, Herr Professor," Heydrich remarked with a cruel smile. "That's the final solution—every man, woman, and brat. That is why I need someone of genius to devise a way to get rid of them—by the thousands. Bullets are expensive. If you get any good ideas, let me know." Heydrich put down his glass and walked away.

Lamm stood there dumbfounded. Kill them all? Disposing of the entire Jewish population of Europe would be no simple task, and the thought of it made Lamm queasy. Heydrich and the others talked about the Jews as if they were cattle. Perhaps some or even most of them would stand and be slaughtered, but what about the rest? They had tremendous influence with the Americans and the British. If Germany were to destroy the Jews, then she would have to be so strong that no one would dare interfere. Troubled, Lamm returned to Irma.

"Who was that you were talking to, Max?" Irma asked before sipping her champagne.

"That was Gruppenführer Heydrich. He's the head of the Sicherheitsdienst."

"He's really handsome, so tall and blonde," she sighed. "His eyes are fascinating. Like a hero."

No, Lamm thought, *like a snake.*

"What did you two talk about?" Irma wanted to know.

"The Jews," Lamm said flatly.

Irma wrinkled her nose. "Disgusting people," she said. "What about them?"

"He wants to kill them all."

"I don't blame him," Irma said indignantly. "After all the trouble they've caused, the world would undoubtedly thank him if he does. Of course, it wouldn't be right if they were like us, but they are different. Maybe we should send them all to America or something."

Lamm stared at Irma. Like so many Germans, she naively believed the whole bunch of racial claptrap. Was there anyone left in Germany who had read something other than *Mein Kampf*?

Heydrich returned to his coterie of SS officers, then turned to look in Lamm's direction. A man like Lamm was useful. Von Bartz was not. Lamm wanted to use the Racial Science Section for scientific experiments, while von Bartz was nothing more than a bureaucrat. It would be better for all concerned if von Bartz were out of the picture. It would take time, but it was worth doing.

On the other side of Berlin, Hauptsturmführer Heinz Otto Schindler followed his Uncle Uwe into a decorated-for-victory party. Like the one at which Lamm was speaking to Heydrich, there were Nazi flags hanging from the ceiling and along the walls. Long tables covered with white tablecloths were laden with food, and white-coated waiters were filling glasses from endless bottles of captured French champagne. At this celebration there were no politicians. Most of the attendees were commissioned army and navy officers, with a sprinkling of Waffen SS officers recently returned from France and some older veterans in civilian clothes. Most of them, like Uwe Schindler, wore their medals.

The elder Schindler was of medium height, bald and portly. A widower, he was an executive at a large publishing house in Berlin, and as befitted his position wore an expensive gray suit. Pinned to the pocket was an Iron Cross he had won as a U-boat officer in World War I. The younger Schindler was a shade over six feet tall, and muscular. He had a square chin, a straight nose, and deep blue eyes. His dark blonde hair, neatly combed back, accentuated his handsome features. Limping slightly from a shrapnel wound in the thigh, he looked around the room with some trepidation.

"Uncle Uwe, there are more generals here than I've seen my whole career."

Uwe Schindler laughed. "That's because most of them are in Berlin, not at the front. Some things never change. Come, there's someone I want you to meet."

Heinz Schindler followed his uncle to a cluster of naval officers, one of whom was an Admiral. The Admiral looked up at Uwe and smiled.

"Uwe," he said to the elder Schindler, "good of you to come."

"Ah, Willi," Uwe replied, warmly shaking hands with the Admiral, "how are you?"

"I'm fine," the Admiral responded cheerfully. "It's been such a long time. A year isn't it?"

"At least."

"How are things in the publishing business?"

"We just printed another 50,000 copies of *Mein Kampf.*"

"Wonderful."

Uwe turned to Schindler. "Willi, I'd like you meet my nephew, Hauptsturmführer Heinz Schindler. Heinz, I'd like you to meet Admiral Wilhelm Canaris, head of counterintelligence."

Heinz Schindler eyes widened. How did his uncle know such important people? As Admiral Canaris extended his hand, Heinz Schindler raised his. "Heil Hitler!" he said.

Annoyed, the Admiral also said "Heil Hitler," before they shook hands. "How do you do, Hauptsturmführer. It's nice to meet you."

"It's nice to meet you, too, Herr Admiral." He looked closely at Canaris. The Admiral, who presented an air of reserved gentility, was heavy-set but not fat, and the features of his round face were pleasant. His thinning hair was gray.

"Are you enjoying the party, Hauptsturmführer?"

"Hauptsturmführer? Hah!" Uwe said. "Call him Heinz. He's like my own son."

"Do you mind?" the Admiral asked.

"No, Herr Admiral." Schindler was uneasy. Uncle Uwe did not have a high regard for the Party, and had not been happy when his nephew joined the Waffen SS. Since Uncle Uwe had raised him, Heinz was determined to show his uncle how wrong he was about Hitler and the Nazi Party.

"I see you were wounded, Heinz," the Admiral said, looking at the wound badge on the SS officer's pocket. "Not severely, I hope."

"A light wound in the thigh, Herr Admiral."

"Runs in the family, I see." Canaris had a twinkle in his eye.

"What do you mean, Herr Admiral?"

"Your uncle never told you?"

Heinz Schindler turned to his uncle, who was blushing. "What does he mean, Uncle Uwe?"

Canaris laughed. "You never told him, Uwe?"

"No, Willi."

"Heinz, you know Uwe was a turret officer on the *Derfflinger* during the Battle of Jutland, don't you?" the Admiral continued.

"Yes, I've heard the story it many times."

"Did he also tell you that he got a big piece of hot English steel right in the rear?"

"No." Heinz Schindler turned to his uncle, who was now bright red.

"He spent two months in the hospital on his stomach. That's why I said it runs in the family."

Heinz Schindler had never seen his uncle this embarrassed, and his discomfort amused him.

"I'm going to get some champagne," Uwe said, still blushing.

Still grinning, Canaris changed the subject. "How much longer do you think the war will last, Heinz?"

"A few more weeks at most, Herr Admiral," was the reply. "Surely the English will see the hopelessness of their position and accept terms. We have no desire to destroy the English. The Führer has said so. The war will be over by Christmas. We have beaten our enemies everywhere."

"And the Americans?" the Admiral asked. "What if they should come into the war?"

"It would be stupid for them to fight against us. Besides, they are decadent and corrupt. Have you not seen the film *The Grapes of Wrath*?"

"Yes, I have. But they do have a tremendous industrial potential. What about the Russians?"

"We are at peace with Russia, Herr Admiral. But if we have to fight them someday, we will be victorious." Schindler's uncle was now returning with champagne glasses in his hands.

"I certainly hope so. Just tell me which is more important, Heinz, Germany or the Party?"

Schindler opened his mouth, but nothing came out. He closed it and thought for a minute. No one had ever asked him such a question. In the SS, it would be unheard of. "The Party is Germany," he finally said.

"Of course," Canaris said, smiling enigmatically at Schindler. "Nice meeting you, Heinz, and it was nice seeing you, Uwe."

"Come and have tea some afternoon, Willi."

"I'll do that, I promise."

The Admiral's question had made Schindler uneasy, and he tried to push it from his mind as Uncle Uwe handed him a glass of champagne.

"Interesting man, isn't he, Heinz?"

"The Admiral? Yes."

"It helps to know people in high places, Heinz. Remember that, especially when things don't turn out well. Right now, with the war going well, it's very exciting. I was young myself once, and the early days of the Great War were quite thrilling, but there is much going on that is not good and one of these days, Heinz, you will have to step back and see what's going on."

"You mean the Jews, Uncle?" Schindler replied sharply. He was irritated with his uncle and people like Canaris. Hitler had made Germany the most powerful country in the world. What could possibly be wrong with that? So a few faceless Jews had to suffer. He didn't know any of them. What of it? "I'm really not in the mood to hear about those damned Jews."

"It's not just the Jews, Heinz. It's about art, music, the law, and science. The Nazis have driven a lot of very talented people out of the country."

"Please, Uncle Uwe. Not now. It's a nice party and I'd like to enjoy it."

"No, but I want you to promise me that you'll think about what's happening in the Reich when you get the chance. Do you remember Mr. and Mrs. Waldinger?"

"Of course," Schindler replied, smiling at the pleasant memory. "They're the nice old couple who used to babysit me when you were away. They always remembered me at Christmas and my birthday. How are they?"

"They were taken away the day before yesterday."

"But why? They were so nice."

"They were Jews, Heinz. Didn't you know?"

Heinz Schindler flushed and didn't look his uncle in the eye. "No, I didn't." Finally, he looked at his uncle. "Why do you insist on bringing up these unpleasantries?"

"Because evil things are happening, and the day might come when you have to make a choice."

"What kind of a choice?"

"You'll know when the time comes."

Hauptsturmführer Heinz Schindler was confused and upset. "That doesn't make any sense, Uncle." He thought, *Why the Waldingers? They never hurt anyone.*

August 1, 1940

Von Bartz read the letter one more time and then put it into his briefcase. He was about to embark on a project that was bound to put him in Himmler's inner circle. Then he would get rid of Lamm very quickly. Six months at the concentration camp at Dachau would do the meddlesome professor just fine.

He pompously called his assistant Lamm into his office. "Herr Professor, you will be in charge while I am gone."

"Gone, Herr Obersturmbannführer?" Lamm asked in surprise.

"Yes. I have been selected to work on a special project for the Reichsführer." His tone was haughty and arrogant.

"May I inquire as to the nature of this project, Herr Obersturmbannführer?" Lamm asked politely.

"It is, of course, confidential, but I suppose you have to know if you are to be in charge." Von Bartz was fairly oozing with self-congratulation, and his grin was overly broad. "I am going with Operation Nord as the Reichsführer's personal observer." Von Bartz threw his head back in a final gesture of superiority.

"Operation Nord? Is that a military operation?"

Von Bartz looked at Lamm condescendingly. "It is not a military operation, but if Dr. Nass's theories are correct, then ancient Aryan civilization in Norway predated that of ancient Greece."

"Oh, I see." Lamm had trouble keeping a straight face as von Bartz snapped his briefcase shut.

"Heil Hitler, Herr Obersturmbannführer."

"Heil Hitler, Herr Professor. Oh, leave any mail addressed to me unopened, and please do something about all these cartons."

"Jawohl." Lamm clicked his heels.

As Lamm returned to his office, the office staff was clustered around the radio, listening to the latest report of aircraft shot down in the battle over England.

September 3, 1940

Royal Air Force Wing Commander Edward Foxx looked up as he had every morning for the past two years, but instead of the sky, he saw only the tin ceiling of the corridor with its shabby fixtures as he limped toward his office. He should have been flying, but that was now out of the question. It was difficult not feeling bitter, because flying a desk was not Foxx's kind of war. He was brought back to the present by a familiar voice.

"Teddy, old boy, how are you?"

Foxx turned. Reggie Farnsworth, now a colonel on the prime minister's staff, was slim and handsome. Walking purposefully erect, he looked born for the uniform, an aspect enhanced by the fact that Farnsworth was rich and had his uniforms custom-tailored. Foxx liked Reggie personally, but the ease with which Farnsworth got anything he wanted infuriated him.

"Well, Reggie," Foxx said, extending his hand, "what brings you to the RAF? Thought you didn't like flying."

"Hate it, really. Can we talk in your office?" Farnsworth asked, suddenly sounding somewhat nervous.

Being agitated wasn't Farnsworth's style, and it worried the wing commander as he unlocked his office. Farnsworth stared at the desk, badly worn conference table with matching chairs, and a cot. The only wall decorations were status charts that displayed nothing but bad news.

He frowned disapprovingly. "Rather shabby for a wing commander, isn't it?"

"If you're expecting the Strand, Reggie, you're in the wrong place. Come in and have a seat. What's going on?"

"Before I get to business, I want to apologize for not coming to see you in hospital. I only found out a few days ago. The Jerries shot you up pretty bad, I gather."

Foxx laughed out loud. "The Jerries, that's a good one."

"What happened?"

"You really want to know?"

"Of course I do."

"All right. Just about the time the Germans broke through the French lines in the Ardennes, I was jumped in my Spitfire. I could run rings around one Messerschmitt, but not two. To make things worse, the two knew their business. I got a burst into the tail of one of them, one with a lot of victory stripes. Unfortunately, the Jerry's wing man was also good. I tried to get away, but a burst from the wing man killed my engine. Oil spewed over all over the canopy, smoke filled the cockpit, and then the engine died, so I bailed out."

"You weren't hurt?"

"No."

"Well how did . . ."

"I felt bloody naked drifting down in the parachute, especially when the two Messerschmitts returned. To tell the truth, I thought I was dead, but one of them flew high cover while the other circled to see if I was all right. The bugger actually gave me a thumbs up, escorted me down, and as I got out of my parachute, the German with the scores waggled his wings and flew off."

"You were still unhurt?"

"Not a scratch. I figured I was behind German lines, so I hid the parachute and waited until night and headed west. A day and a night later, I was caught in a crossfire between German and British patrols. The bullets in my knee and right lung were German. The ones that tore up my spleen and intestines were British. The doctor who removed the bullets said I was lucky. Stupid bastard, if I were lucky, they'd have missed me."

"I really am sorry Teddy. I know what flying means to you. I need a bomber," he said in the next breath.

Foxx stared at him with his mouth open. "Wouldn't you prefer a dozen?" he asked when he recovered his surprise. "They're cheaper that way."

Farnsworth grinned boyishly. "Have you got a drink, Teddy?"

"Not a drop."

Farnsworth reached into his briefcase and pulled out a bottle of cognac. "Have you got two glasses?"

"Yes. Where did you get this stuff?"

Farnsworth winked. "The BEF wasn't the only thing evacuated from France."

"Is this a bribe?" Foxx asked, taking two glasses from his desk.

"No. I need an aircraft, perhaps a Wellington, with an experienced crew. One that can be trusted."

"What's this all about?" Foxx asked, handing Farnsworth the two glasses.

The colonel poured three fingers of the cognac into each glass and handed one to Foxx. "Cheers," he said.

"Cheers," Foxx repeated. He took a long swallow. "Too bad the French don't fight as well as they make this stuff. Now, bombers don't grow on trees. What's this about?"

"All I can tell you is that some of the PM's staff are worried. They think the Germans are up to some funny business in Norway. Place called Vikmo."

"Never heard of it. What's going on?"

"Rumor says it's a site for secret weapons."

"Gas?"

"Teddy, I've told you all I can. Look, I didn't want to use this, but it's probably best that I do." Farnsworth removed a letter from his briefcase and handed it to Foxx. The wing commander looked at the "Most Secret" markings and the signature.

"Dear God," he said. "That serious?"

"That serious. No one is to know the purpose of the flight, so I'll be going along personally. The aircraft should be stripped so it will fly as quickly as possible. If anyone asks about it, it's an experimental anti-U-boat patrol."

"I'll do what I can," Foxx said.

Farnsworth smiled and reached into his briefcase. "Oh, I almost forgot," he said, finishing his cognac. "That bottle is because I didn't get to see you in hospital. This one is the bribe."

"Two bottles?"

"Got twelve bloody cases out." Farnsworth said, securing his briefcase.

"Reggie, you're a cheeky sod," Foxx told him, taking a more leisurely sip of the cognac.

"Call me when you have the aircraft," Farnsworth said, going to the door. "Let's have a drink when I get back."

Farnsworth leaned against the bulkhead of the Wellington. He was thinking about the inequities of life. Foxx loved to fly and couldn't, while he hated it and had to. He sipped some tea to keep from vomiting.

"Coming up on target," the pilot announced over the intercom.

Farnsworth crawled up to the bombsight, pressed his face to the rubber eyepiece, and started the cameras. It was a clear day, so the pilot only had to make one slow pass. A cameraman was in the bomb bay. The pilot flew low over the site and waggled the wings of the aircraft. The Germans on the ground waved, thinking the two-engine craft was one of theirs. Farnsworth leaned back from the bombsight. It certainly looked like an archaeological site. The pilot turned the Wellington toward Scotland.

"Inverness in five hours, gentlemen."

Farnsworth clicked on his microphone. "Has anyone got a bag?"

The films were developed as soon as the aircraft landed. The original plan had been for Farnsworth to fly to London as soon as possible. However, the Scottish airfield was having bad weather and Farnsworth would have to take the train. He was thankful for the respite.

"Bad luck, Colonel," the pilot said.

"God bless the Scots," Farnsworth told him, as he headed for the station.

The briefing in London was given by Mr. Alexander Harris, Farnsworth's superior. A civilian with no military experience, Harris was one of the bright young men in the War Cabinet. His specialty was technical intelligence. While everyone at the briefing knew that Harris was concerned with the development of German "secret weapons" at the Vikmo mine, very few actually knew what kind of weapons were causing so much concern. Farnsworth certainly did not.

After showing films taken during Farnsworth's flight, Harris gave them a surprise. "Our agent in Norway has reported that the mine in Vikmo has not been reopened. He managed to get inside the mine himself. These are photos of the interior." Harris showed four slides in rapid succession, causing a murmur in the room. "As you can see, the mine is empty. The staff of this archaeological dig consists of Doktor Nass, an anthropologist of questionable repute; an SS officer named von Bartz; and fifteen or so assistants."

"Then there's no heavy equipment?" someone asked.

"None, my Lord," Harris said. "My estimate of the Vikmo operation is that it actually is an archaeological dig to prove some absurd racial theory."

Three or four people in the room breathed an audible sigh of relief. *That,* Farnsworth thought, *is that.*

October 2, 1940

In Berlin, Lamm listened to the broadcast by Goebbels. Through all the propaganda, it was obvious Germany had lost the Battle of Britain. Something had to be done, or Germany would lose the war. He was more convinced than ever that a uranium bomb was the key to victory, but he had to begin building it soon.

CHAPTER 4

PROMOTION

Berlin to Nuremberg
February 14, 1941

LAMM READ THE LETTERS BEFORE him a second time, chuckled, and rubbed his hands with glee. Anthropologists at Heidelberg, Mainz, and Göttingen were questioning the artifacts "discovered" at Operation NORD that were now on exhibit at the Germanic Museum in Nuremberg. One of the letters from an expert in pre-Colombian artifacts included photographs of the obsidian knife discovered at Vikmo and one in his museum's collection. Even to the untrained eye, the knives were obviously similar, and if that were not enough, several experts had identified some of the pottery shards found at Vikmo as of Meditterranean origin. Just those facts were enough to convince Lamm that Nass and von Bartz had salted the dig with phony artifacts in order to impress Reichsführer Himmler, but had botched the job completely. It was going to a pleasure watching von Bartz squirm.

Lamm allowed himself one more laugh, put the file back together, and assumed his serious subordinate countenance. He was becoming quite adept at hiding his feelings. *Perhaps, after the war, I should become an actor, or maybe a politician,* he mused, walking to von Bartz's office.

Probably counting his cash, Lamm thought, when he saw the door closed. "Is the Obersturmbannführer busy, Fräulein Trautner?"

"I don't think so, Herr Obersturmführer." The reply was syrupy.

Lamm knocked on the door.

"Yes," von Bartz barked, "what is it?"

Lamm opened the door. Von Bartz was, indeed, sorting his mail, and he placed several letters in a desk drawer as Lamm entered.

"I have the latest letters concerning Operation NORD, Herr Obersturmbannführer," Lamm said calmly.

Von Bartz gave him a dirty look. "Where are they from? Russia, America?" Then he said nastily, "Palestine, perhaps?"

"No, Herr Obersturmbannführer," Lamm said, pretending not to notice the sarcasm. "One is from Mainz, one is from Heidelberg, and one is from Göttingen." Savoring a moment of silence, Lamm saved the best for last. "They have also sent copies to Reichsführer Himmler."

"What?" von Bartz said. He reached for the folder, eyes wide with fear. "Let me see them." Lamm, standing at attention, handed him the file. Von Bartz, who gave most documents little more than a casual glance, read each letter carefully, turning his mouth down in disapproval from time to time.

"Those meddlers," he said, under his breath. Looking up, he blinked, surprised to see Lamm still in the room. Glaring at the subordinate who had dared to bring him such bad news, von Bartz dismissed him. "You may go."

"Thank you, Herr Obersturmbannführer," Lamm replied. "If I can be of any assistance. . . . Heil Hitler!"

"Heil Hitler!" von Bartz shot back. As soon as the door closed he slammed the file onto the desk. *That cursed Nass!*

It was now obvious that the archeologist had indeed salted the dig, and protests from the universities would embarrass the SS. *Reichsführer Himmler will hold me responsible,* von Bartz thought. The first thing he had to do was distance himself from the entire affair. At first he thought of writing a dissembling memo, one that might elicit a mild rebuke, but even that was unacceptable. Von Bartz knew how Himmler thought. From then on, he would be considered unreliable.

He had to get someone else to take the blame. Who else but Lamm? If he could get that bothersome professor involved, at the very least Lamm would be dismissed from the SS and kicked out of the Party. If he could arrange it, Lamm would be blamed for the whole thing and sent to Dachau. But how could he involve Lamm when . . . Von Bartz stopped in mid-thought. Of course. He would send Lamm to Nuremberg to make a full report, then submit the details of the report to the Reichsführer with von Bartz's personal notes. It would seem as if Lamm were involved from the beginning. Von Bartz's mouth stretched in a crooked grin. Yes, it would work. He pressed the switch on his intercom, "Fräulein Trautner."

"Yes, Herr Obersturmbannführer?"

"Get me Obersturmführer Lamm."

"Yes, sir."

Lamm returned to von Bartz's office immediately. "Yes, Herr Obersturmbannführer?"

"I want you to take a trip to Nuremberg and personally look at these artifacts. When you return, I want you to make a full written report on all the artifacts that can be proven to be fakes. Don't be diplomatic. If Dr. Nass is trying to deceive the Reichsführer I, that is we, need to know. However, this must remain absolutely confidential. You are to discuss this with no one, understood?"

"Yes, Herr Obersturmbannführer."

"You will type the report yourself. Neither of our secretaries must see it. Make only one copy for me. No carbons. Is that clear?"

It wasn't clear at all, but Lamm said, "Yes, Herr Obersturmbannführer."

Von Bartz managed a pleasant smile. "We in the SS cannot allow this unfortunate occurrence to embarrass the Reichsführer or the SS as a whole, as I'm sure you will agree."

"Naturally, Herr Obersturmbannführer." Lamm sounded sincere, but wondered what was going on.

"As soon as I review your report, I will forward the details to the Reichsführer and get the exhibit closed immediately. Understood?"

"Yes, Herr Obersturmbannführer."

"I'm counting on your discretion, Herr Professor. No one except we two can know about this. While you are there you must make this appear as if it were just routine. You may go. Heil Hitler."

"Heil Hitler."

Lamm returned to his desk and looked back in the direction of von Bartz's office. What in the world was going on? Why was von Bartz trying to get him involved in this? The answer didn't take a detective to figure it out, and was very discomfiting. This was an excellent way for von Bartz to get rid of him. Lamm was to be the bearer of bad tidings. By the time von Bartz got through rearranging the report, it would look as if Lamm had been associated with the affair from the start.

How very simple, Lamm thought. *Once von Bartz gets hold of my report he can quote from it and blame me. That's why no one else must see it.* That way he would be killing two birds with one stone. Lamm winced at the word "killing." There was no love lost between von Bartz and him, and he didn't think the Obersturmbannführer would hesitate to have him killed. What would be the price for embarrassing Himmler? Dismissal, some time in a concentration camp, perhaps? Lamm broke out in a sudden cold sweat, and his face turned down in a mean scowl. *That conniving weasel!*

Lamm walked into his office. Trude Norbert, who had never seen Lamm look so tortured, asked, "Is something wrong, Herr Professor?"

Lamm, jolted out of his reverie, looked up. "I beg your pardon, Frau Norbert?"

"Are you all right?"

"Yes, why?"

"The expression on your face. You looked as if you were in pain."

Lamm forced a grin. "No, it was just this report I'm working on."

I must be very careful, Lamm thought as he picked up the phone to call the museum to get an appointment with the director. Once the meeting was arranged, he called Irma at the apartment building number. What could seem more routine than taking his wife? Von Bartz would think he had fooled Lamm completely. Besides, if everything went wrong, this might be Lamm's last good time together with Irma.

"Do you want to go to Nuremberg for a few days, my dear?" he asked when Irma came to the phone.

"Don't we have to get a special pass?"

"No, dear. I'm going on official business," he explained. "As long as I pay for your ticket, we can go together. There's no problem. It's done all the time."

"Of course," she said, sounding like a young girl again.

"Pack enough for three days—for both of us. I'll pick you up at seven this evening."

Lamm hung up the phone. Von Bartz's plan was clear. Assassinate

Nass and save von Bartz. At the same time, Lamm would be the bearer of bad tidings, and von Bartz would merely be doing his duty to the Reich. It was a difficult situation, but he saw a way to turn this to his advantage. Lamm decided he and Irma would enjoy themselves in Nuremberg.

At 8:00 P.M., the Lamms arrived at the Tiergarten Railway Station to board the express to Nuremberg, a train that stopped only at Leipzig and Hof. As a member of Himmler's personal staff, Lamm was able to reserve a private compartment.

Irma squealed in delight as she looked around the tiny enclosure. "Max, I've never been in a private compartment. Do we have to go to the dining car or can we have supper here?"

"We can have supper here."

"Oh, Max," she sighed, throwing her arms around his waist. "This is so romantic. When you joined the SS I knew you would become an important man very quickly."

After they ate their supper, Lamm wrapped his arms around Irma. He was pleased she liked the compartment, but he was not in the mood for frivolity. If things went wrong he could be reprimanded or worse. Suddenly the stress of the past few days caught up with him, and, releasing Irma, he stretched out on one of the bunks. He was asleep before the porter arrived to clear away the dishes.

Irma stayed awake much longer, looking out the window at the darkened countryside. Delighted with the private compartment, she wondered how high Max would eventually go in the SS.

They arrived in Nuremberg at four in the morning. The station was empty except for the passengers detraining, and it took a few minutes to hire a porter to help them across the street to the Württemberger Hof, which was within walking distance of the museum. After some difficulty waking the night clerk, Lamm and Irma checked into their room, and were soon sound asleep.

In the morning Lamm let Irma sleep and went downstairs to eat. The Württemberger Hof was known for its hearty breakfast, but Lamm had no appetite. A cup of coffee and a roll with marmalade was enough. The news in the Nuremberger *Zeitung* was upsetting. Beneath all the propaganda, it was clear that Germany had not only lost the Battle of Britain, but the "weakened" Royal Air Force was carrying the war to the Fatherland, and its bombing raids were becoming more of a threat. Lamm was furious. What was wrong with the Nazi leadership? Germany had the largest air force in the world and they were still unable to defeat the RAF. *There has to be a way to bring the British to their knees once and for all,* he thought, finishing his coffee.

Lamm had visited Nuremberg several times previously, and loved the city's medieval buildings with their reminders of the wealth, power, and style of the Imperial free city that had been home to Dürer, Melanchthon, and Adam Krafft. After strolling down the narrow sidewalks of the Frauenthorgraben, he entered the old city wall at Vordersterngasse and walked along the inside of the brown stone wall for 150 meters before turning right on the Vorder Kurthauserstrasse. There stood the museum, a fourteenth-century masterpiece draped in huge lurid Nazi banners. An elderly guard opened the door for Lamm as he walked up. Once inside, Lamm walked over to the desk and asked for the director. Unfortunately, "Herr Direktor" was ill, and Dr. Langsdorf, one of the assistant directors, was expecting him. Lamm knew he should have expected this. He couldn't count the times he had seen this in academia. Everything was delegated to assistants, so they could be blamed if anything went wrong. In this case he could hardly blame the director. A visit by a member of Himmler's staff was nothing to be taken lightly. Lamm sensed he had a tremendous amount of power in this situation, and felt he had to find a way to turn the situation back on von Bartz. It was time to be bold.

As he entered the assistant director's office, he saw an average-sized man, with a bald pate showing above a ring of dense curly hair, rising to meet him. Stooping slightly, the man squinted through thick glasses that made his eyes look unnaturally large. Langsdorf straightened his rumpled brown suit, nervously offering his hand to Lamm. "Herr Obersturmführer Lamm, I presume."

Lamm stiffly raised his arm. "Heil Hitler!"

"Oh," said Langsdorf, taken aback. "Heil Hitler."

Lamm then shook hands with Langsdorf and sat down without being asked.

"I presume you are here concerning the Vikmo artifacts," Langsdorf said.

"Yes, Dr. Langsdorf."

Langsdorf was understandably nervous as he fiddled with two letters on his desk. Both men knew that in the twisted logic of the Third Reich, Langsdorf could be blamed for the entire fiasco and be arrested by the Gestapo if Himmler was displeased. "We were instructed to display the artifacts by the Bureau for Racial Research. The letter is signed by Dr. Nass," he said, handing a copy of the letter to Lamm, who perused it politely.

Langsdorf cleared his throat. "Under normal conditions, Herr Obersturmführer, the artifacts have to be examined and verified by independent experts from several institutions. In this case, Dr. Nass insisted we display them immediately. Naturally, we protested a display of newly discovered items that had not been verified. Here is a copy of the letter." Hands trembling, he handed the letter to the SS officer, who then read it. "Unfortunately, Dr. Nass, who claimed he was representing Reichsführer Himmler, insisted." He sighed and looked at the SS officer across from him.

Lamm had to admit that Langsdorf had courage. For a man who knew he might be arrested at any moment, the assistant director was defending the museum and himself very well. Lamm was impressed. He looked at the letter again, then addressed the situation directly.

"I assure you, Dr. Langsdorf," he said, sympathetically, "the Reichsführer regrets this incident as much as the museum, and would like to see it disappear as quickly as possible." He would soon find out if he were exceeding his authority and whether or not someone liked it.

"The exhibit is to run another month and a half, Herr Obersturmführer." Langsdorf wanted Lamm to make the decision.

"How soon can you dismantle it?" Lamm asked.

"Tonight," Langsdorf replied, with an expression of relieved surprise.

"I think that it would be best. By the way, where is it? I'd like to see it, but if I may, I'd like to borrow your telephone first."

"Please." Dr. Langsdorf handed Lamm the phone. Lamm called the local SS headquarters and had a photographer come to the museum and take detailed photographs of the exhibit. As soon as the photographers were finished, Lamm left the museum and returned to the hotel. The photographs would take two days to process.

"Max, where were you?" Irma asked. "I woke up and you were gone."

"Unfortunately, I am here on business, my darling, but the first part of it is over. Why don't we have lunch at the Deutscher Kaiser restaurant and go for a stroll around the city?"

"The Deutscher Kaiser is awfully expensive, isn't it?"

"Just pretend we're on holiday."

While he and Irma enjoyed a superb lunch of roast venison with potatoes, von Bartz was standing at attention in Himmler's office.

"You dolt!" Himmler shouted. "What did you and Nass expect to do? Did you want to disgrace me in the eyes of the Führer and the world?"

"No, Herr Reichsführer, I thought . . ."

"Silence!" Himmler yelled. "You thought? You thought? Between Nass and you I couldn't make one half-wit. Think! That's the problem. You're on my staff to think. Obviously you didn't. Now I want this mess cleaned up immediately. Do you understand?"

Von Bartz opened his mouth to speak, but was so stunned that words wouldn't come.

Himmler snapped, "Don't stand there with your mouth open like a fish. Answer me! Do you understand?"

"Yes, Herr Reichsführer."

"Dismissed!

"Heil Hitler!"

"Heil Hitler!"

Von Bartz left Himmler's office so hurriedly that he forgot to tell the Reichsführer that Lamm was already in Nuremberg. He had missed an opportunity to involve Lamm, and that made him angrier. On his return to the office, von Bartz called the Württemberger Hof and left a message for Lamm, who returned the call after ten in the evening, when he knew the office would be empty.

The following morning von Bartz received a sarcastic call from Himmler. "I don't suppose you've seen the Nuremberger *Zeitung* this morning, have you, von Bartz?"

"No, Herr Reichsführer."

"Do you have someone in Nuremberg, von Bartz?"

"Yes, Herr Reichsführer. Dr. Lamm."

"Well, I'm happy to see someone in the Racial Science Section has some sense. He managed to get the whole thing closed in a day."

"What?"

"Didn't you know?"

"Oh, of course, Herr Reichsführer. That's why I sent him."

"I want to see him when he returns."

"Yes, Herr Reichsführer."

"Von Bartz?"

"Yes, Herr Reichsführer."

"One more blunder like this, and I'll appoint you head of the RIB."

"RIB, Herr Reichsführer?"

"The Reich Idiots' Bureau." Himmler slammed the phone down.

Von Bartz stared at the phone and fumed. Lamm had stabbed him in the back. He had been trying to make von Bartz look bad since he arrived. First his whining about laboratory space and now this. Von Bartz decided to write a scathing letter to the Reichsführer detailing Lamm's disloyalty. His career in the SS was finished!

Lamm and Irma stayed late at the Café Metropole, but he still woke early. He reached over and touched Irma's soft blonde curls as she slept. He loved her so much, but when it came to parties and uniforms, she was such a little girl. Delighted by the external trappings of power and the constant promise of victory, she was unable to comprehend the reality of the situation. He wondered how many other Germans were just like her, and was not comforted by what he thought was the answer. Putting on his uniform, he went for a last walk in Nuremberg to think.

Lamm stopped at the Marien-Thor, one of the main gates of the old Imperial city, and looked down the Lorenzerstrasse into the old city itself. *Very symbolic,* he thought. *I am standing at the dividing line between the old city and the new, just as today Germany stands on the threshold of a new era.* The Reich had a rich cultural and intellectual history, but the Nazis cared little for intellectual and scientific achievement. All they cared about were their absurd racial theories, and they were willing to spend large amounts of money on projects like Operation NORD while real scientific research went begging. Lamm had joined the Racial Science Section hoping he might do some good, but from his vantage point at the Marien-Thor he had failed. Surely Hitler could not be as deluded or stupid as the other high Party officials he knew.

Then there was von Bartz, with his mistress and the bribes. With him out of the way, the Racial Science Section could become the premier scientific organization in the Reich. With proper resources, Lamm knew he could build a uranium burner. After that, who knew what was possible? The only man standing in his way was Erwin von Bartz, but there was no way the head of the Racial Science Section would give up his lucrative little post voluntarily. To make matters worse, he would, no doubt, make Lamm's life miserable from now on. Von Bartz had to go. But how?

Lamm, deep in thought, didn't see the black Mercedes pull up to the sidewalk next to him. "Herr Professor," someone called.

Lamm looked up and, for a moment, thought it was the Gestapo arresting him for exceeding his authority. Just before he panicked, he realized there were SS Gruppenführer flags on the fenders. Lamm breathed a sigh of relief and walked over to the car.

"What are you doing in Nuremberg, Herr Professor?" Heydrich asked.

"I'm here on business, Herr Gruppenführer."

"Get in. I'll drive you to your destination." It was an order.

"I don't want to put you to any trouble, Herr Gruppenführer."

"Get in," Heydrich insisted.

Lamm got into the limousine and tried to make himself comfortable on the soft leather seat. Heydrich made him uneasy. There was something unsettling about a man who could consider murdering millions of people so matter-of-factly. Worse, Heydrich was sober and in his usual foul mood. "Are you here on the NORD business?" Heydrich asked.

"Yes, Herr Gruppenführer."

"Was it you that got the exhibit closed down?"

"Yes, Herr Gruppenführer."

"Hah. I thought so. Do you know how much embarrassment your friend von Bartz and that idiot Nass have caused in the foreign press?"

"I can imagine," Lamm said.

"That *mischling,*" von Bartz snorted. He had used the term for a half-breed to refer to von Bartz. "Someone ought to put a bullet in his brain," Heydrich said, looking directly at Lamm. "Except in von Bartz's case they'd have to shoot him in the rear." Heydrich laughed nastily.

"If he's so bad, why was he assigned to head the Racial Science Section?" Lamm asked.

Heydrich looked at Lamm. "Don't you know?"

"No, Herr Gruppenführer."

"In 1937, the Reichsführer was attacked by a Storm Trooper—one of Röhm's supporters, I think—who had bided his time to get even. He went after Himmler with a pistol. Von Bartz intervened and stepped between the Reichsführer and the would-be assassin. No one knows whether he did it on purpose or whether it was an accident. Von Bartz was shot once in the leg and in the struggle the Storm Trooper was killed, shot through the temple. Personally, I think he accidentally killed himself when von Bartz fell on top of him. When the Reichsführer learned that von Bartz had 'saved' his life, he was naturally grateful."

"He still has a doctorate in physics," Lamm said.

"That was no feat," Heydrich snapped. "He has a good memory. He probably memorized every example of problems that could be used on exams."

"But what about the orals?" Lamm asked.

"He talked himself into the Racial Science Section, didn't he?" Heydrich replied. "He can be very persuasive in the right circumstances."

Lamm said nothing as Heydrich grinned. "Von Bartz's family is *petite noblesse* from Thuringia. They also have money. Those two qualities made him very attractive to the Party in the early days. Himmler has a fetish about nobility in the SS." Still feeling uneasy about being in Heydrich's presence, Lamm wanted to look out the window, but paid strict attention to Heydrich.

"How did you get the exhibit closed down?" the Gruppenführer asked.

"I just told them the Reichsführer was just as anxious as they were to see it gone and to dismantle it immediately."

"And right you were. Very good, Lamm. Von Bartz would have drafted a dozen memoranda before anything was done. We need your kind of decisiveness if the Reich is to survive. Where are you going now?"

"The Württemberger Hof, across from the station. My wife and I leave for Berlin in another hour."

"If you need someone to help you with your bags, I'll send a car."

"Thank you, Herr Gruppenführer, but the hotel provides a porter."

Heydrich's car pulled up to the curb. "Speaking of the Racial Science Section, do you have a laboratory yet?"

"Obersturmbannführer von Bartz says there's no money for it, and has forbidden me to bring the matter up again until he says so."

Heydrich looked at him. "What would you do if you were the head of the Racial Science Section, Herr Professor?"

Lamm hesitated, then decided Heydrich was his only ally in this business. "There is a new theory that energy can be derived from the splitting of atoms. If we can harness that energy, we might be able to make bombs of incredible power and create electricity without the use of coal or oil. It would free the Reich from any dependence on foreign fuel imports."

"Can we direct this energy at a particular target?" Heydrich asked.

"Honestly, I don't know yet, Herr Gruppenführer. It will take lots of experimentation to find out."

"Interesting," was all Heydrich said.

The car arrived at the hotel, and Heydrich's driver got out and opened the door. Lamm stepped onto the curb. "Thank you, Herr Gruppenführer. Heil Hitler."

"Heil Hitler," Heydrich said, absentmindedly. Then he added. "Herr Professor, be careful. Von Bartz may be stupid, but he's still very dangerous. What you've done won't endear you to him."

"Yes, Herr Gruppenführer, thank you." He watched the Mercedes speed away from the curb. Lamm wondered what Heydrich was trying to tell him. He returned to the room.

"Max," Irma greeted him, "you look upset."

"I am," he told her. "I just saw Heydrich."

"The adorable tall one?"

"The same."

"What did he say to upset you?"

Lamm couldn't explain the complexities of the situation. "He told me to be careful of von Bartz."

"Why?"

"Von Bartz made a mistake, and he may try to blame it on me."

"Well, don't let him. Just go to Reichsführer Himmler and tell him. He'll understand."

Lamm smiled at her naiveté. "Yes, dear. That's just what I'll do."

Lamm was grateful Irma didn't ask any more questions. They packed and went across to the Central Station. They were back in Berlin by ten o'clock, and then they couldn't get a taxi. A British air raid had damaged several buildings, and firefighting equipment and rubble blocked a number of streets. The Lamms' apartment was several kilometers from the nearest bomb craters, but the explosions had broken a window and one of Irma's porcelain figurines.

"Dirty British!" she cried, looking at the pieces of a shattered ballerina.

Lamm thought, *This is only the beginning.* "Irma, maybe we should move to the country."

"No," she was adamant. "I refuse to live on a farm. Berlin is my home. No more British will bomb it. If they try the Luftwaffe will shoot them down. Reichsmarschall Göring has said so, and he's such a nice man."

Lamm smiled at her. He had to get his family out of Berlin now that it was a target, but this was not the time. He would try to convince Irma later. "Of course, my love."

It was a traumatic morning. After calling Lamm into his office, von Bartz stood him at attention.

"How dare you disobey my orders!" he screamed hysterically. If von Bartz had acted like an adolescent in his previous tirades, he went over the edge of hysteria with this one. Startled by the ferocity of the attack, Lamm was silent as von Bartz's face turned purple.

"I told you to get the facts to write a confidential report for me, not close the exhibit down! This is the last time you will disobey me, Professor Lamm. I am recommending you be dismissed from the SS and the Party for your flagrant disloyalty. Is that understood?"

"Yes, Herr Obersturmbannführer."

"You are to report to the Reichsführer immediately!"

"I beg your pardon?" This was a surprise.

"You heard me. I have informed the Reichsführer of your disloyalty and he will deal with you. Dismissed!"

My career is over, Lamm thought, as he walked down the hall into his office and called for a car. *I made a decision without von Bartz's approval and unfortunately it proved to be the correct one.*

It was a short trip to Himmler's headquarters building. Lamm entered the Reichsführer's plush outer office wondering if he would be arrested. He didn't even have to tell the receptionist who he was. She smiled and called the Reichsführer on the intercom.

"Untersturmführer Lamm is here, Herr Reichsführer."

"Good. Send him in."

Lamm clenched his fists to keep his hands from trembling and braced himself. The receptionist opened the door for him, and he strode into the office. It was lavishly decorated, with original paintings and expensive Persian carpets. Lamm determined to take whatever came bravely. He raised his arm in a salute.

"Heil Hitler!"

"Heil Hitler, Professor," Himmler said, mildly. Smiling, the Reichsführer didn't seem at all upset, and Lamm wondered why he was so calm. "Have a seat, Herr Professor. Would you like some tea?"

Lamm's jaw nearly dropped. "Yes, thank you, Herr Reichsführer." Lamm perched rigidly on the edge of the chair.

"Send in two cups of tea, please," Himmler said to the intercom, then walked over and took a chair close to Lamm's. He leaned back and spoke of the weather before getting to the point.

"The reason I called you here was to thank you for your handling of the matter in Nuremberg."

Lamm was dumbfounded. He started to speak, but Himmler held up his hand.

"Let's hear no more about it," Himmler said softly.

There was a knock on the door, and a servant in a white jacket entered with two china cups and a silver tea service on a silver tray. He poured the tea, set the tray on the table, and silently disappeared.

"I think you realize, Hauptsturmführer Lamm, that there are times in the histories of great movements in which individuals are not as important as the movement itself. It may be accurately stated that the efforts of the totality of a movement are greater than the efforts of its individual parts. The National Socialist Party is such a movement. Only one individual is important, and that is our Führer, Adolf Hitler." Himmler's voice was reverent as he mentioned the Führer.

"Other individuals," he continued, "must subordinate their will to his for the good of the Reich. I am not saying that we should not be loyal to one another. As Party members, we must have loyalty to help each other as we struggle toward the final victory. That is why I made the motto of the SS 'Loyalty is my Honor.' However, there are times when one must forsake one's loyalty to an individual in order to obey a higher loyalty to the Party. Do I make myself clear?"

"Perfectly, Herr Reichsführer." Lamm didn't have the foggiest notion of what Himmler meant. And why had the Reichsführer addressed him at a rank higher than the one he held? Lamm decided this wasn't the time to ask questions. He politely sipped the bitter herbal tea.

"Do you like the tea?" Himmler asked.

"Excellent, Herr Reichsführer. It's an herbal tea but I don't recognize the blend."

Himmler smiled blandly and explained that it was his own concoction. "Since you like it I will send you some. I am also pleased to tell you that I have approved your promotion to Hauptsturmführer."

"Thank you, Herr Reichsführer," Lamm said, with genuine gratitude. There was a moment of silence, and he saw it was time to leave. He stood up and raised his arm. Smiling, he and Himmler exchanged "Heil Hitlers" and shook hands.

Lamm left the Reichsführer's office and put on his hat and coat as he walked down the steps to his waiting car. "Racial Science Section," he told the driver as he climbed in. Leaning back against the seat, he tried to sort out what was happening. If his decision to close down the exhibit at the Germanic Museum did not put him on a direct collision course with von Bartz, the promotion certainly would. Was that what Himmler and Heydrich were trying to do? Loyalty to the Party was greater than loyalty to an individual. What was he really trying to say? Heydrich had been considerably clearer, "Someone ought to put a bullet in his brain." Were they telling him to kill von Bartz? If so, it was another example of the murky politics of the Third Reich. Divide and rule.

But if Lamm tried to kill von Bartz and failed, Himmler and Heydrich will be the first to condemn him, and then he would be executed. Certainly von Bartz would not rest until he destroyed Lamm, so life would be a lot easier with him out of the way. And with von Bartz out of the way, Lamm would be free to research the possibilities of atomic energy. *Am I at all like them? Can I bring myself to kill another human being?*

By acting sufficiently cowed when he returned, Lamm made von Bartz believe he had been reprimanded by Himmler, and the office settled down to a guarded calm until news of Lamm's promotion arrived two weeks later.

Von Bartz's tone was bitterly calm as he handed Lamm the letter of notification. "I want you to know that I recommended that you not be promoted. You have been disloyal to me personally, to the Racial Science Section, and to the Party. The only explanation I can see is that the SS is in desperate need of officers. I want you to understand that this is not a sign that your conduct of the past few weeks is condoned. I'm sure when my report of your misconduct reaches the Reichsführer your promotion will be revoked. Do I make myself clear?"

"Perfectly, Herr Obersturmbannführer."

Lamm walked back to his office. Once again someone had asked him if things were perfectly clear, but they weren't. Von Bartz was obviously as stupid as Heydrich insisted. Couldn't he see that Lamm was being rewarded for doing a job he, the director, had failed to do? Then there were Himmler and Heydrich talking in riddles. "*Mischling* . . . someone ought to put a bullet in his brain . . . obey the higher loyalty to the Party." If anyone needed killing, it was Erwin von Bartz.

April-June 1941

The war was going well for Germany. Although England still held out, Bulgaria and Rumania were now allies, Yugoslavia and Greece were in the process of being defeated, and in Africa, an obscure general named Rommel turned the tide of Italian defeat with one armored division. On April 27 German troops marched into Athens, and on June 1, German paratroopers took Crete. The news was not all good, however, as the *Bismarck* had been lost.

On June 22, 1941, Goebbels announced that German troops had crossed the Soviet border to destroy Bolshevism. If the Führer expected the German people to cheer "Operation Barbarossa," he was mistaken. Most Germans merely felt relieved, since they had not understood why the Fatherland had ever signed a pact with Russia. However, cheers did not matter much as long as the German Volk did its duty.

The day after Barbarossa began, von Bartz received a letter from the Reichsführer's office confirming Lamm's promotion, along with a personal greeting for Lamm and a half-pound of herbal tea. Von Bartz forwarded both to his assistant without comment, and from then on refused to speak with him unless he absolutely had to. For the next week, von Bartz tried to see Himmler personally. When he failed, he tried to reach him on the phone. It was to no avail. Von Bartz had fallen out of favor, and he knew it. It was all Lamm's fault. But von Bartz still had friends in the Gestapo. Perhaps they might help. He picked up the phone.

At first he thought it was his imagination, but Lamm realized that he was being followed when he recognized the same two men wherever he went. They were obviously Gestapo, but they made no move to arrest him. They were looking for something. For what? They couldn't have been sent by Himmler or Heydrich. If von Bartz had the kind of power that could bring the Gestapo down on him, he was more dangerous than Lamm thought.

On June 29, 1941, Maximilian Lamm decided to kill Erwin von Bartz. It was the only way he could survive and devote his time to atomic energy. Heydrich had given Lamm a hint when he called von Bartz a *"mischling,"* and that was enough. If everyone could be convinced von Bartz was part Jew, Lamm's plan might work. It would be better, of course, if von Bartz just blew his own brains out. Suicide! That was the answer. The head of the Racial Science Section would kill himself. With Lamm's help, of course. Lamm formulated a plan and mulled it over. He was later astonished that von Bartz himself put the plan into operation.

September 19, 1941

"Have Professor Lamm report to me," von Bartz told his secretary.

Since they rarely met face-to-face, Lamm responded to the summons immediately.

"I want you to go to Regensburg tomorrow." Lamm remained

silent. "A teacher has been charged by the People's Court with using forbidden materials written by a Jewish biologist. The court is holding the papers as evidence, and you are to examine them and give expert testimony—nothing else. In no way are you to involve the Racial Science Section in the case. Understood?"

"Y . . . Yes, sir." Lamm stammered. Regensburg was the key in his plan to kill von Bartz, who took the professor's surprise for fear.

"When you arrive, report to the local Gestapo headquarters. And this time you can't take your wife. Any questions?"

"No sir."

Lamm left wondering if he'd been singled out by fate. Naturally, von Bartz would be too busy to leave the office for such a trivial purpose. He wouldn't want to miss a visit to his mistress or a bribe, and that encouraged Lamm to proceed. Von Bartz refused the funds for an express, so Lamm had to take a series of local trains that stopped at every village along the way. He spent the entire journey pacing the corridors of the moving train, reviewing his plan. Failure surely meant death at the Gestapo's hand, or his own.

Arriving in Regensburg exhausted, Lamm went directly to the Grüner Kranz on the Obermunsterstrasse, where the local Gestapo headquarters had reserved a room for him. It was a picturesque little place a few blocks from the old cloisters, the large square stone abbey built in the thirteenth and fourteenth centuries that had been the residence of the local ruling princes from 1812 to the end of the German Empire.

Lamm had never been to Regensburg, and was fascinated by the idea of a city that had begun life as a Roman camp, but he would have to wait for another time to explore it. His twin missions would take up all his time. Shortly after checking in, he was sound asleep.

First thing in the morning, he visited Gestapo headquarters to identify the offending papers, which turned out to be basic notes on introductory biology written by a Jewish professor, something the poor schoolteacher couldn't have known without extensive research. Lamm knew the way things worked in the Third Reich, and he figured the man had been denounced out of spite, and would now suffer for his ignorance. Lamm felt sorry for the man, but he didn't have time to help him. There were more important things to do, and they had best be done quickly. To gain time, Lamm had the Gestapo make copies of the documents so he could study them in his room and promised he would give them a thorough analysis in two days.

The next stop was the Rathaus, a gloomy, irregular building partially erected in the fourteenth century and finished sometime in the eighteenth. It had been the seat of the Imperial Diet from 1663 to 1806, and its walls were black from years of accumulated soot. Walking in, he found the birth records office and entered to look around and memorize the faces of those who worked there. Occasionally, he checked his watch as if waiting for someone. One receptionist asked if he needed assistance, and he politely declined. No one else bothered the SS officer in full uniform who appeared to be there on official business. When Lamm had learned everything he could, he returned to the Grüner Kranz to take a nap. It was going to be a long two days.

Lamm spent the early afternoon reviewing the papers so he could refer to them with some degree of credibility—not that the Gestapo would notice. Gestapo members were not chosen for their intellect. At three he dressed in civilian clothes and explored the area around the Rathaus for an hour. Then he watched the entrance. At quitting time, the clerks from the records office emerged together. Three of them waited at the streetcar stop while another, a junior clerk if Lamm remembered correctly, went off alone. He followed the man to a small crowded tavern where his quarry found a small table in a corner. Since there was an empty chair at the table, Lamm walked up to it.

"Excuse me, Mein Herr. Is this seat taken?"

"No," the man replied timidly, and looked around. This was an age in which all strangers were suspicious.

Lamm sat down, and ordered a glass of beer. In his fifties, the balding man wore a dark gray suit, old, worn, and shiny from pressing. Knowing the man would not speak first, Lamm used the talents he practiced on reticent students to draw him out. He began the conversation with small talk. "I am visiting for the first time, even though my family is originally from Regensburg. I never realized it was such an interesting place. You're lucky to live here."

The man shrugged. His glass was nearly empty.

"Herr Ober," Lamm called to the waiter. "Two more for my friend and me." The man raised an eyebrow. "It's on me," Lamm assured him. His quarry accepted gratefully as Lamm prattled on. Lamm turned back to the man. "I know you. You're Herr Weiss. You work in the deeds department in the Rathaus."

"Oh no," the man said. "My name is Gartner, and I work in the records department."

"Oh, I apologize," Lamm said. "I had you confused with someone else."

"That's quite all right," Gartner was much less timid as Lamm ordered him another beer.

"You must find your work terribly interesting," Lamm said.

"Oh yes, the records are fascinating." Gartner's words were beginning to slur. He had drunk several of the free beers.

Lamm took a deep breath and asked the question. "Suppose one was a loyal German, but had a relative who was 'questionable'? What could one do?"

Gartner looked around conspiratorially and leaned close. "See Herr Faller in the records department. He is in charge of birth certificates. A hundred marks will fix everything."

"Which one is Herr Faller?" Lamm asked.

Gartner described his colleague, and Lamm pressed a twenty-mark note in Gartner's hand. "You have done my family a great service," he whispered. He left as Gartner told the waiter he wanted to order supper.

Lamm returned to the Grüner Kranz, donned a uniform, and returned to Gestapo Headquarters, where he asked them if he could question Herr Faller of the Rathaus records department concerning a confidential matter. Only too happy to oblige a member of Himmler's personal staff, they picked up the records clerk shortly after midnight. Faller, fat and sloppy, in his mid-forties and still dressed in his pajamas, was absolutely terrified. The Gestapo agents sat Faller down in a chair and left. Lamm walked back and forth in front of the terrified records clerk smoking a cigarette, but said nothing, preferring to let the man stew. Faller's eyes followed Lamm everywhere until he stopped directly in front of the frightened man and crushed out his cigarette.

"Herr Faller," he said quietly, "we have enough evidence of your tampering with records to send you to a very unpleasant place for a very long time." He paused. "And I don't think your family will do too well either."

Lamm was taken aback when the clerk suddenly left his chair and threw himself at Lamm's feet, sobbing and begging for mercy. Disgusted by the clerk's total lack of control, Lamm smiled at the ease with which he had broken the man. This was better than he had hoped for. He lifted him up by the hair and pushed him back in the chair.

"Herr Faller," Lamm spoke softly, trying to calm Faller, but the man was hysterical. Losing all patience, Lamm slapped him several times across the face and yelled, "Stop crying and listen!"

Faller sat wide-eyed, holding his cheek.

"What you have done is inexcusable," Lamm shouted at him. "You are a disgrace to the new Germany and I should have you thrown into a concentration camp." He paused. "However, there is one thing you can do to redeem yourself."

"Name it, Herr Hauptsturmführer." Faller sobbed. "I am yours to command."

"There was a man born in Regensburg in 1896, on October the tenth. His name is Erwin von Bartz. I want you to alter his record."

Faller grinned crookedly. "Has he a Jewish relative?"

"No, but when you get through, he will."

Faller's mouth dropped open in surprise. "I don't understand."

"You're not supposed to understand!" Lamm screamed at him. "Do what you're told and you'll get your usual fee. Fail, and you and your family will never see the light of day again!" The smile disappeared from Faller's face. "Do I make myself understood?"

"Yes, Herr Hauptsturmführer," Faller whimpered.

"Now you will make a copy of von Bartz's birth certificate to reflect that his mother was Jewish. Then you will mail the copy to von Bartz as if he had requested it. Mail it to him at the Racial Science Section on the Wolfstrasse in Berlin. Once I get it safely, you'll get your money, not before. Understood?"

"Perfectly, Herr Hauptsturmführer."

"Send the copy as soon as you can. It must arrive no later than the beginning of October."

Faller shook his head. "Of course, Herr Hauptsturmführer."

"Now get out," Lamm snapped.

Like a weasel, Faller slipped out of the room before Lamm could take another breath. Lamm grinned, wondering how Faller would get home in his pajamas, but a second thought erased his grin. If he were caught calling for von Bartz's records to be altered, he could be beheaded. Involuntarily he put his finger between his collar and his neck.

Lamm delivered a report to the Gestapo to the effect that the papers the teacher used were indeed forbidden, and offered to make a deposition or stay on as an expert witness. The Gestapo thanked him, but said it wouldn't be necessary.

Returning to Berlin late in the evening, Lamm considered the next step of his plan, which was to exchange von Bartz's pistol with his own. Regulations required the pistol to be worn at all times with the service uniform, but von Bartz preferred to leave it hanging on the coat hook in his office.

The next Wednesday afternoon, with von Bartz at his mistress's house, it was a simple task to switch the pistols. Then Lamm settled down to watch the mail. Von Bartz, vindictive and lazy, had given Lamm the lowly task of screening everything except his personal mail, so the letter with the new birth certificate crossed Lamm's desk four days after his interrogation of Faller.

Lamm grudgingly admitted that Faller did first-class work. The birth certificate looked like an original, complete with a Royal Württemberg stamp and signature. Now came the wait for von Bartz to work late, which he did frequently when he was answering bribe letters. It gave the impression he was working hard, and there was no one around the office to ask questions.

The entire time Lamm waited, his stomach was full of butterflies and his legs were like lead. Countless times, Lamm made sure the Walther in his holster was loaded and the safety was off. Von Bartz, noticing his assistant's unease, assumed he had finally brought the professor to heel and was in fine humor.

Two days after the forged birth certificate arrived, von Bartz worked late to "catch up on his correspondence." Lamm left the office at the usual time, but didn't go home. He went to a bar to stiffen his courage, and returned an hour and a half after everyone had gone. The guards saluted him, and since the elevator operator was off, he went up the steps.

"Who's there?" von Bartz called when heard the footsteps.

"It is I, Hauptsturmführer Lamm, Herr Obersturmbannführer."

"What are you doing here?" von Bartz asked suspiciously. The venom in his voice was undisguised.

"I forgot to finish a report, sir. It will take half an hour and I will be gone."

"Humpf."

Lamm unlocked his desk and withdrew the birth certificate and envelope, loosened the flap on his holster, and walked down the hall to von Bartz's office.

"Herr Obersturmbannführer," Lamm said, trying to keep his voice from cracking.

"Yes," von Bartz said impatiently.

"I have something which is vital to the Racial Science Section."

"What is it, more of your atomic nonsense? I'm busy."

"No, sir, it's for you personally. I didn't mean to open it."

"Let me see it!" Von Bartz's eyes flashed angrily, thinking Lamm had discovered one of his bribes. Lamm walked around the desk and handed the letter to von Bartz. Von Bartz glanced at the envelope and birth certificate and, since no cash was in it, breathed a sigh of relief, paying no further attention. "I'll get to it as soon as I can," he told Lamm. "Now leave me alone, I'm busy."

It took an incredibly long time for Lamm to draw the pistol, point it at von Bartz's head, and pull the trigger, but the movement caught the Obersturmbannführer completely unaware. The roar of the pistol in the small room was deafening and, for a moment, Lamm was stunned. Von Bartz's head jerked to the left as blood and pieces of skull and brain spattered on the opposite wall. Lamm had the presence of mind to wipe his fingerprints off the gun and put it in von Bartz's hand. After making sure the birth certificate was on top of everything else on the desk, Lamm trembled and ran out into the hall. The guards were already running up the stairs.

"My God!" Lamm shouted. "He's killed himself!"

"Who?" the Scharführer in command of the guard demanded. He was an older man with the Old Fighter's Chevron. Two guards with rifles were behind him.

"Obersturmbannführer von Bartz!" Lamm shouted.

Lamm followed the Scharführer and a guard into the room. Von

Bartz was slumped in the chair, the gun dangling from his finger. Blood was everywhere.

"Oh my God, " Lamm said, weakly.

"You had better sit down, Herr Hauptsturmführer," the Scharführer said. "You don't look well."

Lamm leaned against the wall, then made for the bathroom, where he vomited.

"That's the new SS," he heard the Scharführer say sarcastically behind him.

Lamm flushed the toilet, closed the lid, and sat on it. It hadn't been the sight of von Bartz's corpse that had terrified him. It was the sight of his pistol, still in von Bartz's holster. Fortunately no one had noticed the gun hanging there, and Lamm retrieved it after the Scharführer left to call the police and the Gestapo, with the guard close behind him.

October 23, 1941

A formal hearing and an investigation of the birth records at Regensburg proved von Bartz's mother was Jewish. Faller had, indeed, done his work well. Lamm testified that he had been outside von Bartz's office on his way to visit the Obersturmbannführer when he heard von Bartz say something to the effect of, "Oh, my God, they've found out." Lamm presented evidence of the bribes and von Bartz's mistress to the board of officers conducting the hearing. The conclusion was that von Bartz, a corrupt *mischling* masquerading as an Aryan, committed suicide when he was discovered. The final verdict was simply suicide, and no mention was made of the birth certificate, the bribes, or anything else, in order to prevent embarrassment to Himmler and the SS. It would hardly look proper if it were discovered that a non-Aryan had gotten by the rigorous tests conducted by the SS. The case was closed quickly. Himmler made no mention of the affair.

Von Bartz was buried quietly, without the usual SS fanfare for a fallen comrade. With few people in attendance, the services were short and nothing was said about the circumstances of his death. Von Bartz's wife, wearing a black veil to hide her lack of tears, tossed a handful of dirt on the casket and left. After the funeral Lamm was officially appointed head of the Racial Science Section. Several days later he received a personal telegram from Heydrich, who was in Prague.

"Bravo. You should visit Passau. It's beautiful this time of year."

Lamm went weak at the knees. Von Bartz's mother was born in Passau, but no one had bothered to check her birth certificate. It was a stupid oversight, and it was obvious that Heydrich had covered for him by not bringing up the mother's birth certificate. Lamm would have to be more careful in the future.

CHAPTER 5

MATERIALS

Berlin to Lübeck
November 8, 1941

AFTER VON BARTZ'S FUNERAL, Lamm was appointed chief of the Racial Science section and, to the satisfaction of Reichsführer Himmler, completed the report on Operation NORD, ending the matter once and for all, except for Dr. Nass, who disappeared shortly thereafter. Lamm rearranged the offices and functions of the Racial Science Section in a more logical manner and requested more help, but was informed no replacements were available due to the needs of the Russian Front. Bittner became the office manager, controlling all the correspondence and reports. Frau Norbert was elevated to head secretary of the section, while Fräulein Trautner became the filing secretary. Visibly miffed at her loss of status, Fräulein Trautner complained to Lamm, who was totally unsympathetic. Since Loring was intelligent and very race-conscious, Lamm made him a review assistant, which meant the Scharführer read the incoming papers for signs of racial impurity and only brought them to Lamm's desk if they required his attention.

Lamm was now free to concentrate on his theory that atomic power was the key to German victory. Although most high Party officials seemed oblivious to the fact, the German offensive in Russia was slowing to a halt. *What the Russian winter did to Napoleon, it is now doing to us,* Lamm thought. If the Wehrmacht got bogged down in that endless wasteland it would bleed Germany white. Lamm had to do something decisive, and do it quickly.

He spent hours reading and rereading every paper concerning atomic physics, searching for clues. A pair of articles about the potential of atomic energy had been written in 1939 by Dr. Siegfried Flugge, a theoretical physicist at the Kaiser Wilhelm Institute. Flugge theorized that each fissioning atom of uranium liberated approximately 200 million electron-volts. Assuming a one-cubic-meter block of uranium oxide contained, theoretically, 9×10^{27} uranium atoms, the energy that would be released from the fission of such a block was mind-boggling. The effect of releasing all that energy in a fraction of a second would be enough to destroy a city or an entire army in the proverbial blink of an eye. *That was it,* Lamm thought. A uranium bomb would be the perfect tool. It would be a victory for German science and a victory for German arms.

But the reality of his situation was daunting, and Lamm's enthusiasm cooled rapidly. The technical problems to be overcome were significant. A cubic meter of uranium oxide would weigh about 3600 kilograms, and no German aircraft could carry that big a load and release it over the target. How to trigger the reaction was another problem, if indeed uranium oxide could be used for an explosion. From his early readings, Lamm had theorized pure uranium 235 would be necessary and would, no doubt, require a large industrial complex to produce.

Once Lamm was finished with everything available in the office, he looked for other sources of information. One positive thing von Bartz had done was to make the German scientific community fearful of the Racial Science Section, so when Lamm requested material, he got it quickly and without comment. What he discovered only made the task more difficult. Separation of the two isotopes of uranium had been accomplished in laboratory experiments, but the amounts of explosive uranium 235 obtained were insignificant. Development of uranium 235 alone would require a huge installation dedicated to uranium isotope separation—and a lot of time.

However, an American publication provided an alternative solution. American scientists experimenting with the new cyclotron at

Berkeley had discovered a new element, which they called uranium 239. Like uranium 235, it was fissionable, but because it was different from uranium, the two could be chemically separated, which was theoretically easier and cheaper.

One thing every report agreed on was that the need for a "uranium burner," or reactor, was the first step in harnessing atomic energy, and the most critical item in the reactor was the moderator. Here was another stumbling block. The only moderator the German scientific community thought usable was heavy water. This deduction was the result of an experiment performed in early 1941 by a Dr. Bothe in Heidelberg. Bothe had concluded that using graphite as a moderator was inappropriate. Lamm wondered if Bothe could have miscalculated. At least Bothe's findings were a good place to start. But he needed to look at the experiment.

"Loring!" Lamm called from his office.

"Yes, Herr Hauptsturmführer."

Lamm handed Loring the information he wanted. "The charter of the Racial Science Section allows us to investigate all experiments. Use it to call the University of Heidelberg and get a copy of the calculations for the experiment I've noted. There shouldn't be any trouble. If there is, tell them they are using Jewish physics and they can give the calculations to the Gestapo."

"Are they really using Jewish physics?" Loring asked.

"I'm not sure," Lamm told him. "That's why I need the calculations."

"Right away, Herr Hauptsturmführer," Loring said, snapping to attention. "Heil Hitler!"

"Heil Hitler," Lamm said absentmindedly.

As soon as Loring left, Lamm checked suppliers of materials. The Number II Works of Degussa in Frankfurt was already skilled in producing refined uranium, but not the explosive kind. The Norwegian-Hydro plant in Vemork was producing approximately two hundred kilograms of heavy water a month, which wasn't enough to supply the thousands of kilograms needed for a reactor. The only bright spot in the picture was that Siemens and Philips could supply all the electrical equipment needed.

Even if Lamm could get equipment, the Racial Science Section was still undermanned and was receiving hundreds of requests a week from scientists and teachers for guidelines on what constituted

Jewish physics. Von Bartz had created an administrative nightmare from which Lamm needed to free himself. With Loring's assistance, he wrote a pamphlet called *The Danger of Jewish Physics,* denouncing Einstein and several others. Scientifically, the pamphlet was nonsense, but the Scharführer was such a gold mine of racial jargon that Himmler was delighted, and wrote a personal foreword for it.

As soon as Loring obtained the calculations for the graphite experiment, Lamm devoted all of his time to checking the calculations. Since he couldn't duplicate the experiment, he had to assume that all of Bothe's observations were correct. It wasn't good procedure, but Lamm had no time to waste.

Only an unannounced visit from Heydrich in the first week of December interrupted the unending series of calculations.

December 12, 1941

Wearing a field-gray service uniform, Heydrich looked forever the archetype Nazi. Lamm stood to attention as Bittner showed him into the office. After the obligatory "Heil Hitlers," Heydrich offered his hand and smiled pleasantly.

"How are you, Herr Professor?"

Shaking hands with Heydrich, Lamm was immediately on his guard. The Gruppenführer was only polite when he wanted something.

"Quite well, Herr Gruppenführer. Please have a seat. May I offer you a cup of coffee?"

"Thank you. Cream and sugar, please."

"Bittner, coffee for the Gruppenführer."

"Yes, sir."

"How are your new responsibilities, Herr Professor?" Heydrich asked as he leaned back in the overstuffed chair.

"The Racial Science Section is nearly caught up after the unfortunate demise of Obersturmbannführer von Bartz," Lamm said blandly.

Heydrich laughed coldly. "I told you I was in need of your talents professor, and the time to start using those talents is now. No one in the Reich is ready to admit it yet, but we've begun to work on the final solution to the Jewish question. All this business of merely evacuating them from all German territory is only for show."

"Final solution?" Lamm had no idea what Heydrich meant.

"I'm talking about killing the Jews—all of them, Herr Professor. We're starting, but nothing really works well. Bullets are too slow and too expensive and carbon monoxide gas doesn't always work. When we kill them we can't bury the bodies fast enough. Crematoria are also too slow. What I need is something that will allow the staff of a concentration camp to kill 10,000 a day without worrying about disposing of the bodies. You mentioned something about atomic energy when we met in Nuremberg. Do you have something I can use?"

Lamm looked at Heydrich. He and the rest of the high-ranking Nazis were obviously insane. The German offensive in Russia had ground to a halt and German troops were freezing in the snow, yet here was Heydrich acting as if the war didn't matter. Killing thousands, perhaps millions, of people when the Reich needed all the manpower it could get was absurd, but Lamm had ceased to wonder at Nazi stupidity. This looked like his chance to get exactly what he wanted, and he was determined to seize it.

Lamm briefly explained, "The energy from fissioning uranium would both kill them and incinerate the bodies at the same time."

Bittner came in with the coffee, bowed respectfully to the two officers, and left.

"Good. When can we test this fissioning?" Heydrich stirred his coffee.

Lamm carefully explained the process, leaving nothing out. Heydrich followed every word, nodding when Lamm emphasized a point. Concluding, the professor waited for Heydrich's displeasure at such a long-term, complex plan.

"I can see why you were such a good teacher, Herr Professor." Heydrich smiled with satisfaction as he set the cup in the saucer. "It's perfectly clear. I will send you an official letter asking for a proposal to do precisely what you have just told me, so I can submit this proposal to Reichsminister Speer. That way we can get a high enough priority to begin the project. You will be in charge, of course. I'll give you three months. That should give you plenty of time to double-check the calculations. Fair enough?"

"Of course, Herr Gruppenführer." What else could he say?

"At last we'll have our victory over the Jews and you, Herr Professor, will make it possible. Heil Hitler."

"Heil Hitler."

After Heydrich left, Lamm shook his head. They were at war in

Africa and Russia, yet they were willing to spend millions of Reichsmarks and divert critical industrial capacity to kill civilians. Let them play their games. Morality no longer mattered. The important thing—the only thing that mattered—was that he would be allowed to pursue atomic energy. Germany would have its bomb, and would have it as soon as possible.

Lamm isolated himself in order to tackle Heydrich's proposal. He spent long hours making calculations, and agonized over simple explanations so that even laymen like Himmler could understand the revolutionary concepts of atomic energy. News of the defeats in Russia spurred him to greater efforts. These weren't minor setbacks. The Soviets were proving tougher than anyone imagined. On Friday, December 12, Loring suddenly turned up the radio in the outer office. Lamm was about to shout for the Scharführer to turn it down until he realized what the announcer was saying. He came out of his office.

"Did I hear that correctly, Loring?" he asked.

Yes, Herr Hauptsturmführer." Loring had a broad grin. "We have honored our treaty with Japan and declared war on the United States. Now we can get rid of all those Jew-lovers at once."

Returning to his office, the professor sat down in dismay. Attack the United States? Hitler was mad. Lamm knew little of military theory, but he did know that America had vast industrial potential. He also knew that the United States could boast some of the world's top scientists, ones such as Einstein, Szilard, Wigner, Teller, and Weisskopf, every one of whom was a Jew who had fled Europe to escape the Nazis. Fermi, the brilliant Italian, was not Jewish, but his wife was. It didn't take a genius to conclude that all of them had scores to settle with the Third Reich. It suddenly occurred to Lamm that the war was two and a half years old, and peace was nowhere in sight.

January 21, 1942

Working long hours at a breakneck pace, Lamm pushed to finish the proposal ahead of schedule. The effort was not without cost.

"Liebchen," Irma pleaded, "you must eat."

Lamm looked up from the desk he had set up in the parlor. It was surrounded by sheets of paper overflowing from the wastebasket. "What is it, Dear?"

"You have to eat something."

"In a minute, Irma."

"That's what you said an hour ago. I made you a nice pork cutlet and you didn't even touch it."

Lamm looked at the cold cutlet sitting on the corner of the desk. He dutifully picked up the knife and fork.

"Don't you want me to reheat it, Max?"

"No, Irma, this is fine." Lamm began devouring the cutlet. He was hungry.

"I know that what you are doing is important, but it's not worth ruining your health over. I'm sure even Gruppenführer Heydrich would agree on that. You've lost weight and you only sleep when you're totally exhausted. You must rest, Max."

"Yes, Dear."

Despite Irma's solicitude, Lamm persevered and finished the proposal early in middle of the month, nearly six weeks ahead of schedule. He forwarded it to Heydrich and wrote Himmler a report explaining the danger posed by the atomic physicists in the United States. He couched it in terms of the dangers posed to Germany by "International Zionism's control of the United States." The report was returned with a letter from a member of the Reichsführer's staff thanking Lamm for his perspicacity. Himmler was busy controlling the newly occupied territories in the east and had little time for physics or chemistry.

Heydrich, though also busy, took time to call Lamm. "It's official," he said, his voice tinged with excitement. "We had a conference at Wannsee yesterday. Deportation of the Jews is no longer an option. Eichmann, Lange, and the rest agreed with me on total implementation of the 'Final Solution.' I am forwarding your proposal to Reichsminister Speer as soon as I finish reviewing it."

"That's good news, Herr Gruppenführer," Lamm said as Heydrich hung up. At last something was going to be done.

February 5, 1942

When Lamm returned to his review of the experiment in which Dr. Bothe concluded that graphite could not be used to moderate a uranium burner, he made two startling discoveries.

"There it is!" he shouted, and Loring, Bittner, and Frau Norbert came running into his office.

"Is anything wrong, Herr Professor?" his secretary asked timidly.

"No" he said, grinning. "This is wonderful. When Bothe conducted his experiment, he failed to take into consideration the nitrogen in the atmosphere and he also transposed two numbers. Look!" He happily held the sheet of calculations up for his subordinates to see. The expressions on their faces were ones of total noncomprehension.

Lamm looked at them and laughed. "Never mind," he said. "I know it's complicated, but if I'm right, graphite of sufficient purity is an acceptable moderator. This means we can make a uranium burner without heavy water. After that the possibilities are endless. Frau Norbert, take a letter."

"Yes, sir."

Lamm mailed the letter to the atomic research team at the Kaiser Wilhelm Institute that same afternoon.

March 10, 1942

When three weeks passed with no reply to his letter about the Bothe experiment, Lamm tried the telephone, but no one could connect him with anyone who knew anything. Exasperated, he went to the institute and ascended brown stone steps to the building that had once housed his office. He felt every inch the conquering hero for what he had discovered. Helga Dorfmann, his former secretary, was now the director's secretary. She looked up without recognizing him.

"Yes?"

"Helga, it is I, Professor Lamm."

Helga blinked, then her eyes grew wide. "Ach, Herr Professor, I didn't recognize you. You look so dashing in your uniform. How may I help you?"

"I sent a letter to this department more than three weeks ago," he explained, ignoring the compliment. "It concerned a graphite experiment conducted in Heidelberg in 1941."

Helga thought for a moment, then smiled. "Oh, yes. I remember. I recognized your signature. Please tell Frau Lamm that we missed the stollen this year."

Lamm was in a hurry, but he smiled. When he had worked with

Frau Dorfmann, Irma had always baked the sweet bread for the staff during the holidays. "I will definitely do that," he said, while Helga looked in the filing cabinet.

"It was given to Professor Fischbein," she told him, after a few minutes of searching. "He is now on Dr. Hahn's staff and has the office three doors down from our old one."

"Thank you, Helga." He had met Fischbein once or twice, but couldn't remember him. He headed for the door without waiting to be announced, an unforgivable breach of academic protocol.

Swaggering down the hall, he opened the door without knocking. Fischbein was a large fat man with dark brown, thinning hair, a round nose, and a bushy mustache. He wore old-fashioned pince-nez eyeglasses. Looking up, he blanched at Lamm's black uniform, and when his mouth opened no sound came out. Lamm didn't apologize for the intrusion. "What did you do with the letter I sent concerning the graphite experiment in Heidelberg?" he asked.

"I . . . Who are you?"

"Hauptsturmführer Lamm," Lamm replied, giving his SS rank. "I am the chief of the Racial Science Section of the Headquarters of the Reichsführer SS."

"Oh, yes," Dr. Fischbein said, sufficiently cowed. "You used to teach physics here."

"The letter."

"Ah. We forwarded it to Heidelberg."

"Heidelberg?"

"Of course. It was their experiment. What use would we have with it?"

"Are you not concerned with atomic physics here at the institute?"

"Yes, but what use would we have for an experiment done in Heidelberg?" Fischbein asked. "We conduct our own experiments here."

Disgusted, Lamm turned on his heel and returned to the office on Wolfstrasse, where he called Heidelberg. After a long wait, a graduate student came on the line to tell him they had just received the letter and would reply in three or four weeks. Furious, Lamm slammed down the receiver, then unsuccessfully tried to contact Heydrich, who was in Czechoslovakia.

On February 26, 1942, the Reich's leaders were invited to a secret conference on atomic energy held at the House of German Research, in Steglitz. Himmler declined to attend. With the Gestapo and SS expanding into the conquered territories, he had other things on his mind. Unimpressed by scientific theories, he didn't think to send Lamm. The attendees were impressed by the potential of atomic energy, but otherwise did little more than talk. Lamm learned of the conference in March, when the Reichsführer's headquarters forwarded the 131-page report from the Army Ordnance Department to him. Lamm was furious when he found that he had been excluded from the meeting.

On March 16 the reply from Heidelberg stated the authorities at the university were satisfied that Dr. Bothe was an expert in these matters and that his calculations were correct. The letter went on to suggest that Sturmbannführer Lamm should consult with someone qualified in the field of physics or mathematics if he had any questions about the experiment. In a towering rage, Lamm shredded the letter and threw it into the waste basket. "Idiots!" he shouted, stalking back and forth in his office. None of the staff went near him for the rest of the day.

May-June 1942

In May, an experiment titled Pile L-IV took place at Leipzig. It consisted of concentric metal spheres containing alternate layers of heavy water and powdered uranium. The separation of the materials was necessary due to the violent reaction of pure uranium and water. The pile was then immersed in a vat of water, for cooling, and a neutron emitter introduced into the center of the pile. Despite stringent measures to prevent leaks, water seepage eventually destroyed Pile L-IV. But before it did the experimenters noted that L-IV was producing 13 percent more neutrons that it absorbed. For Maximilian Lamm this was wonderful news. A self-sustaining chain reaction was not only possible, but practical. He could see the way ahead clearly, and composed a letter to Himmler on the significance of Pile L-IV, but then tore it up. It would do no good. Like most of the high Party officials, Himmler was incapable of understanding.

Instead, he wrote to Heydrich urging him to obtain an SSDE priority for the atomic energy project. This was the highest priority possible, but the Gruppenführer never received the letter. On May 29, Czech partisans threw a bomb under his car, and the man who for so long symbolized the Nazi ideal died a week later in mortal agony. Four days later, Lamm's letter was returned with a cover letter stating that the Gruppenführer had died defending the Reich. Nazi retribution against the helpless population of the town of Lidice, whose citizens were falsely rumored to have harbored Heydrich's assassins, was swift and brutal. All of the town's males were executed, and the town was burned and leveled.

But Lamm took no notice of the retaliation by the SS. Heydrich's death threw him into a fit of depression. The one man who understood what he was trying to do and who had the power to assist him was dead. Any hope Lamm had of getting a coherent atomic energy project through the labyrinth of the Nazi bureaucracy had died with him. To whom could he now turn? With his plans shattered, Lamm's mood swung from depression to fury and no one, not even Irma, knew what to expect next. To make matters worse, on June 23, Armaments Minister Albert Speer briefed a disinterested Hitler on the progress being made in the construction of a "uranium bomb." Himmler didn't attend, and since it was obvious that Speer and Himmler were now rivals, no other high SS officials were invited. Once again, Lamm had been ignored. Hitler took no action, and this depressed Lamm even more. After L-IV only an idiot could fail to see the next logical step.

Lamm's depression troubled Irma. She was quiet and caring when he was angry, and comforting when he was depressed. She sat next to him on the sofa and stroked his hair. But her sweet ways failed to cheer him.

"Max, Liebchen, what's wrong?" she asked one night as he tossed and turned on their bed. "You don't eat or sleep or even want to make love."

Lamm turned on the light and told her everything that had happened, except the murder of Erwin von Bartz. Irma took his hand in hers.

"Max, if they can't understand you must help them to."

He looked at her soft face in the lamplight. "Irma, it's not that simple. These aren't students waiting to be shown how something is to be done. They're politicians. They don't care. It's like the Middle Ages. Each has his own little fiefdom, and ignores the rest. They won't accept anything new unless it's forced upon them. They'll never sanction a uranium burner unless they can see a practical application before them. They can't understand that whoever harnesses atomic power first will control the world. They have no vision."

"If they won't help you build this uranium burner," she told him softly, "then you're going to have to do it yourself. It's your duty to the Reich, Max. Once you begin, you'll feel better."

"Of course," he muttered grumpily. "All I need is a few million Reichsmarks, a staff, a factory, and some minor essentials." He turned out the light, lay back against the pillow, and closed his eyes, until the significance of what Irma said dawned on him. Suddenly he sat bolt upright. "Yes!" he shouted.

Irma nearly jumped out of bed. "Gott im Himmel, Max, are you all right?"

"Yes, perfectly. You are an angel, Irma," he blurted. Kissing his wife, he leapt out of bed and put on his robe.

"Where are you going, Max?"

"I'm going to write up a plan."

Irma shrugged, rolled over, and went back to sleep.

After turning on the living room lights, Lamm lit a cigarette and paced the carpet, angry with himself. He should have considered the alternative of starting his own uranium project months before. Lamm stopped and frowned at the portrait of Hitler on the wall. The Führer and his followers were all dolts and imbeciles. It was impossible to deal with them honestly. They were more concerned with fantasies like Nordic ice cultures and killing Jews than harnessing the power of nature. So he would give them their fantasies, and they would finance his efforts to build a uranium bomb.

When he returned to the office, he would begin laying the groundwork toward that end. The biggest priority was money. Most of the money in the Reich was allocated to the war effort, but there were two sources that were still untouched. One was the funding for the SS, which was controlled by Himmler, and the other was the Adolf Hitler Fund, which provided the Führer with money for his living expenses. Somehow, Lamm had to get money from these sources.

The second priority was people. He had to get quality people and keep them away from meddling academicians and the SS. Materials would come with the money.

Where to build the uranium burner was also a mystery. It had to be safe from meddling by the Nazis and from Allied bombs, which were beginning to fall on the Reich with alarming regularity. Lamm sat down in his favorite chair and chuckled. He knew precisely the place. Vikmo, the site of Operation NORD, would fit the bill nicely. It had buildings, its own generators, and a source of running water. Vikmo was near the Arctic Circle and far away from the prying eyes of SS headquarters. It was close to Vemork, the source of heavy water, which would be required for some experiments. It was also outside the Fatherland, so that if anything went terribly wrong, it wouldn't happen in Germany. In all, it was perfect. Lamm smiled at the irony. This time Vikmo would look not to some mythical past, but to the scientific future. And he, Maximilian Lamm, was going to make it happen.

Lamm arrived at the Racial Science Section earlier than usual and started a notebook listing the requirements of the uranium project, then called for appointments with Himmler and the head of the Racial Research Bureau. Lamm inferred from Himmler's secretary that the Reichsführer was too busy to see him. Holding his temper, he took a deep breath.

"Tell the Reichsführer that I have been working on a project with Gruppenführer Heydrich that will bring about the final solution of the Jewish question years earlier than anticipated."

There was a brief silence, then the secretary replied, "Just a moment."

Lamm wished he could see the expression on Himmler's face. Heydrich's death had made him a demigod, and the "Final Solution" was a term only a few select people in the Reich understood. Himmler would, no doubt, be curious to find out how much Lamm knew. When the secretary returned to the phone, he told Lamm the Reichsführer would see him at eleven that morning. Grinning, Lamm hung up, then called the Racial Research Bureau. They were also too busy, until Lamm mentioned Operation NORD. Suddenly, they would be happy to see him at three that afternoon.

At eleven, Lamm entered Himmler's lavishly decorated office feeling that he was about to succeed where all others had failed.

"Heil Hitler!" Lamm said as he reported to the Reichsführer.

"Heil Hitler." Eyeing Lamm suspiciously, Himmler's reply lacked any warmth. "Please sit down, Herr Professor. I'm afraid I can't spare you much time. I have an appointment with the Führer in an hour, but first tell me what you know about the 'Final Solution.'"

Lamm removed Heydrich's letter from his folder and handed it to Himmler. "Gruppenführer Heydrich came to me and asked my help with the . . . er . . . project. He informed me of the enormity of the task and asked what might be done to speed the process. I naturally told him that the practical application of atomic energy would allow him to destroy thousands in a few seconds, with very little ash."

Himmler's expression changed when he saw Heydrich's signature on the letter. "And what is this application?" the Reichsführer asked, still looking at the letter.

"We will be able to create a ray, a beam of energy, that will be so hot that it will vaporize human beings."

"Vaporize them?" Himmler looked directly at Lamm. His expression was one of mixed interest and confusion.

"Yes, Herr Reichsführer," Lamm said, acting as if he knew exactly what he was talking about.

"What exactly do you mean by vaporize?"

"The only thing left of them will be some ash. No more than what you might find on the end of a cigarette, Herr Reichsführer."

"How many at a time?" Himmler asked.

"At first only a few hundred," Lamm replied confidently. "Later we will be able to dispose of them by the thousands."

"In a few seconds?" The head of the SS was still skeptical.

"Yes, Herr Reichsführer. As you well know, anything hot enough to melt steel will easily vaporize people."

"How does this machine work?"

"It is almost like a bomb, except the explosion is much more intense and hot and it can be directed."

"It would be a definite advantage over what we have now," Himmler mused. "Why is this so much hotter than other explosives?"

"Because it is made with uranium."

"Uranium?" Himmler pronounced the word, which was strange to him. "What is it?"

"It's a very rare metal that does not occur naturally in its pure form. It is in the form of an oxide from which the pure metal must be refined. Under the right conditions the pure metal becomes an explosive that gives off thousands of times more energy than TNT or amatol. Once we learn to break it down," Lamm continued, "we might even make a portable machine that can destroy enemy soldiers and tanks on the battlefield."

Lamm avoided subjects like isotopes and reactors in order to keep the concept within Himmler's grasp. When the Reichsführer continued to look at him blandly, he was afraid he had lost Himmler entirely.

"How much will this machine cost?"

"I believe I can build it for five million marks," Lamm stated authoritatively. He also didn't tell Himmler that the army had a virtual monopoly on uranium metal and heavy water. "In addition to the uranium we will need electrical fixtures, tubing, wire, and scientific equipment." Lamm hoped he wouldn't have to explain about heavy water.

"What firm is going to build this machine?" Himmler asked.

"We in the SS are going to build it," Lamm said, proudly. "We can't afford to have anyone who might be tainted connected with this project and, of course, the SS will hold the patent."

This last part pleased Himmler, who was trying to build an SS industrial empire, despite Reichsminister Speer's objections that it was a waste of manpower and resources.

"Where will you build it?"

"In Norway," Lamm said, omitting any mention of Vikmo. "We can work there undisturbed."

Himmler looked as if he were about to say something about Lamm's choice of location but instead answered, "You'll get a budget of one million marks. We'll talk about the other four once I see what progress you've made."

"Of course, Herr Reichsführer," Lamm agreed. "I will also need a few specialized personnel, and some workers."

"Make up a list," Himmler said.

"I already have," Lamm said, handing Himmler the roster. "I checked qualified personnel as part of Gruppenführer Heydrich's proposal, and these are the best qualified for what needs to be done. Everyone is SS."

The Reichsführer smiled at the last remark and accepted the roster. "And the materials?"

Lamm handed him a list of materials.

"I'll call you in a week," Himmler said. The interview was over.

Lamm got up and crisply clicked his heels. "Heil Hitler!"

"Heil Hitler!"

The meeting at the Racial Research Bureau was pleasant and productive. They were only too delighted to relinquish control of the entire "Vikmo Site," as they called it. Dr. Nass and von Bartz had caused them considerable embarrassment, and they were still very sensitive about the subject. Before Lamm left the bureau, he was assured that all deeds and responsibilities for the site would be turned over to the Racial Science Section in a few days.

Things were going so well that Lamm decided to press his luck and make an appointment with Bormann. The Reichsleiter, who sometimes made people wait weeks for an appointment, agreed to see Lamm in two days after he used the phrase "final solution."

On the appointed day, Lamm was ushered into Bormann's office. Bormann was undoubtedly the sloppiest Party official in the Führer's circle. Goebbels, Göring, and Himmler were always neatly and precisely dressed. Bormann, collar undone on his wrinkled jacket, looked more like a grocer than a high Party official. The Reichsleiter uniform did nothing to dispel the image. Perspiring behind the large dark wooden desk, he did not appear busy, despite the clutter of papers and folders before him.

After the dutiful exchange of "Heil Hitlers," the two men shook hands.

"Well, Herr Hauptsturmführer," Bormann said pleasantly, "the last time we met was July of 1940 after the fall of France. I see you've been promoted twice since then."

Lamm had heard that Bormann had an excellent memory for names and faces and used it regularly to put people at ease or throw them off balance. Today he was putting Lamm at ease. Heydrich had been right. He had impressed Bormann with his little lecture at the victory party.

"What can I do for you today?" the Reichsleiter asked politely.

"I have invented a device which will prove to be the decisive weapon of the war," Lamm said. "And I am in need of monetary assistance."

"Why come to me? Why not Reichsminister Speer? He is charge of armaments."

"Because you are the person who knows how badly the Reich needs such a weapon. The professors and the rich industrialists are not interested. They have their titles and profits and they are only concerned with maintaining them. Sometimes I wonder if they're really interested in carrying on the Führer's struggle against Bolshevism and international Jewry," Lamm said.

Bormann gave him a sharp look. Lamm had carefully hit the right chord. The Reichsleiter was a blue-collar socialist with an inherent mistrust of anyone wealthy or powerful, especially one who had made it on his own.

Lamm continued. "As the custodian of the Adolf Hitler Fund, you are the only one to whom I could turn."

"I understand," Bormann nodded sagely. "But what is this invention?"

"A death beam that will vaporize its target—tanks, airplanes, even cities. It will kill people by the thousands. Imagine what a weapon like this would do to London." Lamm added for effect. "What better place to use it?"

Bormann leaned forward. "London?" Like everyone in the Nazi hierarchy, Bormann was obsessed with the idea of destroying London, although destruction of the city would have little effect on the course of the war.

"Imagine the entire city destroyed in a single blast. They won't be able to grow potatoes in the rubble," Lamm stated fiercely. "That will be our first target. After that we can destroy Moscow and Washington. With that kind of power, no one will stop us."

Bormann, looking stupidly evil, was grinning at the thought of this new device. "If you were to get monetary support, who would hold the patents?" he asked.

Lamm lifted his head. "Our Führer, Adolf Hitler, in the name of the German Volk," he replied proudly.

Bormann looked hard at him. "How much would you need?"

"Approximately five million marks for a two-year research program."

Bormann barked. "Five million? I can give you maybe one and a half."

Lamm shrugged. So the Adolf Hitler Fund had a limit, too. "Any amount will put the Reich that much closer to victory, Herr Reichsleiter." He wasn't exaggerating.

"I will have the paperwork drawn up within the week."

July 16, 1942

A few days later, Lamm had two drafts totaling two and a half million marks, as well as his first staff member. A shade over six feet tall with a stocky build, Sturmführer Friedrich Hammerstein had a round face and short-cropped light brown hair. His blue eyes were bright, as if he had just heard a good joke. He stood before Lamm's desk while Lamm looked at his personnel file in dismay.

"You're a lawyer?"

"Yes, sir."

"Why are you here? I gave the Reichsführer a list of mathematicians, physicists, and chemists, and I get a lawyer? No offense, but I can't use you, Sturmführer."

"Begging your pardon, sir," Hammerstein said, "but I am not one of the people you sent for. SS regulations require that any project of your size or value must have a legal representative."

Lamm looked at him. There was no sense fighting regulations, and it did mean another man. "All right," Lamm said. "Welcome to the Racial Science Section. Have a seat." Hammerstein did as he was told.

"Do you know what we are doing here, Hammerstein?"

"Your charter, which I took the liberty of checking at the Reichsführer's headquarters, says you are supposed to be checking scientific documents for racial correctness, but quite frankly, I don't understand why you have such a large budget. Your staff and surroundings hardly justify a budget of a million marks."

"Two and a half million," Lamm corrected.

"But the records at the Reichsführer's headquarters show you were issued a draft of a million marks."

"That's true. We also received a million and a half from the Adolf Hitler Fund, courtesy of Reichsleiter Bormann."

Hammerstein's jaw dropped, but he said nothing.

"Do you know what an atom is?" Lamm asked.

"No sir."

Lamm gave Hammerstein a quick lesson in basic physics and the possibility of producing a uranium bomb, as well as some of the background of the Racial Science Section.

"It sounds too fantastic," Hammerstein said. "A bomb that can destroy an entire city?"

"Precisely. Now, the question is, what do we do with you?"

"May I make a suggestion?" Hammerstein asked.

"Feel free."

"First we set up a corporation. Let's call it NORD GMBH. We'll issue stock in the names of the SS and Adolf Hitler. Then we get a loan from the Reichsbank for another three or four million marks, to be repaid within five years of the end of the war at two and a half percent interest. That should give us plenty of capital to work with."

"NORD GMBH," Lamm repeated. Hammerstein obviously had a sense of humor as well as a brain. It was Lamm's turn to be impressed.

"I am a corporate lawyer, not a trial lawyer," Hammerstein told him with a smile.

"What are you waiting for, Herr Lawyer?" Lamm asked. "Get to work."

While Hammerstein worked on the loan from the Reichsbank, Lamm turned his attention to the materials required for the reactor, which included powdered uranium, uranium metal, graphite, heavy water, and boron. The installation would need switches, gauges, and wire to start. Later they would need more exotic equipment, so Hammerstein began negotiations with Philips Werke in the Netherlands.

August 3, 1942

Himmler had issued a letter directing local SS commanders to assist the Racial Science Section in every way possible. Meant for Norway, the letter didn't specify a country, so Lamm used it in Germany. After commandeering a Luftwaffe Junkers 52, he and Loring flew to Norway. It was an uneventful trip, until the pilot mistook a BF 109 Messerschmitt for a Spitfire and dove for the deck. Slightly shaken, they landed at a small naval weather station twenty-five miles from Vikmo and borrowed a truck to travel the rest of the way. Vikmo was so near the Arctic circle that it was still light at eight P.M., which allowed them to begin their inspection immediately.

Lamm was pleased to find all the buildings in good repair. Even the maintenance facilities, which had not been in operation since the coal mine had closed, could be made usable with minimal cleaning. The dining hall and cafeteria also needed cleaning, but looked to be in excellent shape. The best part was that the electricity was still working. Lamm smiled at the way things were going.

He and Loring stayed the night and explored the mine the next day. The main shaft looked safe, but the lights didn't work. One of the lower shafts was flooded, and Lamm didn't know if it would affect operations. Where the shafts branched off there was one large chamber. Lamm decided to build the reactor there. Loring made notes constantly, occasionally augmenting them with sketches as he and Lamm paced off a particular area, since neither of them had thought to bring a tape measure. Both thought Vikmo would do very nicely.

When Lamm returned to Germany with a list of requirements for repairs at Vikmo, he was delighted to learn his new subordinates had arrived. Lamm wanted to meet them immediately, but Bittner had other ideas. He was grinning strangely. "Begging your pardon, Herr Obersturmbannführer, but you're out of uniform."

"Oberstur . . . " Lamm said. "Bittner, are you drunk?"

"No, sir." Bittner handed Lamm a letter, which he quickly read. Suddenly his face broke into a grin. He had been given a temporary promotion in order to run the project. Bittner produced a tunic from behind the door with Obersturmbannführer rank on the epaulets and collar. Lamm looked at the four stars and single lace on the left collar and the jagged "SS" on the right. He slipped out of his Hauptsturmführer tunic and put on the new one. It felt good. He smiled happily and he and Loring went in to meet the new members of his staff.

Lamm strode through the door and stopped. He had given the Reichsführer a list of twelve names, and there were only four men in the outer office. As Lamm entered the room they stood to attention and raised their arms in unison. "Heil Hitler!"

"Heil Hitler!" Lamm said, returning the salute. "Are there any more of you?" he asked.

The four officers looked at each other. "No, Herr Obersturmbannführer," one of them said.

Beggars can't be choosers, Lamm thought. "Allow me to introduce myself," he said. "I am Haupt—er, rather—Obersturmbannführer Lamm, head of the Racial Science Section. There were supposed to be twelve of you. Which ones are you?"

"Obersturmführer Horst Nachmann, Doktor of Physics," the first said. Nachmann was of medium height and slim, with dark hair and a large nose. His face showed scarring from severe teenage acne.

"Untersturmführer Friedrich Lindner, Master of Physics," said the second. Lindner was the youngest and shortest of the three. With his light hair and skin, Lamm wondered if he even had to shave.

"Hauptsturmführer Ernst Reinhart, Doktor of Chemistry," was the third. Reinhart was tall and good-looking, with a pleasant demeanor.

"Obersturmführer Alfred Dietrich, doktor of mathematics," reported the fourth. Dietrich had a bulky frame and unruly black hair, and black-framed glasses perched on his round nose. He definitely looked more like an academician than a soldier.

Lamm shook hands with each of them and asked whom they had studied with. Then he got right to the point.

"Have any of you heard of Jewish physics?" he asked them.

The four looked at each other, then Nachmann said, "Of course, Herr Obersturmbannführer. We are all familiar with the fact that Einstein's theories are degenerate and false."

"Are they?" Lamm asked.

The surprise on their faces was evident. "Of course," Nachmann continued. "We were all taught that . . ."

"Gentlemen," Lamm interrupted. "I am a professor of physics, not some stupid Storm Trooper who hasn't read anything except *Mein Kampf* and *The Protocols of the Elders of Zion.* Now, what do you think of Einstein's theories?"

Nachmann swallowed, but didn't answer. "They appear to be essentially correct," Lindner said, finally. The others looked at him.

"What about fissioning the 'basic building block of the Aryan Universe'?"

"Dr. Hahn did it in 1938," Lindner said. "In theory, a large amount of energy is given off during the reaction."

"Not in theory—in fact," Lamm stated emphatically. "Gentlemen, I want you to forget everything they taught you in the Hitler Youth or in SS Cadet School about Jews. You have been told Jews are sly, but rarely intelligent. That isn't true. Some of the finest minds in the world are Jewish. They are currently in the United States and Great Britain—enemies of the Reich—working on a uranium bomb. Have any of you heard the term?"

"Yes, Herr Obersturmbannführer," Nachmann said, as the others nodded in agreement. "The theory is that millions of atoms fissioning at once will cause a tremendous explosion."

"Again not theory but *fact!*" Lamm emphasized. "Gentlemen, the reason you are here is that you are I are going to give the Reich the world's first uranium bomb. Then we are going to drop it on London before the Allies have a chance to develop theirs. Will you help me?"

"Yes, Herr Obersturmbannführer," they replied in unison.

"Good! First, you will review the latest experiments and techniques in atomic science. If others have performed a valid experiment and we can use the information, we will do so. We cannot afford duplication of effort. Later we will discuss our new organization, mission, and base of operations. Then we will get to work. Any questions?"

There were none. "You are dismissed."

"Heil Hitler!" they replied.

Lamm gave them a stern look. "From now on we can dispense with the incessant 'Heil Hitlers.' We are all adults and we all know whom the Führer is. From now on you will treat this as the research organization that it is." Without waiting for a reply Lamm returned to his office, where Bittner was waiting with a smiling Hammerstein.

"You seem to be in a good mood today, Hammerstein," Lamm observed.

"You will also be in a good mood as soon as you have seen this, Herr Obersturmbannführer," he replied, handing Lamm a slip of paper.

Lamm read it quickly and looked up. "This isn't a joke?" he asked anxiously.

"No, Herr Obersturmbannführer. According to the reports, the French had boron rods made for their own experiments."

"Who else knows about this?" Lamm asked.

"To the best of my knowledge, no one," Hammerstein replied. "The rods are just sitting in a depot south of Paris."

"Loring," Lamm called down the hall.

"Yes, Herr Obersturmbannführer?"

"Warm up the aircraft. We're going to Paris."

"At last the SS has recognized my real talents." Loring was grinning.

Lamm had to laugh. "Unfortunately, we're going to get some boron."

"But, Herr Obersturmbannführer . . ."

"Go." He told Loring. "Is there anything else, Hammerstein?"

"All the solid refined uranium metal is earmarked for the army. Powdered uranium metal and uranium oxide are no problem. Heavy water is reserved for experiments conducted by the army and academic experiments approved by Reichsminister Speer. However . . ." Hammerstein let the sentence hang.

"However?" Lamm asked.

"Bittner knows someone in the train yards. The man told Bittner that there is a shipment of uranium metal leaving the Degussa Works in Frankfurt next week. The boxcars are loaded, then they spend two to three days in the yard."

Lamm raised an eyebrow. "Boxcars," he said, to no one in particular. "We're going to have to make up a train anyway. Hammerstein, go to Lübeck and lease office space. Then see if you can charter a ship. We have to hurry. Bad weather in Norway sets in the second week of October. After that we can't expect too much in the way of support by road or aircraft, so I want to get established long before that. Also check on the rail lines to Vikmo—if there are any."

"Yes, Herr Obersturmbannführer. Heil Hitler!"

"Did you hear what I told the others about 'Heil Hitler'?"

"Yes, Herr Obersturmbannführer."

"It applies to you, too."

"Yes, Herr Obersturmbannführer."

Later, as his car pulled away from the curb and headed to the airfield, Lamm looked back at his headquarters building and remembered that it had been covered with anti-Semitic slogans when he first saw it. That world was dead, and the present one would be also, if he didn't succeed.

August 21, 1942

Uwe Schindler emerged from the subway station and looked around to get his bearings. This was an area of Berlin he didn't frequent. When he remembered where he was, he went in the opposite direction from that which he intended to go. It was early evening and he strolled casually, stopping every now and then to look into shop windows. Then he stopped to tie his shoe. Each time he looked around carefully, and when he was convinced that Gestapo men were not following him he headed back to his objective by a slightly less circuitous route. The three-story house was on the Lausitzerstrasse, between the Görlitzer Railroad Station and the Kottbus Ufer. There was nothing to differentiate it from the other gray middle-class houses on the cobblestone street. After one last check, Schindler turned down Lausitzerstrasse and knocked on a door. Sergeant Erich Kraemer, a young Luftwaffe signal specialist, answered the knock. He clicked his heels and bowed stiffly at the waist. It was an old-fashioned courtesy that Schindler appreciated. He, too, bowed slightly.

"Herr Schindler, it's good to see you."

"And you, Herr Kraemer. Is the Admiral in?"

"He's upstairs. May I take your hat and coat?"

"Thank you." Schindler let Kraemer take his hat and coat. He removed his gloves but kept them in his hand, then started up the stairs.

"I'll bring you some coffee directly" Kraemer said.

Schindler thanked him again and went to the first room on the left at the top of the stairs. It was a small room, with two comfortable chairs and one table with a small lamp. In one of the chairs sat Admiral Canaris, smoking a cigar.

"Ah, Willi."

The Admiral half-rose to shake his friend's hand and motioned to the other chair.

"Good to see you, Uwe. Cigar?"

"Thank you." Schindler lit the cigar and puffed until it drew correctly.

"Uwe, what is so important that you risk yourself by coming here?"

"We have a very grave problem, Willi. Are you familiar with the new theories on atomic energy."

"I'm not a physicist, but I understand what some of the theories are."

"I'm not either, but I do know that the first step in capitalizing on this energy to make electricity or a bomb is to build a uranium burner to control the neutrons given off. The SS is trying to build such a burner."

"The SS has been singularly unsuccessful in doing anything commercial or scientific, Uwe."

"This time there's a good chance they may succeed. The man in charge of the project is Dr. Maximilian Lamm. He used to teach physics before he joined the SS. He now has a staff of several young scientists and mathematicians. One of our contacts in SS Headquarters gave me the information."

Schindler put on his gloves and reached into his coat pocket to withdraw an envelope. Canaris looked at it and motioned to the table. "Put it there."

Kraemer brought Schindler's coffee on a small silver tray. "Can I get you anything else, Admiral?"

"No thank you, Kraemer."

The Luftwaffe sergeant quietly withdrew. He was used to such meetings.

"If the SS succeed in making an uranium bomb they won't hesitate to use it, Willi."

"I know, and if they do the Allies will destroy us with theirs."

"Do they have one already?"

"I don't know precisely, but it's only a matter of time. God knows, the Nazis gave them Einstein and all our best talent."

"Lamm has to be stopped, Willi."

"I know. You must leave that to me."

Uwe sipped the coffee. "Excellent, Willi."

The depot, just south of Paris, was commanded by an overweight, forty-three-year-old reserve Hauptmann whom the war had passed by. He saluted Lamm in the military fashion.

"Captain Braun at your service, Herr Obersturmbannführer. What can I do for you?"

"There is some French material which we need," Lamm told him.

Braun smiled bitterly. "This place is full of useless French material. What is it you're looking for?"

Lamm handed Captain Braun the slip of paper that Hammerstein had given him. Braun studied it for a moment, then shook his head. "I don't remember this. Let me see if Feldwebel Koenig does. He's been here since we took this place over from the Frogs.

Sometimes I think he knows every nut and bolt here."

Braun picked up his telephone and turned the crank. "Hello. Send Feldwebel Koenig to depot headquarters. I want him to find something." Braun hung up the phone. "He'll be here in a moment."

Feldwebel Koenig was ancient and shrunken, in a uniform three sizes too large for him. With one look at the paper, he took them directly to a stack of metal tubes behind some cannibalized French trucks. "Why is this so important?" he asked.

Lamm shrugged and smiled. "When the Reichsführer SS says 'get some,' who am I to ask why?"

Feldwebel Koenig was also not one to question the motivation of those in charge, and nodded sagely in agreement.

The boron was light enough to go on the aircraft in one load. Upon returning to Berlin, Lamm made arrangements to store it under guard at Tempelhof. He then returned to the Racial Science Section to supervise the packing for Vikmo.

Hammerstein, delayed by an air raid, arrived in Lübeck too late to accomplish anything, so he checked into a hotel and waited until the next morning to begin his search. The morning ride through Lübeck was an experience. Used to the minor bomb damage in Berlin, Hammerstein was shocked to find many buildings gutted and some completely leveled. The devastation made him determined to help Lamm succeed. Fortunately, the waterfront was only lightly damaged, and work there went on as usual.

Knowing nothing about ports, Hammerstein, using a copy of Himmler's letter, visited the harbor commander, who had nothing to do with the commercial aspect of the port. Wishing to stay on the right side of a representative of the Reichsführer, the commander graciously put him in contact with a firm that had a warehouse for rent and one that had a ship to charter. Neither, Hammerstein discovered, was a prize. The warehouse was a frame of rotting wood covered by rusty tin. The owner claimed the holes in the walls and the roof were caused by bomb splinters, but they looked more like rust holes to Hammerstein. Unfortunately, storage space was at a premium, and he had no time to argue. One bright spot was that the building did have an office area out of the weather, suitable for immediate occupancy.

The SS *Mayerling* out of Bremen was available, although the torpedo damage from her last voyage to Norway had not been completely repaired, and when Hammerstein went aboard her he didn't know what to think. With one stack and bridge amidships, she was gray overall and streaked with rust. Acetylene torches snapped everywhere, and the entire ship smelled of paint, diesel fuel, and grease. To someone who knew nothing of ships and the sea, it seemed like chaos instead of the daily routine of a ship's crew. Her master, Captain Zorndorf, was a short, stocky man with a round face, lined and creased from years on the bridge. Sharp blue eyes set deep in their sockets and gray chin whiskers identified a man who had seen most of the world's oceans. Wearing a battered hat with no insignia and a rumpled blue jacket with four tarnished gold stripes on each sleeve, he was personally supervising the repairs to his ship when Hammerstein came aboard. He greeted the SS officer cautiously.

"This way, Sturmführer Hammerstein." Zorndorf led the lawyer inside his cabin. "What can I do for you?"

Looking around the cabin, Hammerstein found it neat and businesslike, unlike the rest of the vessel. "I'd want to charter your ship for NORD GMBH."

"NORD GMBH," Zorndorf mused. "Don't know of any shipping company by that name."

Hammerstein knew the man was feeling him out. "It's a holding company," he said truthfully. "Over the next six months to a year, we will be shipping equipment and supplies to a research project in Norway. There may also be passengers from time to time."

"I am an independent ship owner," Zorndorf said. "The *Mayerling* belongs to me. The charter is 100,000 Reichsmarks plus the cost of fuel, crew, and maintenance."

"Your price is very high, but I will agree to it if we become your sole customer for the next eighteen months."

"Does that include the protection of the SS?"

"In a matter of speaking, yes."

"Have the papers drawn up for my signature, Sturmführer Hammerstein. The *Mayerling* will be ready to sail in seven days."

As soon as the contract with Zorndorf was signed, Hammerstein used the Himmler letter to obtain an aircraft to fly from Lübeck to Oslo, where he rented more warehouse and wharf space. Noting the name NORD GMBH, British agents were able to track down requisitions for food and clothing only to find that NORD GMBH was an SS holding company, but there was no indication of what it did. Hammerstein telephoned Lamm from Oslo with the names and addresses of the NORD warehouses.

"I am ready to fly back to Berlin," he told Lamm.

"Stay there. You are now commander of the advance party. I'll send Loring up to be your assistant. One of the new men can take over the NORD operation in Lübeck."

"Is there anything you need here?"

"A couple of aircraft and a train."

"I'll see what I can do. The local SS commander has already agreed to let me use two of his platoons. It's about sixty men."

"That's more than we had before," Lamm said. "Keep up the good work and we'll be seeing you shortly. *Auf Wiedersehen.*"

Lamm was pleased. In a few weeks NORD had become an organization of more than a hundred people and millions of marks in assets. Invoices from all over the Reich arrived daily. All of them requested the address to which their products had to be shipped. Bittner answered them with a form letter directing everything to NORD GMBH in Lübeck. The endless list included ore from Belgium, electrical equipment from Holland, and toilet paper from Dortmund. Only one thing was missing—uranium metal.

Berlin
August 31, 1942

Many of the men in the small nightclub looked at the young woman in the strapless gown sitting at the small table with the older man in the evening jacket. She was of medium height, with a nice figure. Her shoulder-length chestnut hair surrounded an oval face with a straight nose and a full mouth. Though most could not see them, her eyes were a deep blue. While not stunningly beautiful, Margit Hassel had good looks and the aura of a confidant woman, which attracted men. Women noticed her too, and were quick to note that her handsome companion was considerably older and, no doubt, rich.

Ignoring the admiring glances and disapproving stares, Margit

Hassel sipped champagne and laughed at the comedian who had just made a subtle mockery of Göring. The man was treading on thin ice, but since Allied bombers had begun appearing in German skies, Göring was fair game. Momentarily, Margit frowned. She hated Nazis and secretly wished the Allies would bomb Germany flat, then hang every one of the Nazi swine from the tallest trees in the Black Forest. At that moment her escort reached across the little table and took her hand.

"You're too beautiful to frown, Margit."

She smiled affectionately at Hermann Rothenburg and squeezed his hand. "You're good for my ego, Hermann." Margit genuinely liked Hermann Rothenburg. He was kind, gentle, and understanding, as well as rich. He was also a member of the very small anti-Nazi Resistance movement beginning to grow in Germany.

"Time to go," he said, placing a one-hundred-Reichsmark bill on the table. "Tomorrow is another work day."

Margit nodded, stood up, and followed him through the crowd to the door. Outside, they climbed into his large Mercedes and drove to Margit's small room near the Wilmersdorf section of Berlin. When he pulled up in front of Margit's apartment. He leaned over and kissed her, and she kissed him back.

"I love you, Margit."

"I know, Hermann. You're a wonderful man." Margit stroked his cheek. She liked him terribly, but there was only one man she really loved, and while there was a chance that Paul Holbein was still alive she couldn't love anyone else.

"I have to go to Wiesbaden for a few days," he said. "When I return there will be another package."

Margit glanced at Rothenburg. "Same delivery?"

"No, I'll give you the instructions with the package."

Margit asked no further questions. It was dangerous to know too much. She and Rothenburg were playing a dangerous game. In the few months they had known each other, they had become lovers, and Margit had developed into a skilled courier for Rothenburg's Resistance cell. She had learned to pass the "packages," as they were called, in dozens of ingenious ways to people she had never met. A remark about the weather and an envelope was discreetly slipped into a gentleman's pocket. She spilled an armload of packages after bumping into a gentleman wearing a carnation in his boutonniere. The gentleman, carrying packages of his own, naturally stopped to help. Who could tell that when they finished she had one less small package and he had one more?

Still, it was dangerous work. Already one of their number, Willi Graumann, had been arrested by a vigilant Gestapo. Fortunately, Graumann didn't know that Margit was also in the Resistance, so he could tell the Gestapo nothing of Margit's activities.

"Be careful, Hermann, dear," she said, getting out of the car.

"You know I will."

Margit walked up the stairs and into her building, then down the hall to her apartment. She stepped inside, closed the door, and lit a cigarette. When would it all end? For six years she had watched the Nazis destroy everything and everyone she loved. The only thing that had been left to her was a bitter enduring hatred of Hitler and anyone who followed him.

The first ones she had lost were her parents. Gottfried and Helga Hassel were devoted parents, but they were also dedicated communists who openly worked for the German Communist Party during the years of democracy under the Weimar Republic. Margit, their only child, grew up in a pleasant middle-class German household with a generous leavening of Marx and Engels. Her father worked in a factory during the day and for the Party at night. Mother was a Hausfrau who passed out leaflets and made up voter lists for her husband. In the years of the Weimar Republic, Margit grew from a happy, precocious little girl to an attractive young woman. Less political than her parents, she studied hard to become a teacher and find her Prince Charming among the boys who courted her. In 1932 she never imagined events in far-away Berlin would destroy her happy life in Munich.

Gottfried Hassel was under no such illusions, and when Adolf Hitler was appointed chancellor on January 30, 1933, he and his comrades knew that political freedom in Germany would be crushed unless all of the other parties organized to resist the Nazis. At first it seemed their efforts would work, but in March Communist deputies were forbidden to take their seats in the Reichstag and special courts were established for the prosecution of the political enemies of National Socialism. Gottfried Hassel never came to trial. After the anti-Communist decree, he and his comrades continued to speak out against the Nazis, but the German populace was terrified on one hand and apathetic on the other, a dangerous combination. Shortly after Margit's sixteenth birthday, Gottfried Hassel was "caught" addressing a public meeting by Nazi Storm Troopers, who beat him so mercilessly he never regained consciousness. Margit had been in school. She arrived home to find the apartment ransacked and blood everywhere. The girl stood in the doorway horrified, and when someone emerged from the shadows, she screamed. The man slapped her, and her eyes went wide. It was Artur Milner, a comrade of her father's.

"Be still, Margit. The Storm Troopers may return. You must come with me."

"Mother and Father . . ."

Milner's eyes were very sad. "I'll take you to them. Come."

He took her to the morgue, where she identified her father's barely recognizable corpse and her mother's bullet-riddled body. She had been killed as the Storm Troopers burst into the door. Milner held Margit as she wept.

"Had you been home, you would have been killed, too."

"Why, Herr Milner, why?"

"The Nazis can't abide any views different than their own, and are prepared to murder anyone who speaks out."

It wasn't an answer she understood. To a teenage girl growing up in a loving home there had to be justice in the world. The next morning, Margit went to the police, who wasted her time filling out meaningless forms. She realized then that they weren't going to do a thing. Clutching the carbon copy of the police report that said her parents had been killed by unknown assailants, Margit could barely suppress her anger. Milner met her outside the station. The expression on her face was one of cold rage. "They'll pay," she swore. "All of them. The Nazis and the whole German Volk!"

In order to achieve her goal, she had to survive, and that quickly became a full-time occupation. As Gottfried's daughter, Milner was afraid she would be arrested, so he sent her to live with another family. It was just in time. The day after she left, Milner and his family were arrested by the Gestapo and sent to a concentration camp. Over the next two years Margit never stayed with one person more than a few days, in order to avoid the Gestapo. Then she met Paul Holbein, who was thirty-two and just under six feet tall. He had dark curly hair and a rugged face, and sincere brown eyes. He was educated, refined, and an energetic idealist who reminded her of her father. Margit listened rapturously as he spoke of the struggle of the lower classes to reach Utopia. Soon he was her guiding light as he introduced her to other communists, with whom she printed and distributed an underground newspaper. She now had the dual goal of avenging her parents and forwarding the cause of international communism. In the midst of the great political struggle against the Nazis, Paul and Margit fell in love. For the next year, she was happy and hoped they might be married until a terrible evening in 1936 when the Gestapo smashed down the door as they were printing the newspaper. Only Margit and Paul managed to escape, but they became separated, and she was once again on her own.

With the only communists she knew already in concentration camps, Margit had no one to turn to. To make ends meet, she found the job she now held in the Melchior Dress Shop, near the Kurfürstendamm in Berlin. She went to work daily wondering if the Gestapo was going to arrest her. They never came. Through a clerical error in the Munich Gestapo office her name was dropped from the list of suspects after her father died, and she was allowed to live and work under her own name. Nevertheless, she remained as unobtrusive as possible until she met Rothenburg, a wealthy attorney, who noticed her at the dress shop while buying a gift for his sister. He was in his fifties, well dressed and extremely polite. He asked her to dinner twice, and the second time she accepted. He had an internal strength that she admired, and she responded to his kindness with affection. When she told him her story, Rothenburg introduced her to the Resistance. The members in Rothenburg's circle were not communists, but Margit was happy to help anyone opposed to the Nazis, and she became their courier.

Three days after Rothenburg had dropped her off from the nightclub, at 7:30 in the morning, Margit Hassel sat in the crowded streetcar with other dozens of other Berliners heading for work. As usual, many of the men glanced in her direction, but she didn't return any of the admiring glances. Instead she pretended to read a copy of the Berliner *Zeitung*, with its cheerful reports of victory on all fronts. From her contacts in the Resistance she knew the real story. The German army was advancing in Russia, but the casualties were numbered in the thousands daily. When the car stopped on the Kurfüstendamm, she descended to the street with a sigh of relief. She didn't like closed-in places like streetcars, but she forced herself to ride in them. There was safety in looking like everyone else in a crowd.

Traffic was heavy and the sidewalks were crowded with pedestrians on their way to work as she walked the block and a half to the small dress shop on Wielandstrasse. Except for the large numbers of men in uniform around the city, it was hard to tell there was a war going on.

Margit tapped on the locked glass door of the dress shop and Frau Melchior, the owner, let her in. Frau Melchior was a plump widow with short, straight hair and a shiny round face that was normally turned up with a pleasant smile. Today she wore a frown. Margit noticed immediately.

"Good Morning. Frau Melchior, are you all right?"

"Oh, Fräulein Hassel, you haven't heard the news?"

"What news?"

"It's terrible. Herr Rothenburg is dead."

"Dead? How?"

"He was taken for questioning by the Gestapo and had a heart attack."

The Gestapo! Margit turned pale and stood absolutely still. It took every ounce of willpower not to flee in utter panic or faint. What was she to do now?

Frau Melchior took one look at Margit and clutched her gently by the arm. "Fräulein Hassel, you look terrible. You must sit down." The older woman led her to an armchair reserved for customers and she sat down. "I'll get you a glass of water."

While Margit drank the water, Frau Melchior prattled on about what a nice man Herr Rothenburg had been. "Yes," Margit said from time to time in agreement. She wondered if Rothenburg had told the Gestapo that she was a courier for the Resistance.

There was a tap on the door and the two women looked up to see two men in leather overcoats standing there. Both were tall. One was heavyset and the other thin. Gestapo. Margit tried not to sweat as Frau Melchior opened the door.

"Heil Hitler," the two men said in unison, with outstretched arms.

"Heil Hitler," Frau Melchior replied.

"Frau Melchior?" one asked.

"Yes?"

"We're looking for Fräulein Margit Hassel. Have you seen her?"

"She's right here." The woman pointed to Margit.

When they approached, Margit greeted them with an enthusiastic "Heil Hitler!" One of them smiled.

"We understand you knew Herr Hermann Rothenburg, Fräulein."

"Very well," Margit relied truthfully. There was absolutely no sense in lying.

Frau Melchior's mouth popped open, and the Gestapo agents looked at each other, smiling. "Would you come with us, please?"

"Certainly."

The two men weren't rough or abusive, and one of them actually held the door for her. Margit was relieved. The heavyset agent's name was Buhne and the slender one's was Arndt. Margit hoped they had nothing on her and were just fishing. When they arrived at their office, Arndt offered her a chair.

"Coffee, Fräulein?"

"Yes, thank you."

While Arndt poured the coffee, Buhne conducted the interrogation. "How well did you know Herr Rothenburg, Fräulein?"

"*Very* well, Herr Buhne. I was his mistress."

The Gestapo agent grinned at her candor. "You're a very attractive woman, Fräulein. Why would you be interested in someone like Rothenburg, who was so much older than you?"

Margit forced herself to look him straight in the eye. "Because he was rich" she said, convincingly.

"Ahh." Buhne grinned. It was what they expected. "What about his other activities?"

"What other activities?"

"Did he belong to any clubs or organizations?"

Margit named the lawyers' club and social club of which Rothenburg had been a member.

"Did you know any of Herr Rothenburg's associates?"

Margit named most of the people whom she had met through Rothenburg, including his sister, and then mentioned Willi Graumann.

She hated to do it, but it brought a positive reaction from the two agents.

"You're sure, Fräulein?"

"Of course."

"When did you last see them together?"

"I don't know exactly. Maybe two months. He hasn't been around lately."

The two Gestapo agents ignored the comment. "Were you aware of any illicit activity Herr Rothenburg might have been involved in?"

"You mean like the black market?"

The Gestapo man shrugged noncommittally.

"He was rich. He didn't need the money."

Buhne and Arndt conferred quietly in a corner while Margit sipped her coffee.

"What do you think?" Arndt asked.

"The information about Graumann is very useful."

"Do you think she's one of them?"

"I don't think so," Buhne told him. "These Resistance types normally don't mention each other's names without persuasion. Anyway we can ask Graumann. He's not going anywhere. What do you think?"

"I think she's a greedy little tramp."

"Only because you don't have the money to keep her."

Buhne and Arndt released Margit late that morning, and she returned to her room rather than go back to work. Then the rigid control she had maintained melted away, and as soon as she closed the door, she threw herself on the narrow bed, sobbing in relief. It was early in the evening before she regained her composure. She removed her tear-stained dress and, with trembling hands, poured a glass of schnapps and lit a cigarette. *So,* she thought, *I've survived again while someone else has had to pay the price.* Where would it all end? Her hands shook so badly that she spilled some of the schnapps as she drank.

September 1, 1942

Major Hans Meiler Freiherr von Rittburg strode up the steps of the High Command Building on the Bendlerstrasse with the confident air of the professional combat veteran. Tall and imposing, the handsome, dark-haired officer with his riding breeches and cavalry boots represented the best of the Prussian officers that had served their country from the days of Frederick the Great. Returning the salute of the guards at the door, he paused to remove his hat and gloves before ascending the broad staircase. When he entered his office in the Intelligence Section, his orderly greeted him.

"Good morning, Herr Major." Gefreiter Weiss clicked his heels and came to attention. Weiss was short and wiry. His brown hair was close-cut, and he smiled easily. There was a twinkle in his blue eyes. Like von Rittburg, he had red piping on his uniform, because he was a cannoneer.

"Good morning, Weiss." The Major returned the salute and looked around. "I see the British left their calling card." There was plaster dust all over the place.

"They also broke two windows, Herr Major. I'll get them replaced as soon as I can."

Major von Rittburg looked up at the ceiling. There were holes where chunks of plaster had come down. The broken widows were already boarded up.

"Still, it's better than the Russian Front, eh, Weiss?"

"I was thinking the same thing, Herr Major. May I take the Major's coat?"

"Thank you, Weiss."

Weiss left to hang up the hat and coat. He liked von Rittburg. The Major was a gentleman in every sense of the word, and treated everyone from the lowliest private to generals with consideration and respect. The Major was pleasant and light-hearted even in the face of danger. Once he had watched the Major single-handedly destroy two Russian tanks that had broken into their position, all the time encouraging his men. Weiss didn't know how many men Rittburg saved, but he cared for all of them and grieved for each man killed. When word had come that his lovely wife had been killed in an air raid, the Major had put on a brave face, but Weiss knew it had changed the man forever. Nevertheless, Weiss had been pleased to accompany the Major to Berlin to his assignment to High Command Counterintelligence, known simply as the Abwehr. It was headed by Admiral Wilhelm Canaris, whom Weiss thought was entirely too mysterious, but then Weiss didn't know that many Admirals.

"Admiral Canaris left a message he wanted to see the Major at 0830 hours. He didn't tell me the subject."

"Thank you, Weiss. He gave me some notes to study." Von Rittburg looked at his briefcase lying on the desk. Von Rittburg's official job in the Abwehr was the assessment of enemy capabilities. In a short time he had mastered the subject and his estimates were highly regarded by the General Staff. Because they were extremely accurate and did not put Germany's position in a favorable light, they were seldom shown to Hitler. The assignment Canaris had recently given him had nothing to do with the enemies of the Reich, but the Reich itself. Von Rittburg had always had nagging suspicions about some of the things going on in the Reich and its occupied territories, but they had been just that—suspicions—and he had hoped they weren't true. But according to the voluminous reports that Admiral Canaris had given him, things were worse than he could possibly imagine.

Von Rittburg might have dismissed it all as nonsense, but he had known the Admiral for a long time. As a Hauptmann, von Rittburg had been Canaris's pupil and served in Counterintelligence right out of General Staff school. When the war broke out he commanded a battery in France and then Russia, until he was reassigned to the Abwehr. Canaris requested him by name to replace another officer killed in an air raid. Canaris had indirectly hinted about some of the things going on, and when he felt von Rittburg was ready for the truth, he had given him the reports the Major now carried in the briefcase.

Canaris was waiting when von Rittburg entered his office. There was no one else in the room.

"Ah, Major, good of you to come." The Admiral was heavyset but not fat. His features were pleasant and his hair gray. He presented an air of reserved gentility and was warm only to those he knew well. "Please close the door."

The Major did as the Admiral requested.

"Have a seat, Herr Major." The Admiral pointed to a comfortable chair. "Coffee?"

"No thank you, sir."

The Admiral filled a bone china cup from a silver pot and sat behind his desk. "Have you read the reports I gave you?"

"Every one, Herr Admiral. Most of them twice."

"And?"

Von Rittburg removed the sheaf of paper from his briefcase. "It's unbelievable," he stammered. "The Reichsbahn isn't shipping enough weapons and ammunition to the front because the orders to deliver Jews to concentration camps are using too many freight cars. This can't be right."

"You've read the report. Do you doubt its accuracy?"

"No, but this is absurd." The Major held up the report for emphasis. "Sending people to their deaths just because they're Jews or Poles is insane. To do it rather than support your own troops fighting a war is . . .is . . ."

"Psychotic? Demented?"

"I cannot think of a word to describe it," he declared, shaking his head. "After the losses in Russia and the heavy fighting going on now at Stalingrad, how can we continue this way?"

"But we do continue, Major von Rittburg." Canaris fixed him with his eyes.

"Only a madman . . ." Von Rittburg was silent. *I have already said too much,* he thought.

"Only a madman surrounded by obsequious sycophants who share his insanity and worship him could carry out such a policy," the Admiral continued. "Is that what you are thinking, Major?"

"I . . ."

"And our beloved Führer, Adolf Hitler, is just such a madman."

Von Rittburg looked away.

"It's time to stop looking away, Major. Did you know that I was once one of Hitler's confidants?"

"No sir, I didn't."

"That was back in 1935. I was a captain then. I became head of the Abwehr because of some counterintelligence work in the Great War. Like many others I thought Hitler was the answer to Germany's problems, but I was wrong. In 1938 I was appalled at Hitler's plan to annex the Sudetenland. I even thought of joining a coup to oust him from office when he failed. None of the coup planners realized he had the Devil's own luck. I was even prepared to change my mind about him, but a short time later I was at his headquarters when he went into one of his incredible rages."

"What was it like, Herr Admiral? I hear they're quite something."

"This one was. I'm glad it wasn't directed at me. I would have been funny if it hadn't been so frightening. He got some bad news and lost all control, screaming and pounding his fist on the table." Canaris shook his head.

"When he ordered the invasion of Russia, it confirmed my worst fears. He has to be stopped. He's a madman, and he won't be satisfied until all of us are either mindless Hitler followers or dead. Even now the Nazis have permeated every aspect of German society so there is no place to hide from a swastika, a portrait of the Führer, or a copy of *Mein Kampf.* Worse, they have even permeated the High Command. Field Marshal Keitel and General Jodl are supposed to be directing the operations of the army. Instead, they are nothing but toadies who let Hitler personally control every battalion from Russia to France. Even I have had to give up some of my control to the Sicherheitsdienst. I thought Reinhard Heydrich was my friend, but even he encroached on the Abwehr. If we are to save Germany, we must stop them, and we must do it soon." The Admiral paused.

"I am sorry to have included the information about your wife. I thought you should know the truth."

"Thank you, Herr Admiral." The Major looked through the Admiral and far beyond. On the Russian Front he had received word that his beloved wife Renate had been killed in an air raid, but among the papers the Admiral had given him was a copy of a police report. Renate had been run down by a drunken Kreisleiter as she walked down the sidewalk in broad daylight. There had been no air raid that month. Von Rittburg was furious. "Was the man charged?" he asked.

"No, the incident was covered up. You were away at the front so they figured you'd never know. I know how much you meant to each other."

"Thank you, Herr Admiral." The controlled rage in the Major's voice was evident.

"I hope you are not considering revenge," the Admiral said. "The Fatherland needs you now more than ever. There will be plenty of time to settle scores after the war. I also have to ask that you reveal the information about your wife to no one, not even your wife's family. If certain people knew you had that information, both of us would be in a lot of trouble."

Puzzled, von Rittburg looked at him, and Canaris voiced his concern.

"Why don't you take some leave and spend some time with your family? It will help."

Von Rittburg nodded. "Have you anything else for me, Herr Admiral?"

"Yes, but not here. Meet me at the Tiergarten Café near the zoo. Do you know it?"

"Yes, sir."

"Meet me by coincidence at one o'clock."

"Yes, Herr Admiral." The Major stood, clicked his heels and departed, wondering what was so sensitive that the Admiral was too cautious to discuss it in his own office.

That afternoon, strolling slowly down the street, the Major kept one eye open for the Gestapo and one for Canaris, whom he found sitting at a table.

Von Rittburg clicked his heels and bowed stiffly. "Excuse me, Herr Admiral, may I join you?"

Canaris smiled warmly "Major von Rittburg, what a pleasant surprise. Yes, please sit down, by all means. Do you come here often?"

"Thank you." Von Rittburg sat down. "I occasionally come here when my boss hasn't burdened me with work."

Canaris grinned. "I hope that's not too often."

"What's not too often, Herr Admiral, the overburdening or the coming here?"

Canaris laughed heartily as the waiter came over. "I asked for that one."

The Admiral ordered another glass of wine and a beer for von Rittburg. They joked, drank, and made small talk, keeping track of two Gestapo agents in leather overcoats who hovered at a table nearby. It became obvious the Gestapo weren't interested in them in a few minutes when the men in overcoats soon hurried down the street on what appeared to be urgent business. The Admiral paid for the drinks and motioned for the Major to accompany him for a walk in the zoo.

"Major von Rittburg, do you know what atoms are?"

"As in basic physics and chemistry? Yes, Herr Admiral."

"Have you ever heard of uranium?"

"No, Herr Admiral. What is it?"

"It's an obscure metal made up of large atoms, until recently only used in the manufacture of pottery and for scientific experiments. In 1938, Professor Hahn of the Kaiser Wilhelm Institute succeeded in splitting uranium atoms, and the forces released compared to the amount of uranium used was enormous. I'm no scientist, but it comes to this: There are two kinds of uranium. One explodes and the other doesn't. If you get a few kilos of the right kind, and make it explode, you could destroy an entire city with a bomb the size of an oil drum."

"A whole city with just one bomb?" Von Rittburg looked at him in disbelief. "That's impossible. One of the Allies' extra-large bombs weighs six thousand kilos, but that's not enough to destroy a city."

"I'm not talking about conventional high explosive. This is something like the power of the sun. My contact says such a bomb would explode with a force equivalent to more than twenty-five thousand tons, mind you, I said tons, of ordinary explosive all going off at once. And it doesn't end there. After the bomb went off, it would contaminate everything with radiation so that those who survived the blast in a radius of several kilometers would sicken and die."

Von Rittburg shook his head. "That's incredible, Herr Admiral. But if that's the case, why doesn't someone build one. Or several?"

"The process to get the uranium that explodes is extremely complex, and we haven't solved it yet. Unfortunately there is someone working on the problem right now." He explained briefly about Lamm and Operation NORD.

"You said 'unfortunately.' I still don't understand."

"Major, if Germany had such a bomb, what do you think would happen?"

"With such weapons, we could win the war."

"Suppose we only had one or two?"

"The Führer would use the first one on London and the second on Washington, if he could get it there."

"Would that end the war or stop the Russians?"

"No, Herr Admiral. But we might get a negotiated peace."

"Do you seriously think the Führer would negotiate peace?"

The Admiral stopped for a moment and Major von Rittburg stopped with him.

"No, Herr Admiral," von Rittburg replied, after a long pause. "I don't."

"You are familiar with the Allies' industrial capacity, Major. What do you think of the possibility of their developing a bomb such as this?"

"About as good as ours," von Rittburg replied. "Maybe better."

"Definitely better," Canaris said, continuing to walk.

"Why are you so sure?"

"Because we gave them all our best talent. The Nazis chased them out from 1935 to 1938. Most of them were Jews. Those who remained were put in concentration camps." Von Rittburg said nothing this time, and Canaris continued. "These scientists, whom we forced out of Germany and the rest of Europe, have no love for us. So there is no reason for them not to build a uranium bomb for the Americans or British. Once we started, what do you think would happen?"

"They would use the same kind of bombs on us."

"Exactly, only they would have more of them, and they would eliminate us, the Germans, from the map of Europe."

"That's a sobering thought."

"The Nazis must be destroyed, von Rittburg. They must be cut out of the German body like a cancer. If we can do it ourselves and eliminate this barbarism that is being committed then maybe, just maybe, we can negotiate a peace with the Allies. If we can't, the British, the Americans, and, God forbid, the Russians, will do it for us. Even if we don't succeed in removing Hitler, we must prevent him from using this uranium bomb, once Lamm and his team succeed in building it."

"With all of the difficulties do you think it's possible?"

"If it were left to others, no. But Lamm is one of the most brilliant scientists in this country. If anyone can do it, he can. He is a protégé of Heydrich and like his mentor, he is totally ruthless."

"What do you propose to do, Herr Admiral?"

"I don't know, yet. It all depends on whether or not Lamm succeeds. If he does, drastic action may be required. Can I depend on you, Major von Rittburg?"

"Yes, Herr Admiral."

Canaris looked at his watch. "It's time for the seals to be fed. Care to join me?"

"Excuse me, Herr Admiral, but I need time to think."

"Of course. *Auf Wiedersehen,* Major von Rittburg."

"*Auf Wiedersehen,* Herr Admiral."

CHAPTER 6

URANIUM

The Frankfurt Rail Yard
September 7, 1942

FRIEDRICH BITTNER LOOKED UNCONSCIOUSLY at the predawn sky, a habit many Germans were developing. No Allied bombers had reached Frankfurt on the Main yet, but the overcast sky still made Bittner feel better. Checking his watch, the SS man scowled. The switch engine was late and Bittner had to finish his work before the day shift returned. Being in the Frankfurt Yards brought an ironic smile to Bittner's lips. Eight years before as a worker in this yard he had been a committed socialist who vowed with his comrades to fight Nazi domination to the death. By 1936 the Nazis were in firm control, and their enemies quickly disappeared. Never a believer in lost causes, Bittner became a member of the Party while the others went to concentration camps or escaped to fight in Spain. As soon as he understood the special status of the SS, he joined, making sure his tracks as a socialist were well covered. The fact the SS paid more than the railroad made it even better. Now, he and Hans Werner were the only two remaining of their old socialist cell, and he occasionally wondered about the others.

Those who had not gone to concentration camps or left the country were now on the Russian Front. It was unfortunate, but in times like these, it was every man for himself, and Bittner congratulated himself on making the right decision. All he had to do was follow orders and mind his own business to succeed. With this last promotion and the assignment to the Racial Science Section, he was in a nice comfortable job, and he intended to stay there. Let the others be heroes. He was thinking of the future. Even if Germany lost the war, the Führer would still need the SS.

Impatiently, looking at his watch again, Bittner shivered, took a cigarette out of his pocket, put it to his lips, and lit it. Being here was crazy, just like Lamm was crazy. Destroy a city with a single bomb—that was crazy, too. Still, one could never tell. Lamm believed utterly in what he was doing, and his enthusiasm for this project was contagious. On his orders the entire section was traveling from Berlin to Norway, stealing things and making deals. *I must be crazy too,* Bittner thought. After all, here he was in Frankfurt to steal a carload of uranium metal, which somehow was supposed to explode. A metal that exploded. What a bunch of nonsense. Just because some Jew named Einstein had a theory. All those Jews were crazy, too. Hitler was right to get them out of the Reich. Life was full of injustice. Let the Jews look out for themselves; he always had to.

The lights of the switch engine suddenly appeared from behind a line of boxcars. *About time,* Bittner thought, tossing away his cigarette. He stepped gingerly over the rails to throw one switch, then ran down the track to throw another. The engine followed the new route onto a small siding containing three boxcars and coupled to the first car with a thud. In the bustle of a yard like Frankfurt, no one noticed the extra activity.

Bittner released the coupler between the first two cars, signaled, and the engine slowly backed away, pulling the car away from its companions. Dropping to the ground, Bittner walked along the side of the moving car, throwing the switches back to their original position, then ran up to the moving boxcar and jumped up, grinning. He hadn't lost the knack. The siding and the other two cars disappeared in the dark maze of the yard. Good old Hans. They had sworn to fight the Nazis together, then they had joined the Party together. Now Bittner was in the SS and Hans was a trainmaster.

The engine slowed and Bittner jumped off to throw three more switches. In a siding as obscure as the first, the boxcar was coupled to three more. As soon as the engine left, Bittner returned the switches to their original positions, then removed the old invoices and replaced them with ones that read "NORD GMBH Lübeck."

In two days the uranium would be in Lübeck, ready for loading on a ship without anyone ever knowing what happened to it—a job well done. Bittner took a shortcut across the yard to thank Hans. His route took him by a little-used platform in an out-of-the-way corner of the yard. There was so much activity there he thought he had lost the way, which was easy for a newcomer to do that in the labyrinth of track and equipment. But Bittner was no newcomer. He knew the Frankfurt yards in his sleep. With little more than an hour until dawn, Bittner checked his bearings by the landmarks showing against the dimly glowing sky.

Curious, he went to investigate some activity that was going on, and stopped when he saw thousands of people on the platform. At first, he thought it was troops boarding a train, but there were guards all around the train, which was made up of boxcars, and people were huddled together in little clumps, each of them clutching a bundle or a suitcase. Moving closer, Bittner saw they were wearing yellow six-pointed stars. Jews!

"Move along quickly now," a voice was saying over a loudspeaker. "We have a schedule to keep. Families remain together."

The Jews moved tamely into the boxcars, each of them with a dazed expression on his or her face as the loudspeaker announced they were going to be resettled in the east. Each car was crammed full of people before the doors were shut, and Bittner wondered if they could sit down. Suddenly realizing what he was witnessing, he shivered. The rumors were true. A guard noticed Bittner standing in the shadows and walked over.

"What are you doing here?" he demanded.

Bittner moved into the light and lit another cigarette, giving the guard a full view of his SS uniform and the armband of Himmler's personal staff.

"I'm from the Reichsführer's headquarters, here to make sure things go smoothly." He hoped the guard didn't notice his nervousness.

Without changing his expression, the guard nodded in recognition and returned to his post. Bittner's hand trembled as he removed the cigarette from his lips. The rumors were true. They actually were going to kill all those people. He braced himself. It was none of his business. After all, they were only Jews. Then he continued on his way to see Hans. The sun was rising and he had to leave.

Hans was still in the switch tower. "Everything go all right, Fritz?" Hans asked.

"Perfectly, Hans, perfectly. The package I left with you is yours."

"Mine?" Hans unwrapped a bottle of Scotch whiskey. "Fritz, thank you. It won't mess up your ration, will it?"

"None involved, " Bittner said, with a wink. "Compliments of NORD GMBH. In remembrance of the bad old days."

"Thank you." Hans returned the grin.

It was light enough for the details of the yard to be visible. A train was slowly moving east and Bittner realized he was looking at the train packed with Jews. Hans noticed Bittner staring at something, and came to the window.

"Oh," was all he said.

"Hans," Bittner asked after a long pause, "where do they take them?"

Hans looked at the sky. "I think it's going to be a nice day, Fritz—a little overcast." The train was gaining momentum.

"I think you're right, Hans."

The train disappeared into the brightening sky. Hans was right. It was nobody's business but those involved. Bittner followed orders and minded his own business.

September 15, 1942

Ernst Reinhart looked out the window as the Junkers trimotor banked for its final approach to the Lübeck airfield.

"My goodness!" Inge Trautner exclaimed. "Look at the damage."

Reinhart and Loring were equally amazed at the destruction caused by the British raids. The Propaganda Ministry had played down the amount of destruction, while pointing out damage to hospitals and churches. If the German public knew the truth, it would have the same question as those in the aircraft: "Where was the Luftwaffe?" The trimotor leveled out and began its descent to the runway. Loring leaned forward to speak with Reinhart. "There should be a car waiting for you and Fräulein Trautner, Herr Hauptsturmführer. There are also two rooms reserved for you at the

Waldhof, outside the city." Reinhart nodded in understanding as the Junkers touched down gently and rolled to a stop.

"Have a good flight to Norway, Loring," Inge Trautner said. The crew chief opened the door and set down a small step ladder. With the propellers still spinning, Reinhart held on to his hat and turned to help Fräulein Trautner down the steps. The prop wash blew her skirt up to her thighs, and he could see the tops of her stockings. When he looked up, Loring, who was grinning in the doorway of the aircraft, gave Reinhart a knowing wink as the crew chief closed the door. The aircraft turned and taxied back down the runway as a young SS man came over to them, shouting over the noise of the Junkers 52 revving up.

"Hauptsturmführer Reinhart?"

"Yes."

"I am Sturmmann Waldmann, your driver." He was speaking to Reinhart, but looking at Fräulein Trautner, and Reinhart realized that Trautner was a bigger asset than anyone imagined. Their first stop was the hotel, which was far enough outside the city to have been spared from British bombs. After freshening up they had lunch and drove to the waterfront through some of the worst damage in silence.

"This is terrible!" Reinhart exclaimed when he saw the warehouse. "We'd be better off in one of those bombed-out buildings. Hammerstein must have been out of his mind to rent something like this."

"He said it was pretty bad," Fräulein Trautner remarked sourly. "He wasn't exaggerating."

The warehouse looked better from the inside. One wall was full of holes, which were repairable, and there were also two holes in the roof, which needed to be patched. It would have to do.

"Let's see what the office is like," Reinhart said, climbing the metal steps to the compact cubicle.

Fräulein Trautner followed hesitantly. "At least Hammerstein thought of the bare necessities," she quipped, looking around her new home. "A filing cabinet, two desks with two chairs, paper, a typewriter, and a framed picture of the Führer."

"What, no Himmler?" Reinhart asked, seriously.

Fräulein Trautner ignored him and picked up the telephone to listen to the dial tone. "It's working," she said.

Reinhart turned the switch and the ceiling lights came on. "The lights work. I wonder if the water is running."

"I'm about to find out," she told him, heading for the bathroom.

The water was on. Hammerstein had left a note that NORD GMBH now had a post box, which Reinhart went to check while Fräulein Trautner established the new filing system. She jumped when the phone rang unexpectedly, and then dutifully picked it up. "Hello," she said from habit, "Racial Science Section." Then she corrected herself. "Excuse me, NORD GMBH. May I help you?"

"Oh, pardon me," a man's voice said, "I must have misdialed. So sorry." He hung up. Fräulein Trautner shrugged, hung up the phone, and returned to her filing. The man on the other end smiled, rather pleased with himself. He now knew that NORD GMBH was connected with the SS. Specifically, it was connected with the Racial Science Section. He would have to get the information to London as soon as possible. The next question was how NORD GMBH was connected to the Racial Science Section, and for what purpose?

The large stack of invoices in the NORD post office box and their contents gave Reinhart cause for concern. Tons of supplies were on the way, and NORD GMBH didn't even have a warehouseman. He went immediately to the employment office to see about warehouse personnel, then stopped at the Reichsbahn office to rent the small siding to the rear of the warehouse. *I wonder if things aren't happening a bit too quickly,* he thought.

Lamm, Nachmann, Lindner, and Dietrich remained at the Racial Science Section office in Berlin to determine the configuration of the reactor.

"As I see it, we have two primary objectives in this uranium burner," Lamm said. "We must surround the uranium with a moderator so the neutrons will be slowed enough to fission the uranium atoms. The reaction in the burner will create considerable heat, so the burner will have to be cooled. Water is the best and most easy to use coolant, but we can't let it touch the uranium. Do any of you have any suggestions?"

Dietrich was frowning, and the others didn't meet his gaze.

"Dietrich, is something wrong?"

"I . . ." he hesitated.

"Speak up," Lamm encouraged. "We won't get anywhere if we can't openly exchange ideas."

"Quite frankly, Herr Professor, the idea of building a uranium burner with no experience is intimidating and dangerous. I recommend that we do something that would give us at least some experience working with uranium and risk fewer resources."

"What do you have in mind?" Lamm inquired, with genuine interest.

"I know you told us not to duplicate other peoples' work, but it seems to me that it would be most useful to reproduce the L-IV experiment. It would give us a controlled environment in which we could gain experience in working with actual materials. As of this moment, none of us has dealt with anything but theory. I haven't been inside a laboratory for over a year, and this goes far beyond test tubes."

They all nodded in agreement.

"Did all of you discuss this?"

They looked at each other and nodded again.

Lamm smiled, "Good!" He was emphatic. "I want you all to use your initiative and work as a team. It's the only way the few of us can succeed."

The young SS officers visibly relaxed. Lamm was, indeed, treating them as scientists.

Nachmann, who had been reticent to speak, now leaned forward. "Since we are going to duplicate the L-IV experiment, what are we going to do for vessels? The L-IV experiment used spherical stainless steel vessels that undoubtedly took a long time to make. To do the same we are going to need a priority from Reichsminister Speer."

"Nachmann's right," Lindner agreed. "We need a priority, but I don't think we really need to bother with the spherical apparatus. Cylindrical should do nearly as well, as they can be adapted from current designs. That still leaves the problem of heavy water. That's the one thing that will be difficult to come by, and we dare not ask for it."

Lamm thought a minute. "I'll wire Loring and Hammerstein in Norway and see if they can help. At the same time, we'll tell Reinhart to see about stainless steel or aluminum vessels for the pit of the uranium burner. Also, I'm going to see the Reichsführer about a priority."

"Isn't Reichsführer Himmler in Poland?" Nachmann asked.

"Yes. I'd completely forgotten. Perhaps the Reichsleiter can help us. Has anyone given any thought to the problem of keeping the uranium away from the water?" Lindner raised his pencil.

"Lindner?"

"I suggest we seal the uranium in cans just like food. As a matter of fact, we could probably use a food canning assembly line from an established factory," he said.

"Too risky," Nachmann interjected. "We'd contaminate the entire assembly line. Heavy metal poisoning is very bad. Besides, we need to keep a low profile, and trying to hire a factory would just call attention to ourselves."

"Nachmann has a point," Lamm agreed.

"Then why don't we modify the plan some way?" Dietrich offered. "We could use aluminum or stainless steel pipe. Perhaps we could use something like one-meter lengths. The pieces of uranium could be wired together and sealed inside. There would be some heat retention in the pipe, but in Norway, we can get very cold water."

Lamm looked around the table. Everyone was in agreement. "Fine. I'll get an appointment with Reichsleiter Bormann. Dietrich, call Reinhart and tell him what we need, then see if you can reach Hammerstein and Loring. I want to be operational at Vikmo before the bad weather sets in."

The night before his departure for Vikmo was almost too much for Lamm. Rarely had he been separated from Irma for more than a few days, and he always missed her deeply. Now he would be away for months. He could not bear her tears as he held her tightly to him.

"What am I to do with you in Norway and Karl in school?" she sniffled. "I can't bear it."

"It's our duty, dearest. I would never go away unless I were ordered to, you know that. I am like a soldier now."

"But you're a professor, not a field marshal. Papa was a soldier and he stayed in Heidelberg the whole war."

"I know, my darling, but this is scientific work."

"Why can't they send someone else?"

"Because it's something only I can do. Irma, what I'm working on is a bomb that is so powerful that it will make will make Germany the most powerful nation on earth. No one will dare oppose us, so there will be peace for hundreds of years. That means that when Karl grows up he won't have to fight in a war. You would want that for him, wouldn't you?"

"Yes, you know that. But why do you have to go to Norway? Why can't you do it here in Berlin?"

"The project must be kept secret and away from prying eyes," he explained gently. He didn't mention it had to be kept away from German as well as prying Allied eyes. "If the Allies found out about this they would attack Berlin incessantly and kill lots of innocent people, and I couldn't bear to have that happen."

"Max, you're so sweet. Promise me you won't do anything dangerous."

"I will be very careful, my dear, I promise." Despite his tears, he grinned. He was going to unlock the very secrets of nature and she didn't want him to do anything dangerous. "I love you, Irma. I love you more than the day we met."

"Oh, Max, I love you so much." They held each other until the car arrived to pick him up.

Loring met Hammerstein in Oslo, then they flew up to the weather station. After remaining overnight, they borrowed a truck and drove to the Vikmo site.

"I'm afraid we've really got our hands full," Hammerstein told Loring. "There's a lot more to reopening a mine than dusting it out."

"What needs to be done, Herr Obersturmführer?"

"To start, the lower section of the mine is flooded, and we have to pump it out."

"Do we have pumps?"

"Since the mine was operational nearly twenty years, the owners left the equipment because it wasn't worth the price of salvage. The original pumps and wiring are still in place, as is the kitchen equipment. I'm looking around the surrounding villages for anyone who worked on the pumps, and offering top wages for those who come here."

"Carry on, then."

The mine complex was small and the layout simple. Near the entrance to the mine were two small buildings. One had been an administrative office and had a switchboard and a window for issuing badges to workers entering the mine. The other building, located near the entrance, was made of stone. It contained the switchgear for all the electrical equipment, as well as an emergency generator.

"I wonder if it works," Loring offered.

"No way to tell. We have no fuel."

The rest of the buildings were tin-covered wood with insulation attached to the inside. Two hundred meters to the north of the mine entrance were three medium-size buildings that could hold twenty to thirty men each. Another hundred meters to the east were two large sheds. A short distance from the sheds was an old dining hall.

"At least there will be enough for housing," Loring said, "but where are we going to store all the equipment when it comes?"

"I guess the mine. That's the most logical place."

Hammerstein replied, "Come here, I have something to show you." He led Loring to the old archaeological dig that had been used by Operation Nord.

"So, this is what caused all the trouble," Loring said.

"Yes, and I intend to reopen it," Hammerstein told him. "With Obersturmbannführer Lamm's approval, of course."

"But why?" Loring asked. "It was obviously a fraud. Besides, it's going to look pretty silly digging up artifacts in the snow."

"Precisely," Hammerstein grinned.

"I don't follow you."

"Everyone will think we're trying to work the same old fraud. At least that's what I hope they'll think."

"Ah," Loring remarked. "It might work at that. If nothing else, it will confuse anyone who flies over."

On a bluff a short distance from the Vikmo mine, a figure with powerful binoculars lay flat on the ground, observing the mine area. Moving his head carefully to ensure the sun didn't reflect in the field glasses, he watched the two Germans walk from building to building. What did they want with the Vikmo mine? They couldn't possibly want to reopen their silly archaeological dig, but there they were, only this time there were more of them. Over thirty SS men were spreading barbed wire and smoothing out an area that could only be an airfield. What was going on? He knew the mine was dead. He worked there before it closed. Geologists and mining engineers from all over Norway had inspected the mine and concluded it was no longer profitable. Yet there the Germans were reopening the mine—and without any heavy equipment. The man with the binoculars wished he could hear what the men at the dig were saying.

"The old line bringing electricity to the mine still works," Hammerstein continued. "So we have plenty of power. There was a railroad spur up to the mine, but they took the track up to use elsewhere. I doubt if we can get another spur laid anytime soon. We'll have to unload at Vikmo, twenty-five miles from here, and truck it in." He looked up at the snowflakes. "That means a lot of work before the bad weather really sets in."

Moving slowly back from the ridge until he was no longer visible to the Germans, the man covered the lenses of the binoculars before carefully returning them to the case. Moving at a crouch until he could no longer be seen, he stood up and began the long walk to the carefully hidden truck. In a little over an hour, he returned to his cottage outside Vikmo, where he removed a panel from the wall in the study and warmed up the transmitter while he checked the codebook. When the radio was ready he expertly tapped the key.

"Activity at Vikmo; mine opened." He stopped transmitting and waited for the reply.

"Activity at Vikmo; mine opened. Roger." He turned off the set and concealed it.

The British submarine retransmitted the message on a different frequency to England. At Gestapo headquarters in Vikmo, a radio-intercept operator put down his headphones and smiled. He took a pencil and made two marks on the map above his radio.

"Did you get him, Franz?" his partner asked, anxiously.

"Not quite, Klaus, but next time for sure." Looking very satisfied, he lit a cigarette.

September 29, 1942

After attending a round of continuous briefings for the past forty-eight hours, Colonel Reginald Farnsworth was ready to go to his London club, have a drink, and go home to get a good night's sleep. The Battle of Alam Halfa was over, Rommel had shot his bolt, and Montgomery was ready to launch the offensive that would break the Afrika Korps once and for all. If that weren't enough, Operation

Torch, the invasion of French North Africa, was on schedule. No one said so out loud, but the tide was turning. *Well someone's out there fighting the war instead of pushing bloody papers,* he thought, filling his briefcase with reports. He was nearly out the door when a woman's voice said, "Excuse me, sir, are you Colonel Farnsworth?"

Even though the headquarters was crawling with Women's Royal Army Corps volunteers, Farnsworth still couldn't get used to women in the army.

"Yes," he told the WRAC corporal. "What is it?"

"Corporal Winters, sir. Mr. 'Arris would like to 'ave a word with the Colonel. At the Colonel's convenience." She saluted smartly.

"Thank you, Corporal." Farnsworth returned her salute. *At the Colonel's convenience, indeed.* Picking up his hat, briefcase, and swagger stick, the colonel headed down the corridor. Whatever Harris wanted, it meant trouble. Farnsworth wished he could find a regiment somewhere and enjoy the war. Instead he was stuck in this twilight world of political liaison and intelligence, with all the top brass worried about the Germans producing some weapon straight out of Buck Rogers. And Harris was the worst of the lot. The trouble was that Farnsworth wasn't exactly Harris's subordinate, but Harris was so high up in the cabinet that there was no way Farnsworth could refuse a request from him. Reaching Harris's office, the great man's secretary was nowhere to be found. "Ours is not to reason why," he muttered, and knocked on the door.

"Come in. Oh, Colonel Farnsworth. Good of you to come." Alexander Harris looked haggard and drawn. He was fighting an uphill battle trying to convince the War Cabinet of Winston Churchill that the Germans were on the verge of several scientific breakthroughs.

"It sounded urgent, sir." Everything Harris wanted was urgent.

"Yes, quite. Please sit down. Drink?"

"No thank you, sir. Been up too long."

"Oh, yes. Smashing briefing you gave on the Afrika Korps. The PM's people thought it quite good."

"Thank you, sir," Farnsworth replied appreciatively. "How may I assist you?"

"Oh, yes. Unfortunately it's the Norway business again."

"Norway, sir?"

"Don't you remember? You obtained an aircraft for a reconnaissance in Norway back in 'forty. Place called Vikmo."

"Oh, yes, sir. I remember," Farnsworth said. God had he gotten sick on that flight.

"Well, unfortunately, Jerry is back at Vikmo, but this time it's not one of those damned fool archeological sites. Our man tells us the SS has reopened the mine and they're moving in all sorts of heavy equipment. The question is what could they possibly be doing there? It isn't the coal. The mine played out ages ago and it's one thing the Germans aren't short of. I'm worried."

Farnsworth hesitated before he spoke. "Do you think it's the long-range rocket we've been hearing about, sir?"

Harris's face seemed to fall. "I'm afraid so, Colonel. No one in London seems to believe in them, but I do. Those last reconnaissance photos of Peenemünde confirm that Jerry has something. As for Norway, what better place to build and launch the blasted things? We'd have to divert half our bombers from Germany to get at them. We have to see what's on the ground, and while I appreciate your help in the previous mission, I have to go on this one myself. You might inadvertently miss something technical. Sorry."

"No need to apologize, sir. When do you need the aircraft?"

"As soon as possible."

"I'll do my best."

As Farnsworth closed the door he looked back over his shoulder. The thought of huge rockets raining down on London from Norway was a pretty grim prospect. He sincerely hoped Mr. Alexander Harris was wrong. The trouble was, Harris was usually right.

CHAPTER 7

THE FATHER OF THE GODS

The Reich Chancellery, Berlin
September 30, 1942

MAXIMILIAN LAMM WAITED IMPATIENTLY OUTSIDE Bormann's office. How did anything in the Reich get done with so many layers of bureaucracy? He was about to design the most powerful weapon in the world and all they cared about was their paperwork.

"Obersturmbannführer Lamm?" someone said.

Lamm turned. The person who spoke was a deputy Gauleiter he had never seen before. "I am Obersturmbannführer Lamm."

"I am Deputy Gauleiter Horstmann," the man said. "Would you come this way, please?"

Lamm followed the man away from the Reichsleiter's office, and his heart sank. He needed to see Bormann, not this deputy Gauleiter.

Horstmann had an office on the second floor. Once inside, the two of them sat down, and Horstmann began speaking. "The Reichsleiter has asked me to extend his apologies on two accounts," he explained solemnly. "The first is that he was unable to see you. The second is that he was unable to get you an SSDE first-class priority. Those may only be obtained directly from the Führer or Reichsminister Speer. He hopes that the SS, which is number-two priority, will suffice."

Lamm fought down the urge to jump with joy as he took the letter from Horstmann. "We shall do our best to ensure final victory," Lamm replied. "Heil Hitler!"

"Heil Hitler!"

Lamm sped back to the office feeling like a little boy who had just been visited by Father Christmas. Any priority would have gotten them the ability to legally draw on reserves of strategic materials, which is what he wanted. An SS priority was a license to steal. Reinhart would have to be notified immediately. Lamm ordered Dietrich to fly to Lübeck with a copy of the priority the next morning.

Reinhart was deliriously happy to see Dietrich.

"Things are getting out of hand, Dietrich. Day and night shipments are coming in from all over the Reich, and I don't have the room to store half of it. The ship will be ready tomorrow, so I'm going to move everything down to the wharf and start loading her. It's going to take two, maybe three runs to Oslo before it's all moved. Fräulein Trautner has been marvelous. If I asked the men to do some of the things she has, they'd mutiny. She can get them to do anything."

Dietrich grinned. "She could get me to do anything," he said. "Tell me, have you ever . . .?"

It was Reinhart's turn to grin. "As an officer and a gentleman, I refuse to speak." They both laughed.

"Seriously, Reinhart, what do you need?"

"Organization mostly, and I need that letter. I've found something that will save us a lot of time, now that we have the SS priority."

"What's that?"

"There's a handling firm here in Lübeck that has a warehouse full of stainless steel vats and tubing. Some are high-pressure vessels of various sizes. They were made for a chemical firm that paid for them and now can't use them."

"Why?"

"The factory was hit in one of the early raids. A bomb hit the shelter, killing most of the managerial and research staff. Another bomb caused a fire in the research department. Whatever plans there were went up in smoke. Now they're trying to sell them for repair money."

"How did you find all this out?"

"When I started asking around, I was approached by the head of the handling firm that is storing all the stainless steel."

"Don't tell me. He wants a bribe to release the stuff."

"Not a bribe," Reinhart said sarcastically, "just a small handling charge for a loyal Nazi."

"Humph! He probably attended a synagogue before the struggle. I'm going to call Professor Lamm. There's little left to do in Berlin. We might as well move up here."

"Fine. I'll get things started with the handling firm."

As soon as Reinhart left, Dietrich called Lamm and explained the situation.

"Excellent." Lamm was satisfied. "I'll leave Bittner here with Frau Norbert. Fräulein Trautner can return to Berlin as soon as we close out in Lübeck. We will need the civilian employees in the warehouse to keep supplies moving. Lindner, Nachmann, and I will be in Lübeck in two or three days. Is there anything else?"

"We need someone to do the welding."

"Don't waste time," Lamm told him. "Create a subsidiary firm and hire a couple of experts. Don't stint on the money. We need good people and if they don't have equipment, buy it."

"Immediately, Herr Obersturmbannführer," Dietrich said. "Heil Hitler!"

"Heil Hitler!" Lamm said into the receiver, wondering if he'd ever get them to stop the incessant "Heil Hitlers."

The following morning, Captain Zorndorf moved the *Mayerling* to the NORD GMBH wharf, where loading began immediately. Reinhart had been correct. One shipload would never move the amount of supplies required by the Vikmo project. Three days later the *Mayerling* sailed with its first cargo for Oslo, and Lamm wired Hammerstein and Loring so they would be ready for her arrival.

Loring grinned as the messenger delivered the telegram to Hammerstein. "Good news?"

"Right you are, Loring!" Hammerstein said as he read the wire. "We're in business," he announced to everyone within hearing. "The *Mayerling* has sailed."

"The airfield will be finished by the time the ship docks," Loring reminded him. "When do you want the trucks at the railhead?"

"Let's see," Hammerstein said, partly to himself. "The *Mayerling* should reach Oslo day after tomorrow, so we're really going to have to move. Assuming three days to unload the ship . . . tell the drivers to have the trucks ready day after tomorrow. As soon as we get the word that the train is on the way, they can drive to the Vikmo railhead. I don't know how many trips we'll have to make. Just make sure we have alternate drivers for each truck so one can sleep while the other drives. And no schnapps!"

"Yes, sir."

Reinhart could not find a firm to do the welding needed in a reasonable time, because all of them had contracts repairing ships and U-boats. There were a number of experienced welders who could be lured away from their employers by higher wages and a higher priority, but they had neither the equipment for special welding nor a shop in which to install it. Reinhart created the NORD Special Welding Company and hired Manfried and Gebhardt Axel, two brothers with over twenty years experience in shipyards in Bochum. They were delighted to start the new company for the money Reinhart offered, and for the challenges of welding stainless steel and aluminum.

At thirty-seven, Manfried was the eldest. Gebhardt was four years younger. They were similar in appearance, tall and lanky with long arms and hands, and hair cut short over their horsy faces. They were dour until the subject turned to welding. At that point their eyes lit up and they were ready to work. After Reinhart explained the problems they faced and told them they would have to buy the necessary equipment, the Axels grinned.

Armed with a copy of the SS priority, orders from the Racial Science Section, and the excellent credit of NORD GMBH, they were on the train to Hamburg the next morning. The items they wanted were unavailable on such short notice if one wanted new equipment, but they found used equipment in excellent condition and had it shipped to Lübeck immediately. They were back on the afternoon of the fifth day.

As soon as the stainless steel vats and pipe arrived, Reinhart knew he had a problem. The original plan had been to send all the materials and equipment to Norway on the *Mayerling*. If they did that, everything would be delayed by the loading and unloading time of the ship. He called Lamm in Berlin.

"Set up a temporary welding shop in Lübeck," Lamm ordered, "and have the Axel brothers make the tubing for the uranium and the vats to replicate the L-IV experiment. Then fly everything, including the Axels and their welding equipment, to the Vikmo mine. I want no more delays."

"Yes, Herr Obersturmbannführer."

"And Reinhart . . ."

"Yes, Herr Obersturmbannführer?"

"I shouldn't have to make every little decision. I have the utmost confidence in you and the others. Use your initiative like Hammerstein." His tone was fatherly but impatient.

"Yes, Herr Obersturmbannführer."

Reinhart attempted to avoid the subject of an atomic reactor by explaining to the Axels that they were trying to measure the release of neutrons, but they looked at him blankly. Reinhart then tried to explain atoms. That didn't work either.

"Look, Herr Sturmführer," Manfried Axel finally said, in his thick Ostfriesian dialect. "You are a scientist and are, we think, very smart. Of this atom business, we know nothing. I think it is best if you tell us what you want us to weld and how the pipes should go. This we understand."

Reinhart looked at Gebhardt Axel, who nodded in agreement with his brother. Reinhart wondered for a moment if he hadn't hired the wrong men for the job. He thought for a moment and then went over and picked up one of the meter lengths of stainless steel pipe.

"What we are going to put into this pipe is a metal called uranium," he said. "When we have a lot of them together, they will create heat, so they must be cooled. We will cool them by immersing them in water, but the pipes must be waterproof because if the water gets to the uranium, it will explode."

The Axels looked at each other, then Gebhardt asked, "So this uranium acts with water like sodium?"

Reinhart blinked, then smiled. The Axels understood. "Yes. The reaction is not as violent, but it's the same principle, and if it happens the whole experiment is ruined."

"This we understand," Manfried said. "We make your tubes, each with a hook on the end and a waterproof cap that unscrews. After we make them we put them in water for twenty-four hours to test them. Is this acceptable, Herr Sturmführer?"

"Yes, marvelous! Clear away the room you need and start as soon as your equipment arrives." He returned to the office.

Gebhardt turned to his brother. "These scientists. They complicate everything. Why didn't he just tell us he wanted waterproof tubes?"

"I don't know, Gebhardt. It sounds like they are trying to reinvent the steam engine."

The welding equipment arrived two days later, and the Axels got to work. In one corner of the warehouse, there were groups of meter-long tubes, each nine centimeters in diameter, with a hook on both ends. The tubes were submersed in a large wooden vat. At the end of the test only one showed leakage, and it was discarded. Nachmann and Lindner quickly became experts at making the wire lattices of uranium that went inside the tubes. Lamm had Dietrich calculate the number of tubes that could be stored in the warehouse and before the number was exceeded, Lamm ordered Dietrich to fly a load of tubes directly to Vikmo.

"And Dietrich," he added, "you might as well stay there and help Hammerstein and Loring in Vikmo. It's about time we had some scientific expertise there."

"Yes, Herr Obersturmbannführer," Dietrich answered.

"We should all be joining you shortly," Lamm added. "I expect the *Mayerling* is on its way back by now."

Hammerstein was appalled at the delays. The cargo had to be unloaded from the *Mayerling* and piled on the wharf. Since there were no tracks on the wharf they had leased, the unloaded cargoes had to be trucked to the waiting rail cars. Labor was extremely limited. Even those out of work hesitated to work for the Germans. Fortunately, at Vikmo it was different. There were very few Gestapo there, and they were engaged in catching partisans, so most people in the area didn't mind the Germans. The *Mayerling* left only a day late. Hammerstein had to use all his influence and a little cash to run a special train to the railhead twenty-five miles from Vikmo. They had to hurry. The weather was closing in.

Dietrich was the first to fly into the airfield at Vikmo, where Loring greeted him, amid snow flurries.

"Heil Hitler, Herr Obersturmführer."

"Heil Hitler," Dietrich replied. "I just flew up from Lübeck via Oslo. There's a load of tubes for the uranium burner on the aircraft. Where do they go?"

Loring shrugged. "I really don't know, sir. I suppose we can store them in the mine since that's where the burner is supposed to go. We finally have lights and pumps working. Are you staying?"

"Yes, I am."

"In that case, welcome to the Reich's northernmost resort."

Dietrich looked around the area and gave Loring an artificial smile. "If you'll show me the way to the ski slopes, I'd be much obliged."

Loring laughed. "You'll be lucky if you find a bottle of schnapps around here, Herr Obersturmführer."

Dietrich reached into his bag and produced a bottle of crystal-clear liquid. "Your wish is my command, Scharführer," he said, tossing Loring the bottle. "But watch it. It's not schnapps. It's Aqua Vit."

"Aqua Vit?"

"Guaranteed to clean the rust off your uranium burner," he told him.

"Ah," Loring said with a grin, "civilization has arrived. I'll show you to your quarters."

The man with the binoculars watched the trucks rolling into the mine area. More Germans were arriving, and judging from the supplies stored everywhere, they were planning to stay the winter. Although the man couldn't see in the crates, it was obvious there was no mining equipment and yet the Germans were pumping out the lower shafts. Why? Despite the pretense of sectioning off the old dig, they weren't the least interested in archeology. Covering the lenses of his binoculars, he carefully put them back in the case and eased away from the edge of the bluff. He couldn't figure it out, but London had to know.

This time it took him less than an hour to get home. He tapped the message rapidly. "Vikmo mine open. Heavy equipment. Type unknown."

"Got him!" Franz said. The radio triangulation had worked. "It's who we thought. Sven Thorvald, the retired mining engineer. Come on," he told the waiting SS squad.

Thorvald was hiding his radio transmitter behind the bookcase in the living room when he heard the truck. *It had to happen eventually,* he thought, grabbing his coat. If he could get to the woods, he had a chance. He almost made it.

"Halt!" one officer shouted.

"Take him alive!" Klaus shouted.

A staccato burst erupted from a machine pistol, spraying dirty snow around the legs of the fleeing man. A shock threw him to the ground. He tried to get up but his legs would not move. Reaching down, he felt blood all over his legs as a group of Germans ran toward him. Reaching into his pocket, Thorvald took out a small white capsule.

"Don't move!" Klaus yelled in Norwegian.

Placing the capsule between his teeth, Thorvald bit down, and was dead before the Gestapo agents reached him.

"We should have known," Fritz swore, shaking his head.

"But why Vikmo, Fritz? There's nothing there but that old mine and that stupid archaeological site."

"Maybe they thought it was something else, Klaus. Whatever, the bastards are minus one radio operator. Let's go find his transmitter. This report is going to make us look pretty good. Who knows. Maybe we'll get a transfer to Holland or France."

"France would be nice," Klaus said with wistful smile. "Southern France, where it's warm."

"Come in, " Harris said in reply to the knock on his door.

Corporal Winters stood in front of his desk, saluted, and handed him a slip of paper. "Another Vikmo message, Sir."

"Thank you, corporal," he nodded, in return to the salute. "Vikmo mine now open. Heavy equipment. Type unknown." Harris cursed silently. There were two things he had to do. It was more imperative than ever that he make the reconnaissance and, as dangerous as it might be, he had to contact the German Resistance.

Farnsworth had difficulty locating Teddy Foxx, who was now a group captain in command of his own bomb group. The air base north of London was smart and clean, with large new bombers lining the runway. Gone was the shabby Battle of Britain look. A flight sergeant led Farnsworth to Foxx's office, which was right on the flight line. The airman grinned and rose to shake Farnsworth's hand.

"Reggie! Good to see you. I was just thinking of you when you called. It's been a long time."

"It certainly has, and you've done well for yourself." Farnsworth looked at the flying suit hanging in the corner. "Teddy, you are a fox, if you'll pardon the pun. I thought you'd never fly again."

Foxx smiled sheepishly. "Not fighters, old boy, but seems there was a clerical error in my medical records." He cleared his throat. "How about a drink?"

"Love one."

"You here to steal another one of my aircraft?"

"Teddy," Farnsworth replied, mock hurt in his voice.

"It'll cost you a bottle of French cognac," Foxx said, pouring a glass of whiskey.

"Do you mind if I go out and come back in?"

"Why?"

"This is too bloody easy."

"Things have changed, Reggie." His tone was serious, but optimistic. "I now have more aircraft under my command than we had in the whole bloody RAF in '40. Then there are the Americans. Good lads, the Yanks. By the time we get through with Adolf's bloody Reich, there won't be two bricks left stuck together. It won't be easy, mind, but we're going to do it."

Farnsworth smiled. Things really were getting better. He pulled the letter out of his briefcase. "This will cover you should anything happen, Teddy."

"Where are you going this time, Reggie?"

"I'm not going anywhere," Farnsworth replied, with a satisfied smile.

"Probably a good thing, too," Foxx laughed. "I understand you soiled the last aircraft you used."

Farnsworth blushed.

"If you're not going, who is?"

"Mr. Alexander Harris, member of the War Cabinet."

"*The* Alexander Harris?"

"Precisely."

"Good Lord. Is that whom you work for?"

"In a manner of speaking."

"What's this all about?"

"I can't tell you, Teddy. It's that hush-hush and that serious."

"Then it should cost you two bottles of the stuff," Foxx grinned. "When do you want the aircraft?"

"The weather chaps say we should have clear weather all the way there and back three days from now."

"Where does Harris want to go?"

"Norway."

"Same place?"

"Same place."

"All right."

October 14, 1942

As the Junkers 52 banked for the final approach, Lamm thought the Vikmo project resembled a giant anthill. Supplies were neatly stacked everywhere, smoke was rising from the chimneys, and the ground was covered with snow. Overall he was pleased, but there were still the problems of getting cooling water to the uranium burner and how to get heavy water to duplicate the L-IV experiment. Nachmann met him at the aircraft. The entire complement was now at Vikmo.

"How are things in Berlin, Herr Obersturmbannführer?" Nachmann asked.

"The bombers are coming more and more often."

"We'll soon fix that."

"What is the situation with the water tower and the L-IV pit?" asked Lamm.

"The water tower is nearly complete, but we have to get a backup pump. Hammerstein is looking for one in Oslo. If we have to, we can let the bottom shafts of the mine flood to take the load off the old one. We'll double up the bunks on the surface."

"There's still the heavy water," Lamm said.

"Can you come over to the L-IV shed, Herr Obersturmführer? There's something I think you should see," Nachmann said, seriously.

"Trouble?"

"I think you should judge for yourself, sir."

Lamm looked at him and wondered what was wrong now. He followed Nachmann into the large shed. A pit had been dug in the floor, and a large stainless steel vat had been set into it. Lindner, Loring, Dietrich, and Reinhart were standing around the pit. They looked up as Lamm and Nachmann entered the building.

"Over here," Nachmann said, leading him to a corner of the building. The others gathered in the same corner. All of them looked extremely grim.

There was trouble. "Well?" Lamm asked.

"I think Loring should tell you," Lindner said, "it's his fault."

"I don't deserve all the blame," Loring replied.

Lamm, irritated from the long flight, wasn't in the mood for any nonsense. "Will someone tell me what's going on?" he snapped, "I'm rapidly losing my patience."

"Tell him, Loring," Dietrich said.

"Tell me what?" Lamm demanded.

"This." Loring pulled back a tarpaulin and Lamm opened his mouth but no words came out. It took a second for the sight of the four gray barrels before him to register. He walked up to the barrels and touched one. On the top of each drum was stenciled "Vemork-Norwegian Hydro-Electric Works, D_2O, Kaiser Wilhelm Institute Berlin."

"Heavy water." Dazed, Lamm looked at them all, grinning as Nachmann opened a bottle of champagne. "Where did you get this?"

"Champagne, Herr Obersturmbannführer?" Nachmann said, handing him the mug.

Lamm took the champagne. "Where'd you get this?" he repeated, indicating the barrels.

"Vemork," Loring said.

"Vemork?" Lamm asked incredulously. "How did you get heavy water from Vemork? I still don't understand."

"Loring and I took two of the guards to Vemork in the truck to scout the place out," Dietrich explained. "We got there on the fourteenth, and asked to see the German commander because we were lost. The guard at the gate let us in to the compound. I'll let Loring tell you the rest, since it was his idea."

"Obersturmführer Dietrich pointed out the electrolysis building to me." Loring continued. "There is a barrack between it and the main turbine station. A few minutes after we got inside, there was a commando alert and all hell broke loose. About a dozen guards came pouring out of the barracks, running toward the perimeter. Obersturmführer Dietrich and I ducked into the electrolysis building. It was empty because all the workers were in their shelter."

"That's when we spotted the four drums," Dietrich interjected. "They were on a platform ready for shipment to the Kaiser Wilhelm Institute."

"As soon as we loaded them on the truck, some lieutenant comes running up and tells us to get the hell out. So we left." Loring finished the story with smug satisfaction.

Lamm sipped the champagne and laughed. "I don't believe it."

"None of us had better go back," Dietrich said. "They probably think we were the British commandos."

"The guards were so anxious to get us away from there that they held the ferry for us."

"You are lucky bastards," Lamm said, "I'll give you that. Now let's see if we can duplicate L-IV."

It took the Axel brothers a week to prepare the cylindrical containers in accordance with designs furnished by Nachmann. The completed vessels were weighted down, sealed, and submerged for seventy-two hours instead of the twenty-four the Axels had originally proposed, after which they were inspected for leakage. They were all dry.

"Fill the vat with water," Lamm ordered. "We're ready to begin, but first I need two volunteers to fill the cylinders with uranium powder. Not only is it poisonous, but in water it is highly pyrophorous. In the L-IV experiment, I understand they filled the sphere with carbon dioxide to reduce the chance of fire. We don't have that kind of luxury."

"I'll volunteer," Nachmann said, without hesitation.

"I will, too," Lindner added, taking a step forward.

"Good," Lamm smiled in approval. "I want the filling done in the other work building. Use the dry air blower to clear it out all night, then we can start filling the cylinders using protective equipment and clothing. No shortcuts. I need you all for this and it's going to take a lot of time. Safety first. Understood?"

They all nodded in agreement.

By the next morning, the building was dried out and Nachmann and Lindner, wearing protective clothing, respirators, and goggles, began their dangerous task. Just enough uranium powder was brought into the building, which they nicknamed the "Powder Magazine," to fill each cylinder separately. As soon as Nachmann and Lindner finished packing a cylinder and sealed it, it was removed to the L-IV shed.

As a safety precaution, Lamm had all the tools and instruments removed from the L-IV shed and stored in the open. Even the barrels of heavy water were stored outside. Only the instruments necessary for the experiment remained. With uranium packing complete, all the parts of "L-IVa" were assembled under the movable crane in the building, and the open spaces were filled with heavy water. Four of the men then guided the L-IVa to the vat. As soon as it was immersed, everyone except Dietrich and Reinhart evacuated the building.

Carefully, Dietrich and Reinhardt inserted the tube that would hold the radium-beryllium neutron source. Once in place, it protruded from the center of L-IVa to about a meter above the surface of the vat. Then they made a last-minute check of the electrical equipment. When they signaled that everything was ready, Reinhardt nodded and Dietrich introduced the radium-beryllium into the tube before joining Reinhart at the instrument panel. In a few seconds the needles on their instruments began to move, and the two men gave the expectant crowd outside two thumbs up.

"It works!" someone shouted. "It works!"

Even the guards at the airfield could hear the cheer that went up. Obersturmbannführer Lamm was odd, all right, but anything was better than the Russian Front.

Alexander Harris, startled out of a sound sleep, was grumbling.

"Sorry to disturb you, sir," the sergeant said, "but you asked me to wake you an hour before we reached the target."

"Oh yes. Thank you," Harris said, "I had forgotten where I was."

"I do that myself on numerous occasions, sir," the sergeant said with a smile. "Can I get you some tea?"

"Yes, thank you."

"Milk and sugar?"

"Yes please."

Harris looked out the waist position of the Wellington. It was near dawn. He had just had his best five hours of sleep since the beginning of the war and was tremendously refreshed. Looking forward to overflying Vikmo, he wondered what he would find. If he found the evidence of large rockets he expected he would need every bit of skill to convince Churchill's staff of the danger. As a civilian and a non-scientist, he often ran afoul of Henry Tizard and Lord Cherwell, neither of whom shared his view of the activity at Vikmo or large rockets, even after the rumors about Peenemünde on the Baltic coast. He knew the pure scientists were too jealous of their own reputations to listen to a non-scientist. When he mentioned rockets, Cherwell scoffed. To him a rocket was a ten-penny firework for Guy Fawkes' Day, and he couldn't conceive of rockets weighing hundreds of tons, carrying thousands of pounds of explosives, arriving at the target at a velocity greater than the speed of sound.

The military was another story. Too many of them were still fighting the Great War. Even after the Germans beat them in Belgium and Africa, they couldn't see the need for armored formations and close-support aircraft. It was incredible.

"Your tea, sir," the sergeant said, intruding into Harris's thoughts.

"Thank you, Sergeant." It was typical service tea—one-third tea, one-third condensed milk, and one-third sugar—but Harris drank it gratefully. When he got back he was going to have a big cup of hot coffee.

"Mr. Harris," the pilot said in Harris's earphones.

"Yes."

"Mr. Harris. Are you all right?"

"Yes, I'm . . ." He realized the pilot couldn't hear him. Embarrassed, he flipped the switch on his mask. "Yes, I'm fine."

"We're going to make a pass over the Vikmo mine in about five minutes. We suggest you get to the bombardier station."

"Thank you."

Harris crawled to the bombardier station and took up his position.

He took a pair of binoculars and hung them around his neck. The cameraman was at the waist shooting pictures. The Wellington came in low and slow. Harris could see the Germans looking up. One waved. The pilot brought the plane around again. This time no one was waving. They could see the roundels on the wings and several Germans raised their rifles. The second pass went directly over the supply dump. Harris took in everything he could. Something down there bothered him, but he couldn't say exactly what it was. The Wellington climbed quickly, getting away from the ground fire. The pilot then headed the aircraft out to sea. "Everyone okay?" he asked.

Everyone answered except Harris, then he remembered the button again. The weather was deteriorating, so the pilot decided to hug the coast for awhile. If trouble developed, there were plenty of clouds to hide in.

The British aircraft disturbed Lamm. Someone was obviously curious about Vikmo, and he wondered why. How could anyone know or even suspect his purpose there? Obviously the Englishman's purpose was reconnaissance. Lamm returned to the L-IV shed, where the LIVa experiment was still in progress. Lindner and Dietrich were discussing the experiment. The results meant that they would have to make changes to the existing design of the uranium burner. When Lamm entered the shed, Loring handed him a cup of coffee.

"You look as if you could use something stronger, Herr Obersturmbannführer," Loring said, reaching into one of the cabinets for a half-full bottle of schnapps. Lamm drank part of his coffee and extended his cup. Loring filled it with alcohol.

"Prosit!" Lamm said, and drank the schnapps-laced coffee. They had come a long way, and they had a long way to go. Lamm reflected upon his awesome responsibility. In his hands and those of his subordinates at Vikmo lay the key to Germany's ultimate victory.

Harris had seen something, and while it registered unconsciously, he couldn't put his finger on it. Concentrating on the last run over Vikmo, he mentally listed everything he had seen, item by item. There were three buildings, a pile of something under canvas, large crates on pallets, gray drums, more large crates, tubing, a group of . . . Harris stopped. The four gray drums. Where had he seen them before? That was it! He hadn't seen anything like that before. He had only seen pictures of the drums from Vemork. No, that was ridiculous. What would the Germans be doing with heavy water in Vikmo? "Oh, no!" he groaned out loud. "Oh, no!"

Ahead of the Wellington, two German Bf-110D twin-engine fighters circled slowly. They were waiting to escort a FW 200C Condor that was due in from a convoy reconnaissance run over the North Sea.

"See anything?" one pilot asked.

"Not a thing. Hey, what's that down there about seven o'clock?"

"Could be her. No, wait a minute. It only has two engines. Looks like a Wellington. That's crazy, what would a lone Wellington . . . Wait! It is a Wellington!"

"Let's get her."

The two fighters peeled off and came in out of the sun. The first warning to the Wellington came in the form of 8mm machine gun bullets and 20mm cannon shells slamming into the aircraft. One cannon shell exploded in the starboard engine and the copilot was killed in that first burst. With flame and smoke pouring from the crippled engine, the pilot yelled, "Bail out!"

Alexander Harris did not bail out. He had been killed by a cannon shell fired by the second aircraft.

"Ach," one of the pilots said, watching the Wellington go down in flames. "I forgot to turn on my gun cameras."

"Too late now," the other said.

The Wellington was a ball of fire trailing a plume of thick black smoke. Two hundred feet before it crashed in the water, the fire burned out.

In England, Colonel Reginald Farnsworth stood in front of a very unhappy General Henry Beresford. Mr. Alexander Harris was missing.

"You did what? You got Harris an aircraft so he could go joyriding over Norway?"

"He was concerned about something in a place called Vikmo, sir."

"Vikmo. Never heard of it," Beresford said. "Is it a naval base or something?"

"A coal mine, I believe," Farnsworth said. "He was concerned about secret weapons of some sort."

"Those damned rockets," Beresford said. "The man is . . . or *was* daft. He actually believed the Germans were building rockets with one-ton warheads that could hit London from more than a hundred miles away. Preposterous, that's what it is." Farnsworth wondered if the general had bothered to look at the latest reconnaissance photos of the German research facility at Peenemünde, on the Baltic coast. "Look, Farnsworth, you've overstepped your bounds this time. I'm afraid we're going to have to transfer you out of here. Lesson to the others, you know. Nothing of this to anyone."

"I understand, sir."

"No time to get you a decent assignment. You'll be going to one of those blasted new armored divisions in Montgomery's Eighth Army. Best I could do, sorry. That's all."

Farnsworth looked properly mortified, saluted, and left. When he got out of the general's office he laughed and ran to pack his kit. An armored division. *Thank you, Mr. Harris, wherever you may be.*

November 24, 1942

"We have serious design problems," Nachmann said. "Our original configuration just won't work. Not because it's theoretically unsound, but because we just don't have the facilities to shape the graphite the way we intended. Lindner has an alternate plan."

Everyone turned to look at Lindner.

"Lindner," Lamm said.

"Cooling the uranium burner with water and using graphite for a moderator is not beyond our capabilities, but it will be more difficult than we thought. I recommend building the burner in a shape as close to a sphere as possible, but we're going to have to build the burner block by block instead of in slabs. I have the diagram here." Lindner laid out the new plan. Lamm and the others looked it over carefully. "I think we can keep the uranium in its current stainless steel tubes. It will make control of the fuel easier," he added.

"It's larger than the original layout," Lamm said.

"Yes, Herr Obersturmbannführer. We'll have to do more digging in the mine, but the time won't be wasted since we're going to have to cut the graphite anyway."

"I can see where the uranium and the control rods go," Dietrich said, pointing to a place on the diagram, "but what are these?"

"Those are holes for the new uranium slugs," Reinhart said. "As soon as we get a constant flow of neutrons, we put in the uranium slugs. Eventually, the uranium will become a new element with the atomic number of 94. It's theoretically more explosive than uranium 235. We can also run a line to make heavy water, should we need to."

"Do we have enough uranium?" Lamm asked.

"We should," Lindner answered. "I think we can use the uranium powder on the outer edges of the burner. The solid uranium we can save for the bomb."

"Can't we take a little more time?" Dietrich asked. "We should conduct a few controlled experiments before we build a burner."

"Have you heard the latest news?" Lamm asked him.

"No, Herr Obersturmbannführer."

"Rommel is in full retreat in Africa, the Americans have landed in Morocco, and von Paulus is cut off at Stalingrad." He paused. "We can experiment as we go."

January-February 1943

The Axels turned from the welding of stainless steel to cutting graphite with a will. Lindner was officially the supervisor, but the Axels provided the impulse and genius behind the work. Dietrich supervised the shaping of the chamber in the mine. Christmas of 1942 was celebrated by continuing to work. On the twenty-seventh of December the chamber was ready, and Lamm ordered the wooden frame for the base of his uranium burner constructed. On the thirtieth, the first graphite blocks were laid around the wooden base. Each block was 25.9 cm x 104.8 cm. Eventually, ten thousand of them, many specially drilled, would make up the reactor. Each layer was tested as it was laid, and as the uranium burner took shape the boron rods were inserted. At level ten the rods were withdrawn slightly and readings were taken.

"Things are beginning to happen." Lamm was exhausted but smiling. "Let's get some rest, and we'll start the last ten layers tomorrow. Then we'll see if all this is for nothing." He looked around and laughed.

"What's so funny?" Loring asked.

"You all look like minstrels," Lamm replied.

They looked at each other and discovered each was covered with a fine layer of shiny black graphite dust. Nachmann's laughter joined Lamm's and soon they were all bellowing as the left the mine to clean up and go to bed.

Lamm woke refreshed from a deep dreamless sleep. As soon as he shaved, he ate a hearty, hot breakfast of canned meat and beans and went to the mine, returning the guard's salute as he entered the shaft. It was level for about ten meters before it descended for seventy-five meters and stopped at the cross tunnel. Ahead of him was the elevator that descended into the lower tunnels. To the left were the barracks and supply rooms. To the right was the chamber that held the reactor. When Lamm walked through the opening, the others were already at hard at work placing the last layers of graphite blocks.

"Hammerstein," Lamm asked, noticing the lawyer, "when did you get back?"

"This morning. Reinhart called me a few days ago. I just got a flight up. I understand we are about to witness an historic achievement."

"That's correct. I'm glad you're here. You deserve to share in it as much as any of us."

"Thank you, sir."

From the corner of his eye, Lamm noticed something written on the wall of graphite blocks. "What is that?"

"What's what, Herr Obersturmbannführer?" Loring asked innocently.

"Let me see it," Lamm insisted.

They parted to reveal the name "ODIN" painted on the uranium burner. The painter must have had a classical education, because he used the ancient Norse name instead of the German one.

"It's appropriate," Lamm remarked. "Odin. The Father of the Gods. I suppose this is your handiwork, Hammerstein?"

"Yes, sir."

"I approve."

Hammerstein grinned.

The last layer of graphite blocks was in place by one o'clock. Sweating and grimy with graphite dust, they broke for lunch and half an hour later were back. Dietrich and Hammerstein were selected to withdraw the rods, since the others were needed to monitor the readings of the instruments. At two o'clock, Lamm ordered Dietrich to withdraw the first nine boron rods. Slowly the instruments registered activity as needles moved and counters clicked. As the rods were removed, the readings climbed. At last there was only one rod left.

"Pull it out!" Lamm ordered.

Hammerstein withdrew the rod and the readings began to climb. When the rod was completely removed, they kept rising. Unlike the previous experiments there was no leveling off. Instead of clicking, the counters were buzzing. Lamm waited fifteen seconds. "Gentlemen, it is self-sustaining."

There was an incredible cheer. Hammerstein, as usual, had brought champagne. They filled their mugs and turned to Lamm. "Kameraden," Lamm reminded them, "let us not forget that this is but a first step toward creating the ultimate weapon for the ultimate victory of the Fatherland." He extended his arm. "Sieg!" He shouted.

"Heil!" the others said, returning his salute.

"Sieg!"

"Heil"

"Sieg!"

"Heil!"

CHAPTER 8

THE RESISTANCE

Berlin
February 26, 1943

OBERSTURMBANNFÜHRER HEINZ OTTO SCHINDLER, in the field-gray uniform of the Waffen SS, stood at attention as the flag was removed from his Uncle Uwe's casket. He was gaunt and thin, and there were dark circles beneath his deep blue eyes. Even his neatly combed dark blond hair served to accentuate the stress etched on his features. It was the face of a man who had too little sleep and seen too much death.

Schindler was able to attend the funeral because he was on medical leave for wounds suffered on the Russian Front, where he was a tank battalion commander in the 2nd SS Panzer Division, "Das Reich." For the action in which he was wounded, he had been awarded the Knight's Cross, which he wore around his neck.

Schindler watched as the oblong black box was lowered into the ground. Uwe Schindler had raised Heinz after Heinz' parents had died in the influenza epidemic of 1919. Uwe was a kind, generous man who was usually surrounded by lots of friends. Today very few of them were in evidence, and that made Schindler angry. A couple of Gestapo agents had made themselves rudely conspicuous during the ceremony, and Schindler wondered why they were there. The Gestapo men looked on disapprovingly as the men folded the flag.

It wasn't a Nazi flag. It was the white-and-black ensign of the Imperial German Navy, because Uncle Uwe had served as a turret officer on the battlecruiser *Derfflinger,* which had blown up the British battle cruiser *Queen Mary* after a fierce gunnery duel during the Battle of Jutland. Heinz Schindler always sat in awe as Uncle Uwe described the mass of British shells hitting the ship, and the rapid fire of the big guns as they sent huge shells toward the enemy. Then Uncle Uwe would generously tell his nephew how brave the British sailors were. Heinz thought it was glorious. Uncle Uwe had been proud of his service on the *Derfflinger,* and kept a photograph of her over the mantle.

After Jutland, Uwe had been transferred to U-boats. Uwe didn't talk about them much, but he received an Iron Cross for serving on them. Having been in the tight, confined space of a tank on the Russian Front, Schindler now had some idea what it must have been like in a turret on the *Derfflinger* or in the cramped hull of a U-boat. Either way you cut it, they were all iron coffins.

One of the few attendees at the funeral was Uncle Uwe's old friend and naval comrade Admiral Wilhelm Canaris. As the Admiral approached, the young SS officer clicked his heels and saluted in military fashion, instead of with the Nazi straight-arm salute.

Canaris returned the salute and extended his hand. "May I offer my condolences, Heinz?"

"Thank you, Herr Admiral."

"Your uncle was a fine man. He had many friends."

"There weren't many mourners, Herr Admiral," Schindler said flatly.

"I know." The Admiral looked around at the Gestapo agents, who were looking their way.

"Gestapo Swine." Schindler muttered. "We're short-handed on the Eastern Front, and they're here getting rich on the black market. I wish they'd send them all to the front."

"Is there somewhere we can go?" the Admiral asked.

"I have to sort out my uncle's things, Herr Admiral. I'm going there now."

"May I join you?"

"Of course."

"We can take my staff car." The two men climbed into the black sedan and headed toward what had been Uwe Schindler's house.

Once they had pulled out of the cemetery and onto the road, the Admiral asked Otto, "Are you all right, Heinz? I heard you were wounded."

"I'm all right." Schindler didn't look directly at the Admiral. "Russian 85mm guns. They're mounted on the T-34 now. The 85 tears through our Panzer IV armor at short range. Killed everyone in the crew except me and the driver."

"What about the new tanks?"

"The new Tigers are fine, except there are very few at the front. We need to use them in mass numbers, and they only come in dribs and drabs."

"When are you due to return?" The Admiral's tone was caring.

"In a few days," Schindler sighed tiredly, feeling worn out and old before his time.

The car stopped in front of Uwe Schindler's apartment house, and Heinz Schindler and Admiral Canaris got out of the car and went upstairs. The door to the apartment was open. "What's going on?" Schindler demanded.

"It's all right, Heinz," the Admiral said. The two men stepped inside. "Is that you Kraemer?"

"Yes, Herr Admiral." A Luftwaffe sergeant wearing the uniform of a signal specialist appeared from Uncle Uwe's bedroom carrying several pieces of wire. When he saw Schindler he saluted.

"Heinz, this is Sergeant Erich Kraemer of the 15th Company of the Luftwaffe Experimental Signals Regiment." Schindler obviously didn't understand. The Admiral continued. "Everyone in the regiment is an electronics expert. Sergeant Kraemer is on loan to the Abwehr. His specialty is the location of listening devices and cameras."

"If you will allow me, Herr Obersturmbannführer, let me offer my condolences. I knew your uncle. He was a fine man."

"Thank you, Sergeant Kraemer."

"What did you find?" Canaris asked the sergeant.

"The usual. There was one microphone in the bedroom, one in the kitchen, and of course the telephone." Kraemer handed the three devices to the Admiral.

"That's all, Kraemer. Thank you."

Kraemer saluted, and as soon as he left, Admiral Canaris closed the door. "Sit down, Heinz."

"What the hell is going on here?" Schindler asked again. "What were these devices doing in my uncle's house?

"The Gestapo put them here."

"Why? What for? My uncle wasn't a threat to anyone."

The Admiral looked at him sympathetically. "Heinz, besides being brilliant, your uncle was a kind, decent man. At one time he had a great many friends; now there are few left. Some fled the country, while others are in concentration camps. The reason the listening devices were here was to get enough evidence to arrest him. That is why your uncle committed suicide."

"No! He wouldn't do such a thing. Why should he? How could anyone question his loyalty to the Fatherland? He won an Iron Cross in the last war."

The Admiral handed Schindler an official-looking envelope that was addressed to "Obersturmbannführer H. Schindler, 2nd SS Pz Div."

"What is this?"

"It's your uncle's death certificate. It's addressed to you, as his nearest surviving relative. Read it."

Schindler opened the envelope that contained a carbon copy of an official form. It was stamped with an eagle and swastika. Under "Cause of death," it read "Suicide." The SS officer said nothing.

"If the Gestapo had arrested your uncle, they would have questioned him under torture. He wasn't worried about himself. He was afraid he might inadvertently betray a friend. That's why he killed himself."

"How is it you know so much, Herr Admiral?"

"I am the head of the Abwehr, counterintelligence. It is my business to know as much as I can. In the case of Uwe, I found out too late to do anything about it."

"But why would the Gestapo want to arrest him?"

"Because he had the courage to work for an end to the terrible things that are going on in our country."

"Uncle Uwe, a traitor? I don't believe it."

"You shouldn't. He wasn't a traitor. He loved Germany more than anyone."

"Then why was the Gestapo after him?"

"Heinz, do you remember when I asked you which was more important, the Party or Germany?"

"Yes."

"Uwe thought Germany was more important."

Schindler shot him a dirty look.

The Admiral continued. "Don't believe it, then. Just think about this. Germany is being destroyed by a few power-hungry men, and soon it will need people willing to see and speak the truth. Can I rely on you when that time comes?"

"You're crazy. If you weren't my uncle's friend, I'd turn you over to the Gestapo myself." Despite his best efforts, Schindler's voice lacked conviction.

"Think about it, Heinz. Germany needs honest men more than ever, and they will have to act soon. Where will you be then?"

Schindler said nothing. He rose when the Admiral rose. "Have a safe trip back to the front, Heinz. I wish you well."

"You, too, Herr Admiral."

The two men shook hands, and then Schindler was left to inventory his uncle's few remaining possessions. For a man who had been an executive in a large printing firm, he had very little. Schindler took one memento and went to his uncle's lawyer.

Herr Winterfeldt, the lawyer, was an old man, with a bald head and white mustache. He explained that most of the Schindler estate had been seized by the Gestapo. Heinz Schindler's share of an estate worth roughly 10,000 Reichsmarks was little more than 500 Reichsmarks.

"I'm sorry," the lawyer said. "These things happen. You can appeal this through the courts if you wish."

"And what good would that do?"

"Very little, I'm afraid, Herr Schindler. I am very sorry about your uncle."

"Did you know him well?"

"Yes, we were on the *U-63* together. He was a fine man."

"Why did he commit suicide?"

Herr Winterfeldt looked at Schindler's uniform as if that were an answer, and then at Schindler's face. "I believe you received a copy of the death report, did you not?"

Schindler understood perfectly. The man wasn't about to impart any information to someone wearing a Nazi uniform. "Yes."

The lawyer made out a check for 500 Reichsmarks, and Schindler bade him *auf Wiedersehen.*

Two days later Schindler was on the train to Poland. If the trip wasn't interrupted by partisans, he would be back with his unit in five days. He couldn't help thinking about the first time he had met Canaris. Just who was the Admiral anyway, and what was he up to?

Schindler absentmindedly wrapped the wire around his hand. It was attached to the tiny microphone that had been planted in his uncle's bedroom. It was the only thing he had taken from what was once his home, and it upset him. Why did the Gestapo think his uncle was dangerous? Why did the lawyer not trust him? There were so many questions and no answers. Heinz Schindler was confused and very angry.

March 11, 1943

Major von Rittburg sat in the chair across from Admiral Canaris sipping his coffee from a china cup. Neither man spoke. Something was going on, but the Major didn't know precisely what. In the past few months he had become well aware of the shadowy world in which he and the Admiral lived, but there was more to Canaris than counterintelligence. The Admiral corresponded with and met numerous people during the course of the day, but there were several that did not lie within the circle one normally assumed for a head of an organization such as the Abwehr. One was Oberst Count von Stauffenberg, an officer badly disfigured by wounds, and another was General Hans Speidel, Rommel's chief of staff. Von Rittburg was convinced this meeting had to do with the removal of Hitler, or perhaps even his assassination. The Major wondered just how many people were involved in Canaris's scheme.

The Admiral was playing a dangerous game, and the strain was beginning to tell. In a few months the Admiral had aged perceptibly, and now looked increasingly worn. So far the Admiral had given von Rittburg a lot of very sensitive information, but had not asked him to do anything overtly disloyal to the Reich. The Major had thought about it, of course, and was ready to accept whatever assignment Canaris gave him. Long ago von Rittburg decided that

Germany would be much better off without Hitler or the Nazis. Part of his decision stemmed from his sense of duty to the Fatherland, and part from a desire for revenge for the senseless murder of his wife by that drunken Kreisleiter.

Canaris finally spoke. "The Gestapo is taking an increased interest in me, Herr Major," he told von Rittburg. "It is most necessary that you not be seen as my shadow or even a close associate."

"I understand, Herr Admiral. Can you tell me why the Gestapo is taking such an interest?"

"It would be best if you don't know any details. Whatever happens will be self-evident. But there are a few things I want you to do."

"What are they?"

"From now on, we must appear to be occasionally at odds. I want you to attend some of the cabarets that Hitler was supposed to have closed, but which party officials keep open because they like to have a good time even if the Führer doesn't."

This brought a grin from von Rittburg.

"It would help if you began seeing a number of attractive women, and to be seen publicly inebriated from time to time. For this behavior I will occasionally reprimand you and you will complain about it publicly."

"I understand."

"Hereafter when you enter this office, consider that the Gestapo is listening."

"Yes, Herr Admiral."

May 17, 1943

"This is your bed, Fräulein Hassel," Frau Schulz said, pleasantly. "All the comforts of home."

Margit Hassel looked at the single bed with its nightstand and wardrobe and smiled at Ingrid Schulz' little joke. She was the head of all the Luftwaffe female auxiliaries at the headquarters of the Air Defense Control Center of the Fifth Air Division.

"I suppose you'll want to freshen up a bit, Fräulein. The shower is down the hall. Supper is at 6:00 in the evening and breakfast is at 6:30. Your briefing begins at 7:30. If you need me, I'm in the next building." She continued. "It's not bad here. Linz is about twenty kilometers northeast from here, and it's a nice city. There's plenty of social life and the pilots are young and attractive."

"Thank you, Frau Schulz," Margit smiled. "I'm here to serve the Fatherland, and, if the pilots are as cute as you say, then it will be a double pleasure."

Frau Schulz returned the smile and then raised her arm. "Heil Hitler."

"Heil Hitler," Margit replied.

Margit leaned back on her bed and lit a cigarette, thinking about Frau Schulz. *Stinking Nazi.* She not only hated the goose-stepping thugs, but their mindless women as well.

It had taken nearly nine months for Margit to recover from the shock of Hermann Rothenburg's death and her brush with the Gestapo. After that she withdrew, simply living from day to day, until she was contacted by Adolf Steuben, a friend of Rothenburg's who was a member of a different Resistance group than the one headed by Margit's late lover. Steuben was looking for someone to become a Luftwaffe female auxiliary, in the Fifth Air Division Control Center at Schleissheim, just north of Munich. With the Luftwaffe's manpower stretched to the breaking point, they were happy to get female volunteers. After some hesitation, Margit decided to keep fighting the Nazis. The man whose place Margit took showed her what to do, then left for the Russian Front, and Margit settled down to the easy routine. Putting any reticence behind her, she met and dated some of the officers from the nearby group, taking turns liking them for who they were and hating them for what they stood for.

Steuben introduced Margit to Herr Waldemar Wirth, a jolly older man who had lost a leg in the Great War. Wirth worked in a warehouse on the airbase and sported a large Nazi Party badge in his lapel.

"It's very simple, Fräulein Hassel," he explained. "After every mission, I will meet you accidentally at the Golden Ox. We are old family friends. Occasionally you will join me. You will give me the actual number of planes destroyed and damaged as well as pilots killed and injured. If you hear anything interesting you may include that too. You will give the report in writing and it will look like a shopping list for ladies' makeup or other articles. For example, ten grams of bath powder means ten planes shot down, and five packs of cigarettes, five planes damaged. This way if the Gestapo stops you, they will see nothing unusual.

"I understand, Herr Wirth. When do I start?"

"Today, Fräulein Hassel."

"All right." She wondered if Paul Holbein was still alive.

June 22, 1943

Major von Rittburg flipped through his notes and looked at the clock. It was eight in the morning, and he had to give a briefing to Admiral Canaris and some other high-ranking officers in half an hour. Weiss hurried into the office.

"Herr Major, that was the Admiral's secretary on the phone. She says you're late for the eight o'clock briefing.

"Eight o'clock? It's for eight-thirty." Von Rittburg checked his calendar, then gathered his notes and charts and headed for the conference room near the Admiral's office.

When he entered the room, the Admiral said sharply, "You are late, Major von Rittburg."

"My apologies, Herr Admiral."

"Get on with it," Canaris told him. "We all have other things to do."

Von Rittburg gave the briefing skillfully and quickly.

"Are you sure that is the correct number of tanks the Allies have in England?" an army general asked.

"It is not an exact number, Herr General. It's our best estimate based on agent reports. Without aerial reconnaissance, there is no way we can confirm it."

"Thank you."

"Are there any other questions?" von Rittburg asked.

"When do you think the Allies will invade the continent, Major?" another general asked.

"In about a year, Herr General Admiral. Late spring or early summer of 1944 at the latest. It would give them an entire summer with good weather for their air forces to fight their way across France."

"Thank you."

"Any other questions?"

There were none.

The Admiral rose, as did the rest of the officers in the room. "Thank you for coming, gentlemen," he said politely. Then tartly he quipped. "Major von Rittburg, I want to see you in my office, now."

"Yes, sir."

Von Rittburg followed the Admiral into the office and Canaris pointed to the ceiling. There was a microphone in the chandelier.

"What do you mean by coming to the briefing late, Herr Major?" he shouted.

"I apologize, Herr Admiral."

"Perhaps your duties are interfering with your night life."

"No, Herr Admiral."

Canaris took a slip of paper out of his pocket and placed it on the desk. "If your duties here are too strenuous," he continued, "I can find you another assignment."

"That won't be necessary, Herr Admiral." Von Rittburg picked up the paper."

"See that this doesn't happen again, Herr Major. Dismissed"

Von Rittburg clicked his heels and left. When he returned to his desk he looked at the paper. It was an address on the Lausitzerstrasse, between the Görlitzer Railroad Station and the Kottbus Ufer, along with the time "7:00 P.M." *It must be a safe house,* he thought.

Von Rittburg worked late, had a light supper at a restaurant, and took the subway to his destination. It was an uncomfortably warm evening to be in a wool blouse with a buttoned collar, but von Rittburg wore his uniform properly. He walked nonchalantly down the darkened street. There were numbers of soldiers, sailors, and airmen on the street, some of them with women who were obviously prostitutes. Even the drunks saluted politely. It was very dark due to the blackout, but he occasionally stopped to peer into a shop window to see if he was being followed. He saw no one.

Like the houses around it, the house he wanted was weathered. There was a little splinter damage along the street, and one building at the end of the street was completely gutted. The house had a mechanical bell, and von Rittburg turned the handle twice. He didn't know what he expected but it certainly wasn't the young woman who answered the door. She was blond with a round face, a generous mouth, and sparkling eyes that von Rittburg learned were gray when he saw them in the light. Her hair was shoulder-length, and she wore a wool sweater and skirt.

"Major von Rittburg?" Her voice was lovely, too.

The Major recovered quickly. "Yes. Who are . . ."

"Come in quickly. It isn't good to loiter."

Von Rittburg entered, and she closed the door behind him. "May I take your hat? The Admiral is waiting." He gave her the hat and she hung it on the hall tree. "Follow me."

He followed her to a small room at the top of the stairs. Blackout curtains hung over the windows and only a dull lamp glowed on a table. In one of the two comfortable chairs sat Admiral Canaris in civilian clothes, smoking a cigar. Von Rittburg stood in the door, clicked his heels and bowed stiffly. "Good evening, Herr Admiral."

Canaris nodded. "Major, this is Fräulein Lise Elbing. She's with us."

Fräulein Elbing extended her hand. When they shook hands, von Rittburg found her grip strong and confident. "Nice to meet you, Major. The Admiral has told me a lot about you. Happy to have you with us."

That was the second time someone had said "us." "If I may inquire, just who is the 'us' everyone is with?"

Fräulein Elbing smiled briefly, and then looked at the Admiral, who nodded. "I'll explain," the Admiral volunteered. "Would you like something?"

"Tea, please."

Fräulein Elbing left, and von Rittburg sat in the chair indicated by Canaris.

"What do you already know and what do you suspect, Herr Major?"

Von Rittburg listed his suspicions about a conspiracy to remove Hitler and who might be involved.

Canaris puffed on his cigar. "It's a good thing the Gestapo isn't as astute as you, or our lives would be more difficult than they are."

"What do you want me to do, Herr Admiral?"

"I have a special assignment for you." The Admiral took a large thick envelope from the table beside his chair. "It concerns Operation Nord."

"The project that is trying to build a uranium bomb?"

"Exactly." Canaris handed the Major the envelope just as Fräulein Elbing arrived with the tea.

"I thought you might like some, too, Herr Admiral."

"Yes, Lise, thank you."

Von Rittburg noticed the familiar form of address and wondered if the young woman was Canaris's mistress. When Lise sat down with them, von Rittburg realized she must be a person of importance in the Resistance.

"In the envelope is a list of names. Those are the people you can depend on if you need to destroy Operation Nord."

"Destroy?"

"Yes. This is something we must do on our own. The only man in England who might have helped us was shot down while doing an aerial reconnaissance over Norway. It was a foolish thing to do, and he was killed in the process. Nevertheless, he's dead and we're left to our own devices." Von Rittburg couldn't conceal his surprise. Just how far had all this gone? Canaris continued without comment. "If Lamm succeeds in building an uranium bomb before we can remove Hitler, then his project must be destroyed. He cannot be allowed to get that bomb into an airplane. Is that clear?"

"Perfectly clear, Herr Admiral." Canaris was perspiring. *This uranium bomb really has him worried,* von Rittburg thought. Did he really believe one of them could destroy an entire city?

Canaris sipped the tea. "From now on our association will only be in the office. Whoever is watching must believe I don't approve of you. You will be divorced from everything the Resistance does. No matter what happens, your only mission is to prevent Lamm from making that bomb. Even if your comrades are beheaded, you must deny them and be ready to do this one thing. Do you have any questions?"

"No, Herr Admiral."

Canaris finished the tea and stood up. "You must go now, Major von Rittburg. What we do is dangerous, but it is necessary to preserve something of the Fatherland. If Hitler is allowed to continue his mismanagement of the war and his cruel racial policies, Germany will lie in total ruin at the end of the war, and we will never recover."

"I will do my best, sir."

Canaris smiled. "I know you will."

At the door, Fräulein Elbing helped the Major on with his coat. About her was a faint scent of bath powder. It reminded him of Renate. "Thank you, Fräulein Elbing. I doubt that we will see each other again. *Auf Wiedersehen.*"

"Go with God, Herr Major."

She waited until he had gone and then went upstairs. Canaris was putting on his coat. "Well, Lise, what do you think of my new recruit?"

"Next to you he must be the loneliest man on earth."

Canaris gave her a wan smile. "You are very astute for one so young." He kissed her cheek. "I must go. Give my regards to your father."

July 9, 1943

The envelope was sealed and von Rittburg did not open it. He didn't want to. He didn't know whether his reluctance was because he hoped he wouldn't have to go through with it, or perhaps the fact that if he didn't read it he could deny he knew anything about the contents if the Gestapo arrested him. For the first time in years, von Rittburg was unsure of himself. It was one thing to face oncoming Russian tanks in combat. It was quite another to hide one's feelings and deny one's friends merely to survive. But the Nazis had left the Reich without honor. They had to be destroyed.

One thing was clear—von Rittburg had to hide the envelope. But where? The Gestapo would search his apartment at the first hint of suspicion. They would look for loose floorboards or new plaster. There was no place in the office and there was no one he dared ask to hide it for him. After wracking his brain for several days, von Rittburg found the perfect place. He accidentally pulled a drawer completely out of his desk, spilling the file folders onto the floor. He cursed and started to slide the drawer back into the desk when he realized that it was deep enough for a false bottom and could still hold file folders. Taking the measurements, he purchased a small piece of wood, a coping saw, and sandpaper. In the evenings he cut and sanded until the piece fit perfectly in the bottom of the drawer. One evening, after everyone had gone, he slipped the envelope into the secret compartment.

August 10, 1943

Lamm and his officers stood grimly in the parking area as the supply convoy drove into the compound. Supplies were normally greeted with great rejoicing, but riding with this convoy was Deputy Gauleiter Johannes Sobel, Bormann's personal representative, who was at Vikmo to inspect the project and report on its progress directly to Bormann. Lamm received the news of Sobel's visit with mixed emotions, but after some soul-searching, he decided to give Bormann's representative an honest appraisal.

As Sobel stepped down from the truck in his brown dress uniform, be looked totally out of place. He was a thin older man in his sixties, with gray hair and sharp features. He had dull brown eyes and thin lips. Before working his way up in the Party hierarchy, he had been a shoemaker. Lamm shook his head when he read that. Typical Nazi choice. He was trustworthy, loyal, and unquestioning. Who better to inspect the most advanced scientific installation in the world? Lamm and his staff greeted him with the Nazi salute.

"I am happy to be here, Herr Professor," Sobel told him, "but I only have two days, so I would like to start immediately."

"Of course, sir," Lamm told him. "If you will come with me, we will start at the beginning."

First they gave Sobel a tour of the installation to show him how they were organized. After a light lunch Lamm took him to the L-IV shed, where they gave Sobel a brief overview of atomic physics. Rather than bury him with technical jargon, they explained as simply as possible the process of nuclear fission and showed him the pit and the duplication of L-IV. Throughout, Sobel paid close attention and occasionally nodded his head in understanding.

"And now we'd like to show you 'Odin,' the uranium burner," Lamm told him. Sobel dutifully followed. A short way behind walked Reinhart and Lindner.

"He looks like he understands it," Lindner said. "This may be easier than we thought."

"I think so, too." Reinhart agreed.

They walked down the shaft to the gallery where Odin hummed. As Lamm started to explain the purpose of the reactor, Sobel stopped him.

"This won't do, Herr Professor," he said.

For once Lamm was caught totally unaware. "What won't do?" he blurted.

"The storage battery is much too large. Reichsleiter Bormann said your machine is supposed to be portable, but you couldn't even put this on a truck. You will have to make the battery much smaller,"

Sobel said, gesturing to ODIN. "We can't be building these things all over the Reich. It's too expensive."

"Herr Gauleiter," Lamm tried to explain calmly, "this isn't a storage battery. It's an atomic reactor."

"It makes electricity and you have wires running from it. It doesn't burn coal like a dynamo, so whatever you call it, it's a battery. Whoever this ODIN company that makes it is, they'll just have to make it smaller."

"Herr Gauleiter, why don't we take a break? We can show you to your quarters and then my staff and I can give you a better demonstration of what we do here."

"Oh, thank you. It's getting a bit close in here."

Lamm had Nachmann and Loring take the gauleiter to the mess hall, while the rest of them went to the work shed.

"He's an imbecile!" Lamm screamed in frustration. "A battery! Just because it's big and black the dolt thinks it's a battery. What are we going to do?"

"No wonder he's no longer a shoemaker," Hammerstein quipped. "He probably isn't smart enough to make change or keep his books. Too bad we can't show him a real death ray."

The others buzzed for a moment, then Reinhart spoke. "I have an idea," he said. The others looked at him hopefully. "It's not exactly ethical," he said.

"Reinhart," Lindner said condescendingly, "we have stolen uranium from Degussa, heavy water from Vemork, and set up a holding company that is a house of cards and you're worrying about ethics? What is it?"

"If he wants to see a death ray, why not give him a death ray?" Reinhart reiterated.

"We can't. There's no such thing," Nachmann replied.

Reinhart explained, "Sobel doesn't know that. Look, it's very simple. We make a stand out of a non-flammable substance like graphite and drill holes for a hose and electric filament. At the same time, we rig a bright light to throw a pencil beam. You see, the hose is attached to an oxygen tank, and the filament is attached to the switch for the lamp. We put one of the white rats in a bell jar over the hole and turn on the oxygen. As soon as there is a pure oxygen atmosphere under the bell, we throw the switch. The beam comes on and the rat burns."

"It lacks something," Hammerstein told them.

"O-ho," Lindner guffawed, "since when are you a technician?"

"I'm not. I'm a lawyer. Technically there's nothing wrong with your plan, but it lacks drama."

"Drama? What is this, the Berlin Opera?"

"He's right," Lamm interjected, obviously intrigued. "Go on, Hammerstein."

With some relish Hammerstein outlined his plan.

That evening the apparatus was set up in an unused shaft of the mine. Before they descended, everyone was required to put on protective clothing. It was bad enough seeing through the faceplates of the asbestos helmets in the open. In the badly lighted shaft it was nearly impossible. Sobel's eyes remained fixed on the bell jar. The rat was introduced by Dietrich right after he turned on the oxygen. Reinhart waited a few seconds, then flipped the switch. The beam flashed to the bell jar and the poor rat burst into flames. The effect that the demonstration had on Sobel was incredible. After they removed the heavy suits and returned to the mess hall, Lamm attempted to explain the power problems with the "storage battery," but Sobel was too appalled to listen.

"That poor animal." Sobel shook his head. "I know the Reich needs such things, but this is terrible. I will report your progress to Reichsleiter Bormann."

He left the next day and two months later NORD GMBH received a deposit of half a million Reichsmarks from the Adolf Hitler Fund. Lamm and the others gave Reinhart, Hammerstein, and the late lamented rat a testimonial.

November 2, 1943

"I have a blip on the radar!" The loudspeaker crackled and the Fifth Air Division of the German Luftwaffe sprang to life. The personnel in the air defense control bunker at Schleissheim, just north of Munich, hurried to their places. The Americans were coming to deliver another blow to the heart of the Reich. This time they were coming from the bases they had recently captured in Italy. Responsible for tracking Jagdgeschwader 57, an interceptor squadron from nearby Fels am Wagram, Margit Hassel finished her cigarette, put on her earphones, and grabbed the long stick she used to push the flags of JG 57's wings across the big map of southern Germany and Austria.

"We're airborne," reported the squadron, and Margit pushed the JG 57 flags toward the American flags Kristin Finster was shoving toward the Messerschmitt factory at Wiener-Neustadt. She knew what was about to happen. Before they reached the bombers, the German fighters would be shot up by the American fighter screen, then they would have to face the huge American bombers bristling with heavy machine guns. The price for shooting down a few bombers would be very high.

At its arrival at Fels am Wagram in 1942, JG 57 was represented by a flag for each wing. There were still three flags, but instead of the 450 operational aircraft the Geschwader was supposed to have, JG 57 had barely 116.

"I see them," the leader said. "About two hundred bombers and fifty fighters." A small raid for the Americans.

Listening to the mission made Margit's stomach churn. She wanted to see the Nazis defeated, and every German aircraft shot down brought the Reich closer to defeat, but listening to the reports of planes lost was hard. She knew most of the pilots personally and had loved a few, but if this was the way to destroy Hitler and his gang, so be it. She moved her markers into direct contact with the American flags. She listened as she made a mental note of the planes shot down and damaged. Later she wrote her shopping list for 5 grams of bath powder and 2 packs of cigarettes. As she did it she thought of Paul. His absence left her soul empty. Would she ever see him again?

The following evening she met Herr Wirth at the Golden Ox. Their usual greeting was a kiss on the cheek from Margit, at which time she slipped the note in his pocket. She didn't know who was getting the information she provided and she didn't care, as long as they were using it to kill Nazis. She leaned over to kiss her friend and he said jovially, "Good evening, Margit. Sit down and join me."

Margit was flabbergasted. This was a Major deviation from routine. What was wrong? She sat across from him. "Ah, Herr Wirth, so good to see you again. How is Frau Wirth?"

"In the best of health, thank you."

"What's going on?" she asked quietly.

"You are to cease all your activities immediately and stay out of sight."

"What?"

"You have been selected for a special project. That's all I know. From now on you are not one of us until you get your orders."

"What's going on?"

"I honestly don't know."

After more small talk, Wirth took his leave and went home. Bewildered, Margit looked out the window into the night. She didn't understand.

November 29, 1943

A bitter wind ripped down the Kiel Fjord as Naval Weapons Specialist Dieter Meiner strode across the vast expanse of concrete and cranes that comprised the Germania shipyard in Kiel. To date, Allied air raids had been infrequent, and had done little to interrupt the steady hum of jackhammers as the shipyard turned out U-boats for the Reich's war against the Allies at sea. In the blackness of early morning, acetylene torches from a thousand different places flashed and snapped like earthbound stars. Meiner entered the small building in the heart of the yard that comprised the control center for him and the other the naval inspectors attached there.

The office was an informal affair headed by Korvettenkapitän Stauffer, an engineering officer. Like most naval officers, Stauffer was not a Nazi, and that made him a lot easier to work for. Meiner's specialty was inspecting the repairs on warships ready to be returned to sea. As usual, he was one of the first to arrive at the office. Stauffer and a yeoman were already there making out the assignments for the day.

Stauffer looked up and smiled as Meiner entered and saluted. "Ah, Meiner," the Korvettenkapitän remarked. "Grab yourself a cup of coffee. I'll have the paperwork ready in a minute."

"Yes, sir." Meiner went to the pot perking on a hot plate and poured thick black coffee into a white ceramic mug. "What's it going to be today, sir, that minesweeper that got strafed?"

"No," Stauffer replied somewhat reluctantly. "It's *U-751.*"

"The *751?*" Meiner was so incredulous he spilled some of his coffee. "After that last depth charge attack it was ready for the scrap heap. God only knows how Captain Beimler got her home."

"I know," Stauffer said calmly. "Now she's been repaired and we're to make sure she's ready for sea." Like Meiner, Stauffer knew that *U-751* was a wreck, and he didn't sound too convincing. He handed Meiner a thick folder containing the specifications. "Do you know where she is?"

"Aye, aye, sir."

"Take the Kübelwagen." Meiner saluted and left.

The *U-751* was anchored at a small wharf at the eastern end of the yard. Meiner parked near the boat's wharf. Before going aboard he opened the file Stauffer had given him and checked the list of what tests were to be run. The tests did not indicate a Major shakedown for a ship that had been rebuilt, but a check after routine maintenance for a seaworthy vessel.

In 1941, sending a submarine in the condition of *U-751* to sea would have been considered negligence. With the Allies sinking U-boats at an ever-increasing rate since May 1943, however, the German Navy was now short of boats, and what mattered was numbers, not men. But the Nazis never cared about men, or women, for that matter. That inhumanity was why Meiner had joined the Resistance.

He came from a simple seafaring family. His father, a ship captain, was a square-built man with a graying beard. He was hard-working, deeply religious, and had a stern sense of duty. Dieter's mother was a thin, caring, Christian woman with a wry sense of humor, who believed the only way to spread God's word by was by acts of kindness and mercy. With a father and grandfather who were ship captains, Dieter Meiner grew up listening to the wind in the sails of his imagination. The sea was a great equalizer of men, because it was what they did, not who they were, that made them important. Dieter's father brought home crewmen of all shapes, sizes, and colors for the holidays, so that by the time he was sixteen, Dieter Meiner had heard dozens of languages without leaving the family home in Brake on the Weser. In high school, he knew he wanted to design ships to sail the seas. He wanted to be a marine architect.

With such deep moral convictions, the Meiners found National Socialism loathsome, and while many of their friends were compromising their beliefs, they spoke out when the Nazis attacked religion. For his condemnation of the Kristalnacht, Meiner was severely beaten by Storm Troopers, some of whom had been boyhood friends. While he was hospitalized, a high-school teacher who was also a member of the Nazi Party won Meiner's confidence. The teacher introduced him to members of the Resistance as soon as he left the hospital.

Drafted into the navy shortly before the war, Meiner found the life agreeable. The naval officers he served under rewarded Meiner for his hard work and attention to duty, so he rose rapidly from torpedoman to gunner to artificer on the destroyer *Anton Schmitt.* The officers encouraged Meiner to submit his application for a commission, but he was denied officer status and offered a warrant because of his denunciation of the Kristalnacht.

Assigned to the *Wilhelm Heidkamp,* he quickly found how unprepared the German navy was for war when the destroyer was sunk at the Battle of Narvik. After two months in the hospital for wounds and exposure, he was assigned to the naval base at Kiel as a naval inspector, pending the completion of a new minesweeper. Thanks to his detailed knowledge of ships, Meiner remained at Kiel when the minesweeper left for her sea trials, and he was later reassigned to the Naval Liaison section at Germaniawerft. Meiner's superior in the Resistance at the Germaniawerft was Bruno Zeitzler, a foreman in the U-boat construction yard. Meiner expected to perform acts of sabotage, but the Resistance only wanted information, such as which ships were ready for sea and which were not. Here, he was in a perfect situation to give such information.

Meiner turned from his reverie, closed the file, and he and Beimler boarded the U-boat. With a fresh coat of paint she looked ready to sail, but Meiner knew better. Instead of a voyage lasting several days, they were only to go out into Kiel Bay and return. Once inside the boat, Meiner could see that it was worse than he had thought. There were leaks in the forward torpedo room and binding in the periscope. Worse, the engine could not develop full rpm. However, upon his return to the wharf, Meiner found supplies and munitions stockpiled on the dock and an adjutant waiting for him. They were going to sail.

"Looks like good news," Beimler quipped sarcastically.

The adjutant saluted Beimler, and handed the U-boat skipper an envelope. "I have your sailing orders, Herr Kapitän. You are requested to attend a briefing with your officers at 1900 hours this evening."

"Thank you."

"Not if I have anything to say about it, Herr Kapitän," Meiner said. Determined to keep the boat from going to sea, he headed down the gangway, jumped into the Kübelwagen, and sped for the office.

When he arrived at the office, he rushed in, and Stauffer looked up.

"*U-751* can't pass the technical inspection," Meiner told him. "It can't be allowed to sail."

Stauffer looked at him blandly. "It's already been decided," he said.

"But . . ."

"Meiner, there is nothing either of us can do. She's going to sail."

"But sir . . ."

"Meiner!" the Korvettenkapitän snapped uncharacteristically, "I know how you feel but there's no sense in getting in hot water over this one. It's done. Now, take a deep breath and calm down."

Meiner looked at him for a moment and took a deep breath.

"Fine," Stauffer sighed. "Now go over to the mess and get a nice stiff drink."

"Aye, aye, sir." Stauffer was right, of course. There was nothing he or anyone could do for the men of the *U-751.*

Dejected, Meiner shook his head and walked out of the office. He decided he would go to the mess. He was about to get into the Kübelwagen when a familiar figure appeared out of the darkness.

"Oh, hello, Bruno."

"You seem dejected, Dieter. What's wrong?"

"The *U-751* has orders to sail."

"That's too bad. Those poor sailors," Bruno said, under his breath.

"Isn't there anything we can do, Bruno?"

"Nothing, Dieter. Nothing at all. It would be foolish to try."

"Ach," the weapons specialist swore. "It's so frustrating."

"Yes it is, my friend, but I have news for you that will be even more frustrating."

"What?"

"You are to cease all activity. I can't even speak with you about our work any more."

"Why? Can't I be trusted?"

"On the contrary. You have been selected for a special project."

"What is it?"

"No one knows yet. The orders are for you to disassociate yourself and wait for orders."

"That's it? Just wait?"

"We all have our parts to play, Dieter. Goodbye." Bruno turned and walked away.

It's insane, Dieter thought. What good was it having a Resistance if they didn't resist? He put the Kübelwagen in gear and drove to the mess.

December 2, 1943

In France, Infantry Sergeant Stephan List also got instructions not to have any further involvement in the Resistance, as did Sergeant Gerhard Freitag, a Luftwaffe ground crew chief in Russia. None of the men understood what was happening.

CHAPTER 9

ONE EXPERT

The High Command Building, Berlin
February 6, 1944

THE ABWEHR SECTION OF THE HIGH COMMAND building was swarming with SS officers as von Rittburg arrived for work. "What is going on, Weiss?" he asked his Gefreiter.

"The Sicherheitsdienst has taken us over. We are now subordinate to them," Weiss replied, taking the Major's hat and coat.

"I have to see the Admiral, then." Von Rittburg bristled at the thought of serving under the SS Security service, or Sicherheitsdienst, as they were called.

"That's quite impossible, sir. I called the Admiral's secretary this morning to find out what was going on. What she told me was that the Admiral was meeting with SS Obergruppenführer Kaltenbrunner and Gruppenführer Müller."

"I wonder if that now means we are to be in the Gestapo, Weiss." It was meant to be a joke and Weiss dutifully laughed, but neither of them actually saw anything funny in it. The Admiral was meeting with some very powerful men. Kaltenbrunner was the head of the Reich Main Security Office, and Müller was the head of the Gestapo.

Von Rittburg was now very worried, and he forced himself not to glance in the direction of his desk where the envelope was hidden. The SS would execute him if they ever found it.

In Canaris's office, the Admiral spread folder after folder before the two men in black uniforms who sat on the other side of his desk. No surprisingly, both were polite. *Why shouldn't they be?* thought Canaris. They had won a Major power struggle within the Reich, even though Germany's forces were in retreat on all fronts.

Müller picked up a folder with von Rittburg's name on it. "This Major von Rittburg, Herr Admiral. It says here that he is your officer in charge assessments of foreign armies. What type of man is he? Is he a member of the Party?"

"No, Herr Obergruppenführer. As far as his job, he is brilliant. The High Command relies absolutely on his accuracy. As far as I know he has never been wrong."

"You said 'as far as his job, he is brilliant.' What do you mean?"

The Admiral scowled disapprovingly. "He is, to put it mildly, a womanizer and an habitué of nightclubs and cabarets."

Kaltenbrunner and Müller looked at one another while Canaris pretended not to notice. Then the two visitors turned their attention to other officers in the Abwehr.

July 20, 1944

At one in the afternoon, Weiss entered Major von Rittburg's office without knocking.

"Herr Major, someone has just tried to kill the Führer."

"What?" The Major dropped his pen. So this was what all of Canaris's meetings with Stauffenberg and Speidel were about. "You said 'tried,' Weiss. Is he still alive?"

"It's a miracle. Someone planted a bomb in a building the Führer was in. It exploded but he is still alive."

Von Rittburg couldn't think of anything worse than this. The retribution would be terrible.

Von Rittburg listened to the radio as the situation deteriorated. Stauffenberg, who had planted the bomb, believed Hitler was dead and flew to Berlin. Generaloberst Fromm, commander of the reserve army, and himself one of the plotters, found out Hitler was still alive and had Stauffenberg shot to save his own skin. Major Remer, head of the Watch Battalion of Berlin, made sure the city was secured while his subordinate, Leutnant Hagen, went to the propaganda ministry to confirm the fact that Hitler was still alive. Since Hagen was a member of the ministry in civilian life, he easily got the news that the Führer was indeed still alive.

As ordered, von Rittburg stood aside and let events take their course. That evening he went to a cabaret where they celebrated Hitler's narrow escape from death. When they shouted, von Rittburg's voice was among the loudest.

Late August 1944

Lamm nodded to the guard who stood at the entrance to the mine and then walked down the shaft. The condensation on the walls sparkled in the light of the bare bulbs that hung from wires that had been quickly strung months before. Superficially the mine compared unfavorably with the laboratories in most universities or government-funded projects housed in clean new buildings, but Lamm didn't care. It was his! He alone had made it work and he and his dedicated band of researchers would succeed in creating the world's first uranium bomb, just as they had given the Fatherland the world's first atomic reactor. And they had done it under the most primitive and austere conditions. It was pure science, unlike the politics-ridden research going on in the heart of Germany.

When he reached the chamber, he stood for a moment and gazed with pride upon the gleaming black wall of graphite. The name "ODIN" that had been painted on the wall was no longer stark white. It was smudged by the countless sleeves of scientists and technicians brushing up against it. But decoration didn't matter. Like a young child learning to walk, the reactor was maturing. Reinhart and Nachmann stood at the wall of gauges making calculations on their slide rules. Their faces showed considerable concern, and their expressions didn't change when Lamm approached. They had been working together in the confines of the Vikmo mine so long that they no longer had to explain their moods to each other.

Lamm walked over and leaned between the two younger men. He was too short to peer over anyone's shoulder. Reinhart looked at Lamm and continued as if the professor had been there the entire time.

"Dietrich is the mathematician. He should check these calculations to see if they're correct. If they are, we'll have less of the 94 metal than we planned. I can't say how much less right now, but it may mean we'll only be able to make one or two bombs instead of several."

Lamm smiled, and Reinhart and Nachmann looked at him with puzzled expressions. Lamm pulled several sheets of paper from the pocket of his tunic. "You have to look on the bright side, gentlemen. Here we are concerned with the number of bombs we're going to make while our esteemed colleagues in the Reich are still trying to make a reactor with heavy water. Here's their report. It's top secret of course."

Reinhart and Nachmann flipped through the report swiftly, chuckling as they went. "Maybe we could sell them some of our heavy water," Reinhart quipped. "We could take the money and build a nightclub."

"Listen to you." Lamm shook his head. "I wish we could. It would be worth it just to see the expressions on their faces. But the last thing we need is all those researchers crawling around Odin telling us what we've done wrong when they maintain what we're doing is impossible. No, it's best to be quiet about Operation NORD a little longer."

"They probably wouldn't believe it anyway," Nachmann sighed.

Lamm left them to their calculations and returned to the surface. It was eight o'clock in the evening and it was still light. Soon the season would change, and it would be dark most of the time. Hammerstein approached him with a sheaf of papers and a scowl. *Undoubtedly another defeat,* Lamm thought. The lawyer, who was normally the lighthearted one of the group, had been thrust into the depths of despair after the assassination attempt on Hitler in July. Lamm, however, was dumbfounded that the conspirators hadn't just shot Hitler and been done with it.

"The Allies have captured Paris, Herr Obersturmbannführer." Hammerstein handed Lamm four pages of Teletype messages.

"Thank you, Hammerstein." Glancing through the pages, Lamm could see that every one held uniformly bad news for the Reich.

"Is there any way we can accelerate building the bomb, Herr Obersturmbannführer?" Hammerstein asked. There was desperation in his voice.

"I'm afraid not, Hammerstein. We are experimenting as we go, so we can proceed just so quickly. We are all as concerned as you are.

Cheer up. Remember the Führer survived the attack and he still leads us."

"You're right, of course. Thank you." His arm tensed, and for a moment Lamm thought he was going to give a Nazi salute. He didn't.

The lawyer disappeared in the direction of the mess hall while Lamm continued toward the shed that housed the office area. Hammerstein was right, of course. Time was running out and even fanatics like these young SS men were beginning to realize it. They were taking as many shortcuts as they safely could. Was there anything he had missed? There had to be a way to speed things up.

Lindner was bent over a desk, busily operating a mechanical calculator. He pressed several buttons and pulled the lever. The machine spit out more paper tape. Lindner leaned back and sighed.

"Problems?" Lamm asked.

"Oh, Herr Professor. I've been making some calculations on the bomb casing and, quite frankly, it's going to be huge." Lamm looked at the young man and Lindner continued. "There are still so many unknowns about the design of the bomb to be precise, but what it comes down to is this: The 94 metal and the triggering device will be relatively small. Probably two men will be able to carry it. However, once you put it into an aerodynamic shell with the proper fusing and shielding, it will probably weigh close to a ton. Another problem is the design of the outside of the bomb itself. I am not an aerodynamicist, but I do know the shape of the bomb will have to be tested in a wind tunnel to insure that it falls correctly and doesn't flip over. If it does, it might interfere with the fuses and the bomb would be a dud."

"Very good, Lindner. You have done excellent work."

"Herr Professor. I don't understand. What I have been telling you is that we may have the explosive without being able to deliver it."

"What you have done is help me define the delivery problem. Now that the problem has been defined, we can begin to solve it."

"Yes, Herr Professor. I hadn't thought of it that way."

"Go get yourself some something to eat. God knows you need a break."

"Thank you, Herr Professor." Lindner headed out the door. The professor was usually very positive and encouraging. Lindner had never met anyone like him. He was like a mentor and a father rolled into one. If anyone could get this bomb built and delivered, he could.

Lamm waited until the door closed before sitting at his desk. In the top drawer was a copy of a report to Himmler about a long-range rocket called the A-4 that was about to go into action against London. It had a range of 160 miles and carried a warhead with a ton of amatol, a conventional explosive. With the Luftwaffe defeated in the air, the idea of using a conventional bomber was out of the question. If the report was correct, the A-4 could not be intercepted. Lamm was positive he had found his delivery vehicle, and he was very pleased. The delivery system would be as revolutionary as the bomb.

September 11, 1944

Gruppenführer Heinrich Müller's office in the Reich Security Office showed no signs of the damage visible in other parts of Berlin. The paintings on the walls were extremely valuable and, no doubt, looted from some occupied country. The carpet was Persian, and the chairs covered with soft leather. These were certainly much nicer surroundings than those von Rittburg had experienced in his previous visits to Gestapo headquarters. Müller sat behind a large oak desk in his black dress uniform.

After entering the office, von Rittburg clicked his heels and raised his arm. "Heil Hitler."

"Heil Hitler, Herr Major. Thank you for coming." Müller indicated a chair. "Have a seat."

"Thank you, Herr Gruppenführer. Always willing to help the Gestapo," von Rittburg replied. "Although I must say this is a much nicer place that the last two offices I visited."

Müller laughed. "I hope they weren't too unpleasant."

"Your men were only doing their jobs, sir. After the terrible business with those men trying to kill the Führer, it had to be done." Von Rittburg hoped he sounded casual. The last two times he had met with the Gestapo he had been scared to death. They had stopped just short of torture, but von Rittburg told them nothing because, thanks to Canaris, he knew nothing.

Müller opened a box on his desk and pushed it toward von Rittburg. "Cigarette?"

"Thank you." Von Rittburg lit it and took a drag. "M-m-m. Turkish?"

"Yes, as a matter of fact." the Gestapo chief changed the subject quickly. "You know Admiral Canaris has been arrested?"

"I had heard a rumor to that effect, but I hadn't seen him since he was replaced in June of this year. Went to the War Economics Office, didn't he?"

"Yes. Were you and he close when you worked for him?"

Von Rittburg laughed. "The Admiral and I close? That's a good one."

"Didn't you two get along?"

"In the office it was all right, but you know he was very stuffy."

"Was he?" Müller feigned ignorance.

"Objected to everything I did after hours. I mean there's a war on. A man has to have some diversion. There are a lot of beautiful women in Berlin, and a lot of good nightclubs . . . "

"Did the Admiral have any contact with Oberstleutnant von Stauffenberg?"

"I saw him in the office a couple of times, but never realized what he might be up to. Makes you wonder, doesn't it?"

Müller wrote this last comment down. "Was there anyone else unusual who visited Canaris?"

"Quartermaster General Wagner also visited the Admiral. In fact I briefed him once."

"Were you aware that General Wagner committed suicide?"

"No, I wasn't." Von Rittburg was well aware that Wagner had killed himself.

"Anyone else?"

"No one," von Rittburg smiled. He hoped he appeared cooperative by implicating Wagner. Even though the general was dead, von Rittburg knew it would go badly for Wagner's family, but it was a matter of choices. If possible he wouldn't implicate anyone who was still alive and who might have escaped the Gestapo's clutches. More importantly, he had to save his own skin.

"Thank you, Major. You've been most helpful." Von Rittburg was obviously being dismissed.

"Please call on me anytime, Herr Gruppenführer. Thank you for the cigarette. Heil Hitler!"

"Heil Hitler."

Von Rittburg left Müller's headquarters trying not to sweat. He had escaped their clutches again, but for how long?

As soon as von Rittburg left, Müller picked up the phone and asked the operator to get him Kaltenbrunner. Kaltenbrunner was soon on the line, and the two men discussed von Rittburg.

"I can't find any reason to arrest him, Herr Obergruppenführer," Müller reported. "He's not trying to cover for Canaris, and what the Admiral said about him appears to be true. If there's any question about his loyalty, why not send him to the Eastern Front?"

"I would," Kaltenbrunner replied, "except the High Command, which includes the Führer, depends on his assessments. Let him think he's free and clear, then have some men watch him at random intervals."

"I agree, Herr Obergruppenführer."

November 25, 1944

Major Hans Meiler Freiherr von Rittburg strode up the steps of the High Command Building on the Bendlerstrasse. After returning the salute of the guards, he paused to brush the sleet from the sleeves of his coat before ascending the steps to his office. The door was open and Gefreiter Weiss was starting a fire in the fireplace.

"Good morning, Herr Major." Weiss clicked his heels and came to attention.

"Good morning, Weiss." The Major returned the salute and looked around. "I see the British knocked out the heating system again."

"Not only that, Herr Major, they got the last window and most of the plaster from the ceiling."

Major von Rittburg looked up at the ceiling, where there were more empty spots than plastered ones. All the office windows except one had been boarded up, and now that one would also be covered.

"At least this foul weather will keep the Americans away today," Weiss said. "May I take the Major's coat?"

"No, thank you, Weiss. I'll keep it on until the room warms up. I'm not like you. Sometimes I think you actually enjoyed those winters in Russia."

Weiss's round face smiled. "Not really, Herr Major. Too many Russians."

Smiling at the joke, von Rittburg walked to his desk, the glass on the carpet crunching beneath his feet. With his gloved finger, he drew a line in the layer of finely powdered plaster that covered the shiny surface of his desktop.

"They always leave a mess. I'll have it cleaned up in a moment, Herr Major." The Gefreiter poked the fire and stepped back to admire his handiwork as flames from the paper and wood licked around the lumps of coal. He turned to von Rittburg with a look of satisfaction. "Would the Major like some coffee? Real coffee?" Weiss asked softly.

"Real coffee? Where did . . . Never mind," von Rittburg put up his hand. "I don't want to know. Yes, thank you, Weiss."

Weiss grinned and went out of the office, closing the door behind him. The Major turned to the shattered window where the view of Berlin had once been obstructed by other buildings. Now, through the frame of glass shards, he could see for blocks. A once beautiful Berlin was now trying bravely to retain a last flicker of life amid the ruins. A native Berliner who grew up and married in the great metropolis, he watched columns of black smoke, reminders of the latest bombing, flow skyward as sleet poured down. Only weather kept the Allied air forces away from the Reich. The Luftwaffe, that invincible arm of conquest, could not even defend its own capital.

"Your coffee, Herr Major." Weiss placed a steaming mug on the desk.

Von Rittburg, grateful for the interruption, smiled and nodded. "Thank you, Weiss."

"You really shouldn't dwell on it, Herr Major." Weiss hung a piece of canvas over the window and tacked it into place. "Besides, it lets out the heat."

The Major sipped the coffee. "This is very good, Weiss."

"Thank you, sir. Would the Major like me to take his coat and hat?"

"Yes, thank you. It's getting warm now."

Von Rittburg removed his cap, put the gloves in it and handed them to Weiss, who helped him off with his coat. The Major was an aristocrat. Even amid all the destruction and deprivation, he was elegantly dressed in a custom-made tunic and handmade riding boots. And, of course, the gold-rimmed monocle. Weiss gave him a concerned look.

"I'm fine, Weiss, really."

Weiss left to hang up the hat and coat. Von Rittburg picked up the mug of coffee and walked to the fire to relish its warmth. Savoring the aroma, he sipped at his mug. *Incredible,* he thought, *real coffee.* It was uncanny the way Weiss obtained the little things that made life bearable. Even during the darkest hours of the first Russian winter, Weiss was somehow able to procure canned food, fuel, and other things. There was often coffee, a sweet, or an occasional bottle of schnapps to remind them they were alive. Von Rittburg took small sips to make the coffee last.

The coffee brought him out of his reverie. In eleven years the Third Reich had sunk from the lion of nations to the point that a cup of real coffee was an unknown luxury. Hitler had promised so much, and they had all believed him. By 1936, with the nation prosperous and powerful, everyone was willing to turn a blind eye to the sufferings of a large portion of the population. After all, who cared if a few Jews were inconvenienced if it meant the greater glory of the German Reich and its New Order? The Germans were a stupid people who turned their backs on centuries of culture and humanity to trade honor and decency for the promises of a false prophet who led them to a level of barbarism unknown in human history.

And now the Führer had called for one last great offensive in the west, one that might be the nation's death rattle. The Third Reich probably had less than a year to live, and the German Volk still could not see Hitler for the monster he was. Those who had understood and were willing to act had failed to kill Hitler and were now dead, along with thousands of innocent people. The country that had the physical courage to conquer Europe, then keep the world at bay for three years didn't have the moral courage to see the truth. Admiral Canaris had seen the truth early in the game, and no one would believe him. More correctly, no one wanted to believe him. Now Canaris was gone with the rest of the conspirators. Von Rittburg wondered if the Admiral was still alive, but he dare not find out. Anyone who had any contact with Canaris was watched day and night after the plot to kill Hitler failed.

When the plot to assassinate Hitler failed, the Major's life turned to hell. For months he played a deadly game with the Gestapo, who followed him constantly and arrested him twice. Questioning him once for two days and again for three, they let him go, hoping he would lead them to more conspirators. They finally gave up in October when Müller, the head of the Gestapo, tried to lull him into thinking he was safe. Von Rittburg was amused by one Gestapo report that referred to him as a General Staff officer who lacked the convictions to be a National Socialist, and recommended he never be allowed to join the Party. He knew why he hadn't been sent to the Eastern Front. Also, he was in Berlin where the Gestapo could watch him. His thoughts drifted to his wife Renate. After three years, the pain of missing her had not stopped.

"Herr Major? Herr Major, are you all right?"

It was a moment before von Rittburg realized that Weiss was speaking. "Sorry, Weiss. Were you speaking to me?"

"Yes, Herr Major. Are you all right?"

"Yes, of course. I was just thinking of the things I had to do today." He looked into his empty cup. "Is there any more coffee?"

"Not real, just ersatz. I can put some schnapps in it, though."

"That will do."

"I have cleaned off the Major's desk." Weiss gestured to the desk, which he had dusted and polished while the Major was lost in thought.

After sitting at the desk, which was still surrounded by broken glass and plaster, von Rittburg opened a notebook and took the pen from its stand. Before he dipped in the inkwell, Weiss returned with the mug of schnapps-laced coffee. Carefully sipping it, the Major coughed. "Here, Weiss. You'd better get rid of this before the Gestapo arrests you for stealing rocket fuel."

Weiss laughed. At least the Major could still make jokes. "It's not so bad once you get used to it, Herr Major. Shall I have someone clean the carpet?" he asked.

"No," von Rittburg told him. "I've got some very important business to attend to. Close the door and see that I'm not disturbed. And don't come in without knocking."

Weiss raised an eyebrow. Since the SS had taken over, the Major never had business important enough to close the door. The Gefreiter was curious, but knew enough not to ask questions. "Yes, Herr Major."

Weiss's boots crunched across the carpet as he left the room and closed the door. Taking another sip of the vile mixture, von Rittburg leaned back in his chair and waited for the door to close before he pulled the drawer completely out of the desk. Taking everything out of the drawer, he removed the false bottom and withdrew the envelope he had placed there in July 1943. Over a year had passed, but it seemed like only yesterday.

Von Rittburg sighed in relief at the fact that everything was as he had left it. The Gestapo, convinced the Major had some incriminating documents, had searched high and low, ransacking first von Rittburg's apartment and then his office. During the search they had pulled all of the drawers from the desk and dumped their contents on the floor. They also checked the desk for secret compartments, but had failed to find the well-concealed false bottom in the drawer. *Perhaps after the war, I'll be a cabinetmaker,* von Rittburg thought. The Gestapo had no idea that they had been within inches of enough evidence to have him beheaded or hanged with a piece of piano wire.

Throughout, the envelope had been safe, except for one scare. After the failure of the plot to kill Hitler, the SS moved into the building in droves and took over nearly every military intelligence function except von Rittburg's. Offices and desks were shuffled around and the incoming SS men were given the largest offices and newest desks. Von Rittburg was moved to a smaller office, and was informed that he would get a smaller desk. Von Rittburg smiled and thanked the SS Sturmbannführer in charge of the reorganization for replacing his old scratched desk. Instead, the Sturmbannführer had smugly told him that there was a war on and made it absolutely clear that von Rittburg did not deserve the luxury of a new desk, and he would have to make do with his old one. On the last day, workmen moved the old desk into von Rittburg's tiny new office. When they left, von Rittburg closed the door so no one could see him perspiring.

The SS now had control of all the security and intelligence services of the Reich and were demonstrably triumphant. They didn't know that the Resistance movement had one more card left to play, but there was little time left in which to play it. If Lamm and his assistants were on the verge of creating a uranium bomb, he had to stop them quickly. With his miniature saber letter opener, von Rittburg slashed open the envelope and spread its contents on the desk. It contained a detailed history of the Racial Science Section and Operation NORD, as well as biographies of Lamm and his associates. On a separate page was another list of names and addresses. The first name on the list was an officer in the Waffen SS, and von Rittburg stared at it in disbelief. He hoped the Admiral knew what he was doing.

Von Rittburg recognized two names. One was Erich Kraemer, the Luftwaffe sergeant who worked as an electronics expert in High Command Headquarters. The other was Lise Elbing, the Resistance member whom Canaris had introduced to von Rittburg. Three were listed as inmates in the Bergen-Belsen concentration camp. There was nothing else, not even a note from Canaris. Von Rittburg sighed. He would have to make this up from whole cloth. He jotted the names onto another piece of paper before returning the envelope and its contents to the secret compartment.

How could he get a bunch of Resistance people into a secret SS research facility? He looked back at the list. The SS officer. That was it. Send an inspection team. The Major went to the door.

"Weiss?"

"Yes, Herr Major?"

"I want priority orders for all these people to report to this headquarters immediately. This is a confidential operation that is to be divulged to no one. These people are to report directly to me. Draw the orders up at once."

Weiss looked bewildered. "*Jawohl*, Herr Major. I'll send them this morning."

"Also, I want two transport aircraft, if the Luftwaffe has any left. This is a special team that's going to Norway for training."

"Norway, Herr Major? At this time of year?"

"Yes. Now get going. There isn't much time."

"Yes, Herr Major," Weiss said. "Right away."

December 3, 1944

In a habit essential to survival on the Western Front, Obersturmbannführer Heinz Otto Schindler scanned the evening sky. The meteorologists reported overcast skies for the next day, which meant another day without dodging American fighter-bombers. Schindler returned to his billet, a small hotel where the staff, who didn't like having a hotel full of Waffen SS officers, made themselves as unobtrusive as possible. Schindler crossed the deserted lobby and went up the stairs. He looked shorter than his 1.8-meter height, because the pressure of the bandages over the recent wound in his shoulder made him stoop when he walked. It seemed he got wounded wherever he went. He had been wounded in France in 1940 and in Russia. Then he had been wounded again in early November, when a British fighter-bomber hit the vehicle he was riding in with rockets.

Now, he was thin and wan and his eyes were sunken from too little sleep, because the pain of his wound kept him awake. He was obviously a man nearing the end of his endurance. He opened the door to his room, took off the camouflage jacket, and tossed it on the bed without lighting the candle on his table. Wincing from the pain, he sat down, drew a cigarette from the pack, and put it to his lips. Even the act of lighting it took some effort, but the doctors had declared him fit for duty, and he had returned to find the 2nd SS Panzer Division, "Das Reich," refitting south of Blankenheim, a small town not far from the Belgian border. The others in the room were in worse condition than he and they also had been declared fit for duty.

"That you, Schindler?" It was Franz Degenbach, like Schindler a tank battalion commander. He and Schindler had been in the hospital together, and now they shared the room with two others.

"Yes."

"Got a cigarette?"

Schindler tossed him the pack.

"Thanks. The canteen was closed by the time I woke up."

No wonder, Schindler thought. Degenbach was recovering from multiple shrapnel wounds and needed a lot of rest. "Keep the pack."

"Mmmm." Degenbach lit up and drew deeply. "I'm glad I got out of the hospital. I can't wait to jump off and capture some more of those American cigarettes. Everyone's ready. I haven't seen this much new equipment since we refitted before Kursk. We're going to push those Allied swine right into the sea, like we did to the British in 1940."

"I'm sure we'll do it faster," Schindler said, without conviction. He went to the window and opened the blackout curtain to look out into the dark, overcast night. Unable to see a thing, he knew that just outside the window lay "Das Reich." Had it been daylight, he still would have seen nothing. Nearly twenty thousand men and two hundred tanks with all their supporting artillery and equipment lay out there, perfectly camouflaged and waiting. Schindler closed the curtain, drew on his cigarette, and returned to bed. The 2nd SS Panzer was a good division. He was there when it was formed in 1940. He had been a platoon leader in France, and then a company commander in the Balkans. After three short years he was commanding a battalion, but he was no longer the idealistic young officer that had eagerly joined the SS. Unlike his comrades, he no longer had blind faith in the Führer. That faith had been shattered by one cataclysmic event after the other, but he was too busy fighting for his life to give much thought about his uncle or Admiral Canaris until he was badly wounded.

In the hospital, he had had plenty of time to reflect. The Russian Front had been a meat grinder, and Schindler was one of the few original members of the division to survive it. Das Reich was shot up, but its spirit was unbroken.

Earlier that year, Das Reich had been pulled out of Russia and sent to France for refit and recuperation. After a little rest, they were determined to return to Russia and show the Soviets a thing or two, but they never made it. On June 6, the day the Allies invaded Normandy, Das Reich was in its rest area just north of Toulouse in southern France when it was ordered north to Normandy to stop the Allied invasion. A journey that should have taken two days became ten days of hell as French guerrillas cut the road and sniped constantly. If Schindler thought things were bad in Russia, he was mistaken. At least there the Luftwaffe was still in evidence. When the division arrived at Caen, the sky was black with Allied aircraft. It was impossible to move without drawing the attention of Allied fighter-bombers, and there were no German aircraft to contest the skies.

It was stupid to fight without air cover, but the Führer ordered them not to retreat, and for a time they stopped the Allied onslaught. News of the attempt on the Hitler's life only made the troops more determined to hold on. Finally, they were forced from their position and ordered to counterattack in the direction of Avranches. It was another blunder. They were caught in the killing ground of the Falaise Pocket, and Schindler watched hundreds of his comrades die in the relentless Allied bombardment as the Canadian, British, and American armies closed the pocket and squeezed. Schindler and some of the experienced tank crews abandoned their vehicles and fled on foot as the Western Front collapsed. He escaped, even though he was wounded, and Das Reich was taken out of line for refit in September. By then, the division boasted a total armored strength of three tanks. If the Russian Front shook Schindler's faith, the Western Front shattered it. Allied material superiority left the Germans with no hope of winning the war.

Yet, with no air support and the world against them, here they were in Belgium, getting ready for a new offensive. Degenbach was right. There had not been this much new equipment since 1943, and it didn't take an intelligence expert to figure they were getting ready to attack. All units were brought to full strength, and the unreliable "Racial Germans" from Alsace and Transylvania were pulled out and sent to units in the rear. Schindler knew that no one did that for defense. There was an abundance of everything—food, uniforms, new tanks, artillery, ammunition, and above all, fuel. Morale was high and everyone was ready to push the Allies into the sea.

Schindler thought it was madness, sheer madness. Some new equipment and some hot food and they were ready to beat the world. Couldn't any of them remember the past few months? The past three years? The Führer's promises were worthless. Schindler understood that now, but what difference did this enlightenment make? He was a combat officer whose sole function in life was survival.

"Degenbach?" The tank commander was asleep again, and had dropped his cigarette on the floor. Schindler crushed it out, finished his own, and leaned back on the pillow. He fell asleep instantly.

"Obersturmbannführer Schindler?" An orderly shook him by the shoulder.

Schindler woke instantly and bolted upright in pain. He howled, waking up the others. "What are you trying to do?"

"Sorry, Herr Obersturmbannführer, but I have a priority reassignment for you. You're being sent to Berlin."

"What?" Schindler asked groggily.

"Did you hear that?" Degenbach said. "Schindler's going to Berlin."

"He's going to miss all the fun," another quipped.

"Let me see those orders," Schindler demanded. "It must be a mistake."

"There's no mistake." The orderly handed the orders to Schindler, who lit a candle. His roommates left their beds to look over his shoulder.

"The Abwehr?" Degenbach asked, after seeing the letterhead. "You, Heinz?"

"I don't understand it," Schindler repeated. "It has to be a mistake."

"There is no mistake, sir. These orders were sent by priority message. I have a car waiting outside to take you to the railway station. I am to help you pack your things."

"There's nothing to pack. It's all in my blanket roll." He dressed and in an hour was headed for Berlin. The Abwehr. Who but Canaris? Yes, that was it. But Canaris had been arrested. If not Canaris, who? As he boarded the train, he was more puzzled than ever.

Staring out the window of the train, Schindler didn't notice it was getting light. He was thinking about his uncle and Mr. and Mrs. Waldinger. They had babysat Heinz on evenings his uncle had to work and always bought him a gift on his birthday and for Christmas. Sometimes Mr. Waldinger had taken him to the cinema. Schindler wanted to recall Mrs. Waldinger's pleasant face when she baked cakes, but all he saw was the hurt in her face when she saw him in his Hitler Youth uniform. He never even knew they were Jews. He wondered where they were. Thoughts that were superfluous in a turret of a tank during combat now came in a torrent, and for the first time in years, there were questions, endless questions. What was this assignment to Berlin for? Was he doing the right thing? He felt so guilty leaving his comrades just before the big offensive. At twenty-seven, Schindler had spent nearly a quarter of his life in the SS, whose motto was "Loyalty is my Honor." For the first time since joining the Party, Schindler wondered what loyalty and what honor the motto referred to. If he did the right thing, would he ever be able to look his comrades in the eyes again?

December 12, 1944

Margit stood dumbfounded. She had gone to the party with Captain Klaus Meinz, a Luftwaffe pilot who was actually rather nice. When he saw someone across the room, he took her by the arm. "Come on, I want you to meet someone. Herr Paul Weber, I'd like you to meet Fräulein Margit Hassel."

It was Paul! He had a beard, but it was definitely Paul.

"Herr Weber is one of the few intellectuals in Schleissheim," Meinz remarked.

Margit stared at Paul with her mouth open. She wanted to throw her arms around him to make sure he wasn't a mirage, but he shook his head ever so slightly.

"Uh-er-yes. Nice to meet you, Herr Weber," she stammered, pretending not to know him.

"Charmed, Fräulein Hassel." When he bowed and kissed her hand, goosebumps broke out on her arms.

Later, when she had a chance, she cornered him alone. "What are you doing here, Paul?"

"Not here, Margit. Come by the Weber Book Shop on the Hauptstrasse near closing time on your day off. I'll explain everything."

"Why didn't you let me know?"

"Later," he whispered, as Meinz approached. "The book business is not as dull as people imagine, Fräulein Hassel," Paul said pompously.

"Well," Meinz inquired, "how are you two getting along?"

"Fine," Margit sighed. "I just don't see what's so exciting about running a book shop."

"Why don't you visit me sometime, Fräulein?" Paul said graciously. "We have just received a new volume of poetry released by the Ministry of Culture."

"Would you like to dance?" Meinz asked. Margit turned to him.

"Of course." She smiled broadly, but she was looking at Paul. "I'd love to."

Margit traded days off with Kristen so she wouldn't have to wait too long. Her legs were rubbery with excitement and her heart raced as she entered the bookshop to see Paul carefully wrapping the book of poetry an older woman had just purchased. "Thank you, madam," Paul said with a bow.

"Heil Hitler," the woman said.

"Heil Hitler." Paul smiled sweetly and followed the woman to the door, where he greeted Margit.

"Ah, Fräulein Hassel. I'll have your copy of *Mein Kampf* in a moment." Waiting until the woman walked out of sight, he locked the door and turned the "Closed" sign around. "Come in back, quickly."

Margit followed Paul through a door in back of the shop. It was a storeroom with a flight of stairs that led to the second story. Paul closed the door and grabbed her around the waist. She threw her arms around his neck and kissed him. "You do still love me, don't you, Paul?"

"Yes, more than you can know. I never stopped thinking of you. But I never thought I'd see you again." His eyes were misty.

"Nor I you." Tears of joy ran down her cheeks as she rested in his arms. "Where have you been, Paul? Why didn't you try to let me know?"

"Do you want me to explain right now?" he whispered, caressing her.

Margit giggled nervously. "Later. If you don't make love to me right now, I'll never forgive you."

After their frenzied lovemaking, Paul explained what had happened to him. "After we were separated, I looked for you, but I couldn't stay long. Friends got me out of the country, and I went to fight against the Fascists in Spain. When the Republicans lost I had nowhere to go, so at a suggestion from a comrade in the trenches I went to the Soviet Union. They trained me to return here to work against the Nazis. In my present guise, I am a longtime member of the Nazi Party who can't be drafted because of a history of tuberculosis. So, I run a bookshop, and meet numbers of officers who, without knowing it, give me lots of valuable information." He gave her a satisfied little smile.

"I'm working for the Resistance, Paul. Or at least I was."

"What do you mean?"

"I was providing the underground with information about the fighter squadrons. Then one day they told me to stop."

"Stop? Why?"

"I don't know. I was told that I had been selected for a special assignment and was to contact no one."

"What kind of assignment?"

"I don't know. My contact was Waldemar Wirth, a nice old man with a wooden leg. He was the one who told me to cease all operations. That saved my life, because Wirth and number of others were rounded up after the attempt to kill Hitler."

"Curious." He nuzzled her neck.

"Oh, Paul, I love you so much. Now we can finally stay together."

"I love you too, Margit. I always have."

"Mmmm." Margit was happy. She had Paul were together again. Soon the war would be over and they would get married in a peaceful world.

Holbein stroked Margit's hair. He loved her more than he ever imagined he could love anyone, and he wanted to protect her from ever having to do anything dangerous again. But what could possibly be so important to the Resistance that they would withdraw a member from intelligence gathering? Until the Gestapo shattered it after the aborted attempt on Hitler's life, the Resistance had thrived on information. This had to be important.

The following day Margit was back at her post. She was intently watching the flags and markers on the map board and following the instructions in her headset when a Luftwaffe sergeant walked up and handed her a slip of paper.

"Fräulein Hassel?"

"Yes." Terror struck her. She desperately struggled to maintain her composure. *Oh no, they've come to arrest me,* she thought. *I mustn't betray Paul.*

"You have priority orders for Berlin," the sergeant said quietly.

"Berlin? Why Berlin?" *They must want to arrest me,* she thought.

"It doesn't say, Fräulein. Only that you are to report to High Command Headquarters in Berlin at the end of your shift."

She took the paper, thought for a second, and then breathed a sigh of relief. If the Gestapo wanted her they wouldn't have sent a Luftwaffe sergeant, and they wouldn't give her orders to Berlin. They would have arrested her immediately. But the relief at not being arrested didn't last long. Once again she was being torn away from the man she loved. Her first impulse was to ignore the summons and stay with him, but she couldn't. This wasn't some clandestine meeting in a gasthaus. These were official orders from the High Command. She had to tell Paul.

The Luftwaffe broke contact with the Americans half an hour later, with the Reich thirty-one aircraft and nineteen pilots poorer. Margit handed her pole and headset to her relief and went to her room. Packing the things she needed in a small cardboard suitcase, she caught a bus for the train station. She had barely enough time to call Holbein.

"Hello, Weber Bookshop."

"Paul, darling," she said.

"Margit. Why are you calling?" he asked.

"I have priority orders to report to Berlin."

"Berlin?"

"Yes, I've been transferred to High Command Headquarters."

"High Command? Well that's wonderful, dear. I envy you being in Berlin so close to the Führer." *That's for the benefit of the Gestapo if they're listening,* Margit thought. "Don't forget to look up my dear friend Emil Gruber. He'll take good care of you." Paul gave her the number and the address and she wrote it down.

"I love you."

"I love you, too."

She boarded the train for Munich wondering what she had been chosen for.

December 16, 1944

Schindler, the first of the group to arrive from outside Berlin, was late because his train had been delayed at Koblenz. Unable to get a car from the local SS headquarters, he risked a courier plane, since the weather over most of Europe had grounded the Allied air forces. It was the weather that hundreds of thousands of Germans in the Ardennes were waiting for, and on December 16, 1944, Hitler gave the order for his Panzer divisions to drive for Antwerp. Schindler, knowing the offensive was suicide, but wanting to be with his comrades, listened to the news with mixed emotions. Arriving at the Bendlerstrasse, Schindler showed his orders to a guard, who directed him to see a Major von Rittburg, upstairs.

Weiss looked up in surprise as the haggard SS officer entered the office. "Yes, Herr Obersturmbannführer. May I help you?"

"I'd like to see Major von Rittburg," Schindler snapped.

"Do you have an appointment, Herr Obersturmbannführer?"

"No, I just arrived in Berlin. I was ordered to report here," Schindler said irritably. He showed Weiss his orders. "What is this about?"

"I'm sure the Major will explain everything, Herr Obersturmbannführer. Just have a seat. I'll see if the Major is available." Weiss took the orders into the office and then came right back out. "Please go in."

Major von Rittburg saluted as Schindler came through the door, then extended his hand. "Ah, Herr Obersturmbannführer. It's good to meet you."

Schindler eyed the Major with the suspicion most front-line soldiers had for general staff officers. "How do you do, Major?"

"Fine, thank you," von Rittburg replied, ignoring Schindler's attitude. "You must have had good connections to get here so quickly."

"The tracks were cut near Koblenz, so I took a courier aircraft."

"That did take courage. Can I get you a schnapps or something?"

"If you don't mind."

"Weiss!"

The Gefreiter stuck his head in the door.

"Do we have anymore of that Canadian whiskey?"

"Yes, Herr Major."

"Two glasses, please."

"Right away, Herr Major." Weiss disappeared.

Von Rittburg turned to Schindler. "Why don't we sit by the fire, Herr Obersturmbannführer? It's more comfortable."

"Thank you, Herr Major. Now please tell me what is so important that I was taken away from a tank regiment prior to an important offensive."

"I can't reveal the nature of the operation for which you have been selected until you help one of our operatives carry out a simple task. After that you will be fully briefed."

"What's so secret?" Schindler demanded. "I didn't ask for this."

"What I can tell you, Herr Obersturmbannführer," von Rittburg told him solemnly, "is that the fate of Germany depends on the operation about to take place."

"The fate of Germany hinges on the offensive you took me away from, Major." Schindler, suffering from the pain of his wound and tired from his journey, was unable to control his temper.

Von Rittburg calmly looked Schindler directly in the eye. "You and I both know that's not true," he said.

Schindler just stared at von Rittburg. The Major's calm made him even angrier, but he knew the man was right.

Weiss knocked on the door and stuck his head in. "Whiskey, Herr Major?"

"Yes, Weiss, come in."

Schindler and von Rittburg each took a glass of the amber liquid from the tray. "Prosit," von Rittburg said.

"Prosit," Schindler repeated. The whiskey warmed his stomach and reminded him he was hungry. "If you want to know the fate of Germany, Major von Rittburg, look out your window. You can see we're losing the war. It's only a matter of time."

"I'm not concerned with the war. I'm concerned with the fate of the Germans as a nation and as a people." Von Rittburg's voice was calm as before.

"But what could be worse than losing the war?" Schindler's interest was suddenly piqued. He couldn't imagine anything worse than losing the war.

"The death of every man, woman, and child in the Reich."

"What are they going to do, gas us?" Schindler was annoyed. "It's not possible to gas people on a large scale. Besides, no one is crazy enough to try that."

Little do you know, von Rittburg thought. "It's not gas, but it's worse than your most terrible nightmare, Obersturmbannführer Schindler."

Schindler glared at von Rittburg and shouted, "Then at least tell me what it is!" He banged his fist on the arm of the chair, then stood up and stalked across the room.

Worriedly, Weiss poked his head in the door. "Anything wrong, Herr Major?"

"No, Weiss. Everything is fine." Von Rittburg waved his hand and Weiss closed the door. Schindler was tired and upset and the Major had to calm him down before he did something to put them all in danger.

"Sit down, Herr Obersturmbannführer, please." Schindler glared back at him. "I'll tell you what I can."

Still glaring, Schindler sat down, picked up his glass, and swirled the remaining whiskey around in it.

"Have you ever heard of a uranium bomb?" the Major asked.

"No," he replied curtly.

"A uranium bomb is theoretically so powerful that a single bomb the size of a pineapple could destroy an entire city."

Schindler looked at von Rittburg for a moment and took a deep breath. The Major obviously believed what he was saying and didn't appear mad. "You're not joking?"

"No," von Rittburg said. "We're fairly sure that the Americans have succeeded in making such a weapon. We are close to making one."

"Then why don't we use it?" It was a reasonable question.

"You've been in combat on both fronts. What happens when we send one gun, one plane, or one tank to the battlefield?"

"The Allies send more."

"Precisely. Their industrial capacity grows every day, while ours is crippled. If we use one bomb or two against England, the United States will not leave one city standing. And there's another thing."

"What's that?"

"According to some scientists, wherever one of these is dropped it leaves radiation, which lasts a long time and can kill people for generations."

Schindler took another deep breath and another swallow of whiskey. "I still don't understand."

"For now, all I can tell you is that we're going to ensure that no uranium bomb is used against us."

"All right, Major, I'll do what you ask—the first thing, I mean. Then I'll decide whether or not you're crazy. What do you want me to do?"

"I want you and an assistant to get three prisoners from Bergen-Belsen Concentration Camp."

"Who are these prisoners?"

"They're physicists—all Jews. They're the only ones we know who can say for sure whether the bomb will work without raising suspicion."

"Do I just walk in and say I want three Jews?"

"No. The paperwork signed by the Reichsführer has been forwarded. All you have to do is arrive and take them away. You will have an assistant who will be wearing the uniform of a SS Sturmführer."

"Once I get them, what do I do with them?"

"Kraemer, the Sturmführer, will help you every step of the way."

"I don't like this. Whose bomb are we talking about?"

"I've said enough. When you return from Bergen-Belsen, you will know everything."

"What's to prevent me from going straight to the Gestapo?"

Von Rittburg looked directly at him. "Nothing, except I'll deny I ever heard of you and tell them you deserted your unit before the big offensive."

"I have orders."

"This office has no authority to issue orders. May I remind you that

I am where I am supposed to be and you are quite a distance from your unit."

"You swine."

"Do I have your word that you will do this one task?"

"As an officer in the SS."

"After Bergen-Belsen, you may not wish to use that expression again," von Rittburg said.

"What do you mean?"

"You'll see." Von Rittburg went to the door. "Weiss, get me Sergeant Kraemer."

Schindler looked at Kraemer as he entered the room. "Don't I know you?"

"Yes, Herr Obersturmbannführer. I found the microphones in your uncle's apartment."

"I thought you were in the Luftwaffe."

"I am."

"Then why are you wearing a SS officer's uniform?" Schindler demanded to know.

"Because, like you, I have a role to play. Shall we go? It's a long drive."

Professor Jakob Levinsky, Doktor of Physics, handed shovels to the members of the road crew passing by the window.

"Hurry up, we don't have all day," the kapo yelled, occasionally hitting one of the pathetic bags of bones with his truncheon to demonstrate his power. The kapos were prisoners themselves, but were given privileges in return for supervising other prisoners. Many of them were criminals before they were imprisoned, and treated their charges unmercifully.

The SS guard, submachine gun at the ready, looked blandly on, then followed when the road gang trudged out the gate to repair the damage done by Allied bombers the night before. Closing the window, Levinsky turned to his colleague, Professor of Physics Joachim Geyer, who was busy taking inventory of the tools remaining.

"They say the Allies are getting close, Joachim. Maybe we'll survive this yet."

Geyer looked at him. "For what? To be the only Jews left on earth? Maybe they'll stuff us and put us in a museum."

"Joachim, you don't have to be bitter with me. We've been through this together."

"I know, I know. My God, Jakob, there has to be some justice in this world. Look at us. We were professors, men of learning. Then one day a crazy Austrian comes across the border and the country we love turns on us. I hope the Allies kill them all, and salt the soil for the next twenty years. I hope they shoot anyone who whispers the word 'German.'"

An SS guard threw open the door. "Hey, you two. Over to the tailor shop. A couple of officers need fittings."

"Right away," Levinsky replied, keeping his expression neutral. Tailoring was another one of the never-ending tasks they had. Still, it was better than being on the road crew.

Geyer put down the inventory and the two of them pulled their blankets around their shoulders, checked their straw sandals, and trudged across the snow-covered yard, avoiding the piles of bodies waiting for cremation.

"One good thing about the cold weather," Levinsky said, "it cuts down the stench."

"Why do they do it, Jakob, why do they hate us so?"

"Does it matter? Maybe it's because after five thousand years we're still Jews, or maybe it's because we have brains and talent. What we don't have is the will to fight."

"Like they did in Warsaw? Would that help, Jakob?"

"Yes it would. At least if we fought instead of going passively along, they might have left us alone or at least come to an agreement. From now on we must fight. We must."

"I don't know, Jakob. I don't know."

"Joachim?"

"Yes?"

"Did you ever wonder if someone is keeping us alive?"

"What are you thinking?"

"Every time something bad happened to those around us, we were excluded. When they sent all those people to Auschwitz, we were sent to Theresienstadt."

"Yes, and when people from Theresienstadt were sent to Auschwitz, we were excluded. The three of us were always excluded—Georg, you, and me."

"Doesn't it make you wonder?" Levinsky asked.

"No," Geyer replied, "it frightens me."

There were no officers in the tailor shop, and the two moved immediately to the stove. "I hope those officers take their own sweet time," Geyer said, soaking up the warmth.

Outside the camp, Schindler stared unbelievingly into the barbed wire enclosure. He had seen German and Allied soldiers dead in the snow and mud, but he had never seen emaciated corpses stacked row on row as far as he could see.

"Mein Gott!" he exclaimed. "What is this place?"

"This," Kraemer said blandly, "is how the New Order deals with its enemies. This is only one camp."

"There are others?" Schindler was unable to hide his disbelief.

"Dozens. You ought to try the stench in the summer."

"How do you know so much?"

"I had to get some information for the Resistance, so I've been to several."

"Resistance?"

"I'll explain later. Here comes our escort."

A Hauptsturmführer and an armed guard approached the gate. "Heil Hitler," the Haupsturmführer said. "May I see your identification?"

Kraemer and Schindler returned the salute and handed him their pay books, which he examined cursorily before returning them.

"What's your business here?" he asked.

"We're here to pick up three prisoners," Schindler said, recovering from his astonishment. He handed the Haupsturmführer a copy of the orders.

"Oh, yes," the man said. "We got your message. Unfortunately one of them died of pneumonia last month. Damned frail, these Jews." He laughed.

"Perhaps you'd like to explain the death to the Reichsführer SS. I assure you he won't be too happy about it," Schindler said, grateful to have a worthwhile target for his frustration. "Maybe you think the Russian Front would be funnier."

"Uh, yes . . . er . . . no," the SS officer stammered. All traces of his grin were gone. "This way, gentlemen," he motioned as the guard opened the gate.

"A couple of our ovens have broken down," the Haupsturmführer explained apologetically, motioning to the bodies on the ground, "and it's hard to dispose of the corpses any other way." Schindler wanted to kill the man slowly.

When they arrived at a small building with benches inside, the Hauptsturmführer saluted. "I'll have them for you in a minute."

Schindler, a sickly shade of pale, avoided Kraemer's inquiring eyes and stared out the window.

"What's the matter, Herr Obersturmbannführer? Does the scenery bother you?"

"I-I can't believe it," Schindler said, unable to tear his eyes away from the window.

"Take a good look," Kraemer continued evenly. "That is our very own Third Reich in action. Never in human history has there been such calculated barbarism. You ought to see their production figures. At Auschwitz, they brag about cremating over ten thousand a day. In how many battles have we lost ten thousand a day?"

"Not many."

"None." Kraemer continued as if lecturing a child. "At Stalingrad it got as high as eight thousand a day, but that included wounded and missing."

Schindler sat down and put his face in his hands. "I didn't know."

"You didn't know. How nice. Tell that to the world when the Allies liberate these places. How many of us do you think they'll hang?"

"Hang?"

"After all this, don't you think they'll try us for war crimes?"

"I had no idea."

Kraemer laughed sardonically. "When Hitler and his crew started talking about getting the Jews and other subhumans out of Germany, what did you think they meant? Did you think that once they started beating up innocent people in the street, they'd stop once they came to power?"

"I told you I didn't know!" Schindler shouted defensively.

"Well, now that you do know, will you help us?"

"I . . . all right, but . . . someone's coming."

The Haupsturmführer returned with two emaciated men draped in blue-striped pajamas and wrapped in blankets. On each uniform was a six-pointed yellow star with the word "JEW" in the center. The SS officer stepped inside with them and closed the door.

"Leave us alone," Schindler ordered.

"Sorry," the Hauptsturmführer said. "It's against camp regulations."

Schindler grabbed him by the tunic. "I've had all I can stand from you," he said between his teeth. "If you don't watch your mouth, you'll be transferred to the Russian Front tomorrow. If you think I'm joking, just try to be funny again." Schindler turned him loose, and the frightened man left quickly.

Kraemer turned to Geyer and Levinsky. "We're taking you out of here," Kraemer told them.

"Why?" Geyer asked.

"We'd like you to do something for us."

"What makes you think we'd do anything for you?"

"For one thing, it will get you out of here. For another, we promise that you'll be put across the Swiss border as soon as the job is finished."

"What guarantee do we have?" Geyer asked.

"Only our word," Kraemer said.

"The word of SS men?" Geyer said, laughing.

"If it gets us out of here, Joachim . . ." Levinsky said.

Geyer looked at Levinsky and then at Kraemer and Schindler. "What do you want us to do?"

"We can't tell you that until we are out of here, but you may not leave Germany until everything is accomplished."

"In other words, we're still prisoners," Levinsky said.

"In a manner of speaking, yes," Kraemer told them.

"Why us?" Geyer asked.

"You're physicists. You're the only ones who can tell us if we're looking at what we want."

"No," Geyer said emphatically.

"What?"

"You want us to develop a new weapon for you. Why else would the SS want a couple of Jew scientists? No, we won't do it."

"That's not it at all," Schindler blurted out.

"The weapon is already developed," Kraemer added. "We're trying to prevent the SS from using it."

"But we've never done weapons research," Levinsky said. "We couldn't possibly help you."

Kraemer looked directly at Levinsky, but said nothing.

"Wait a minute," Geyer injected. "Wait just one minute. Jakob, what were you doing when you lost your position at Heidelberg?"

"Nothing special, except the separation of isotopes by electrical means."

"What were you using?"

"What difference does that make?"

"What were you using?" Geyer insisted.

"Uranium, of course. It has the biggest cross section of any available atom."

"Uranium," Geyer repeated. "I was using uranium, too. Only I was trying to measure the amount of energy released by the fissioning uranium nucleus. There was some discussion about it before I was dismissed, but I think these supermen are worried about an atomic bomb."

Levinsky was almost stunned. "Joachim, is it possible?"

Geyer turned to Kraemer and Schindler. "Tell us, my Aryan friends, is it possible?"

Schindler looked at Kraemer, who said nothing.

"Your silence is eloquent."

Schindler moved toward Geyer, but Kraemer restrained him.

"We don't expect you to love us, Professor Geyer," Kraemer said.

"Professor?" Geyer's voice was high-pitched. "Now it's 'Professor.' That's the first time one of you has called me anything other than 'Jew' since 1939. No name, no number. Just 'Jew.'" Geyer's voice raised and his eyes began to burn. "Let me tell you what you are. You're afraid! You're afraid that if Hitler uses the bomb, the Allies will have more and they will bomb you out of existence. Isn't that it?"

"Yes," Kraemer admitted.

"Well I hope they do!" Geyer screamed. Levinsky stared in disbelief. His friend, the man who had been his strength throughout their ordeal, had become unhinged.

"Joachim, sit down. You're upset,"

"Upset? Upset?" Geyer laughed hysterically. "Look at them, the Master Race. They can't even solve their own problems. They need subhumans to do that." Geyer spat at Kraemer and Schindler. "I hope you use the bomb, then I hope the Allies destroy every city in this accursed country. You scum, you filth, I hope you all die a slow lingering death!"

Schindler and Levinsky watched Geyer's breakdown so intently that they didn't see Kraemer draw his pistol. Geyer was ranting and raving, saliva pouring from his lips as Levinsky tried to restrain him. Geyer, imbued with maniacal strength, threw him across the room and screamed in triumph as Kraemer pulled the trigger. The first bullet caught Geyer in the mouth, and the second in the forehead. The frail professor's body jerked backward, and he sprawled against the wall.

Levinsky crawled over to him. "Joachim," he cried, running his hand through Geyer's blood-soaked hair. "Speak to me. How am I to survive without you? Please, Joachim, tell me."

"Grab him." Kraemer ordered the stunned Schindler. "Here comes that stupid Hauptsturmführer."

Schindler picked up the weeping Levinsky by the waist, surprised at how light he was.

"What's going on?" the Hauptsturmführer asked as he burst into the room?

"Stupid Jew," Kraemer replied coldly. "He went for my gun."

Kraemer spit on Geyer's corpse and said, "Well, since there's only one left, we'll have to take him. Clean up the mess." They left the SS officer with his mouth open.

Schindler wrapped the weeping scientist in a warm blanket and put him in the back seat as gently as he could, and then locked both back doors.

"You look like you need a drink, Herr Obersturmbannführer," Kraemer said, starting the engine.

"I do."

"There's a flask in the glove compartment."

Schindler pulled out a small silver flask and took a stiff drink, which burned the inside of his mouth, his throat, and his stomach. The fumes rose in his nostrils and his eyes filled with tears. "My God, Kraemer, what is this stuff?"

"Something Weiss gets."

"Who's Weiss?"

"Von Rittburg's orderly."

"Oh, yes."

"It seems that Gefreiter Weiss has a talent for coming up with the finer things in life, and he's quite devoted to von Rittburg."

"Do you want any of this?" Schindler asked.

"Are you kidding? Once was enough."

Schindler screwed the top back on the flask and returned it to the glove compartment. "Where are we taking Levinsky?"

"Are you with us?" Kraemer looked into his eyes when he asked the question.

"Yes." Schindler replied without hesitation. He looked back over his shoulder toward the concentration camp.

"We are taking the professor to a safe house the Gestapo knows nothing about."

"Then what happens?"

"We clean him up and treat him like a human being for a few days, and if he responds, we get him a new identity and he comes with us."

"And if he doesn't, we kill him," Schindler said.

"I hope not, Herr Obersturmbannführer."

"I've never killed a man in cold blood, Kraemer."

"Don't worry about the incident with Geyer. He's one of the lucky ones."

"Have you been in the Resistance long?" Schindler asked.

"Long enough."

"Are there a lot of you?"

"No. The few who weren't caught after the twentieth of July are too terrified to do anything. One cell was kept alive solely for this purpose. It's been inactive for over a year to keep it out of sight. Most of the members don't even know what it's about."

"Then why do they do it?"

"Because anything is better than what's back there. You know what crime most of those people in the camp committed?"

"No."

"Being human."

Schindler did not reply. In silence they drove to a house on the outskirts of Celle, owned by the Elbings, a couple in their fifties. Herr Gert Elbing was of medium height and slightly stout. He had a long, friendly face with a square jaw and a flat nose. Frau Olga Elbing was small and spare. Her eyes were tired but pleasant. Her once dark brown hair was heavily streaked with gray.

"Heinz Schindler," Kraemer said, "Frau and Herr Elbing."

"How do you do?" Schindler said, supporting a half-conscious Levinsky.

"Upstairs, please," Frau Elbing said. "Follow me."

Schindler put his arm beneath Levinsky's legs, then carried him to the bedroom Frau Elbing indicated and laid him on the bed.

"We'll take him from here," Frau Elbing said. "Why don't you two wash up and our daughter Lise will get you something to eat."

"Thank you, " Kraemer said, leading Schindler to the washroom to clean up.

"Now what?" the SS man asked.

"We wait. They're going to clean up Levinsky and feed him. At first he'll get dependent on the Elbings, then they'll make him do things for himself. After that we should be able to reason with him."

"What if he gets like Geyer?"

"We'll worry about that when the time comes. Let's go eat, I'm starved."

Schindler wondered how someone who had just killed a crazy man in cold blood could be hungry until he realized how hungry he had been after a lot of killing in combat. When he looked in the direction of the kitchen, he gasped. When the Elbings mentioned their daughter, Schindler expected a little girl, not the lovely young woman who stood before him. Her round face surrounded by shoulder-length blond hair made him think of an angel with a halo.

"Lise," Kraemer said, "Heinz Schindler."

"Oh, hello," she said sweetly, and extended her hand. "You must be new. Welcome."

Schindler was impressed by her beauty and the strength of her hand. "I . . . I'm glad to be here." He stammered.

"Sit down," she said. "I'll get you something."

Schindler watched her. She was graceful, charming, kind, beautiful, and everything else Heinz Schindler had missed in nearly five years of war. There had been women in the past five years, but they, like he, were only seeking temporary tenderness and a moment of release. His reaction to her was emotional, not sexual. It had been so long since he had just sat and talked to a woman about little things like the weather or a film. He just wanted to be near her, listen to her voice and feel civilized again, in the security of her family's house.

Supper consisted of cold cuts, cheese, and bread, a feast for any soldier, but Schindler wasn't hungry. Lise looked at him. Like so many young men, he would have been handsome had it not been for the gaunt face and the distant look in his eyes. She wondered what had brought a SS officer into the Resistance. As an attractive young woman she had met a lot of them. Despite the hardships and obvious signs of defeat, most retained their unyielding faith in Adolf Hitler and the Nazi Party. Schindler's faith had been shattered.

"Don't worry," Lise told him, trying to make conversation. "There's plenty."

"Sorry, Fräulein, but I'm just not hungry." He managed a flicker of a smile. He glanced at Kraemer, who was tearing into his portion, letting the two of them talk.

"You went to Belsen, didn't you?" she asked. Before he answered, the pain in his face answered for him.

Schindler looked into her eyes. She seemed to understand, or wanted to understand. "Yes."

"Didn't you know?" Her voice was full of sympathy.

Schindler shook his head. The piles of corpses intruded into his thoughts. "If I hadn't seen it with my own eyes I never would have believed it."

"Because you couldn't believe it or didn't want to believe it?" Her voice was soft. There was no hint of accusation.

"I don't know. After seeing that, I don't know what to believe any more."

"Is it any different than Russia?"

"Different?" He resented the question. "Of course it's different. In Russia it's war. There are weapons and foxholes and if you're hurt someone tries to help. They don't just kill them and stack them naked in the cold. I thought I knew what butchery was, but that camp is worse than anything Dante could have imagined." His voice was rising.

She leaned over and put her hand on his arm. "It's all right. I didn't mean to upset you."

Under normal circumstances, Schindler would have enjoyed her touch, but at this moment, there was too much to cope with, so he moved away. "I'm sorry. I didn't meant to raise my voice. The whole world is falling apart and I don't know what to do." He felt like hiding.

Despite the uniform, Lise liked Schindler. He was a boy, really. A boy who was in the middle of nightmare he thought he could control and then found out he couldn't. "Do you think the war will be over soon?" she asked, changing the subject.

"Within a year," he sighed.

"You sound sorry it's going to be over."

"It's all I've known," he told her truthfully. "My comrades and I have fought from one end of Europe to the other. And for what?" he said, more to himself than to her. "I thought I was doing my best for my country and believed that what I was doing was right. All the time I was fighting to support mass murder. What do I have left?"

"Heinz," she said. "Do you mind if I call you Heinz?"

He smiled. "No, of course not. It's much easier to say than Obersturmbannführer."

She smiled warmly. "Good. The fact that you can understand what is happening means you still have your soul. That is the most important thing right now."

"My soul?"

"Yes."

"I haven't thought about my soul in years." He sighed heavily. "Look, I'm very tired. Is there some place I can lie down?"

"I'll take you to your room."

"My room?"

"Yes. Come with me."

He followed her up the stairs. The room was tiny. It had only an armoire, a washstand, and a single bed, but to Schindler it was a room of amazing luxury. No matter how good accommodations had been in the past, he always had to share them with other SS officers. This was the first room he had had to himself for as long as he could remember.

Lise Elbing wished Schindler good night and looked at the door after it closed. There was so much good in Schindler and it wanted to get out. She wanted to help.

That night, Schindler's dreams were filled with stacks of corpses, all of them with Geyer's bloody face. He woke from his nightmare in a sweat, and then paced the floor while he smoked a cigarette and thought of Lise. When he went back to bed, the corpses left him alone.

Levinsky recovered so rapidly that by the second morning he was sitting up feeding himself. After a doctor examined him, a photographer took pictures for a new identity card in the name of Professor Heinrich Buchner, a research physicist from Heidelberg University. On the fourth evening, Kraemer asked Levinsky the crucial question.

"Are you ready to travel, Herr Professor?"

"Do I have a choice, Herr Kraemer?"

"None of us really have any options in this, Herr Professor. I least of all. If you wish, we can wait one day more."

"No," Levinsky said, "I'll go."

"There's one thing I'd like to say to you before we go any further, Herr Professor, and that is I regret having had to kill Professor Geyer. I want you to know that."

"Does that make any difference, Herr Kraemer?"

"I hoped it would."

"It doesn't." Levinsky sat flatly.

Schindler took Lise's hands in his before he said goodbye. "May I see you after all this is done?" he asked.

"Yes, I'd like that very much."

"Thank you. Auf Wiedersehen."

"Auf Wiedersehen."

Once the three men were in the car, Levinsky asked, "Where are we going?"

"Professor Buchner," Kraemer replied, "we are going to Berlin."

CHAPTER 10

THE TASK

Berlin
December 20, 1944

THE SKY ABOVE BERLIN WAS no longer a uniform gray, and the dim yellow light between the massive clouds meant American and British bombers would once again rain bombs on the factories and railways of the Reich. At the front, fighter-bombers had already forced the offensive in the Ardennes to a halt. The war was irrevocably lost, and von Rittburg gave the Reich no more than six months while Hitler and his entourage moved nonexistent units back and forth on the maps in the command bunker. The only valid question was whether the Russians or the Americans would be first in Berlin.

"Excuse me," Weiss said. "Would the Major like some coffee?"

"Real or ersatz?"

"Ersatz, Herr Major, but I can put something in it."

"More rocket fuel?"

"No, Herr Major," the Gefreiter grinned. "You have my word."

"All right." Closing the shutter on his desolate view of Berlin, von Rittburg walked over to the fire. Speculating about the Reich didn't relieve his concern about the fate of his fellow conspirators. In the two weeks since the orders had gone out only Schindler and Kraemer had shown up. The one beneficial side to the delay was that Levinsky was getting stronger. Weiss returned with the coffee and handed the steaming mug to von Rittburg. The Major lifted the mug hesitantly to his lips and tasted it.

"Not bad," he told a smiling Weiss. "When did we send those priority orders out?"

"Twelve days ago, Herr Major," was the reply. "Is something the matter?"

"It's just that only two of the people on the list have shown up."

"I wouldn't worry too much about that, Herr Major. My brother-in-law works on the Reichsbahn, and he says that things are far worse than the radios and newspapers say. Sometimes they can only use the tracks four or five hours a day. Six months ago, it took me three days to see my sister in Hanau. It used to be an overnight trip."

"I suppose you're right." Von Rittburg didn't want to think about the alternative if one of them fell into the hands of the Gestapo. The personnel he had so far gave him cause for hope. Kraemer, familiar with the SS and the Wehrmacht, was a dedicated member of the Resistance and an invaluable asset. Schindler was also coming around, but Levinsky was another matter. How could anyone predict what a man who had been through so much hell would do? Hopefully he wouldn't go the way of Geyer. Kraemer had done the right thing by killing Geyer, because a lunatic would have endangered the entire project, but having to murder a crazy man made the Major shake his head. What had they become? "Weiss, check on those people and see if any of them have been killed or wounded in action."

"Yes, Herr Major." Weiss was beginning to wonder what was going on.

The Major sipped his coffee. *I wonder if I'll live through this insanity,* he thought.

Von Rittburg would have been more nervous had he known the true state of communications and rail traffic in the Reich, which was the reason that only two of the selected project members had shown up. Although he had sent the orders out on December 10, only Schindler and Kraemer had received them within the allotted five days. The others did not receive their orders until much later.

The Reichsbahn was under a triple load. Its primary function was to support the offensive in the Ardennes. Day after day, trainloads of tanks, artillery, and ammunition headed west and returned with wounded soldiers, damaged equipment, and prisoners. Bad weather gave the battered Reichsbahn a temporary respite to repair roadbeds and rolling stock damaged by daily air raids, but not all the rolling stock was used to support the offensive. Valuable trains and cars were needed for the transport of Jews to death camps, and to Hitler's Third Reich that had priority even over survival. The remaining rolling stock transported war materials in ever-decreasing amounts to the Eastern Front and Italy. The Reichsbahn, like the rest of Germany, was being called upon for one last effort, leaving passengers like Margit Hassel and Stefan List sitting in railway cars on sidings hour after hour while trainloads of war material rolled by. Priority orders meant nothing. The Reich was bleeding to death, and the Reichsbahn was trying to bind its wounds.

On the twenty-eighth of December, von Rittburg breathed a sigh of relief when Stefan List, the last to arrive, showed up at his office.

"We must get started immediately, Kraemer," von Rittburg insisted. "We are running out of time."

"Do you think the Gestapo are on to us, Herr Major?"

"The Gestapo is the least of our concerns right now," the Major said. "What worries me is the way the war is going."

"I don't understand. There isn't any way we can win, is there?"

"That's just it. The propaganda ministry is still giving glowing accounts of the Ardennes Offensive, but it's no longer announcing the number of kilometers advanced or the names of the towns taken. It's obvious the Americans have stopped us cold at Bastogne."

"Herr Major, I still don't understand. This means the war will be over that much sooner. Isn't that good news?"

"No, it's just the opposite. The Führer is a man of limited technical imagination, and his comprehension of new technological developments is nil. He has twice rejected weapons of incredible potential because they were beyond his ability to grasp their significance in modern warfare. The first was the rejection of the A-4 guided missile, which is now called the V-2. He summarily rejected any thought of the rocket after he visited the rocket test site at Kummersdorf in 1941. It was an impressive demonstration, but Hitler watched, unmoved, as a rocket engine was fired from the test stand. Despite the evidence of raw power demonstrated by the trembling earth, and the column of flame that thrust nearly thirty meters from the motor, he was unimpressed. He later told one of his aides that he dreamed a rocket would never reach England.

"He did the same thing with the M-262 jet fighter, an aircraft superior to anything the Allies could put in the air. In sufficient numbers, it could have gained the Reich some valuable time. After a successful demonstration in November 1943, Hitler asked if the aircraft could carry bombs. When a surprised Professor Messerschmitt replied it could, the Führer astonished all present by telling them to use the M-262 as his new 'blitz' bomber. The technical difficulties of converting the aircraft to a bomber were extensive and delayed its production for months.

"Hitler reversed his decisions on both these weapons only after it was too late. So you see Kraemer, the quicker the Ardennes Offensive comes to a halt, the more probable it is that our Führer will look for some new miracle to turn the tide."

"Then we'd better not delay."

"How is Levinsky?"

"Much better and very cooperative," Kraemer assured the Major.

"Tomorrow we will drive everyone to the safe house in Steglitz. We'll introduce the team members to each other and brief them. There's bound to be a good deal of uneasiness and suspicion, but that can't be helped."

The next day, the briefing was held in the basement, which had at one time been a root cellar. It was cramped and dank, but also soundproof, and Kraemer inspected the entire area to ensure there were no microphones. Von Rittburg began his briefing with what he knew about the bomb and noticed Levinsky paying particular attention. Several times the professor raised an eyebrow and jotted something in a small notebook, which was more reaction than he had showed to anyone since his rescue from Belsen. Finally he raised his hand for a question, stopping von Rittburg and making Kraemer and Schindler turn their heads.

"Yes, Herr Professor?"

"Herr Major, if this group in Norway has, in fact, constructed this uranium burner or reactor, where did they get their heavy water?"

Von Rittburg gave him a weak smile. "Unfortunately, Herr Professor, I'm not a scientist." He shuffled through his notes. "Are you speaking of using heavy water for a moderator? Is that the word?"

"Yes."

"If I am reading this correctly, they use graphite for a moderator."

"Interesting. How do they separate the isotopes of uranium?"

Von Rittburg gave him a blank look. "Herr Professor, at the risk of sounding extremely ignorant, I don't even know what an isotrope is."

"Isotope," the professor corrected.

"Isotope," von Rittburg repeated, like a dutiful student. "None of us have any background in atomic physics, which is why you are here. You are the only one who can tell us whether or not they're capable of making a uranium bomb, as our contact says."

"How do you expect me to tell you anything without seeing any calculations or experimental results, Herr Major?"

"You will have all the information you need when you get there, Herr Professor."

"Where?"

"Vikmo, where the bomb is being made."

"Go there?" Only Schindler and Kraemer were not taken by surprise.

"Yes," the Major said, waiting for the murmur to die down.

"Your sole purpose is to get to Vikmo and find out if they have succeeded in creating a uranium bomb. If they have, you are to destroy everything and everyone there. We have already lost the war, and every day we delay suing for peace our country becomes more devastated. If Hitler and his followers are allowed to use this bomb, the Allies will retaliate with numbers of them, and Germany will be no more."

"Are we just going to walk in and say, 'Hello, may we look at your place before we blow it up?'" Freitag asked.

"I'll get to that in a moment." Ignoring the sarcasm, von Rittburg placed a large diagram of the layout of Operation NORD at Vikmo on an easel. In a corner of the chart was a small inset of the map of Norway that showed the location of Vikmo.

"This is Vikmo," he continued. " At one time it was a prosperous mining community. The mine petered out a few years ago and most of the people left. Even the short rail spur that led to Vikmo was taken up. In 1940, Vikmo became an archaeological dig when one of Himmler's cronies claimed it was the site of an Ice Age Aryan culture. The claims were false, and when it was discovered that the mine had been salted with artifacts, it led to considerable embarrassment for the Reichsführer. It was forgotten until 1942, when it was taken over by the Racial Science Section, headed by Maximilian Lamm, who, before his induction into the SS, was a professor of physics at the Kaiser Wilhelm Institute. To state that Lamm is a genius would be an understatement, because uranium research was floundering until he established NORD GMBH, the holding company that has organized and financed this operation. He is also completely ruthless and well-connected. From a check of birth certificates in Regensberg and Passau, we think he murdered his former boss, and made it look like suicide, with the tacit approval, if not encouragement, of Himmler and Heydrich. You don't happen to know him, do you, Herr Professor?"

Levinsky thought for a moment and then shook his head. "No, Herr Major."

"Good. One thing we don't know is where Lamm gets his financial support, which must amount to millions, or how he manages it. Whereas other SS financial and industrial endeavors have failed miserably, NORD has flourished. However, that's not the point. You must get inside the Vikmo complex and destroy it if they have a uranium bomb."

Schindler raised his hand.

"Yes, Herr Obersturmbannführer?"

"Major von Rittburg, all we have heard so far is speculation. What solid evidence do you have that anything is happening at Vikmo? Couldn't this be another false archeological dig?"

"We have an agent at the Racial Science Section who worked with Lamm and his associates in organizing NORD GMBH and shipping the material to Vikmo. I have copies of several of the manifests here." Pulling a sheaf of papers from a folder, he handed them to Levinsky. "Do you think a uranium burner could be built with this material, Herr Professor?"

Levinsky flipped through the papers with a frown. "If what you have told me about graphite being an adequate moderator is correct, and the materials on this list are of sufficient chemical purity, I don't see why not."

"Is there enough to make a bomb?" Schindler asked.

Levinsky shrugged. "At this point who can say?"

"We have just learned something else that is equally disturbing," the Major added. "The SS is evacuating everyone within an eighty-kilometer radius of a point about sixty kilometers north of Vikmo.

Since the area is nearly within the Arctic Circle, it is very sparsely populated, but the amazing thing is that the SS from Vikmo are being very civil about the whole thing, paying people top price for their property. The local rumor is that the area will be used as a training area for troops going to the Russian Front. They're also employing a lot of Norwegian labor to make it all seem less mysterious. Why clear an area like that unless you are going to test a massive weapon? Neither the Army nor the SS has the manpower to run such a large training area."

There was a slight buzzing among the conspirators and Meiner asked, "Herr Major, how do you expect to get us in there without being detected when none of us are commandos?" He looked directly at Levinsky.

"You will not be going in as a commando team, Oberwaffenwart Meiner. As I told you, we don't have any detailed information about Vikmo. This map is made up from descriptions given to our agent during polite conversations. You will all be going to Vikmo on official business."

Everyone looked at him in surprise.

"Obersturmbannführer Schindler will be the head of an inspection team from the Reichsführer's headquarters. Vikmo, after all, is an SS installation, and the Reichsführer has the right to keep up with what goes on there. You will all be in SS uniform and have your own names, except Professor Levinsky, who from now on will be Professor Heinrich Buchner, the scientific advisor to the inspection team. Fräulein Hassel, you will wear the uniform of an SS Hilferin. Professor Buchner, you are from Heidelberg University so that you can speak of your colleagues with accuracy if Lamm questions you. You'll get more detailed information during the training week, which begins tomorrow morning." Von Rittburg paused. "Professor, you will be the one who makes the decision whether or not to destroy the Vikmo project."

"Why me?"

"At the risk of repeating myself, you are the only one who will know what's going on at Vikmo. The visit is scheduled to last four days, so you will have ample time to determine the status of Lamm's project."

"Where are we going to get the weapons and explosives to do the job?" List asked.

"You will all carry your assigned weapons. After all there is a war on."

Everyone tittered nervously.

"The officers will carry P-38 pistols and the enlisted men will carry MP-42s. Fräulein Hassel and Professor Levinsky, excuse me, Buchner, will carry 9mm PPKs so the ammunition will be compatible. All the luggage will be lined with plastic explosive. None of you should really notice the weight, and it will give you nearly fifty total kilos of explosives. One of you will have detonators, fuses, and blasting caps. The training program at the Kummersdorf testing grounds near the Tegeler See will show you how to handle and use all of it. While you're there don't talk about your mission. The instructors know better than to ask.

"For transportation, you will be given special passes signed by Reichsführer Himmler himself, which will identify you as a member of the Reichsführer's personal staff, but you are not to use them unless you get separated. You will travel under priority orders by rail to Lübeck, where you will take a ship to Oslo. Going by aircraft is out of the question. We can't afford the risk of flying. Maritime travel is dangerous enough. You may travel to Vikmo from Oslo by aircraft if the weather is clear enough. If not, you will have to take the supply train that travels to the Vikmo railhead once a week. From the railhead you must travel overland by truck. The arrangements have been made by the staff at Vikmo, who know you're coming."

Freitag raised his hand.

"Yes, Freitag."

"Major von Rittburg, let us assume that what everyone has said about this bomb is correct, and we do have to destroy the bomb and this uranium burner. What happens afterward? I mean, what if we have prisoners?"

Major von Rittburg chewed on his bottom lip, then took a deep breath and looked up. "If there are no prisoners, then you can tell the authorities, should any arrive, that the Vikmo mine was attacked by British commandos."

List asked bluntly, "How do we get out?"

"There are enough facilities and supplies at Vikmo to keep you comfortable until relief comes. If the opportunity presents itself there is usually at least one supply aircraft at the Vikmo airfield. If you have a truck, you may reach the railhead."

When von Rittburg finished the room was silent. Each member of the team would individually have to wrestle with the idea of killing fellow Germans.

Schindler finally took charge. "We all need a good night's sleep. Once our training begins there won't be much time to do anything but think about the mission."

There was a general agreement in the room and von Rittburg opened the door and led them upstairs. "Before we go to bed," von Rittburg said, "we should all get acquainted. There's food in the parlor."

He led them to a table with generous helpings of bread, sausage, cheese, wine, and beer. The group mixed freely except for Levinsky, who took some bread and cheese and retired to a corner.

"Do you think we can trust him?" Schindler asked Kraemer.

"Not a bit," Kraemer answered truthfully, "but we've piqued his curiosity and that should get us some mileage. I don't care if he hates us as long as he tells us what we need to know."

"Do you think he'll actually tell us?"

"Oh, yes. Despite all he's been through, the poor devil is still an honest man, while we are not."

Von Rittburg watched List walk over to the professor. It wasn't hard to imagine what the conversation would be about. The infantry sergeant was in the Resistance for a reason that the Major could easily understand. Just before he was drafted, List was engaged to a Jewish girl. He served with distinction in France and returned home to discover that the woman he loved and her parents had been taken away to a concentration camp. Von Rittburg knew he could depend on List.

List stopped a respectful distance from the professor, who looked up at him with the neutral expression one quickly learned in the concentration camp if one wanted to survive. A blank expression was one less reason for the guards to beat a prisoner if they needed a reason.

"Good evening, Herr Professor. My name is Stefan List."

Levinsky, betraying no emotion, kept his eyes on List as he would on anyone wearing a German uniform.

"I heard you were in one of those camps. My fiancée and her family were Jewish. Their name was Rosenberg. I was wondering if . . ."

Levinsky slowly shook his head.

"Thank you," List said, his eyes moist. "I had to ask."

He was about to turn away when Levinsky spoke. "You mustn't think about it. There were so many."

List nodded and left him alone. After an hour, the gathering broke up, with the men going to double rooms and Margit going to her own private room with a single bed, a table with chair, and a wardrobe. The room, with its pink bedcover and delicate wallpaper, had once belonged to a young girl. Stuck to the wall were black-and-white photographs of movie stars Renate Mueller, Conrad Veidt, Grete Mosheim, and Gary Cooper. Margit allowed herself a short chuckle at that one and shook her head, wondering if the girl were still alive. Kicking off her shoes, she sat on the bed wondering what kind of world this was where you wondered if a young girl were still alive.

Before she undressed for bed, she decided to have a cigarette and went to the wardrobe. When she retrieved a half-pack of cigarettes from her coat, a crumpled piece of paper fell to the floor. When she picked it up, she remembered it was the name and address of Paul's friend. She had completely forgotten. There wasn't much time. If she were to do anything she would have to do it tonight. She sat back on the bed and lit a cigarette and waited until she was sure everyone was asleep.

Putting on her coat, she stepped quietly out of the room and down the stairs. Checking once more to make sure no one was watching, she slipped out of the house, leaving the door unlocked. The night wind was so bitterly cold it sliced right through her Luftwaffe overcoat. She walked for a long time through streets flanked by huge piles of rubble that had once been homes and businesses without once seeing a public telephone. She was about to turn back when she noticed two drunken soldiers coming up the street. One of them had a bottle of schnapps.

"Ah, Fräulein," one of them said. "Would you like to come to a party with us?"

"No thank you. I must get to a phone. I can't find my mother."

"Oh, there's one in the subway station just up the street. Want us to wait?"

"No, you've been too kind." The soldiers went off singing.

Margit would have missed the subway station if she had not been looking for it. Once inside, she was totally unprepared for what she found at the bottom of the steps. The platforms on both sides of the track were packed with people who made the station their home. She appeared confused and a policeman noticed her and asked, "May I help you, Fräulein?" Margit jumped.

"I'm sorry," he said. "I didn't mean to startle you. You looked lost."

"I am," she said. "Can you tell me where to find a telephone?"

"Of course. There's one right down the platform," he said, pointing. "I hope it works." A narrow walkway was the only route through masses of ordinary people who had lost everything except a few blankets and a pot. Children and injured people were lying everywhere. At the opposite end of the station, on the other side of the tracks, was an operating table. Listening to make sure the phone worked, Margit checked the number and dialed. It rang for a long time and she was about ready to give up when a sleepy voice answered.

"Hello, Herr Gruber?" she asked.

"Yes," the man on the other end replied. "Who is this?"

"I am Margit Hassel. Paul Hol . . . er . . . Weber asked me to contact you."

"Yes, he told me. Can we meet tomorrow morning?"

"No, this is probably my last chance to see anyone. Our schedule is pretty full."

After a moment of silence Gruber asked, "Where are you?"

Margit looked around for a sign. "I'm at the Breitenbach Platz subway station," she said.

"Stay where you are. I'll be there in about half an hour."

He hung up and Margit walked back to the entrance to sit on the steps. The policeman was gone and no one else in the station paid any attention to her as she sat trying to cope with the latest events in her life.

"Fräulein Hassel? Fräulein Hassel?"

It took a second before Margit realized that someone was speaking to her. She first noticed the brown boots and then the brown uniform of a Kreisleiter with its ornate Nazi armband.

"I'm Emil Gruber," the Kreisleiter said.

"Oh, my God," Margit whispered and began to cry. "Oh, my God." *It's all over,* she thought.

Gruber lifted her gently to her feet and embraced her. "It's all right," he whispered. "It's not what you think. I guess Paul didn't tell you. We all have our roles to play."

Margit sobbed in relief as the policeman returned. "Is everything all right, Herr Kreisleiter?" he asked.

"Yes, yes, everything's fine. This is my sister—we each thought the other had been killed in the last raid."

"Then you are indeed fortunate," the policeman said sympathetically and went on his way.

"Can you walk upstairs?" Gruber asked.

"Yes. I-I'm all right. I just thought . . ."

"I know. I thought Paul told you. Otherwise I would have warned you on the telephone. Come on, let's get out of here. Have you eaten yet?"

"Yes, thank you, but I could use a drink."

"I have something in the car."

As soon as Margit leaned back in the plush seat of Gruber's black Mercedes, he started the car. "There's a flask in the glove compartment," he told her. "Now what's so important?"

Margit took the silver flask out of the glove compartment, unscrewed the top and took a long drink. "Excuse me for being unladylike," she said, taking another swallow. "This is good. What is it?"

"Scotch. A souvenir of Africa."

Margit let the Scotch warm her for a moment. "Have you heard of something called the uranium bomb?" she asked.

"Ura . . . you mean the atomic bomb?"

"Yes, that's another name they used."

Gruber's eyes opened wide, and his attitude changed from polite civility to intense interest. "What do you know about it?"

"Not much," she said, taking another drink of the Scotch, "except that the SS is building one someplace in Norway."

"This is incredible," Gruber said. "What is your part in it?"

Margit quickly explained the mission to Vikmo. "They're afraid if the bomb is used, the Allies will retaliate with more bombs and Germany will be wiped out."

"Whatever it takes, you must get the plans to that bomb," Gruber insisted. "Was there anything to indicate that the British and Americans also have atomic bombs?"

"Nothing concrete, but Major von Rittburg seems positive they do."

"I've heard of von Rittburg. He's the best analyst they have for the British and American armies. Call me whenever you can, day or night. I will give you the name and address of a place to go in Oslo after you have the plans. Our people there will get you to the Soviet Union."

"Is it that important?" Margit asked.

"Yes, it's that important. If we have this bomb we can keep the capitalists from taking over the world."

"Oh."

"It's time you got back, Margit. Where are you staying?"

"It's not far from here, but I'll have to direct you. There are no signs and the streets are just wide places in the rubble. Go down this way and take a left where the lone lamppost is standing."

"For whom are you working?" Gruber asked.

"The Resistance."

"The Resistance? I thought it was destroyed after the attempt to kill Hitler last July."

"Apparently they kept this one cell away from the others in case they needed it to deal with the bomb."

"That's a group we'll have to see to after the war," Gruber muttered. "This bomb is the weapon we'll use to end capitalism once and for all. You'll see."

"There's the house," Margit said, pointing it out.

Gruber drove to the block beyond it before stopping. Margit took another swallow of Scotch before she returned the flask to the glove compartment, opened the door, and stepped out on the curb.

"Don't forget to call," Gruber reminded her. Margit nodded and walked quickly to the house. The door was still unlatched and she slipped back inside. Removing her shoes she quietly and cautiously returned to her room. When she undressed and slid beneath the covers, the Scotch put her right to sleep.

The following morning everyone except Margit, Levinsky, and Schindler were fitted for SS field uniforms. Margit was fitted for an SS Hilferin uniform, and Levinsky got a brown suit that was too large for him. Breakfast was a quick affair of tea, bread, and marmalade before they boarded the bus for the testing grounds.

December 27, 1944

In the dark Vikmo morning Horst Nachmann hurried to the building next door to the L-IV shed. "Good morning," he called, entering the building.

"Good morning," Hammerstein replied flatly. The long hours they were spending trying to hurry the development of the bomb were telling on all of them, as was evident by the dour tone of the normally cheerful lawyer. "Have some soup," Hammerstein said.

"Any hot coffee?" Nachmann inquired.

"No coffee."

"Tea?"

"Or tea."

"How do they expect us to win this war without tea or coffee? Fiendish, these Allies." That was his only attempt at humor.

"We would have had supplies a few days ago," Hammerstein explained, "but *Mayerling* was hit by a bomb just as she was leaving Lübeck. She should be back under way by now."

"Who would want to waste a bomb on that old tub?" Dietrich asked. "It's a wonder old Zorndorf doesn't just scare the planes away."

"Or bribe them," Lindner quipped. "The way he's making money off us, I wonder if he isn't a Jew."

The others laughed a little.

Loring entered the shed. "What's going on? I thought Obersturmbannführer Lamm was holding a meeting here this morning. If you can call anything around here morning."

"That's just one of the charms of living near the Arctic Circle this time of year," Nachmann said, in mock condescension.

"Charm, my rear end, if you'll pardon the use of such an indelicate expression, Herr Obersturmführer. Besides, I have just come from the radio room with a message that will delight you all."

"And what is this wondrous piece of news?" Reinhart asked.

"In about ten days we will be visited by an inspection team from the Reichsführer's headquarters, so everything has to be neat and tidy. After all, this is an SS installation."

"Marvelous," Nachmann said. "We can't get coffee, but we can get inspectors."

"The way of war, my son," Hammerstein said, putting a comforting hand on his shoulder. "Are we going to give them a demonstration of the 'death ray'?" Lindner asked.

"No. We should be able to demonstrate the real thing," Nachmann assured him.

"Too bad," Hammerstein lamented. "I sort of liked the death ray. It had style."

The others laughed, recalling how the "death ray" provided them with a rare moment of humor amid the incessant work. They were still laughing when Lamm walked in the door.

"Well is something funny, or have you all gone off the deep end at once?"

Loring stopped laughing first. "We got notification of an inspection team coming to visit us. We were wondering if we could demonstrate the death ray again." Loring handed him the notification.

Lamm smiled, remembering the joke, and went through the list quickly. "I hate to disappoint you, but this time they're sending a Professor Buchner from Heidelberg with the team. Hopefully he'll understand us a lot better than Sobel. Loring?"

"Yes, Herr Obersturmbannführer."

"This place is going to have to start looking more military. We hardly have any regulation overcoats or parkas, but we'll have to get some insignia sewn on. Some of the guards should have some decent uniforms. Make sure they wear them when the inspectors are here. Start getting the place cleaned up now."

"Yes, Herr Obersturmbannführer."

Loring left and Lamm turned to the others. "Now that that's taken care of, let's get down to business. Is there any coffee?"

"Only soup, Herr Obersturmbannführer," Lindner said.

Lamm made a face. "What kind?"

"Bouillon or vegetable."

"Bouillon, please."

They all sat at the table, and Lindner handed Lamm a steaming mug. "I'm sorry I'm late this morning," Lamm said, "but I was up until about four going over the reports and calculations. I assume that you have been discussing the problem with each other."

"Would you like me to leave, Herr Obersturmbannführer?" Hammerstein asked.

"No, Hammerstein. I realize you are not a scientist, but that is why I'd like you to stay. Sometimes you have a perspective that we do not." Hammerstein nodded and Lamm continued. "I don't have to tell you the war is going badly for the Reich. The Ardennes Offensive has ground to a halt in the west and the Russians are in Poland in the east. It won't be long before Germany itself is invaded. The only thing that can change the situation in our favor is our bomb. Even if we don't defeat the Allies we will be able to get a negotiated peace on favorable terms. We must decide *today* how we will proceed. Specifically we must determine the amount of 94 metal available, decide the configuration of the bomb, and decide whether or not we should test an actual bomb.

"Nachmann, you've been monitoring the conversion of the uranium into 94 metal. How much is there?"

Nachmann cleared his throat. "At this point, we have enough 94 to make two bombs, with enough at the end of February to make another. In May we will have enough for two more and that will be the last of it."

"Does that include the uranium oxide?"

"Yes, Herr Obersturmbannführer. We have already smelted all the available uranium oxide we had. Due to our crude processes and the requirement for purity, the wastage is very high."

"Still, that will give us five bombs by June," Lamm said confidently, "even if we test one that will enable us to take out London, Moscow, and Washington, and leave one in reserve. Now what about the design problem?"

Lindner took out his handkerchief and blew his nose. "Basically, Herr Obersturmbannführer, we have a choice between atomic efficiency and mechanical reliability. Until now, we have been able to cope with crude devices in creating the uranium burner and developing the 94 element. The bomb needs to be a precision instrument with redundant circuits for reliability if we are to get its full potential. This is doubtful in any case, because our 94 metal invariably contains some traces of U-238 impurities.

"The ideal configuration for the bomb is spherical. The sphere of 94 would be surrounded by another sphere of high explosive, with detonators at critical points, which we would have to calculate. The prerequisites for a reliable weapon are: high explosive of uniform thickness; consistency and purity; uniform detonators; and an electrical detonation system that will fire all of the detonators in the same microsecond. If the 94 metal is not uniformly compressed simultaneously at all points, it will be pushed out the side of the explosive and there will be no atomic detonation. Frankly, we do not have the facilities to build a weapon this sophisticated."

"What's the alternative?"

Lindner smiled. "The alternative is crude but effective. All we do is place one half of the material required at one end of a tube and suspend the other half at the opposite end on shear lugs with a high explosive charge. When the high explosive is detonated, it smashes one-half against the other and you have an explosion. This weapon we can easily build here at Vikmo."

"How much wastage will there be?"

"The calculations I gave you, Herr Obersturmbannführer, are based on the tube weapons," Nachmann replied.

"How powerful would the bomb be?" Lamm asked.

Dietrich cleared his throat. "We calculate that the explosion would be in excess of the equivalent of 10,000 tons of conventional high explosive."

"What does that mean to us poor lawyers?" Hammerstein asked.

Reinhart turned to Hammerstein. "When we say it would produce the equivalent explosion of 10,000 tons of TNT, we mean 10,000 tons of TNT exploding simultaneously, which is chemically impossible because there is always unexploded material left over. Imagine if you will, 14,000 B-17 bombers dropping 50 percent high explosive and 50 percent incendiary, all of which explodes at the same second."

"That's hard to imagine. Are you sure it will work?" Hammerstein asked.

"At this point we are as sure as we can be, but remember, no one has done this before. Until we actually explode a uranium bomb, it's just theory."

"I take it you feel we should test the bomb first," Lamm said.

"Yes." Reinhart was emphatic. "And as soon as possible."

"What about you, Lindner?"

"Yes, Herr Obersturmbannführer."

"Nachmann?"

He nodded. "I don't see that we have a choice. If we have made an error and the bomb doesn't go off at the target, it will tell the Allies everything about our bomb. It might also give them a clue they need to complete their own bomb, if they have not already done so."

"Good point," Lamm agreed.

Reinhart continued, "I suggest we have the Axels build two prototypes with which we can test the concept with non-explosive masses. That will give us some experience designing the shear lugs. In the meantime, Nachmann can cast the four cylinders of 94 metal we need for the bomb."

"Good. Have it done immediately. We haven't a moment to lose," Lamm told them. "Does anyone wish to add anything else?"

"Well," Hammerstein said lightly, "we haven't selected an appropriate target. I'm for Piccadilly Circus."

"With a bomb of this magnitude, we don't have to be that accurate," Lindner said.

"I know, but it's the principle of the thing."

"How about Big Ben?" Reinhart asked.

Hammerstein looked at Reinhart. "You know, Reinhart, you've just christened our project. Who will toast Operation Big Ben with me?"

They laughed and raised their mugs of tepid soup.

January 3, 1945

Only Schindler and List were in any kind of shape for the morning calisthenics and the run. Meiner, Freitag, and Margit dropped out before they were over. Levinsky was excused from the calisthenics but was required to walk around a track. After their workout, they began with weapons familiarization for their assigned weapons, plus others they would encounter, such as the KAR 98 service rifle and the MG42. The instructors helped them every way they could and asked no questions. Levinsky showed a definite interest in the weapons. He asked List very pertinent questions, then disassembled and reassembled them rapidly.

"You look as if you've done that before, Professor." List was impressed.

"Actually no. I always felt using them was wrong. Now I find them fascinating. When do we learn to shoot them?" Next to the discussion of the uranium bomb, it was the most animated anyone had seen Levinsky.

"Tomorrow, I think," List replied.

On the way back to the barracks, Schindler and Kraemer stopped List.

"What did you talk about with the professor, List?"

"Nothing. Why?"

"You're the only one he talks to. We have to be sure about him, that's all."

"He's been stripping and reassembling weapons like he's been doing it all his life. He likes them and he's even looking forward to using them tomorrow."

"Did he say anything else?"

"No."

That evening List sat on his bunk smoking a cigarette while Meiner, Freitag, and Kraemer slept. Schindler had gone to call Lise, and Margit was sleeping in a woman's barracks. Levinsky sat on the bunk opposite List.

"Did I make trouble for you, Sergeant List?"

"No, Professor. Since I'm the only one you talk to they wanted to know what you said. They're not sure of you, that's all."

"None of them are sure around people with minds of their own."

"Get some sleep, Professor. You should enjoy tomorrow."

Schindler, List, and Kraemer found most of the second day boring. They all had their share of firing weapons. Meiner, Freitag, and Margit did reasonably well, but Levinsky took to it with an unnerving coolness. By the time the training was over, he could pick up any weapon and hit his target with unerring aim.

"What do you think?" Kraemer asked the SS officer.

"I don't know," Schindler replied with a puzzled look. "I never thought about Jews with guns. I can't say it's a comforting thought. If they're all like the professor, we may have the devil to pay."

"We will. Don't forget, we've already taught them the consequences of losing."

Schindler, who didn't want to think about Belsen, shrugged and turned away.

The range practice continued in the frigid, cold night with fleeting silhouettes of dark cloth stretched over a wooden frame. Whenever one of the trainees waited too long to fire, an instructor screamed "Now you're dead! Dead!" Levinsky never missed.

The explosives orientation began before dawn of the third day. Cold numbed their fingers as they tried to cut fuses and crimp blasting caps. Learning the numerous ways to light fuses in the cold and dark, they set off small charges that flashed orange in the gray light of the overcast day. Once again Levinsky's aptitude surprised them.

That night, everyone went right to sleep except Margit, who slipped off to make a phone call to get the Oslo address from Gruber. She wrote the address on a slip of paper and hid it in her holster.

The fourth day consisted of instruction in basic hand-to-hand combat. Levinsky did poorly, and Schindler, worried the physical exertion would adversely affect the professor's health, excused him for the afternoon. Their final exam was on the fifth day. They hiked out to the range with packs, weapons, and a full load of explosives. Levinsky carried only his pistol, but barely kept up. List fell back to make sure he was all right.

"You're used to this, aren't you Sergeant?"

"I guess I've walked from Leningrad to the Atlantic and back here."

"Why did you fight for them?"

"Germany is my country, professor. For good or ill, just like it's yours."

"Not any more, it isn't."

"I guess I would feel the same way if I went through what you did. Do you have a family?"

"I don't know, sergeant."

"I'm sorry, Professor. I really am."

"I know. I wish I hadn't met you."

"Why?" List was hurt.

"I can't hate you the way I hate the others. What was she like, your fiancée?"

For the first time in years, List spoke of Hannah, his fiancée, and he was grateful for the opportunity.

"Sounds like she was a very nice girl, Sergeant." Levinsky's voice for once was warm and sympathetic.

"Thank you, Professor. That means a lot."

When they returned to the main training area and turned in their equipment their instructor said. "I can't tell you whether you've passed or failed. We'll know that if you return alive from where you're going."

Von Rittburg allowed them some time for rest because of Levinsky, and then they boarded the train for Lübeck on the evening of January 8. On the following morning, they were met at the station by Sergeant Klepper, a Wehrmacht truck driver with a wooden leg. They quickly discovered that a leg wasn't all he was missing, but he was a careful driver, and they endured their ride through the ruins of the old Imperial Free City in grim silence. The center of the Hanseatic League had endured nature's wrath and man's folly for eight centuries, and now the Royal Air Force had laid it low. The desolation made Schindler particularly morose now that the offensive in the Ardennes had failed. He couldn't shake his emotional ties with Degenbach and his other comrades in Das Reich. They were being torn apart by American planes, and there was nothing he could do. With his thoughts and emotions in constant turmoil, he was beginning to understand why so many German officers committed suicide. Honor and decency did not mix with Nazi doctrine.

The waterfront was badly damaged, but the destruction was under control as shops and cranes continued to function. Rails were kept clear and in good repair and several wharves were still in operation, building and repairing U-boats and small craft. Schindler now understood that people were coping with the war, and the ability to manage in this hopeless situation gave people the illusion that the situation was not as bad as it was. Klepper drove the truck to a wharf far upriver.

"This is it," he said, pointing to a ship.

Schindler and the others dismounted from the truck and stared at the vessel. Wallowing in the oily water, it was covered with rust and dirt.

"It doesn't exactly inspire confidence, does it?" Kraemer said.

At closer inspection, barnacles could be seen above the waterline and her hull was a combination of black paint, red lead, and rust. The superstructure had been over-painted gray, but the original white showed through. On the stern the name *Nordstern* Hamburg was partially concealed with rust.

"I wonder how badly she leaks?" Schindler said.

"That's one thing most Germans don't realize," Meiner said. "Our merchant fleet is either interned in neutral ports or on the bottom of the sea."

"Well," Schindler sighed, "let's go see the captain."

Schindler, Kraemer, and Meiner went up the gangway together and stared when they discovered that what they thought was dirt was something entirely different.

"Splinter damage," Meiner remarked. "You can tell by the pattern that the damage was done by bombs. Most of our U-boats that make it back have the same problem."

There was no guard at the gangway so the three of them looked for someone who could tell them where the captain was. They found two crewmen working a winch about halfway to the bow.

Like most non-sailors, Schindler's image of the sea and sea life was tinged by romantic films and books. One look at the crewmen showed him reality. Dirty, they worked in slow motion, their faces drawn and expressionless. They reminded Schindler of his tank crews after weeks of continuous combat had pushed them to the limits of endurance.

"Excuse me. Where can I find the captain?" Schindler asked. Surprised to see a uniform, the crewmen stood and removed their caps. "Are you the Gestapo?"

"No," Schindler replied. "We're supposed to be taking this ship to Norway."

"Oh, I'll get the captain," one man said, moving toward the bridge.

"Excuse me, gentlemen," the remaining sailor said. "If you want my opinion its safer to fly." The crewman had little confidence in his own ship.

"Yes, what can I do for you?" came a thick, booming North Sea accent. "I'm Captain Olsen."

They looked up and discovered a man as large as his voice. As they shook hands Schindler told him, "We've booked passage on your ship, and we'd like to board now."

Olsen shook his head. "I'm sorry," he said, "you'll have to stay ashore until tomorrow, because we'll be unloading all night."

"Can we at least bring our luggage aboard?"

Olsen shook his head again. "It's company policy that no passengers or luggage be brought on board ship during the loading or unloading of cargo. It's for your own safety."

Schindler wanted to ask Olsen if he knew there was a war on, but judging by the damage to the ship, he obviously did. He also looked like a man unimpressed by rank.

"Be here at ten tomorrow morning," Olsen told them.

Schindler thanked him and they retreated whence they came.

List and Freitag had unloaded all the luggage from the truck. Schindler told them to put it back. "We can't board until tomorrow."

"Where are we going to stay?" Margit asked.

"I haven't the foggiest idea," Schindler told her, "maybe at a hotel."

"Begging the colonel's pardon," Klepper said, using the army equivalent of Schindler's rank, "but I think I know a place we can stay."

"Where?"

"South of town there's a Luftwaffe barracks with a ladies' dormitory. There aren't too many people because they sent them all to the Russian front." Klepper laughed as if he had told a joke.

"Okay, take us there."

Once the luggage was back on the truck, Klepper drove them to the barracks, which had only a small caretaker detachment. Schindler wondered why the space wasn't used for shelter for refugees, but he could guess the answer. Civilians weren't allowed on Luftwaffe property.

They spent a boring evening with no supper only to be interrupted by an air raid.

"Don't bother," Klepper said, as they rose to go to the air raid shelter. "The British are on their way home from Berlin and some of the bombers that didn't drop all their bombs drop them here."

"How considerate," Margit said. No one remarked on the sarcasm.

The "all-clear" sounded shortly after midnight, and they went to bed.

They greeted the dismal morning by washing in cold water and sharing some stale rolls Klepper managed to get.

"I get these from a woman who runs a bakery near here." Klepper told them. "You don't need a ration ticket. The woman likes me. I was supposed to marry her daughter until I got hit in the head." Klepper wept for a few moments, then stopped as if nothing had happened.

The following morning there was a huge column of black smoke coming from the direction of the *Nordstern*'s wharf, and a military policeman stopped them at a barricade over a hundred meters from the wharf. Several large sheds were in the way, and Schindler couldn't see anything.

"I'm sorry, Herr Obersturmbannführer," he said respectfully. "You can't go any further."

"We're supposed to sail on the *Nordstern* today," Schindler protested.

"No one is sailing in her anymore, Herr Obersturmbannführer," the MP replied, gesturing at the column of smoke. "See for yourself."

Schindler got out of the truck and realized the ship wasn't there.

"Where did she go?" Schindler asked, not quite understanding.

"To the bottom, sir. She took a direct hit last night and broke in two. No survivors."

Schindler stared uncomprehendingly at the smoke. What were they going to do?

"I'm sorry, Herr Obersturmbannführer," the MP added politely, but you'll have to move your truck. We have to keep the road clear."

"Of course," Schindler replied wearily, and returned to the truck.

"When do we board?" Margit asked. "I'm cold."

"Never. We have to find another ship."

"What's wrong?" List asked.

"Everything. She was hit with a bomb last night and broke in two."

"And the crew?" Meiner asked.

"That sailor was right. It's safer to fly. They're all dead. Let's go back to the barracks." Klepper laughed and put the truck in reverse.

CHAPTER 11

THE INSPECTORS

Lübeck
January 11, 1945

SCHINDLER WONDERED IF THEY'D EVER get out of Lübeck. There were no ships due to leave until the nineteenth. Freitag found out that a Focke Wulf FW 200C Condor was scheduled to go to Norway from Berlin, but it was attacked and crash-landed at Lübeck. The ground crew estimated at least a week for repairs. One look at the aircraft told Freitag they were hopelessly optimistic.

Four days after they arrived they managed to find a ship sailing to Oslo. It was not listed in any of the notices because it was under special contract to NORD GMBH. When the port authorities informed Schindler and Kraemer that the *Mayerling* did not accept passengers, they went directly to the ship. Crewmen were everywhere repairing bomb damage.

"What a tub," Schindler said. "This rust bucket makes the *Nordstern* look like a luxury liner."

"Except this ship is afloat." Kraemer observed.

"Where's the captain?" Schindler asked a crewman.

The man pointed to a figure on the bridge. "That's him."

"Thanks." Schindler headed up the steps, with Kraemer close behind.

"Hello," Captain Zorndorf said, calmly puffing his pipe. "Is there something I can do for you, Herr Obersturmbannführer?"

"I'd like to book passage on your ship to Oslo," Schindler told him.

"NORD GMBH does not allow passengers," Zorndorf said calmly.

"I have the authority of the Reichsführer SS to seize this ship." Schindler said with authority.

"Seize away," Zorndorf replied quietly, "except you'll have to sail it yourself with me and my crew in jail."

Schindler leaned toward Zorndorf, but Kraemer grabbed his arm and said calmly, "There's no sense in losing our tempers. NORD is a business, and the captain here is their agent, so I am sure we can reach a business-like agreement that will satisfy all parties."

Zorndorf raised an eyebrow. "Perhaps we might be able to arrange something."

"It's awfully cold on your bridge," Kraemer remarked.

"My cabin is this way."

Zorndorf's cabin was a small cubicle with a desk, a wash basin, and a bunk where he indicated Schindler and Kraemer should sit. Kraemer, always prepared, drew a small bottle of schnapps from his jacket. "Do you have any glasses?"

"Only two." Zorndorf produced two water glasses and Kraemer filled them a third of the way. Schindler gave him a dirty look.

"Prosit," Kraemer said. He nudged Schindler to drink from a glass while he drank from the bottle.

"Prosit," Zorndorf repeated, and drained his glass. Then he said, "Five hundred Reichsmarks or one hundred Swiss francs per passenger."

"Wha . . ."

"Agreed," Kraemer said loudly, before Schindler could protest.

They sealed the bargain with another glass of schnapps.

"We sail at 1500 hours on the ninth, which allows us to do most of our traveling in the dark. Bring the money with you when you board."

"You bribed him," Schindler said as they walked down the gangway.

"Yes."

"Why?"

"Because it's the easiest way."

"Asking for foreign currencies in the Reich is illegal."

"Herr Schindler," Kraemer purposely dropped the SS rank. "What do you think we are doing, going to a Fasching party? Illegal? Are all the Waffen SS as naive as you? Anyone who can trades in foreign money, because the mark is worthless."

"Where are we going to get the money?" Schindler asked, suddenly unsure of himself.

"Von Rittburg gave me enough for emergencies. We have plenty."

The others greeted the news with stoicism.

"Well, don't everyone thank me at once," Kraemer said

"What are we going to do about getting something to eat?" List asked him. "The Luftwaffe won't feed us because we have SS ration cards. We gave Klepper a little money but he couldn't find anything. The stores are empty. He's honest, I'll say that for him. He actually brought the money back."

"I bet there's food in the cellars of these bombed-out buildings," Levinsky offered. "Sometimes the road gang guards would let us look for food in such buildings. Of course they took most of it. Still, it was more than we got in the camp."

"But that's looting," Meiner protested indignantly.

"So starve," Levinsky told him. "We can always tell people we're looking for firewood, which is legal, and we can use some of that, too. Besides, who's going to question the SS?"

"He's right," Kraemer said. "What do we have to lose?"

They all looked at Schindler, and he nodded in agreement. The entire group made their way out of the installation to the deserted piles of rubble that had once been buildings. List and Meiner searched for firewood on top of the rubble and acted as lookouts while the rest tried to find their way into the cellars. Their first booty consisted of seven cans without labels. Returning to the barracks, they feasted on beans, cabbage, and fruit, grateful to Levinsky for their windfall.

The following morning all of them except Schindler and Margit went looking, and they struck it rich in the cellar of what had probably been the home of a wealthy businessman. There were many cans of food, bottles of wine and schnapps, and burlap bags to carry everything in.

On the way back, Kraemer carried a bundle of firewood, as did Levinsky, who had grown progressively stronger, while Meiner and List traded off carrying the heavy burlap bag full of cans and the lighter one that contained the bottles. Incredibly pleased with themselves, they were walking back to the Luftwaffe barracks through the rubble when two men in overcoats spied them from the street.

"You there!" they called.

"Gestapo," Kraemer whispered.

"What do they want?" Meiner asked.

"Probably what we have," Levinsky snarled.

Snow was beginning to fall as the two heavily built men approached. One had dark hair and a Hitler mustache. The other was clean-shaven and sandy-haired. Neither was smiling.

"What are you doing here?" the dark-haired one demanded.

"Just getting some firewood, sir," Kraemer replied, meekly.

The Gestapo agent with sandy hair flashed his identity disc. "Gestapo. Let me see your identification."

One by one they handed him their identification books. He looked at each one carefully, then scowled and gave it back to its owner. His expression changed to a cold smirk when he examined Levinsky's.

"You are Professor Buchner?" It was a snide question.

"Yes." Levinsky's face and expression remained neutral.

"It says you work on the Reichsführer's staff."

"That's right."

"What do you do?"

"I'm a scientific advisor for this inspection team. We are waiting for our ship to leave for Oslo. Would you like to see my orders?"

"No, that's not necessary. Do you teach?"

Kraemer, List, and Meiner looked at each other. Where was this going? Something was wrong.

"Not any more," Levinsky replied calmly.

"Where did you teach before the war?" It was obvious the Gestapo man already knew the answer, but how?

"Heidelberg."

"Heidelberg, hmm?"

"Yes, sir." Levinsky's voice betrayed no sign of concern.

"I was at Heidelberg," the sandy-haired Gestapo agent remarked. "I was majoring in physics, but I was kicked out because some Jew professor said I cheated on an exam. That professor's name was Levinsky. Remember, Professor?"

Everyone's eyes turned toward Levinsky.

"Yes." Levinsky responded as if he were answering a question in the classroom. "Your name is Reinhard Bohlen, and you did cheat."

Kraemer, List, Meiner, and the other Gestapo agent stared incredulously at the unruffled confession. Was Levinsky crazy?

Gestapo Agent Reinhard Bohlen grinned broadly. "You're all coming with—"

Bohlen never finished the sentence. There was the crack of a pistol and his eyes opened wide in surprise. A huge smoking hole appeared in the pocket of Levinsky's coat. Bohlen collapsed like a rag doll. Before the other agent could recover, he was staring down the muzzle of Kraemer's P-38.

"Please," the other agent begged in panic, "I didn't see a thing. I won't tell, I promise."

"This way," Kraemer said, motioning him further back in the rubble. Levinsky followed."I need his coat," Levinsky said coldly.

"Take it off."

"Please, I have a wife and two children. I won't say anything, I promise. You'll be gone, no one will know."

"Take it off and I'll consider it."

The man quickly removed his coat and handed it to Levinsky.

"Please, I have a family." He reached into his pocket to get his wallet. Opening it, he showed Kraemer a photo of a woman and two children.

"Very nice." Kraemer put a bullet through the man's head. "Do you think anyone heard?"

"Not in this maze." List yawned.

They looted the bodies of the dead Gestapo agents for their money and identification to make it look like robbery, then dragged them into the rubble and covered them carefully. Levinsky put on his new coat.

"It's a little big for you, Professor," List grinned. "But it doesn't have a hole in the pocket."

Levinsky gave the sergeant a cold, satisfying smile. Killing the Nazi had made him feel very good. It was after dark when they returned to the barracks.

"You should have been back long ago," Schindler said. "Is anything wrong?"

"No," Kraemer, lying back on his bunk, assured him. "We had to bury two Gestapo agents, that's all."

"What? What happened?"

Kraemer told him precisely what had occurred.

Schindler's jaw dropped in shock. "Are you crazy, Kraemer? You can't just kill Gestapo agents." He was displaying the raw nerves they all had.

"Did you want them to arrest us?"

"No, I . . ." Schindler was exasperated with him. "Sometimes I think you like killing."

"Of course, he does," the usually quiet professor added sarcastically. "He's a German."

"You killed the first one," Schindler shot back.

"I'm a German, too, or have you forgotten?"

"I think we need a hot supper and some rest," Meiner interjected. "We're getting on each other's nerves, and we have a big day tomorrow."

The next day, the Gestapo were not in evidence as Schindler and his group boarded the *Mayerling* at two in the afternoon. There were not even any customs inspectors present. After an impatient wait of an hour and a quarter, the engines began to throb. A few minutes later the lines were cast off and the redoubtable old *Mayerling* moved away from the wharf. Churning grayish-yellow foam from her single propeller, she headed for the middle of the channel. As soon as the ship cleared the headlands, Schindler and his companions heaved a sigh of relief and went to their cabins to think about the coming mission.

Lamm's face was grimly set as he trudged through the deep snow toward Lindner, who was standing with the Axel brothers and three demolition men from the security company. At their feet was a prototype of the bomb that, in one stroke, would reverse the Reich's waning fortunes on the battlefield and restore the Fatherland to her rightful place as the head of the scientific world. Lamm should have been exhilarated, but he was too aware of time slipping away. The Reich was dying and only he could save it. They were now but a step away from doing just that. Lamm wondered what the expressions on the faces of fools like Fischbein would be like when they discovered that he had succeeded where they had failed miserably.

The SS men came to attention as Lamm approached, so he waved his hand and they relaxed. Except for ceremonial purposes, the troops at Vikmo had dispensed with saluting and the incessant "Heil Hitlers."

"Good morning, Herr Obersturmbannführer," Lindner said, exhaling a cloud of white vapor.

"Good morning. Are you ready?"

"In a few minutes we'll know if we are correct," Lindner replied. "Based on your instructions we had to make two modifications to the shear lugs, but that should do it. I still don't understand why they have to stand ten Gs for sixty seconds."

"All in good time," Lamm said, watching the Axel brothers screw a block of steel into a shiny metal tube.

"All the dimensions are the same as the actual bomb," Lindner continued, "but until now we couldn't get the weight correct. Now that we have the actual 94 metal, we were able to approximate it with steel and lead. If the shear lugs work we can build it."

As soon as the Axel brothers and the demolition men carried the tube to the firing pit, they attached the detonators and sandbagged the tube so it wouldn't blow away when it exploded. The Axels returned to the firing position and the demolition men followed, laying the wires carefully on the snow.

"We'd better step behind the sandbag revetment, Herr Obersturmbannführer. Sometimes we get big pieces."

Following Lindner's advice Lamm moved to the revetment and crouched behind it as the demolition men attached the wires to a blasting machine. They looked at Lindner, who nodded. One of the demolition men pushed the handle of the blasting machine and there was a loud "crump," followed by falling snow and ice. Looking over the revetment they saw a black circle in the snow surrounded by shredded sandbags. About three meters from the firing pit lay a blackened, twisted metal tube.

"Get it analyzed!" Lamm told his assistant.

"We'll know in about an hour." Lindner's voice was tinged with excitement.

Lamm nodded and returned to the L-IV shed, where Nachmann was checking the dimensions on the last cylindrical slugs of 94 metal. To keep from having to put on a bulky protective suit, he went to the side window and watched. *Soon,* he thought, *soon.*

The following day Professor Maximilian Lamm watched intently as the component parts of the two bombs were laid out on special platforms constructed in the L-IV shed. He wanted a cigarette desperately, but he had to wait until he took off the protective suit.

The external configuration of the bombs consisted of one short and one long cylinder, both of equal diameter. The crews took the first cylindrical slugs of 94 metal and slid them into the long cylinders. Next, they placed thick lead discs over the 94 metal to keep the two parts from forming a supercritical mass. These safety discs would have to be removed for the bomb to work correctly. From the lead discs protruded a long threaded rod. A clamp went over the opening of the long tube and a wing nut screwed on to the rod. The second piece of 94 metal was slipped into the short tube and rotated ninety degrees so that it engaged the shear lugs. The high-explosive charge designed to propel the movable slug was also screwed into the short section of the tube, and a plug was placed in each of the four detonator holes. The detonator retaining cap screwed on, and the small section of tube screwed on to the long section. Each gleaming, stainless steel tube was slipped into an aluminum one that had an access plate for the detonators. The aluminum tubes were then set in lead-covered steel tubes with carrying handles. Hammerstein had been at it again. One bomb case was decorated with the name "Thor," after the Norse god of thunder, and the other "Loki," after the imp of discord. After checking the building with his Geiger counter, Lindner gave the signal that it was safe, and everyone removed his or her headgear.

"Well, I see you've been at your poetic best again, Hammerstein."

The lawyer beamed. "Thank you, Herr Obersturmbannführer. If all goes well, Thor will thunder at the test, and Loki will send our enemies into confusion. Heil Hitler!" Hammerstein shouted.

"Heil Hitler!" the others echoed.

Lamm's arm shot up along with the others, but he wondered how intelligent men like Hammerstein and the rest could remain so fanatically loyal to a regime that was militarily, socially, and intellectually bankrupt. Perhaps he would never understand, but together they had worked well and had accomplished the impossible. Lamm removed the rest of his protective clothing and hung it up before walking outside. Taking a cigarette out of the pack, he put it to his lips and Lindner leaned over and lit it for him before lighting his own.

"Thanks, Lindner. You know, you and the others have done very well."

"Thank you, Herr Obersturmbannführer, but none of us would have accomplished anything without you. The Führer will be indebted to you for saving the Reich. I can't imagine what your reward will be."

"My reward will be London disappearing in a blinding flash," Lamm told him. *Then I'll probably spend the rest of my life trying to explain atomic physics to Nazi dolts like Sobel,* he thought. "Those inspectors should be here in a few days, so we're going to have to prepare the test site as quickly as possible." Lamm looked over at the other end of the shed. "Reinhart?"

"Yes, Herr Obersturmbannführer."

"Come here for a minute."

Reinhart trotted over. "How far is the test site from completion?" Lamm asked.

"Two days. The tower is completed. All we have to do is move the instruments from the L-IV shed to the bunker. I wish we had another set, but we've got just enough for Odin and L-IV. All the brackets are in place and the lines are run. Give us the word, and we'll turn on the bunker heat and install the instruments.

"Start on it immediately. Work in shifts around the clock. I don't want any delays. Is there any more schnapps?"

"No, we're out of everything except rations and water," Lindner said.

"The *Mayerling* should be in Oslo in a day or two," Reinhart added. "Old Zorndorf hasn't failed us yet."

January 13, 1945

Aboard the *Mayerling,* the evening meal was eaten in silence. The crew resented having members of the SS on board and ate at their own table, while Schindler and his group were relegated to another table with their own rations because the price of the passage did not include meals. At Schindler's insistence they had brought the looted food and wine, so no one went hungry, but the meal was gloomy and quiet, each member of the team lost in his own thoughts. They were finally on their way.

One by one each drifted off to his cabin except for Margit, who decided she needed some air. It was bitterly cold on deck and the sky was overcast but the air was free of cigar smoke and engine fumes. With the ship blacked out, it was darker than Margit could imagine, yet the ship's wake was phosphorescent. Margit thought it was pretty until she realized it was perfect marker for enemy aircraft. In the darkness she tripped over a toolbox on the deck and cursed it loudly, wriggling her pain-wracked toes in her boot to make sure they weren't broken. Looking up, she realized that someone else on deck was approaching her. She reached into the tool box, felt a heavy wrench and picked it up, determined not to be raped on the cold deck. Hiding the wrench behind her, she finally recognized who it was. "Oh, hello there, Kraemer," she said, smiling.

"Hello, Fräulein. I heard you yell. Are you all right?"

"I'm fine. I just stubbed my toe on this toolbox."

"Ahh," he said flatly.

"I was afraid you might be one of the sailors. This is my first time on a ship. It's a little rough, but I like it."

"For whom are you working, Fräulein?" Kraemer asked bluntly.

"I-I beg your pardon," she said, taken aback.

"For whom are you working?" he repeated.

"I don't understand the question." She was trying to stay calm but her voice betrayed her nervousness.

"The first night we stayed in Steglitz, you left after the others went to bed and did not return for over three hours. I saw you leave and come back. You were driven back in a large black Mercedes," he said.

"You're crazy," she said, turning away from him. Kraemer grabbed her left wrist in a steel-like grip. "You're hurting me," she gasped.

He held her tight. "Who was it?"

"All right," she said. "I went to see a friend."

"Are all your friends high Party officials? That car had a Kreisleiter's license plate."

"It's not what you think, Kraemer. He's in the Resistance."

"We are the Resistance," he said. "Only we seven. The others are dead or in prison waiting to die. Now tell me the truth. Who is your Nazi friend? I don't like the idea of walking into a trap."

"He's not a Nazi, and there's no trap. Honestly, he only wanted to help."

Kraemer said nothing for a moment. He seemed to want to believe her. "If he's no Nazi, what is he, an Allied agent?"

Margit said nothing.

"Then he's got to be a communist. They're as bad as the Nazis."

"They're not!" Margit replied defensively.

"So, that's what you are, a communist." Kraemer snapped harshly. "None of you can be trusted. I'll make sure you don't continue on this mission."

Not continue? What did that mean? Was he going to kill her? Margit had to think quickly. "All right, I'll tell you."

For a moment, Kraemer relaxed his grip and she turned, kicking him in the shin as hard as she could. Kraemer yelled in pain.

Margit swung the heavy wrench as hard as she could, hitting Kraemer a glancing blow across the skull, which opened a gash on his head. Stunned, he fell to his knees, and Margit used the opportunity to bring the wrench down on his head again and again with a sickening crunch until he lay motionless on the deck. Grabbing him by the foot, she dragged him to the edge of the deck and pushed him under the railing. Feeling sick, she tossed the wrench after him, then leaned over the rail and vomited.

As soon as she collected her wits, she found a fire bucket and splashed water on the patch of Kraemer's blood on the deck. Then she screamed, "Help! Help! Please, somebody!"

After a moment, Captain Zorndorf, Schindler, and some crewmen came running up.

"It's Kraemer," she gasped. "He fell overboard. I heard him call and he was gone. You've got to go back and find him."

"If he fell overboard," Zorndorf said, "he's already dead. In this water he wouldn't last ten minutes. Besides, I'm not going to jeopardize my ship for some idiot who didn't have brains enough to stay in his cabin. Everyone go below. I'll get your statement later, Fräulein."

"Oh, God." Margit threw herself into Schindler's arms, sobbing in relief. The tears were genuine, but they were not for Kraemer.

"The captain's right, Fräulein Hassel. There's nothing we can do. I'll take you to your cabin."

"Thank you," she said, between sobs. Schindler put Margit in her cabin and closed the door. He wondered how something so stupid could have happened to someone as careful as Kraemer. It didn't make sense. Could Kraemer have been pushed? On the way back to his own cabin he met Levinsky in the passageway.

"What's all the commotion?"

"Kraemer just fell overboard," Schindler said.

"I'm not sorry."

"You were the one with the motive, Professor. Did you push him?"

Levinsky laughed. "Can you imagine a bag of bones like me wrestling with Kraemer? Be serious."

"You could have shot him."

"Did anyone hear a shot?" Levinsky pulled his gun out of his coat, and offered it to Schindler. "Sniff it to see if it's been fired, then search me for a knife, Herr Ober-Detective."

Schindler ignored the professor's snide tone and returned to his cabin, locking the flimsy door behind him. Stripping off his boots and tunic, he slipped his automatic under his pillow and stretched out on the hard bunk. The atmosphere among the team members was thick with tension and distrust. What had he gotten into? It was so much simpler in combat. You had yourself and comrades you could trust against the enemy. It was all so clear. Life and death. He didn't sleep.

The sky remained overcast and the sea got rougher as the *Mayerling* zig-zagged in a random pattern, often seeking rain squalls to avoid detection by Allied aircraft and submarines. Thirty-six hours after leaving Lübeck, she berthed in Oslo. When unloading was underway Captain Zorndorf took Margit to the authorities so she could sign the affidavit concerning Kraemer's death. It took only a few minutes for the typist to tap out the form on a battered old machine as Margit dictated her story. When she was finished, the typist removed the carbons and asked her to sign all three copies. *So, that's it,* Margit mused. Three signatures and Erich Kraemer ceased to exist. She felt nothing.

When she returned to the ship, she was greeted by List, Levinsky, and Meiner, shivering over their luggage on the dock.

"Where's Schindler and Freitag?"

"They're at the airfield," Meiner told her. "But I don't think they'll be able to get an aircraft with the weather closing in like this. Our best bet is the train. All these supplies are headed for Vikmo."

Margit turned. Crate after crate marked "TO NORD GMBH, VIKMO, NORWAY" was already piled on the dock. Civilian laborers, under the watchful eyes of SS guards, loaded them on flatcars.

When Schindler returned, he confirmed Meiner's prediction. "They're completely fogged in both here and at Vikmo, so we'd better see about getting ourselves accommodations on the train."

"Is there any food?" Meiner asked.

"I was wondering the same thing," Margit said. "I'm starved."

"We should be able to find something. Fräulein Hassel, why don't you and Meiner take the truck and get some food. The driver should know his way around. Here's some money," he said, handing Margit a small wad of Reichsmarks. "We'd better spend it before it's no good."

"Is this enough to go to Paris?" she joked.

"They don't take Reichsmarks there any more," List told her.

"Well, you can't have everything. Come, Dieter, let's go find a nightclub." As they left she smiled at Schindler, who gave her a disapproving look.

Schindler found a warm building in which Levinsky and the others could watch the luggage and then went to see the transportation officer responsible for loading the train to Vikmo. The Scharführer in the front office officiously asked him to wait, but Schindler was now an expert in the game. Removing his orders from his coat, he tossed them on the Scharführer's desk so he could see the Reichsführer's signature.

"I'm Obersturmbannführer Schindler, and my team and I are on a special mission for the Reichsführer. I want transportation to Vikmo and I want it now!"

The Scharführer glanced at the signature, then stood to attention and clicked his heels. "At once, Herr Obersturmbannführer. I shall inform Untersturmführer Bulow immediately."

Picking up the orders, the Scharführer knocked on a door marked "NORD Transportation Officer" and opened it. There was a soft feminine shriek and a muffled "I told you I wasn't to be disturbed." Then the Scharführer mumbled, "Oh."

A plump brunette with her hair in disarray emerged from the office and, without looking at Schindler, sat at a desk and began typing.

Behind her emerged an overage Untersturmführer straightening his tunic, a spot of lip rouge at the corner of his mouth.

"Ah, Herr Obersturmbannführer Schindler," he said, extending his hand. "How may I. . ."

"Heil Hitler!" Schindler snapped a rigid straight-arm salute.

The Untersturmführer came to attention. "Heil Hitler. How may I be of assistance to you, Herr Obersturmbannführer Schindler?"

"As you can see by the orders, we need transportation to Vikmo immediately. My team consists of myself and five others, one of whom is a lady."

"A lady?"

"She is my secretary and a personal friend of the Reichsführer's wife." Schindler had decided that if he was going to lie, he would make it a big one.

"Of course," Bulow said, "but there's only the supply train and it's completely booked. Perhaps in a few days we could make up a special train . . ."

"The supply train will be fine."

Bulow smiled nervously. "But it's booked."

"Then unbook it!"

"Yes, Herr Obersturmbannführer, of course. I'll make the arrangements immediately."

"Thank you, Untersturmführer Bulow. I'll mention your cooperation to the Reichsführer personally when I return." Bulow beamed. *You idiot,* Schindler thought. *You wouldn't last five minutes on the Russian Front.* "Heil Hitler."

"Heil Hitler, Herr Obersturmbannführer."

By the time Margit and Meiner returned with enough food for the trip, the others were boarding the train's only passenger car. The train's platoon of forty guards normally occupied the entire seating area of the car, but with guests, they doubled up to make room. Margit was given the small compartment reserved for VIPs and at 1315 hours, January 19, 1945, the supply train began its last trip to Vikmo.

To guard against partisans and pilferage, two guards were constantly on duty outside on the flat cars. Because of the bitter cold, they could not be in the open for more than an hour, so there was a constant change of shift. Inside one of the cars an alert team with a machinegun remained awake and ready. The car was heated by a stove at each end, which burned coal stored in one of the open cars. Each guard coming off duty brought in a bucket of coal to keep the stoves going. The guards were issued assault rations, which they supplemented with food they purchased or "found," and they were allowed a glass of beer when they came off duty.

The highest-ranking man in the guard force was a non-commissioned officer. Except for Schindler, there were no officers on the train. Anyone familiar with the fierce reputation of the Waffen SS in battle would have laughed at the guards on the train. They were all men old before their time, used and cast away by an unfeeling Third Reich. A determined group of partisans could have easily destroyed the train, but with the surrounding population so totally dependent on it, no one dared damage the train or its cargo.

Schindler sat by the window. The few villages around Oslo were quickly left behind, revealing the endless snow-covered landscape that reminded him of Russia. The Ukraine was flatter, but it was still an inhospitable white void, one that covered equipment and the men, both living and dead. From a distance the war in the deep snow had a deceptive neatness. Shells gouged huge brown holes in the white carpet, which turned red with men's blood, and it always turned white again. The wounded often froze to death before they could be rescued, and then the snow covered them too.

In the spring the snow melted and men crawled out of the thick, padded suits they had worn for five months to greet the ruined equipment and the forgotten dead.

While remembering the events he had lived through, Schindler's melancholy took full possession of him and he looked over at Levinsky sitting by the stove. They had more in common than anyone realized. Both Germans, they had lost their country and their ideals. He got up and walked over to the stove.

"Pull up a stool, Herr Obersturmbannführer," Levinsky said blandly.

Will there always be a wall between us? the SS man wondered. "You know," Schindler said, "I'm beginning to think I ought to change my name. No one's called me anything but 'Obersturmbannführer' for years, except Lise."

"The girl in Celle?"

"Yes."

"I barely remember her."

"You were in pretty bad shape."

The professor shrugged. "Not as bad as some."

"You know, I think being cold is somehow a frame of mind," Schindler said, gazing out the window. Levinsky didn't reply. "You stay cold for so long that even in the summer you stand by a fire because the cold is embedded in your soul. But at least in Russia, we had some control over our own destinies not like that . . . that . . . "

"Death factory?"

"Yes. I wonder what history will say of us."

"Your Führer put it quite succinctly: 'Who after all remembers the Armenians?'"

"Why the Armenians?"

"Because the Turks tried to do to the Armenians in 1915 what you are now doing to the Jews. Fortunately for the Armenians, the Turks were not as efficient as the Germans."

"Will you tell me something, Professor?" Levinsky looked at him with his practiced neutral expression, which Schindler took as an affirmative. "Why did you come with us?"

"Did I have a choice?"

"I guess not. Why didn't you try to escape?"

"Perhaps I was in the camp so long I didn't even consider it. Besides, where could I go?"

"Could it be that you consider what we are doing worthwhile?"

"No. The only reason we are going to destroy this bomb is that you are afraid of what it will do to Germany. If you thought for a moment that you might be the exclusive owner of such weapons you would use them without hesitation." Schindler said nothing, and Levinsky continued. "And if we destroy this one, that doesn't mean that another one won't be built by someone else. If the Allies have such a weapon they might use it on us or the Japanese. Who knows? My only desire is survival. That's the only reason I've come this far."

He got up and returned to the bench he shared with List. Schindler was left to himself. First he wondered what was happening to his comrades in Das Reich, and then he wondered how high the bodies were piled in Belsen.

The journey to the railhead passed slowly and without incident. At last, the train pulled into a snow-covered siding where trucks were already lined up for their cargo. The guards dismounted and formed a perimeter as the men from Vikmo unloaded the train. A thin wisp of smoke from the nearby village was the only sign of civilization across the horizon. *Lamm has chosen his base well,* Schindler thought.

An officer wearing Obersturmführer sleeve insignia on a Norwegian parka dismounted from a truck and made his way to the passenger car. Entering the passenger area, he greeted Schindler cheerfully. "Heil Hitler," he said. "You must be Obersturmbannführer Schindler."

"Heil Hitler." Schindler returned the salute. "Yes, I am."

"Glad to meet you," the officer said disarmingly. "I'm Obersturmführer Friedrich Hammerstein." They shook hands.

"Glad to meet you, Obersturmführer. Why don't you stand by the stove?"

Grinning, Hammerstein moved to the stove. "I'd like to welcome you to Vikmo, or at least to the Vikmo railhead. The mine is another thirty-five kilometers up the road. It's not much of a road either. Obersturmbannführer Lamm would have been here himself, but none of the scientific types can be spared right now. They're getting ready for your inspection."

Schindler took out a pack of cigarettes and Hammerstein's eyes followed it. "Cigarette?"

"Thanks." Hammerstein took one gratefully. "We've been out for almost a week."

Schindler lit both their cigarettes and Hammerstein took a long satisfying drag.

"I suppose you're out of schnapps, too?"

Hammerstein nodded, and Schindler handed him a bottle that was still half-full. "Sorry, no glasses."

Hammerstein uncorked the bottle and tilted it back toward Schindler. "Prosit." He took a long drink before handing it back to Schindler. "Thank you, Herr Obersturmbannführer."

"Don't mention it. What's your function here, Hammerstein? I take it you're not a scientist."

"I'm the legal representative of NORD GMBH, chief errand boy, and supply officer," Hammerstein replied.

"What do the others do?"

Hammerstein held up his hand. "Don't ask me. The stuff they talk about when they're fiddling with their slide rules looks worse than the books of NORD GMBH. I hope you're not here to look at them."

Schindler laughed. "I can't balance a checkbook. I'm here to inspect the troops. Let me introduce you to the others. List, Meiner, Freitag, Professor Buchner, Fräulein Hassel, come out here. Our reception committee has arrived. Unfortunately Obersturmführer Kraemer fell overboard and was lost at sea."

Hammerstein nodded until he saw Margit. At the sight of the attractive young woman, he removed his hat, clicked his heels, bowed, and kissed her hand.

"Fräulein Hassel, may I welcome you as the first woman to visit Vikmo."

Margit smiled. "Thank you, Herr Ober . . ."

"For you, it's Fritz."

"All right."

"Should we get on the trucks now?" List asked.

"We'll be here loading until tomorrow morning, so you might as well stay put. Well, how was your trip?"

Schindler and his group looked at each other and then began to laugh. Hammerstein was puzzled.

"Sit down, Hammerstein." Schindler began to tell the story, leaving out the parts about the dead Gestapo agents.

"Sorry about your comrade," Hammerstein said. "I can't believe Zorndorf and the *Mayerling* are still afloat. What did he charge you for the passage?"

"Five hundred Reichsmarks."

"Five hundred Reichsmarks? That's pretty reasonable."

"Five hundred per person."

"Ah, that sounds more like Zorndorf. I'm surprised he didn't make you pay in Swiss francs. How bad are things in the Reich?" he asked. "None of us have been back in over a year. Every so often one of us gets to go to Oslo to meet the supply ship and escort the train back, but that's all."

"If you remember what it was like when you were there, it's ten times worse." Schindler said. "The Luftwaffe has been shot out of the sky, our U-boats can't move without being detected, and the army and SS are being pushed back to the borders of the Reich. I doubt if we can hold out another year."

Hammerstein looked very sober, but then he smiled. "I think things are about to change."

"Then you do have a new weapon," Margit said.

"Fräulein Hassel, if I told you, Obersturmbannführer Lamm would cut off my toes. He will have to explain what's going on. However, I will say this. If what we are doing here has any significance, Germany will win this war." Hammerstein said nothing else about the matter and left the car to oversee the loading of the trucks.

Dawn could hardly claim the name. It was only a dim twilight when Schindler got into the truck with Hammerstein. "Day is upon us," the Obersturmführer said.

"Is it always this dark?"

"Most of the time. We can travel now but not when it's really dark, because you can't see any terrain features to navigate by. We originally thought about putting sign posts up along the road, but Obersturmbannführer Lamm is a stickler for secrecy."

"Have you had any trouble with air raids or partisans?"

"Absolutely none. The Gestapo found some Norwegian with a radio set spying on the place a couple of years ago, but they shot him. The last time an enemy aircraft flew over was in '42. I imagine nothing ever came of it because we were trying to look like an archaeological site."

"Archaeological site?" Schindler pretended not to know.

"Yes. Remember that flap about the phony artifacts a few years ago?"

"Not really."

Hammerstein told Schindler the story of the first Operation Nord.

"That's why we named the holding company NORD GMBH. All the stock belongs to the Führer and to Reichsführer Himmler."

"I see."

Hammerstein and Schindler stopped talking a few kilometers from the railhead, and Schindler gazed at the white landscape, trying to keep from feeling sick. He had killed a lot of men in this war, every one of them an impersonal brown lump shouting in languages he couldn't understand. He suddenly realized that he would have to kill the man sitting next to him. Only Hammerstein was no lump. He was a cultured, urbane, and charming brother officer. And yet they were all responsible for camps like Belsen. He wished he didn't have to think about it. Slowly the little convoy bumped and rattled its way toward Vikmo, using up the four hours of twilight.

Walking over to the truck to greet Schindler, Lamm saluted with the obligatory "Heil Hitler. I'm Maximilian Lamm. Welcome to Vikmo."

"Heil Hitler. I am Heinz Schindler. I guess I'm supposed to say I'm happy to be here."

Lamm laughed heartily. "If you had, I'd have sent you to the army psychiatrist in Oslo, under guard."

From the few descriptions he had read Schindler had gotten the impression that Maximilian Lamm was larger than life, and now he understood why. In his uniform, the scientist was physically unimpressive, but he had an awesome presence that reflected his will. No wonder he had accomplished with a very small staff what no one else in Germany's scientific community had been able to do with large budgets.

"Bring your party inside, Herr Obersturmbannführer. I'd like you to meet my staff, and I'm sure they'd like to meet yours, especially the lady."

All of Lamm's assistants were lined up inside the L-IV shed, half of which was taken up by the Axels' workshop. The only reminder of the repeat L-IV experiment was the stainless steel cylinder, which was still in the pit, and the empty heavy water barrels. While Lamm's staff was fawning over Margit, Levinsky walked over to the pit. Lamm smiled. At least the man was interested in something other than the woman. He joined Levinsky at the edge of the pit.

"Most interesting," Levinsky muttered, looking around. "What is this for?"

"This was for our initial neutron experiment. It was a duplicate of the L-IV experiment in Leipzig. Are you familiar with it?"

Levinsky turned to face Lamm and smiled. "My dear Professor Lamm, to tell you the truth, I haven't done a thing in this field for over five years. I haven't the foggiest idea why they sent me. In my last position I was . . . er . . . overseeing excavation work."

Buchner was open and honest. Lamm liked him. "Typical of the bureaucracy, Professor Buchner. This evening you can borrow my files and catch up."

"That's most kind of you."

"Why don't we join the others and get a mutually satisfactory schedule arranged?" Lamm suggested.

"Wonderful."

"As a matter of fact, I was going to give everyone a tour of the entire installation tomorrow, but I'll have one of my officers give the others the tour and take you around to the most interesting areas myself. That's if Obersturmbannführer Schindler doesn't mind."

"Oh, I'm sure that can be arranged. Schindler's a little stiff and unscientific, but nonetheless a fine fellow." Despite himself, Levinsky found Lamm quite charming. He was looking forward to spending time with a fellow scientist who had unlocked one of nature's secrets.

Lamm smiled wryly. "I know exactly what you mean. I used to have a superior like that."

Schindler and Lamm agreed to start the inspection the following morning, in order to give them time to unload the convoy. The inspection team was given one of the smaller buildings for its quarters and office, while partitions were brought in to give Margit some privacy.

"I wish someone had told us that the 'Hassel, M.' on the message we received was a charming young woman," Lamm said. "We could have provided you with much better accommodations."

"It's quite all right, Herr Obersturmbannführer. We've been able to manage quite well under less fortunate circumstances," Margit told him. "This will do fine."

The first item on the agenda was lunch. They waited until the guards ate, then had the mess hall to themselves. The meal consisted of bread, canned ham, vegetables, and fruit.

"Do you always eat this well?" Schindler asked.

"Are you asking as an inspector or a gourmet?" Lamm asked.

Ordinarily Schindler would have appreciated the joke, but he decided it was time to play his role. Feigning irritation, he snapped at Lamm. "Herr Obersturmbannführer Lamm, I am here as an official representative of the Reichsführer SS. It is my duty to see that the soldiers of the SS are properly fed, clothed, and cared for. I have heard nothing but complaints about shortages since I arrived. Half of your personnel do not appear to have the proper overgarments. They may be warmly dressed, but a Reich eagle and sleeve insignia on a Norwegian parka is not a proper SS uniform."

Lamm looked at Schindler icily. *Another arrogant bureaucrat,* he thought. Buchner was right.

"Then in answer to your question, Herr Obersturmbannführer Schindler, we do not always eat this well, but no one here has starved. Beginning tomorrow morning I will have Obersturmführer Hammerstein take you around so that you can talk to every man personally and see our file of unfilled requisitions for clothing and equipment. Now if you will excuse me, I have work to do." He turned to Levinsky. "Professor Buchner, I will send someone over with the files. Good day."

List chuckled quietly as Lamm left. "You had me believing you were an inspector myself, Herr Obersturmbannführer."

"Let's hope they all believe it," Schindler said as they rose to return to their building. "I want everyone to be very critical of everything, except you, Professor. You'll have to play your own role."

"I understand."

CHAPTER 12

THOR

Vikmo
January 22, 1945

THE INSPECTION BEGAN WITH SCHINDLER'S tour of the barracks and the guard force. He noted every minor deficiency, from patches on trousers to holes in blankets.

"You'd think the meddling idiot was on the parade ground in Lichterfeld Barracks," Reinhart remarked after the evening meal. "Do you know they actually measured the heels on the guards' boots? They claim they're three millimeters too high. Then he asked if anyone at Vikmo had a proper SS uniform."

"That's nothing," Loring said. "That Scharführer List wrote so many deficiencies on the guards' weapons, I thought they were going to have to be junked. Where does he think we are?"

"I suppose it was inevitable," Lamm sighed. "Remember they're bureaucrats. It's all their petty minds can grasp. Just be thankful the Reichsführer didn't send a team of scientists to meddle with our work. Besides, they'll be gone soon, but before they do, we'll soon show them something that will make them forget every rust spot on a machine pistol and every missing button on a parka. Loring, I want you to take my personal files over to Professor Buchner."

"Yes, Herr Obersturmbannführer."

Meiner was sitting on his bunk writing his report on the filing system when Loring entered. Schindler's act and their subsequent nit-picking were working perfectly. Loring was as irritated as anyone could be at a group of bureaucratic paper-shufflers intruding upon his world.

"Yes?" Meiner said when Loring entered.

"Where is Professor Buchner? I have some papers for him."

"That's his bunk," Meiner said. "He'll be right back. He's using the head."

Loring gave Meiner a funny look, then laid the briefcase full of papers on the bunk and walked out. Grinning, Meiner noted that the troops at the site were not greeting their comrades with the proper salute and hearty, "Heil Hitler." It had always seemed so stupid.

Levinsky returned from the latrine and noticed the briefcase on his bunk. "What's this?"

"Loring left them. I think they're Lamm's papers.

"Oh." Levinsky sat on his bunk with his back against the wall. "Hmmm," he remarked on reading the results of Hahn's experiment. Soon he was in deep concentration.

"Professor," Schindler said, touching Levinsky on the shoulder. It took a moment for Levinsky to acknowledge Schindler.

"What? Oh, hello, Herr Obersturmbannführer."

"Would you like breakfast?"

"Breakfast?"

"It's 0700. Seven A.M. You've been reading all night."

"Oh, I . . . this is fantastic. Incredible. Mathematically everything checks."

"I don't understand."

Levinsky held up the ream of paper.

"After reading this file, I have no doubt that a uranium bomb is possible. Once the reactor is finished, it's merely a mechanical process. With this file and the proper materials, any nation could build one."

"Really, Professor?" Margit interjected, as she emerged from behind the partition.

"Oh, good morning, Fräulein Hassel."

"You mean that those are the instructions for a uranium bomb?"

"In a way, yes, Fräulein. All the theory has been resolved, but sometimes the mechanical difficulties and human concepts are insurmountable problems. Leonardo da Vinci is a typical example of what I mean. Da Vinci conceived the airplane, the parachute, and the tank, to name just a few things, but he didn't invent them. On the one hand his era did not possess the technological knowledge to build a tank that would work. On the other hand, even if he could have built a working aircraft, the people of his time thought that it was against God's will to fly. As a result they would not have let him build it. Do you follow me?"

"So far."

"Using the airplane as an analogy, this group of papers represents all the current theory in the field—all that we know anyway. All the problems of aerodynamic lift and stability have been solved mathematically, and the Wright Brothers are in the process of constructing their rather crude first 'aircraft.'"

"And?" Margit asked.

Everyone had gathered around the professor's bed. "And, while the Wright Brothers are tacking their bits of wire and linen to a wooden frame, Maximilian Lamm has drawn up the plans for a rocket to fly to the moon, and may have already built it."

The others were stunned.

"Don't look so shocked," he told them calmly. "Isn't this what we're here to find out?"

"Yes," Schindler nodded, after a long pause.

Levinsky sat up and put on his boots. "I'm hungry. Let's get some breakfast."

They went to the mess hall in a group, but Levinsky was the only one with an appetite. At eight Reinhart arrived to give Schindler and the rest of the group a tour of the area and as arranged, Levinsky went directly to Lamm's office in the large building next to the L-IV shed.

"Well Professor, how did you sleep?" Lamm asked.

"I didn't." Levinsky said. "It wasn't that I was uncomfortable. I stayed up all night reading your file. It's absolutely fascinating. I wasn't through with it so I left it in our barracks. If you don't mind, I'd like to finish it this evening."

"By all means," Lamm replied. "It's so pleasant being able to converse with a fellow scientist with some experience and depth. I'm not speaking ill of my assistants, by any means. What you are about to see today could not have been accomplished without them. Each one is quite brilliant in his own way, but they have the limitations of so many scientists."

"And those are?"

"They don't look beyond their fields of endeavor. It's as if they exist in a test tube, but don't know enough to crawl out of it, or even look through its glass walls."

Levinsky nodded. Lamm was correct in that regard.

"Come, I'll take you on a technical tour of this place. First, we'll go next door, then I'll take you into the mine. After that we'll have lunch and I'll take you to the test site."

"Test site?"

"Yes. I'll let you wait for that." Lamm had a grin on his face. "I want you to enjoy the surprise."

"Nothing you do would surprise me, Doktor Lamm," Levinsky told him truthfully. Regardless of the circumstances, Levinsky was fascinated by Lamm and his accomplishments. The man was not modest and had no reason to be. In his way Lamm was extremely honest. He freely admitted using other people's ideas, and vehemently criticized those whose limited foresight and imagination had not been able to give the Reich superior weapons before this.

"They are all prima donnas," Lamm explained. "Each scientist wants to work on his own little project, at his own snail's pace. God forbid you should ask them to accomplish something. They had the answer with L-IV and they messed it up. Come. Let me show you the mine."

They walked across the field to the mine entrance, the snow crunching softly beneath their feet. At the entrance to the mine, the guard recognized Lamm and gave him the Nazi salute and a crisp "Heil Hitler."

"We hardly saluted at all until your friend Schindler arrived," Lamm said.

"He's hardly my friend."

"Sorry, figure of speech. But, he's typical of the other problem."

"What problem?"

"He's the type that's holding Germany back," Lamm said, holding up his hand. "I know what you're going to say. He's a tank commander, brave to the point of insanity. Wounded in action, Knight's

Cross, etc., etc. But the battlefield is where he belongs, not investigating scientific projects. They don't expect us to fight their battles. Why should they interfere in our experiments?"

"I agree."

They entered the mine and started down the shaft. "You'll notice that it's warm in here."

"Yes."

"That's ODIN."

"ODIN?"

"That's the name Hammerstein gave to the uranium burner—'Father of the Gods' and all that. Charming fellow Hammerstein, but no scientific aptitude whatsoever. Turn right at the bottom of the shaft."

They entered the large chamber containing ODIN and Levinsky stared in wonder and awe at the shiny black wall of graphite blocks. The name "ODIN" stood out in large white letters. Walking over to the controls, Levinsky examined each meter and dial carefully.

Lamm continued his commentary. "We had an inspector from the Reichsleiter's office who thought that this was a large storage battery."

The witticism was lost on Levinsky, who stared in wonder at the reactor. For the first time since he had been sent to a concentration camp, he found his intellect stimulated. "Amazing. An infinite flow of neutrons. A controlled chain reaction."

"As you can see, Professor Buchner, our facilities are extremely limited. We had hoped to hook ODIN up to a generator for our own electric power, but it's near impossible to get anything in the way of heavy equipment from the Reich in the present circumstances. Lindner, put in the control rods to show Professor Buchner how well we can control ODIN."

Lindner complied and Levinsky watched in fascination as each of the dials witnessed the absorption of the neutrons. "Incredible."

Finally the instruments stopped humming and audible clicks could be heard as the reaction slowed. Levinsky sighed and shook his head as Lindner slowly pulled out the rods, causing the needles on the meters to rise. In a few seconds the instruments were humming again. Lamm took Levinsky for a walk on the platform above ODIN to see the configuration of the reactor.

"We're using the heat generated by the reaction to heat the mine.

In the summer we have to use water to cool it. That's what the pipes with the vanes are for. The water goes through the pipes and cools ODIN. After a few runs through we have more heavy water than we can use. We've been trying to get more uranium, but the scientists in the Reich have convinced Reichsminister Speer the SS shouldn't have any of the precious stuff. Fat lot of good they're doing with it."

"Tell me," Levinsky said, puzzled. "You're here to build a bomb, but you haven't shown me any isotope separation process. How can you build a bomb unless you have enough U-235?"

Lamm grinned. "Professor Buchner, I am so glad you're here. It's refreshing to find an inspector asking intelligent questions. Our last official visitor was a shoemaker. Since you asked, I'll have to spoil your surprise. We have built a bomb, two, in fact, but we don't use uranium."

"Don't use uranium?"

"No. We can't. We simply don't have the facilities to separate the isotopes of uranium. I imagine it would take some sort of gaseous diffusion process. That would take more money and equipment than the Reich could or would possibly invest. Bureaucrats don't believe in theories. That's why they never progress."

"If you don't use uranium, what do you use?"

"We called it 94 metal, because that's its atomic number. It's an element that does not occur in nature, but if you put uranium into a uranium burner, it slowly turns to 94 metal. The 94 metal is easy to separate because it's chemically different from the uranium. It's a lot easier than trying to separate chemically identical isotopes. Theoretically, the 94 is a more powerful explosive. We'll find out just how explosive tomorrow morning."

"What? You're actually going to explode a bomb tomorrow?"

"Of course," Lamm said, matter-of-factly. "I'm going to take you out to the test site this afternoon, and we're going to assemble one of the bombs. I'd like you to see it. I hope you're up to climbing a 30-meter tower."

"For that I'd climb a 100-meter tower."

Lamm and Levinsky ate lunch apart from the others.

"What did you say you were doing before this?" Lamm asked.

"I was doing stress tests on concrete roads in northern Germany."

That's as good a description as any for breaking rocks along the Autobahn, Levinsky thought.

"Too bad. I could have used you here. You were at Heidelberg before that, weren't you?"

Levinsky wondered if Lamm was testing him. "Yes. I did some isotope separation research with a Professor Levinsky."

"I've heard the name. There were two others, Bermann and somebody."

He was testing Levinsky. "Bergmann," he corrected. "And Geyer."

"I wonder what kind of work they're doing now."

"They're most likely dead," Levinsky replied "All three were Jews. They were dismissed in '39. They're probably all up the chimney, if you know what I mean."

"I know exactly what you mean. The Reich under Hitler had to pay a price for greatness, and the Jew happened to be it. Still, it was an incredible waste. The Fatherland must be intellectually the strongest nation on earth. Nothing else matters. All of that brainpower killed or run out of the country is inexcusable. The problem with the Nazis is they have no intellect or imagination. Take your case, for instance. I could have used you here. Instead they had you doing stress work on the Autobahn. Incredible."

"Yes, it was." Levinsky had passed the test, and he now gave Lamm his practiced neutral look. Lamm spoke of the dead and missing scientists as if they were a commodity, like steel or uranium, instead of human beings. Like so many Germans under the Third Reich, Lamm had lost his humanity. Levinsky wondered if Lamm realized it. Lamm's view of intellectual strength was equally disturbing. Science for its own sake with no regard for the consequences was a monster.

The long drive to the test site first took them to the bunker where Reinhart and Nachmann were making last-minute checks on the newly installed instruments before they went to the tower. "Where's Dietrich?" Lamm asked.

"He's up in the tower with a few of the guards, rigging a pulley for THOR."

"THOR?" Levinsky inquired.

"Hammerstein again. He names everything. The burner is ODIN, one bomb is THOR, and the other is LOKI."

"I see."

"When are you going to emplace THOR?" Lamm asked.

"In about fifteen minutes, Herr Obersturmbannführer," Nachmann replied.

"Good. I'll show Professor Buchner the other test facilities in the meantime."

The bunker was a concrete structure with several small windows that faced the area of the test tower. Hinged above each window was a pane of smoked glass designed to swing down and cover it.

"There's a high probability," Lamm explained, "that the flash will be tremendous, so we're using the smoked glass and dark goggles. There are two independently operated cameras to record the explosion."

"You speak as if there were no doubt in your mind that an explosion will occur."

"There isn't." Lamm's utter confidence was chilling.

Levinsky decided to test Lamm, using an improbable theory that had been raised in the late 1930s. "Aren't you afraid it might cause a chain reaction with the carbon atoms in the atmosphere?"

Lamm dismissed the question with a wave of his hand. "That's a preposterous theory, Professor. I'm surprised you paid any attention to it." From that point on, Levinsky instinctively knew Lamm was on the right track. Lamm showed Levinsky the rest of the bunker and the concrete-reinforced trenches outside. In one corner of the bunker a guard stood in front of a locked steel door. The guard snapped to attention and saluted as Lamm entered. "Heil Hitler!"

"Heil Hitler!" Lamm replied, irritably. "After Schindler leaves it will take six months to stop that business."

Levinsky chuckled and Lamm looked at him. "I apologize, Herr Professor, but it is funny when you think about it."

Lamm had to laugh, too. "Yes it is." He looked at his watch. "Reinhart, Nachmann, are you ready?"

Lamm's assistants appeared with the keys and the guard stood aside as they opened the door and retrieved the cylinder named THOR.

"It's heavy," Reinhart grunted. Lamm and Levinsky each took a handle and carried it to the truck, where Nachmann fastened it to the bed.

"We'll follow you," Lamm told them.

Even though the bomb had been developed for the most evil

regime the world had ever seen, Levinsky was excited at being on the threshold of a great new discovery. For good or ill, the world would never be the same if THOR worked.

The snow on the road was packed down from the numerous trips made to and from the test bunker to the tower, which looked foreboding as they drove up to its base. Levinsky stared at it for a second, intimidated by its height, but the thought of watching them emplace the bomb made him forget his apprehension, and he stepped gingerly onto the ladder. Lamm moved quickly up the ladder behind him.

On the ground, the guards helped Reinhart and Nachmann unload the bomb from the truck, fasten it to a sling, and manually pull it up to the top of the tower. The gray lead cylinder passed Levinsky as he climbed the last ten meters.

"Hello, Professor," Dietrich said, giving Levinsky a hand into the shed on top of the tower. "Welcome to the top of Norway."

Once inside, Dietrich took Levinsky around the tower and pointed out everything that could be seen from it. There were several abandoned villages at different distances from the tower, which would enable them to judge the dissipation of the bomb's effects. They stood aside as Nachmann and Reinhart reached the top and hauled the bomb onto its cradle. THOR was disassembled, the lead disc removed, and THOR rapidly reassembled, minus the detonators. The bomb was then securely bolted to the cradle.

"For safety reasons, the detonators won't be placed into the bomb until tomorrow morning," Dietrich explained.

"Until tomorrow, then," Lamm said, motioning Levinsky to the ladder.

"Well, Professor?" Lamm asked, glancing back up the tower.

"Professor Lamm, you have no idea how much I'm looking forward to tomorrow."

Lamm was beaming as they climbed into the truck for the return trip.

Schindler and the others were waiting impatiently for Levinsky to return.

"Thank God you're all right," Margit sighed as Levinsky walked through the door. "We didn't see you at all this afternoon."

"There was no need to worry. I spent the day with Professor Lamm."

"They took us on a tour, but we didn't understand half of it," List divulged.

"I went out to the test site. We are going to witness something incredible tomorrow."

"What?"

"The world's first man-made uncontrolled chain reaction."

"You mean they have the uranium bomb?" This time it was Schindler who was curious.

"Yes and no."

"What do you mean by 'yes and no'?"

"Yes, they have a bomb, and no it isn't made with uranium."

"What?"

"Never mind, it's a small point," Levinsky said, lying back on his bunk. "I'm very tired. Thirty meters is a long way to climb."

"Perhaps we ought to destroy the place tonight," Meiner said.

"No," Levinsky snapped. "We could never get both bombs. They're far away from here. Besides, we still don't know if they'll work. Why put everyone in danger when we don't know?" He closed his eyes. "I'm so tired."

"What's Lamm really like?" Freitag asked earnestly.

The question woke Levinsky up. He opened his eyes and propped himself up on one elbow. "Right now Obersturmbannführer Maximilian Lamm is the most dangerous man on planet Earth. He is excessively brilliant, and yet he is absolutely amoral."

"Typical Nazi," Meiner muttered.

"No, my dear Meiner. That's where you're wrong. He's not a Nazi in the philosophical sense. He has a view of the Fatherland that can only be called fantasy. For him, it is only important that Germany be strong intellectually. That is all. He is also urbane and charming, but he has no warmth or human substance. He would kill the Führer tomorrow if he thought it would create the kind of Germany he envisions."

"What do you propose we do?" Schindler wanted to know.

"Wait and see what happens tomorrow."

"Are you delaying this because you're curious to see whether this works?"

Levinsky smiled and lay back on the pillow. In a moment he was asleep.

January 24, 1945

Levinsky and Schindler were the only two members of the inspection team allowed in the test bunker, arriving shortly after the tests began at 0500. Dietrich and two of the guards went to the tower to install the detonators, and returned to the bunker forty-five minutes later. The technicians made a final check of the circuits and cameras, while the others screwed the smoked glass down over the windows and put on their dark goggles.

At 0629 hours, January 24, 1945, Maximilian Lamm pressed the firing switch, and the world's first atomic bomb flashed in the dark Norwegian morning. Even those observing through dark glasses and smoked glass were dazzled. The ground trembled, and a few seconds after the blast the deafening roar reached the bunker, along with the first shock wave. Everyone stopped what he or she was doing to watch the glowing fireball lift skyward. A column of smoke thrust up into the center of the cloud, giving it a mushroom shape. In the bunker and in the trenches of the test site Schindler and the members of his team stood in awe at the raw power THOR unleashed. Gradually they noticed incongruous sounds amid the rumbling. At first there was cheering, but as the roaring subsided it was replaced by singing. The SS were singing a song of victory. It was the "Horst Wessel Song," the anthem of the Nazi Party.

"*Die Fahne Hoch, die Reihen fest geschlossen.*
SA marschiert mit ruhig festem Schritt.
Kameraden die Rotfront und Reaktion erschossen,
Marschieren im Geist in unseren Reihen mit!"
("Raise up the flag, and firmly close our ranks.
Storm troopers march with firm and steady stride.
Comrades killed by reactionaries and the Reds.
In spirit march with us side by side!")

THOR's fireball rose majestically, its internal fire lighting the sky, riveting the attention of everyone in the bunker and the trenches except Levinsky, who watched it with a strange detachment. To the soldiers it was an awesome weapon that would decide the war, but Levinsky and Lamm knew it was more than that. With the flip of a switch Professor of Physics Doktor Maximilian Lamm had changed the world and pushed an unwilling mankind into a new age. No matter what von Rittburg or Schindler did, the clock could not be turned back. Killing Lamm and his team might prevent the Nazis from using it, but the Americans or Soviets would eventually discover the atom's secrets also.

The thought of the Soviets brought Levinsky back to his surroundings. The pandemonium and the singing had ceased as technicians diligently recorded the readings of the instruments in the bunker. Levinsky looked away from THOR to observe Lamm. The father of this awesome thing did not shout or sing. He watched the fireball intently, with an expression of cold satisfaction.

Noticing Levinsky's gaze Lamm turned and smiled. "Well, Professor Buchner, are you still skeptical?"

"It's difficult to be skeptical when you're confronted with irrefutable evidence."

Lamm chuckled. "We have merely opened the door on one of nature's tiny secrets."

"And also Pandora's box." Levinsky was prodding Lamm, although the other man did not realize it.

"Professor, I like you, but like so many others you want to impose ethical and moral considerations on science by saying this is good or that is bad. The Christians, the Nazis, the Communists, they all do it. It's stupid and childish."

"What would the world be without moral considerations?" Levinsky asked him.

"You've missed my point, Professor. I'm not saying that we don't need moral considerations. Marx was correct when he said that religion was the opiate of the masses. We need that sort of control, but morality adapts to science, not the other way around. The vaccination for smallpox was proscribed by the Church. What good did that do? Now the Church encourages vaccinations. Look at Schindler."

The Obersturmbannführer was riveted to the spot, mesmerized by THOR's radiant sphere. With beads of perspiration covering his brow, he was oblivious to everything but the demonstration of raw, naked power before him. Schindler was terrified, not only for himself but for Lise. They must never be allowed to use anything like this on her.

"He's awestruck," Lamm continued. "His puny mind cannot cope with what he is seeing. Were it for the likes of him, we wouldn't be this far along. And this is only the first step."

"What's next?"

"A fusion bomb that will make THOR look like a New Year's Eve firecracker. With the proper resources we could have it in two years. Let me show you." Levinsky followed Lamm as he made his way around the technicians in the crowded bunker and into the office adjoining the instrument room. On the desk were several pages of calculations, which Lamm put in order before handing them to Levinsky. A cursory check was all he needed to confirm Lamm's statements.

"Dear God," Levinsky said. "You're right."

"God has nothing to do with it, Professor." Lamm's voice was calm and cool.

"You're probably correct there, as with most things, Professor Lamm, but haven't you overlooked one important item?"

"I don't think so," Lamm assured him. "To what do you refer?"

"To put it quite bluntly," Levinsky said, "the Allies own the air. The chance of a bomber getting through to the target, which, I assume, is London, is minimal."

Lamm's face erupted into a broad smile. "That's what I meant about my assistants' limitation. You're the only one, besides myself of course, to consider the delivery problem."

"Considering it doesn't alter the fact that the bomber will most likely be destroyed over its own airfield."

Lamm was still smiling. "We're not going to use a bomber, Professor."

"I don't understand," Levinsky said, puzzled. "Once this bomb is shielded and put into an aerodynamic shell with the proper fuses, it will weigh nearly a ton. A fighter with that kind of load would be more vulnerable than a bomber."

"Professor," Lamm chided, his voice tinged with condescension, "we are not going to use an aircraft. There is only one thing suited for this task."

"And that is?"

"A guided missile, the V-2," Lamm said simply. "It travels at three times the speed of sound and cannot be detected except by the most advanced radar. Even if it is detected, it cannot be intercepted. The only way to stop a V-2 is to bomb it on its launch pad, and that, Professor Buchner, the Allies have failed to do."

"Why is that?"

"Because the launchers move constantly."

"I've heard it's not too accurate."

"It's accurate enough to hit London, and with the power of these bombs that's all we need. Once London is destroyed, the Allies will beg for a negotiated peace."

"What if the Allies also have a 94 bomb? Won't they retaliate?"

"Bah!" was Lamm's reply. "If they had it they would have used it. We must strike first."

Levinsky made no comment. After a certain point discussion with Lamm was useless.

"I hope you won't think me rude," Lamm told him, "but I have to send you and Schindler back to Vikmo. We have a great deal of work to do and you and Schindler would only be in the way. I'll fill you in on the details later."

"Thank you. I fully understand. Besides, we do have a report to complete for Reichsführer Himmler. It's a pity that he couldn't have been here personally," Levinsky said. *Too bad he couldn't have been right under it,* he thought to himself.

Lamm looked at him as if he knew what Levinsky was thinking. "Of course," was all he said.

Schindler was still shaken as they climbed into the truck.

"How did you like that?" the driver said, grinning. "I'll bet Obersturmbannführer Lamm takes the next one to London and shoves it up that Jew Churchill's behind personally."

"Of course," Levinsky said.

Neither Levinsky nor Schindler said anything else as the driver rambled on about the final victory of the Reich. Schindler asked the driver to let them off near the airfield.

"Do you want me to wait, Herr Obersturmbannführer?"

"No, they need you back at the test bunker right away."

"Yes, Herr Obersturmbannführer. Heil Hitler."

"Heil Hitler."

As the truck drove away, Schindler took a deep breath of the cold twilight air. He was trembling. "I hope it's no inconvenience, but I need to walk."

"It's no inconvenience," Levinsky told him. "Did the explosion disturb you?"

"I can't . . . it's absolutely incredible," Schindler stammered. "It's not only the explosion, it's everything. Admiral Canaris, Uncle Uwe, Belsen, and now this. Man and nature have gone insane. I'm not at all religious, I never have been, but when that thing went off, I thought the world was coming to an end, and I wanted to get down on my knees and beg forgiveness. It was like the gates of Hell opening up." There were tears in his eyes.

"Let's go get some lunch," Levinsky said. "You'll feel better."

Schindler stopped. "Lunch? How can you be so calm?" he screamed. "That thing is evil and you're talking about lunch?"

"Shut up!" Levinsky yelled, slapping Schindler across the face. The Obersturmbannführer's eyes popped open and he blinked. "Get hold of yourself, Schindler!"

The SS man blinked again.

"Are you all right?" Levinsky asked.

"Yes." Schindler took a deep breath. "Thank you."

"Then gather your wits about you. That 'thing,' as you call it, is nature, and man is learning to control it. It is neither good nor evil. It's like a pistol. You can use it to commit a crime or support a just cause. It remains a pistol. The user may be good or evil, but the pistol remains a pistol. Lamm and his comrades now have an extremely powerful pistol, and it is up to us to keep them from using it."

Schindler, unable to refute Levinsky's logic, looked at the professor and sighed. "Let's go back to the barracks."

The others were waiting for them, and one look at their faces convinced Levinsky they were as shaken as Schindler by the detonation.

"Are you two all right?" Margit asked, her voice quivering slightly.

"Yes, we're fine," Levinsky told her.

"It was terrible," she said.

"How much explosive did they actually use?" Meiner asked.

"The bomb could have been carried by four of us with little difficulty," the professor told him. "It was no trick."

"It's hard to believe," List said. "I can understand why they were so terrified of gunpowder in the Middle Ages."

"I think we should act tonight," Schindler insisted, regaining his composure.

"I agree completely." Levinsky was relieved Schindler was returning to normal.

"Thank you, Professor. You don't know how much I appreciate your help."

"You're most welcome. Shall we have lunch?"

"Yes, let's all get a good meal and return here. We have a lot to do."

CHAPTER 13

THE COMMANDOS

Vikmo

LAMM STOOD AT THE DOOR of the control bunker as Reinhart returned from his tour of the destroyed area. "Well?"

"Absolutely fantastic, Herr Professor." Lamm's assistant was grinning from ear to ear.

"Let's go inside. I want all the details."

Once the two were inside the bunker, Reinhart reported his findings. "Basically, it's what you predicted, Herr Professor. The point of detonation is still too radioactive for us to approach, but the tower was completely vaporized and there is a crater approximately thirty-five meters across by twenty meters deep. We'll get the actual measurements as soon as the radiation is at a safe level."

"What about the villages?"

"It's difficult to tell anything in the two villages within two kilometers of the detonation point. Only the stone foundations are left, but in the others most damage was caused by vertical stress overloading from forces of about .3 kilograms per square centimeter over-pressure or higher. Below that, damage decreases dramatically."

"Thermal damage?"

"These are only hand calculations with a slide rule, but slightly beyond one kilometer from the detonation we had about fifty gram calories per square centimeter. This drops very rapidly to a factor of three gram calories about two kilometers from the detonation point. Of course, we have no information on what any of this will do to humans."

Lamm smiled grimly. "We'll let the British do that."

"Nevertheless," Reinhart continued, "there was a tremendous amount of damage done by fire. Although some structures were ignited directly by the blast, most were damaged by the contents like the furniture bursting into flames. The entire area is blackened, even though it was covered by more than a meter of snow before the blast. In a major city, there would have been serious fires within a two-kilometer radius from the point of detonation."

"This will make them pay for Dresden," Dietrich interjected.

Lamm ignored the remark. "Is there anything else?"

"Not until our camera crews process the film. Were the inspectors impressed?"

Lamm chuckled. "You should have seen that dunce, Schindler. He nearly crapped his pants."

"What about Buchner?" Nachmann asked.

Lamm shrugged. "He's a scientist. He doesn't worry about Norwegian parkas and missing buttons."

Schindler's team went to the mess hall together and, except for three off-duty guards drinking tea, had the place to themselves. Only Levinsky enjoyed his meal and felt like talking. The rest just quietly picked at their food and absent-mindedly watched while the cooks packed food in thermal containers for transportation to the test site. When they returned to their barracks Schindler explained his plan.

"Meiner and List, you stand at each end of the barracks to ensure we're not interrupted. Speak out if you see anyone coming. If you do I'll go into a tirade about the inspection. I know the explosion was pretty awesome and affected most of us. Is everyone all right?"

They nodded.

"We have to break into three groups of two in order to have the flexibility to do what's necessary. List and Meiner will be in the first section, Fräulein Hassel and Freitag the second, and the professor and I will make up the third. Since there are so few of us and everything is so spread out, we will execute the plan in two phases.

"List and Meiner, you will go out to the control bunker and destroy the second bomb. Make some excuse to go out there this afternoon to familiarize yourselves with the route and layout and come right back. Don't hang around or arouse suspicion. At 2200, return to blow up the bomb. You will have to eliminate the guards, so take two pistols with silencers and one machine pistol. For the bomb, use one kilogram of the explosive, with a mechanical detonator set for an hour. The rest of us will wait here until Meiner and List return or until 2400, then Group One will attack the guard barracks, Group Two will attack the L-IV shed and the workshop, while the Professor and I take the mine. Do any of you know any English?"

"A few words," Freitag said.

"A little," Meiner nodded.

List shrugged.

"Shout English words, whatever you can, to make them think they're being attacked by British commandos. At the same time yell that commandos are attacking. Remember, we must get all of them. After the attack we'll meet at the airfield. Oh, don't destroy any of the trucks unless someone tries to get away. If for some reason we're not rescued by the Luftwaffe, we'll have to drive to the railhead."

"When should we start?" Meiner asked, gesturing to List.

"Leave as soon as you can. Just be back here by 2400. If for any reason there's a foul-up, the remaining four will have to do the job alone."

"We could use some hand grenades," Freitag suggested.

"I'll see what I can do," List said. "I'm supposed to inspect the ammunition today. I think they may have some."

"Good," Schindler said. "Remember, surprise and coordination are our best chances for survival. Are there any questions?" There were none, and Schindler looked at each of them. They understood what they had to do. "We'd better get back to inspecting," he said.

One by one they drifted to their bunks and put on their parkas.

Levinsky couldn't suppress a shiver of excitement. Since he no longer had any duties, he made himself comfortable and began reading the rest of Lamm's notes, which were logically and clearly done. Lamm had that rare combination of intelligence, organization, and determination that made men great. THOR was proof positive of Lamm's capabilities, and his point about the V-2 proved that his genius pervaded every aspect of the problem. It was a shame his intellect was so cold and unfeeling, because he could have done so much good. Unfortunately, for Lamm science and intellectual power had become ends themselves, and he would happily set the world ablaze and cause untold human suffering just to prove one of his theories. Human beings were not a factor in his equations and for that he, along with his Nazi superiors, had to be destroyed.

Levinsky suddenly realized that he had been staring at the same page for sometime and that Margit was speaking to him.

"Professor, are you all right?"

"Oh," he said, looking up at her. "Yes, of course. I was just absorbed in my reading."

"I'm going to the mess hall for some tea," she said. "Would you like me to bring some back for you, too?"

"Yes, Fräulein. That would be most kind, thank you." Levinsky watched Margit leave the barracks. There was another problem he intended to solve.

Lamm was sitting at his desk in the control bunker comparing his calculations to the test results of Reinhart's initial report when Nachmann entered with a sheet of paper from the Teletype.

"Herr Obersturmbannführer, I hate to disturb you, but this is important."

"What is it?"

"The weather report from the Navy meteorological station."

Lamm took the report and read it carefully. "Ach," he said, then called for Dietrich, who appeared immediately at the door. "Find the pilot and tell him to get the Junkers ready. We have to fly LOKI out right away. There's a gale heading this way."

"Yes, Herr Obersturmbannführer."

"What time is it?"

"It's about 2000."

"I'm starved."

"No wonder. You haven't eaten since breakfast," Dietrich said. "Your lunch is still in the container."

Lamm looked in the container and made a face. "Cold noodles. You'd think this was the Russian Front! Let's go to the mess hall and have a decent supper. Then we can move LOKI."

Nachmann followed Lamm to the truck. The twilight had turned to darkness again. "Do you want the inspectors to fly out with LOKI, Herr Obersturmbannführer?" Nachmann asked.

"No. They can get another aircraft or take the train. I'm taking LOKI to Germany personally."

"Wouldn't it be safer to go by ship?" Nachmann asked.

"Yes, but we can't afford the time. The Russians are already in East Prussia."

"Of course, Herr Obersturmbannführer."

Lamm and Nachmann got in the truck and drove to the mess hall. Loring and Hammerstein were already there and Reinhart and Dietrich came in shortly after.

"Lindner is on duty with ODIN," Dietrich said. "I'll replace him right after I eat."

"Where are the inspectors?" Lamm asked.

"They already ate," Loring told him. "Strange lot. Especially Meiner."

"What's so strange about him?" Nachmann asked.

"I didn't notice it at first, but he keeps referring to the latrine as the 'head.' That's a navy term."

"I wouldn't worry too much about that," Hammerstein said. "We're getting a lot of transfers from the navy these days."

"I suppose," Loring said. "Still . . ."

For a moment Lamm thought about investigating Loring's suspicions, but he had to get the bomb out tonight, and there was so much to do. "Hammerstein's right, Loring," Lamm added. "I asked Buchner about Heidelberg, and he knew the people who were there and what their fields were. You've just been at Vikmo too long."

"You're absolutely correct. Herr Obersturmbannführer, does that mean I get a leave?"

"No, but you can go to Oslo and return with the next supply train."

"I'll take it." Loring smiled, but he wasn't convinced. Navy or not, SS training would have driven that nautical crap out of anyone in a short time. There had to be a way to make sure the inspectors were who they said they were without making Schindler and his crew suspicious or making Lamm and the officers angry.

The cooks brought the meal to the officers' table and Lamm inhaled. "Let's eat. I'm starved. Now, you unscientific folk, what do you think of THOR?"

"It wouldn't have worked without the name," Hammerstein pontificated, "or this." He produced a bottle of schnapps, and began filling the glasses on the table. "Here's to the Führer, to ultimate victory, and the man who made it possible," Hammerstein said, holding his glass high. "Obersturmbannführer Lamm."

"Obersturmbannführer Lamm," they repeated in unison. They began to sing and Loring joined them, but he glanced at the door, wondering what to do.

Margit and Levinsky acted as lookouts as the others opened up the luggage, carefully removed the linings, and took out the centimeter-thick padding of plastic explosive attached to the top and bottom of each suitcase. List cut it up into the proper-size charges while Meiner removed the mechanical timers, fuses, and blasting caps from Kraemer's bag. Freitag screwed silencers on the pistols.

"Once the shooting starts, no matter what the cause, we go into action immediately," Schindler instructed. "You all know your assignments. We will be able to meet at the airfield at 0030 hours, or thirty minutes after the attack begins if it doesn't go on schedule."

Meiner pulled a box out from under his bunk. "They only had six hand grenades," he said, "but they also had some American thermite incendiary grenades."

"Those are wonderful weapons," List said. "We captured some of them in France. They'll burn anything."

"Good. How do they work?" Margit asked.

List picked up one of the red cylinders in his right hand. "Just pull the ring," he said. "As long as you hold down the lever, nothing will happen. You can even put the pin back in the little hole and it's safe again. As soon as you release the lever, the striker flips over and hits the primer. That starts the powder train and three to five seconds later it shoots burning thermite from the bottom. It doesn't explode, so you can just lay it on top of something and walk away from it. Got that?"

"Yes," Margit said, weakly. Suddenly dizzy, she put her hand to her head and sat down.

"Are you all right?" Schindler asked.

Margit nodded her head. "It's probably a cold coming on or something I ate. Believe me, I'll be fine for the fireworks."

"Good. I want each of us to take one grenade."

Dietrich went to the mine to relieve Lindner while Hammerstein held court speculating on Churchill's expression when LOKI exploded in London. Schindler, lying awake in his bunk, could hear the laughter all the way from the barracks. Hammerstein stood on the chair with the fingers of his right hand raised in a "V" and his left holding a cigar. "All I can promise you," he said in a thick British accent, "is blast, heat, and radiation. If the empire should last for a thousand years, which I doubt, they will say, never have so many been killed by so few."

Ignoring the raucous laughter, Lamm turned to Nachmann and asked the time.

"It's 2137," he said, tears of laughter running down his cheeks.

"Let's get LOKI out of the control bunker," Lamm said. "It will take some time to get it the airfield and I want to make sure everything is ready before we go to bed."

"Yes, Herr Obersturmbannführer." He was still laughing as he put on his parka.

"Carry on," Lamm told them. "We're going to get LOKI and come right back."

Nachmann was still laughing, so Lamm offered to drive. "In your condition we're liable to end up at the North Pole."

"I'm sorry, Herr Obersturmbannführer, but Fritz sounds just like Churchill."

"I know. That's what scares me."

After they drove a short way, Nachmann stopped laughing and yawned.

"Are you all right?"

"With all the laughing I forgot how tired I was. As soon as we get LOKI loaded, I'm going to crawl into bed for a week."

"We're all tired, but we have to get LOKI out of here before that storm hits. Otherwise we won't be able to leave for a week."

"Whom will you take with you?"

"Reinhart, I think." Lamm said. "He's a scientist, and he knows as much about the uranium bomb as any of us. I can leave him with Brigadeführer Kammler, who is the head of the V-2 program, so he can answer any questions. Also, I can spare him, but I can't spare you or Lindner, and I need Dietrich for the calculations."

"Ernst is a good man," Nachmann agreed.

"He's also good at translating scientific information into layman's terms. He even made Hammerstein and Loring understand what we were doing."

Nachmann yawned again and Lamm followed suit.

"Stop that, or you'll put us both to sleep."

Nachmann stifled another yawn.

List and Meiner made a final check of their gear.

"All set?" Schindler asked.

"If we're not now, we never will be," Meiner told him.

"Good luck," Freitag whispered.

"Yes," Margit said.

"How do you feel?" List asked her.

"Much better. I took a short nap."

"Get going. It's nearly 2200," Schindler ordered.

List and Meiner left the barracks. With their boots crunching in the snow, they walked across the compound to the motor pool looking for the same truck they had used in the afternoon, because it ran well.

"There it is," Meiner said. "Right where we left it."

"Did you notice that it has a Wehrmacht license plate?"

"Yes, now that you mention it. Nothing here really belongs to the SS. It's all Luftwaffe, Wehrmacht, or Kriegsmarine."

"These people must be the biggest thieves in the Reich." Meiner climbed into the driver's seat and started the engine. "Plenty of gas," he said.

Climbing in next to him, List let out a big sigh. "Let's go."

Putting the truck in gear, Meiner headed for the test bunker. "Stefan?"

"Yes, Dieter?"

"Have you killed a lot of men?"

"Enough."

"What's it like?"

"Depends. Sometimes it's a game and you enjoy the hunt. Sometimes you're fighting for your life and you don't even think about it. Sometimes you have to kill some poor man who doesn't have a chance, but it has to be done."

"I've never killed anybody," Meiner said.

"Hah. You were on a destroyer in a battle, and later you loaded those U-boats with torpedoes and sent them out. Those weren't just ships they sent to the bottom."

"I suppose you're right, but for me it's never been face-to-face."

"Don't think about it. You'll feel depressed after the first time. That's natural. You only have to worry if you start to like it."

Meiner looked at him and said nothing.

Lamm pulled the truck up to the test bunker, and the guard saluted. "Good evening, Herr Obersturmbannführer."

"Good evening. Help us get the bomb on the truck. We want to fly out first thing in the morning."

"My Scharführer has the key. I'll get him."

The Scharführer was in the instrument room and the other guard was standing in front of the locked steel door. The Scharführer stood at attention, clicked his heels and reported, "Everything in order, Herr Obersturmbannführer."

"Good. Help us get the bomb out. I want to keep it at the airfield tonight."

The Scharführer unlocked the door and held it open while Lamm, Nachmann, and the two guards lifted LOKI by the handles and carried it to the truck.

"Can we get some sleep now, Herr Obersturmbannführer?" the Scharführer asked.

"Yes, but one guard must stay awake to guard the instruments."

"Yes, sir. Heil Hitler!" He gave the Nazi salute.

"Heil Hitler!" Lamm returned the salute. *Those inspectors,* he thought. *It will take me another two months to stop this nonsense.*

"I'll drive," Nachmann told him.

"All right." As tired as the rest of his staff, Lamm dropped off to sleep before they had gone a kilometer. He didn't see the other truck as it passed.

"I wonder who that was," Nachmann said, absentmindedly.

"What?" asked Lamm, now partially awake.

"Never mind, Herr Obersturmbannführer. It's not important."

Meiner and List wondered the same thing as they passed the truck containing LOKI. Meiner drove right to the door of the test bunker.

"Who's there?" called the guard.

"Night inspection," Meiner replied, dismounting from the truck. "Heil Hitler."

"Heil Hitler," the guard replied cheerlessly. "I thought the inspection was finished."

"Not until tomorrow morning."

Meiner and List walked over to the guard, notebooks in hand.

"Are you the only guard?"

"Oh, no. The Scharführer and the other guards are inside asleep."

"What's your tour of duty?" Meiner continued.

"Two hours."

"Do you get a night meal?"

"If you call assault rations a night meal." The guard was completely relaxed and trying to see what Meiner was writing in his notebook, so at first he didn't see List pulling his pistol. Then he must have seen something in his peripheral vision, because he turned his head just as List pulled the trigger. The gun made a dull thump, the guard's head jerked back, and he collapsed in a heap, the side of his head a bloody pulp. Meiner looked at the steam rising from the warm blood as it flowed out on the snow.

"I forgot to ask him his name," he muttered, realizing he had not followed the proper inspection procedure.

"Let's go," List whispered, pulling him by the sleeve.

Cautiously entering the bunker, they moved quietly to the guard's sleeping area. Only one man was in his bunk asleep. Meiner put his pistol behind his back and leaned over the man. He shook his shoulder.

"Hey," he said, "where's the other man?"

"Uh, latrine, I guess."

"Thanks."

List's gun thumped twice and the man jerked. Meiner, intent on the man in the bunk, didn't see the Scharführer return.

"What is going on here?" the Scharführer shouted. Meiner whirled and pulled the trigger, the Scharführer's body jerking each time the gun thumped, until the magazine was empty.

"Very good, but you don't to use a full magazine."

The Scharführer, now lying back across a chair, stared glassily at the ceiling as blood poured from his wounds. Trembling, Meiner bent over and closed his eyes.

"Forget that," List told him. "Let's set the charges on the bomb and get back to the mine."

Snapping out of his daze, Meiner followed List to the vault room, where he stopped and stared at the open door.

"It's gone." Meiner's mouth gaped open. "My God, where could it be?"

"That truck we passed. They must be taking it to the airfield."

"We have to tell Schindler," Meiner told him.

"Get the guards' weapons and ammunition," List ordered. "I'm going to get the explosive and blow this place anyway."

"Good idea." Meiner collected three machine pistols and six magazines from the corpses, as List set the fuse for an hour and a half and placed it on the control panel.

"We've got to hurry. The others have to know something's wrong."

Meiner tossed the weapons in the back of the truck and got behind the wheel. He hit the accelerator as soon as the truck started, spraying dirty snow over the body of the first guard.

Nachmann pulled up to the Junkers 52, and the stop woke Lamm.

"What happened?" Lamm said, groggily.

"Nothing, Herr Obersturmbannführer. We're at the airfield."

"Oh, I must have dozed off," Lamm said. He stretched and yawned. "I'm stiff."

"No wonder, the way you were sleeping."

Lamm climbed down from the truck and walked stiffly to the aircraft. The ice-cold air cleared his head and he reached for the door handle. It was locked. Lamm stalked back to the truck. "The cursed thing is locked. We need the pilot or crew chief. Do you know where they are?" he asked Nachmann.

"They're staying next to the L-IV shed, on the opposite end of the building from our offices and quarters."

"I hope they're sober. Let's go find them."

Sitting in the mess hall while the others drank and joked, Loring's restlessness grew until he had to do something. After too many drinks, he had decided it was time to inspect the inspectors.

Nachmann stopped the truck in front of the crew's quarters and then went inside to find the aircrew, but the building was empty. He returned to the truck. "There's no one there," he told Lamm.

"They're singing in the mess hall, let's try there," Lamm told him. "I'm so cold I could use a cup of something hot—even if it's only soup."

"I'll drink to that," Nachmann said.

A figure staggered in their headlights as they drove to the mess hall.

"It's Loring," Nachmann said. "Looks like he's fortified."

Loring weaved his way across the compound, avoiding the truck as it went by. With some difficulty, he climbed the two steps of the tin building and knocked on the door.

Everyone inside froze. Pretending to be in their bunks asleep, no one made a sound, hoping whoever it was would go away.

Loring pounded on the door more loudly. "Meiner, are you in there?" he slurred. He called a second time and when there was no answer, he went in.

Hammerstein was still going strong and the mess hall was jammed. Lamm and Nachmann each got a cup of coffee and sat next to Reinhart, who was laughing hysterically. "We need you at the airfield," Lamm told him.

"What's going on?" Reinhart asked, between guffaws.

"A front is moving in, so we're going to have to leave very early in the morning. I want to load LOKI tonight. Do you know where the pilot is?"

"Yes, that's him over there. The one with the Luftwaffe eagle on his parka, Stabsfeldwebel Kranz. Shall I get him for you?"

"Please. Nachmann and I want to warm up with this coffee."

Reinhart returned with Alois Kranz, a grizzled, heavyset transport pilot with red eyes and a day's growth of beard. "Yes, Herr Obersturmbannführer. What can I do for you?"

"There is a gale moving this way so I want to load our cargo tonight in order to get a very early start in the morning. I would have done it already but your airplane is locked."

"My crew chief and copilot are a little drunk," Kranz told them. "I'll send them to bed then go with you to see that the cargo is properly secured."

Loring looked around the inspectors' barracks, waiting for his eyes to become adjusted to the dark. As soon as he could make out the figures in their bunks, he walked over and shook the nearest one by the shoulder.

"Meiner," Loring said, in a loud whisper.

Freitag sat up. "What do you want?" he snapped.

"You're not Meiner."

"Brilliant."

"Where's Meiner?" Loring's word were slurred.

"On the night inspection."

"Night inspection? What is that?"

"We pull one surprise night inspection on every trip to see if the troops are on their toes."

"Oh." Loring clumsily sat on Freitag's bunk, forcing the Luftwaffe man to sit up. He drunkenly took a cigarette from a pack, put it to his lips, and flicked his cigarette lighter. When it flamed, Loring glanced at Freitag, who was wearing a plain sleeveless undershirt. He took a second look and held the lighter higher to get more light.

"Where's your tattoo? You're not SS."

Freitag lunged for Loring and grabbed him around the middle. Dropping his lighter, Loring hit Freitag on the shoulder with both fists. Schindler left his bunk and moved around behind Loring, then covered the Scharführer's mouth with his hand and stabbed him in the back. Loring gurgled, then relaxed, and Schindler and Freitag let go. Loring hit his head on the bunk as he fell.

Levinsky asked, "Is he dead?"

"Yes, I think so," Freitag said. He and Schindler pushed Loring's body under a bunk.

"What are we going to do?" Margit asked.

"I don't think we should wait for List and Meiner," Freitag said.

Schindler looked at Levinsky.

"I think he's right," the professor said.

"Okay, get your gear."

They hurried to their bunks, dressed, and gathered up their equipment and weapons, hiding the grenades and other bulky explosives beneath their parkas. Still not wanting to attract attention, they filtered out of the barracks by twos.

Kranz glanced at the sky disapprovingly as he climbed into the back of the truck with Reinhart. "The weather should stay decent for a while. Looking forward to seeing Germany again?"

"Yes," Reinhart replied excitedly. "I haven't been back for a couple of years." He relaxed, putting his feet up on LOKI.

"Then prepare yourself for a shock."

"I've heard it is bad," Reinhart declared.

"It's worse," the pilot told him. "If it were up to me, I'd wait out the war right here."

"How can you say that? Especially when this bomb is going to win the war."

"Sounds like a crock to me," the pilot quipped.

"Didn't you see the test this morning?" Reinhart asked.

"No. I only flew in this afternoon. But I don't care what you say, no single bomb is going to win this war."

Lamm said nothing during the exchange. He had better things to do than talk to a pilot about the war.

The truck stopped and Lamm got out. "Let's get LOKI on the aircraft."

The last person out of the inspectors' barracks was Freitag, who pushed the door shut without bothering to make sure it was latched. As soon as he moved away it swung open a few inches and cold air blew across Loring's face. His eyes opened slowly and wouldn't focus. It took a few seconds before he realized he was under a bunk, but he couldn't remember why. When he tried to move there were hot flashes of sharp pain in his back and a dull throbbing ache in his head. Then he remembered. *No tattoo!* As his head cleared, Loring moved his hand to the pain in his back and found the floor was wet. It was blood, and the pain told him whose. He slid out from under the bunk gasping and moaning, and when he tried to roll over on his stomach he nearly passed out again. The second time he succeeded, but the pain was so acute it made him urinate. Loring pushed himself up on all fours and crawled to the door, staying in the cold air. The pain was no longer as sharp and his legs were getting numb. It would be so easy to sleep. Reaching the door Loring paused, drinking in the icy air, and with a superhuman effort he grabbed the doorknob and pulled himself to his feet. Leaning against the doorframe for support, he drew his pistol.

List and Meiner drove up to the barracks as other members of the group were leaving and then stopped in front of Schindler.

"We have problems, Herr Obersturmbannführer."

"What's wrong?"

"The bomb wasn't in the test bunker."

"Where could it be?"

"My guess is they have already taken it to the aircraft," Levinsky suggested.

"Well, we have to move up the schedule anyway."

"Why?"

"Loring came into the barracks looking for you and saw that Freitag didn't have a tattoo. He started to make a fuss so we had to kill him."

"Oh, my God!" Meiner exclaimed, looking at the door of their barracks. "I thought you said you killed him."

Everyone turned to look at Loring standing on the top step, pistol raised above his head. Firing two shots, he hoarsely shouted, "Commandos!" and pitched face-forward in the snow, dead. There were shouts in the distance and a siren blew.

"Quick," Schindler ordered, "your positions!"

"Commandos!" someone cried.

List and Meiner bailed out of the truck and began firing at the guards trying to leave their barracks. Freitag and Margit hurried to the mess hall, where they opened up on the people trying to get out. Hammerstein and a guard fell with the first burst.

"Go burn down the sheds," Meiner told Margit. "I'll hold them here, but I'll need your hand grenade."

Margit gave him her grenade, and then they both scampered for the cover of some crates and steel drums. "I'll give them a burst and throw a grenade to cover you," Meiner said. "Then run."

Margit nodded and Meiner pulled the pin on a hand grenade and hurled it toward the mess hall. Then he fired his machine pistol as Margit fought back nausea and ran toward the sheds. The grenade exploded behind her and she could feel its concussion.

"I'll take care of the mine," Levinsky told Schindler. "Get the aircraft."

Schindler nodded and ran for the airfield while Levinsky headed for the mine.

Lamm and his two assistants were in the process of lowering LOKI from the truck when they heard Loring's shots.

"What's that?" the pilot asked, as more shooting was heard over the siren.

"Shooting!" Nachmann shouted.

"Commandos," Reinhart said.

"Quick," Lamm yelled, "get LOKI on the aircraft so we can get out of here!"

"I've got to get my copilot and crew chief," the pilot said.

"No," Lamm snapped, "we're getting out of here now!"

"But . . ." Stray bullets hit the aircraft. "Okay," the pilot said, throwing open the door of the Junkers.

"Get the plane started," Lamm ordered. "We'll tie LOKI down."

The pilot climbed into his seat and started the engines, which blew snow over Lamm, Reinhart, and Nachmann, who were struggling with LOKI.

"Don't shoot," Levinsky said. "It's me."

"It's one of the inspectors," one of the guards at the mine told his companions. "Don't shoot."

Levinsky ran toward them. "My God! There are commandos everywhere," he said. "Some of them are wearing German uniforms."

"We'll keep them out," a Rottenführer said.

"With only three men?"

"There's an officer and two more in the mine, " replied the Rottenführer. "But we have a good position here and we're prepared. No Tommy is going to get in here. You'd better get down, Professor, it's safer."

"Yes, of course." Levinsky moved behind them, raised the machine pistol from the folds of his parka, and pulled the trigger. The Rottenführer and his two subordinates jerked in the muzzle flashes until the firing pin hit an empty chamber. Levinsky dropped the empty magazine, then inserted a full one and pulled the bolt to the rear. It felt good killing Nazis, especially this SS scum. Heading down the shaft to take care of the reactor, he stooped short as someone fired a pistol. In the confined space of the tunnel, the report was deafening.

"Don't shoot! It's me, Buchner."

"Don't come any further." Lindner's voice was tinged with panic as he fired twice more. Levinsky could see the muzzle flashes as ricochets tore dirt and rock from the ceiling above his head. *There's no sense in getting killed over this,* he thought. Pulling the string on his only hand grenade, he heaved it down the shaft as hard as he could.

The first shed Margit entered was deserted and, after a brief search, she found Lamm's papers. *Paydirt,* she thought, and stuffed them into a briefcase. Leaving the briefcase near the door, she went to the rear of the building and tossed a thermite grenade onto some scrap lumber. It worked as List said it would and she stood mesmerized until she could feel the heat of the flames on her face. She hurried to the door, then picked up the briefcase and dropped a second thermite grenade in Lamm's office.

She walked carefully through the door of the L-IV shed and saw something move.

"Hello," she called. "Is anyone in here?"

The Axel brothers, who had been hiding behind a workbench, stood and smiled in relief.

"Oh, it's you Fräulein."

"Are you all right?" Margit asked, moving closer.

"Oh, yes. What's happening?"

"Commandos. Are you by yourselves?"

"Yes, there's no one else here."

"Good," she smiled, cutting them down with a single burst, then set her last incendiary grenade.

Dietrich looked around him. There were several people still alive after the second grenade went off. Four were on their feet. "It looks like there's only one out there," he said. "Two of you go to the window and start firing. You two follow me. We'll rush him as soon as his head is down. Can you tell where he is?"

"Behind the drums, sir," one of the men at the window reported.

Dietrich crawled toward the door with two SS men behind him. He got into a crouch and pushed the door slightly to be sure it would open. "Now!" he yelled, springing forward as the guards at the windows peppered the ragged drums.

It was a trick Freitag was waiting for. Dietrich tripped on Hammerstein's body and Freitag's bullets caught the man behind him in the face. Dietrich, firing from across the body of the man killed with Hammerstein, hit Freitag with a ricochet that tore the side off the Luftwaffe sergeant's head.

"I think I got him!" Dietrich yelled. "Cease fire!" As soon as the firing stopped, he moved toward the drums in a low crouch, with the other SS man following. Dietrich stood up as he neared Freitag, lying facedown in the snow. "He's dead."

The other two SS men came out of the mess hall. Margit set down the briefcase and watched them standing around the body as Dietrich turned it over with his foot.

"It's one of the inspectors," Dietrich exclaimed. "What's going on?"

Margit stepped out of the shadows so she could see all of them clearly.

"I'd better tell Obersturmbannführer Lamm about this," Dietrich said. He looked up just as Margit opened fire. He and three of the SS men dropped with the initial burst. The fourth man dropped his gun and threw up his hands.

"I surrender."

Margit shot him in the stomach with her last shot, then reloaded and finished him off while he lay pleading for his life.

"That's for my father, Nazi."

Levinsky lay on his back, covered with a layer of dust, looking at the ceiling of the tunnel. He should have known better than to throw a grenade in a confined space. When it went off, it knocked him down and stunned him. The grenade had also taken out the lights. The only illumination came from the fires outside the tunnel. There was a roaring in his ears that wasn't from the explosion, and fine dust was pouring from the ceiling. The shaft was collapsing! A rock hit the professor on the shoulder as he stood up to orient himself. All he could see now was a little glow in the dust, and he ran toward it as fast as he could.

When he reached the mine entrance, all of the firing was in the distance. People were moaning and begging for help, but he couldn't go to them. Exhausted, he sat down just outside the entrance and put his hand to his face, only to discover it was wet with blood. *I'm shot,* he thought in a moment of panic, then he realized the concussion from the grenade had given him a bloody nose. Putting his head against the rock wall he began to laugh softly.

"There must be a dozen of them in each building," Meiner said. "Good thing they don't have any machineguns."

"How do you know?" List shouted as he sprayed the door of one building.

"When I inspected them, I took the firing pins out."

"Good thinking. We can't stay like this, Dieter. They're bound to get organized. Cover me on the left building. I'm going to try and lob a grenade in there and reduce the odds."

"Okay, but it had better work. This is my last full magazine." When he fired, chunks of wood flew off the building. List sprinted to the cover of their burning truck, then paused to take the grenade out of his coat. Just as he sprinted for the building on the left, some of the men in the building on the right rushed Meiner, while others gave them cover. They were getting organized. List pulled the pin on the hand grenade, counted two seconds, then flipped it in through a smashed window.

"Grenade!" someone screamed. The explosion blew the flimsy building apart, killing or wounding all of the men inside. Meiner cut down two of the men rushing him before he was hit in both shoulders and the chest. He lay behind the small barricade of empty drums and sandbags, unable to take deep breaths. Frothy blood escaped his lips. List's ears were ringing and he was covered with debris from the building. Shaking his head, he saw five guards heading for Meiner's position. He hit one man with a burst and fired at the others until his gun was empty. He was killed instantly as he reached for a full magazine.

Schindler was out of breath when he reached the airfield. There was a truck on the runway already and another was driving up. Two SS guards dismounted and ran to the aircraft.

"What's going on?" Lamm demanded.

"Commando attack, Herr Obersturmbannführer."

"We've got to back and help," Reinhart said.

"Don't be stupid," Lamm snapped. "They want LOKI." He turned to the guards. "Cover us so we can take off."

"*Jawohl,* Herr Obersturmbannführer. Heil Hitler!"

"Heil Hitler!" Lamm said, closing the door.

The guards returned to their truck and drove it off the runway. They caught Schindler in their headlights.

"Who's that?" the driver said.

"I'm not taking any chances." His companion leaned out the window and fired a burst at the shadowy figure. Schindler went down with a burning pain in his thigh as the rest of the bullets passed over his head. Despite the pain, he got up on one knee and took careful aim at the truck bearing down on him. Waiting until it got within twenty-five meters, he gave it burst that shattered the windshield. The truck swerved and crashed into some crates piled on the side of the runway.

The was no time for Schindler to check his handiwork. The trimotor taxied to the end of the snow-covered runway on its skis, preparing to take off. Schindler rose to his feet and limped painfully to the runway. Every time his wounded leg touched the ground, an agonizing jolt tore through him. The aircraft turned around at the end of the runway and revved its engines. It was too far for a grenade and Schindler knew he would have only one chance to keep the plane from lifting off. Inserting a full magazine, he waited until the plane was almost upon him. Leading it by a couple of meters, he let the aircraft have the entire magazine.

Glass shattered in the cockpit and bullets thudded along the fuselage, but the Junkers continued to ski down the runway and lift off. For a moment Lamm thought they hadn't made it, and ran to the cockpit.

"Are we all right?" he shouted above the roar of the wind and the engines.

"It's a little drafty," Kranz yelled, "but we're gaining altitude. I think we took a hit in the starboard engine, because we're losing oil pressure. If you can get rid of anything back there it would be a help, but don't worry, these 'Tante Jus' are tough old birds. We'll get there."

Lamm nodded and returned to the cargo compartment. "You all right?" he asked Reinhart.

"A couple of cuts, that's all." He turned to Nachmann. "Horst, are you all right?"

Nachmann sat silently, looking at LOKI.

"Horst!" Reinhart touched Nachmann's shoulder and the young SS officer fell forward. The back of his head was missing. "Horst," Reinhart said. "He's dead. I've known him since we were in the Hitler Youth." Reinhart was weeping. "We even attended the academy at Bad Toelz together."

"Give me a hand with him," Lamm said.

"What are you going to do?"

"We're going to throw him out to lighten the aircraft."

"But he's a fallen comrade," Reinhart protested.

"And if we don't get LOKI to its destination, he'll have died in vain. We need every advantage we can get."

"I . . . I suppose."

"I will personally see the Reichsführer and recommend him for an award when we get back."

"All right," Reinhart said, wiping the tears from his eyes.

They dragged Nachmann's body to the door and Lamm rolled it out as Reinhart gave the Nazi salute and said, "Go now to Valhalla."

What a bunch of dolts, Lamm thought, looking down as the aircraft banked over Vikmo and headed for Oslo. The light of the two burning sheds illuminated the destruction of his dream. "They'll pay," he muttered, "they'll pay."

CHAPTER 14

TWILIGHT OF THE GODS

Vikmo
January 23, 1945

SCHINDLER CURSED LAMM'S NAME AND MUTTERED as he limped toward the barracks. Now Lamm had LOKI and he was on his way to Germany. All of this for nothing.

There was still gunfire. Everything was illuminated by the glow of the flames from the shed fires. As he passed the truck that had fired on him, he heard a moan and limped over to the wreck. The driver's head rested on the steering wheel at an odd angle, but his passenger was still alive, his face covered with blood.

"Help me," the man moaned. "Oh, God, please help me."

"Are you hurt bad? " Schindler asked.

"I can't see," the man whined. "and I can't move my legs."

"Just relax," Schindler said softly. "We'll get you out of there in a second." Schindler drew his pistol and stepped up on the running board.

"It hurts," the man said.

Schindler shot him in the head and the man slumped against the driver. Limping with difficulty, Schindler headed for the barracks, where the firing had stopped.

One of the guards went over to see if List was still alive. "This one's dead," he called, kicking List over. "Look. He's one of the inspectors."

"So's this one. Only he's still alive."

A Rottenführer, the highest-ranking officer left, knelt over, grabbed Meiner's collar, and pulled him to a sitting position. "Who are you?" he demanded.

Meiner blinked and coughed painfully, frothy blood escaping his lips. Smiling at him crookedly, Meiner rasped in hatred, "Your mother was a Jewess."

The Rottenführer screamed in anger. He pushed Meiner back and stood up, putting the muzzle of his MP-42 against Meiner's face. His firing covered the sound of the bolt closing on Schindler's machine pistol. By the time Schindler stopped firing the remaining guards lay in a silent heap. A man who had been hit in the legs was trying to crawl away and Schindler limped over to shoot him in the back of the head.

Levinsky finally struggled to his feet. Except for a few desultory shots, the battle seemed to be over. Dazed and unable to see clearly because his glasses were broken, he intended to head for the airfield, but someone called to him.

"Professor."

He didn't need glasses to recognize the voice. Margit Hassel stood unsteadily before him, pistol in one hand and a briefcase in the other.

"Ah, Fräulein Hassel. I see you got what you came for."

Her jaw dropped in surprise. "How did you know?"

"Does it matter?"

"Not really," she said. "You're coming with me, Professor."

"I don't think so," he told her.

Margit stepped closer. "You're one of the few people who understands all this. We need your expertise."

Clumsily, Levinsky lunged for her gun and she instinctively shot him in the stomach. He fell forward, lay still for a few seconds, then rolled over and sat up with his back against the wall of the mine guard shack.

"You fool," Margit said. "You could have been a Hero of the Soviet Union."

"It doesn't matter," Levinsky said, attempting to hold back the blood pouring from his middle. "I was living on borrowed time and so are you."

"What do you mean?"

"I mean you'll never make it. You'll be dead in a few days at most."

"You're out of your mind."

He coughed. "No, I put a radioactive substance in your tea yesterday. There's no cure."

"You're lying. Why would you do such a thing?"

"You killed Kraemer. I saw the whole thing."

"So?"

"The Russians have persecuted us Jews for years. I didn't want them to have this weapon, either." Levinsky coughed softly. "Also, you cheated me. I wanted to kill Kraemer myself."

"You're crazy," Margit screamed, shooting him again. He slumped over and she walked away, heading for an undamaged truck near the mess hall. As she climbed into the cab, she was overcome by a wave of nausea and had to step down to vomit. *It's only a cold,* she told herself. *The old fool was just trying to frighten me.* Making sure she had enough gas, Margit started the truck and headed for the Vikmo railhead.

Schindler's leg was stiffening badly, and he tied a bandage around it to stop the bleeding. Using a short piece of pipe for a crutch, he limped around making sure the SS men were dead while he tried to find Levinsky and Margit. He limped over to the mine and stopped when he heard a moan. Cautiously he pulled his pistol and stepped over to where Levinsky was slumped against the wall of the guard shack.

"Professor?"

"Is that you, Joachim?"

"It's me, Schindler." Schindler leaned down and pulled Levinsky to a sitting position. One look at Levinsky's face told him the professor didn't have long.

"Oh." Levinsky recognized him through half-open eyes. "Do you have a cigarette, Schindler?"

"Sure, Professor." Schindler sat beside him, put a cigarette between the professor's lips, and lit it. Levinsky took a drag and coughed softly.

"I have to tell you something, Schindler."

"Save your strength," Schindler told him.

"For what? I'm dying and we both know it. Remember I've seen people die just like you have, only in the camps it takes a little longer than it does on the Russian Front, because they kill your spirit before they kill your body."

Schindler listened while Levinsky told him about Margit and Kraemer.

"Professor?"

"Yes?"

"Do you think the world will ever forgive us?"

There was no answer.

Schindler turned to look at him. "I said—"

Levinsky's sightless eyes were staring straight ahead, and the cigarette that had fallen from his lips was burning a hole in his parka. Schindler closed the professor's eyes and flicked the cigarette from the parka. Snow was beginning to fall as he got up and limped toward the shattered mess hall. He had work to do.

A little over eleven kilometers from the mine, the engine of Margit's truck seized up. The bumping of the road had loosened a stray bullet lodged in the radiator and the engine had lost its coolant. Undeterred, Margit cursed, grabbed the briefcase, and dismounted from the vehicle. Before she could take a step, she had to set the briefcase down, lean against the side of the truck, and vomit again. She felt weak, but knew she couldn't rest. There was a village near the railhead and all she had to do was keep the glow of the mine at her back and she would make it. Picking up the briefcase, she headed into the night, the snowfall covering the imprints of her boots as quickly as she made them.

The Junkers fought for altitude as Nachmann's body plummeted to earth, and for his dirge, the wind whistled and moaned through countless holes in the corrugated metal skin of the aircraft. As soon as the door closed both Lamm and Reinhart found some shelter from the icy wind knifing through the cabin in small places where there were no bullet holes. Each huddled silently in his parka, unable to shout over the whine of the rushing air even if they had wanted to.

Reinhart found a place near one of the few unbroken windows and looked down at the flames consuming the buildings of OPERATION NORD. He had liked the project because he knew he was making a contribution to the ultimate victory of National Socialism. Years of work and hope destroyed so quickly. How did it happen? Who was alive? Who was dead? Was ODIN still intact? There were so many questions unanswered.

Saddened at the loss of his comrades, and the feelings of guilt by not sharing their danger, he knew Lamm was right. LOKI was their only hope, and their duty was to ensure LOKI destroyed London. When he could no longer see Vikmo, Reinhart looked out at the sky. Storm clouds were approaching rapidly.

Lamm did not look back. He had no desire to see his greatest intellectual achievement, perhaps the greatest intellectual achievement of all time, consumed by flames. Even his notes and calculations were gone. He could recreate them, of course, but it would take time. His one consolation was the darkened cylinder fastened to the floor. He could see neither the name nor the details of its carrying case. Like its creator, it silently brooded, waiting for its moment of revenge, a moment which would come soon. The British would pay, and pay dearly.

The pilot flew lower and lower to avoid the storm clouds, but the Junkers cargo plane was at the mercy of the elements, bobbing up and down and sideways, like a cork on the sea. When the pilot radioed the Oslo tower, the controllers were appalled anyone was in the air, since all aircraft had been grounded for the past twenty-four hours. They gave him landing instructions, and when the Junkers reached the airfield, they turned the runway lights on, but it did little to improve the pilot's morale.

There was a vicious wind blowing snow directly across the runway. As the aircraft banked to start its approach, the starboard engine coughed and stopped. Despite the freezing cold, Kranz was sweating. A missing engine normally didn't bother him. In Russia he had flown on two and even one engine, but in weather like this he needed all the power he could get. He fought to keep the aircraft between the rows of runway lights, descending more rapidly than he liked.

The aircraft hit with a thud, bounced into the air, and came down again, skidding sideways and only narrowly missing a row of parked aircraft. The pilot reduced power and taxied up to a row of hangars and sandbag revetments, where shadowy figures moved out to meet them. He followed the one with a flashlight and positioned the Junkers over a set of tie-down points. The flashlight made a final signal and the pilot cut power. As the two remaining engines sputtered to a stop the ground crew swarmed around the Junkers to tie it down. Remaining in his seat, the pilot removed his helmet, earphones, and goggles, and, oblivious to the cold, lit a cigarette with trembling hands. Even with the aircraft stopped, the wind continued to play its eerie tune through the bullet holes in the aircraft's fuselage.

Lamm had watched the landing through a broken window, and like the others had breathed a sigh of relief as they taxied to the tie-down point. As soon as the pilot lit his cigarette, he went to the cockpit.

The pilot turned in his seat. "Miracle of miracles, Herr Obersturmbannführer, we made it."

"How long will it take to gas up and take off again?" Lamm asked.

The pilot looked at him, breaking out in raucous laughter, as the pent-up tension of the flight expended itself. "You're serious," he said, looking at the determined expression on Lamm's face.

"We must get to Germany," Lamm insisted. "It's a matter that may decide the fate of the Reich."

The pilot got up and snuffed out his cigarette on the floor of the cockpit. "That may be, but you're not going to fly out of here tonight, even if this crate could fly, which it can't."

"Why not?"

"Hasn't anything that occurred just now registered? There's a full gale blowing ice and snow out there and every aircraft is grounded. Nothing is flying! It doesn't matter whether it belongs to man or God, it's all grounded! Ships don't even sail in this weather." The pilot walked down the center of the aircraft, stepped around LOKI, and jumped to the ground.

Lamm watched him disappear in the darkness and swirling snow.

"What do we do now?" Reinhart asked.

"Stay with LOKI. I'll find someone to help us. If anyone asks what it is, tell them it's a special apparatus for the Reichsführer."

Schindler made one more circuit of Vikmo. There were two more SS guards still breathing so he finished them off with a pistol shot to the head. There was nothing else he could do. It was better than letting them slowly grow numb as their blood seeped into the snow and they froze to death. His leg was beginning to stiffen badly as the wind blew ice and snow across the ruined installation, but Schindler knew his work was only beginning if he were going to survive.

He selected the mess hall as his headquarters, because it was still intact and had a lot of undamaged food. He carried as many loads of wood and coal as he could bear and took blankets from the inspectors' barracks before it, too, began to burn, ignited by sparks from the adjoining buildings. Returning to the mess hall, Schindler kept the fire in the stove going and dragged the dead outside. The bodies of those killed early in the evening were already covered by snow when he emptied the mess hall. He thought of doing something for Levinsky, but he was exhausted and lay down on a pile of blankets next to the stove to sleep.

Infuriated by Kranz' attitude, Lamm looked around for an officer, but found no one.

"There has to be someone on duty in the tower, Reinhart. Keep an eye on LOKI while I try to find someone with authority."

"Yes, Herr Obersturmbannführer."

The harsh wind blew ice crystals straight across the open spaces of the airfield, stinging Lamm's cheeks. The wings of tied-down aircraft swayed in the wind. The cold reminded Lamm of the night he had gone to see Schiller's lecture. It seemed like centuries had passed since then. As he entered the base of the tower, several Luftwaffe enlisted men came to attention.

"How do I get in touch with the commandant?" he asked what looked like the senior sergeant.

"Oberst Lusser is in his quarters, Herr Obersturmbannführer."

"I want to call him."

"He's probably retired for the night."

"Now!" Lamm shouted.

The sergeant swallowed. "Yes, Herr Obersturmbannführer," he said, and picked up the phone. "Operator, get me Oberst Lusser. Yes, now."

When the commandant came to the phone, the sergeant handed it to Lamm.

"Oberst Lusser here." The man was sleepy and obviously peeved at being called in the middle of the night. Lamm quickly explained the situation. "There's nothing I can do now, Herr Obersturmbannführer. Come to my office in the morning and I'll see if there is anything I can do."

Before Lamm could say a thing, he hung up.

Maximilian Lamm was surprisingly calm. He tapped the cradle twice to get the operator back. "Gestapo Headquarters, please."

The Luftwaffe men looked at one another wide-eyed.

A clerk answered. "This is Obersturmbannführer Lamm, commandant of the SS installation at Vikmo."

"Yes, Herr Obersturmbannführer. What can I do for you?"

Once again, Lamm rapidly explained the situation. "Under personal orders from the Reichsführer himself, I need a squad of SS men to guard a priority cargo while my plane is being repaired. I also need someone to speak with Oberst Lusser about cooperation."

"I'll need confirmation of your orders, sir."

"Then send a car and I'll present them." Lamm let his irritation show.

"I'll have one there in an hour."

"I'm at the tower. Heil Hitler."

"Heil Hitler."

The Gestapo still had a firm hold on Norway. In forty-five minutes two Gestapo agents arrived to confirm Lamm's orders. A few minutes later, he was on the phone with Standartenführer Schiltz, the assistant SS commandant of the Oslo area, explaining his situation once again.

Schiltz hung up and called Oberst Lusser's quarters. He really didn't care about Lamm's secret project, but the Reichsführer's orders now gave him an opportunity to get partial control of the airfield, something he had been unable to do for the last two years.

"Oberst Lusser." The man was obviously irritated at having been rung up twice during the wee hours.

"Ah, Herr Oberst," Schiltz said with smooth menace. "This is Standartenführer Schiltz."

Lusser knew exactly who it was without being told. "Yes, Herr Standartenführer. How can I help you?"

Schiltz explained about Lamm and concluded, "I assured him you would give him your utmost cooperation."

"Of course, Herr Standartenführer." *What choice do I have?* Lusser thought. *If I don't drag my men out in the middle of a gale to satisfy this lunatic, I get hanged.*

An hour and a half after Lamm's conversation with Schiltz a squad of SS troops arrived to carry LOKI into a hangar and guard it. Two hours after the conversation with Schiltz, Oberst Lusser arrived at the tower. He was a spare man with a bald head, a long hooked nose, and a pointed chin. He had dark piggy eyes that showed nothing but hatred for Lamm. Lamm didn't care.

"I need the aircraft repaired immediately, so I can fly to Germany," Lamm told him.

"Of course, Herr Obersturmbannführer. We'll start immediately."

A few hours later, Lamm watched with grim satisfaction as a ground crew pulled the damaged Ju-52 into a heated hanger to begin repairs. Exhausted, he and Reinhart finally went to bed in the Luftwaffe visiting officers' quarters. Listening to the wind howling outside, he fell into a deep, dreamless sleep.

In the morning Schindler's leg hurt terribly but he felt better mentally because he had survived. He began boarding up the broken windows and patching the bullet holes in the wall to better his chances of survival and to keep himself occupied. Then he set up a table and chair to write his after-action report. That also would keep his mind occupied. Everything went well until the fifth day. With the storm still raging, his leg swelled up and his temperature rose. Able to move only with great difficulty, he lost his appetite, but forced himself to take nourishment, invariably throwing it up a little later. Except for fueling the stove, Schindler did nothing but lie on his blankets. On the seventh day, he lapsed into delirium, and the fire went out.

When he awoke, Lamm discovered things were not much better than when he went to bed. He had succeeded in compelling the Luftwaffe to cooperate, but he could not control the weather or the Luftwaffe's shortage of spare parts. The damaged engine had to be rebuilt, and that could only be done by cannibalizing the engines of non-flying Ju-52s at the airfield. That meant dismounting engines in the howling wind and bitter cold. Operations that should have taken hours took days. Finally, the storm abated and with a volunteer crew that wanted to return to Germany, Lamm and Reinhart tied LOKI to the floor of the plane. During the storm, Lamm changed his flight plan to go directly to Groningen, Holland to meet Gruppenführer Kammler's engineers, who would put LOKI into the warhead of a V-2.

On February 10, 1945, the Junkers taxied to the end of the runway and revved its engines. The pilot released his brakes and the homely trimotor skied down the runway and lifted into the sky. Luckily, the sky was still overcast and when they reached the Norwegian coast, the pilot descended to an altitude of one hundred meters. The Junkers was easy prey for any Allied fighter and flying low and slow was her only chance for survival. At a low altitude, the plane could ditch easily, but in the cold water they wouldn't last half an hour.

As it turned out, there was little need to worry. On their agonizingly long trip there were no enemy aircraft to be seen. As the whitecaps sped by their windows Reinhart dozed, and for the first time in months, Lamm thought about his wife and son. Irma was still in Berlin and had regularly sent letters and photos until shortages of chemicals made having them developed nearly impossible for the average person. On his sixteenth birthday, Karl had joined the Waffen SS. Lamm worried about him. Lately the letters had grown less frequent, and Lamm was anxious to get home to see if they were all right.

"Excuse me, Herr Obersturmbannführer," someone was saying. Lamm looked at the copilot. "We can't get you in to Holland because of the weather. We have to land at Oldenburg."

The conversation woke Reinhart from a sound sleep. "What's wrong?" he asked groggily.

"We can't get into Holland because of the weather."

Reinhart made a face. "Where are we going, then?"

"Oldenburg." Lamm told him.

"Oh." Reinhart brightened. "If we can get a truck we could be in Groningen in an hour or two."

Lamm thought for a moment. "That's a good idea. We should be able to get something when we land."

The Junkers landed safely, then taxied under a camouflage net. Reinhart and a handful of guards from the airfield guarded LOKI while Lamm went on a search for a truck.

The airfield commandant was Hauptmann Goltz. "Obersturmbannführer Lamm, as a member of the Party and a loyal German, I would like to help you, but I can't. The only two vehicles I have operational are my fuel truck and my supply truck, and I can't spare either. The Army confiscated all of my running vehicles weeks ago, and they stripped the parts they could use from the broken ones. I can give you the last few liters of aviation fuel so you can fly out of here. That's the best I can do."

Lamm was too frustrated to get angry. "All right, fuel the plane. We're taking off immediately."

"Of course."

Once again, Lamm found himself frustrated by the weather. The snow changed to sleet, turning the dirt runway into a quagmire and rendering the skis on the aircraft useless. The ground crew fitted the Junkers' landing gear with wheels as Lamm fumed. Their short wait was four days long.

On the morning of the fifth day, they took off again with the sky safely overcast above fifteen hundred meters, but when they reached nine hundred meters, light was beginning to show through the clouds. Ten minutes later the clouds broke, revealing a big patch of blue sky with dozens of tiny specks.

"Hold on," the pilot yelled back to Lamm and Reinhart, "we have company."

The pilot put the Junkers in a steep bank and headed back to the clouds. Several little specks separated from the others and grew larger until the gray of the cloud enveloped the tri-motor.

"Everyone keep a lookout," the pilot said.

Lamm, Reinhart, and the crew chief stared out of their windows into the gray haze, and suddenly they were bathed in daylight.

"Seven o'clock!" the copilot shouted. The pilot, unable to return to the cloud he just left, put the aircraft into a climb and headed for another cloud, with the fighters closing the distance quickly. As soon as they were enveloped by the gray haze, the pilot changed course, hoping to shake their pursuers.

"Why are they chasing us ?" Reinhart asked the crew chief.

"Germany doesn't have that many planes left and all of their pilots want to finish the war as aces. Oh no," he said, as they emerged from the cloud.

It was no longer a game of cat and mouse. There were four fighters, two of which were posted high to observe their quarry, with the other two positioned to move in quickly. This time there was no room to maneuver. Lamm watched in dismay as the fighters came in with their wings twinkling. Fifty-caliber machinegun bullets and twenty-millimeter cannon shells slammed into the tri-motor, tearing huge pieces of corrugated metal from the side of the fuselage. Lamm and Reinhart instinctively hit the floor next to LOKI, amazed the cylinder had not been hit. The pilot put the Junkers in a steep dive and the fighters roared by, caught off-balance by the sudden move. Making wide turns, they were now out of position, and for a moment it looked as if the Junkers would escape, but the upper pair of fighters decided to get into the act and machinegun bullets and cannon shells tore into the aircraft once more. Pieces flew off each wing, and the starboard engine burst into flame. The copilot was killed by two bullets in the back of the head and the pilot was hit in the shoulder. Hit in the chest by a twenty-millimeter shell, the crew chief died instantly.

The pilot screamed as the mortally wounded tri-motor went into a steep dive. Thick black smoke filled the cabin and Lamm knew they were doomed. There was a tearing sound as the Junkers hit the ground. A fraction of a second later, Maximilian Lamm was plunged into a black abyss.

Oslo
February 15, 1945

A sharp white light that Schindler could only assume was the sun reflecting on the snow intruded upon his consciousness. There were voices buzzing and he wanted to throw up. A logical section of his brain told him there was no sun in Norway this time of year.

"You're dying," it said. "You're having hallucinations, then you're going to die."

A purple ring closed in around him. *This must be death,* he thought. The ring grew tighter and tighter until everything went black. At some indefinite time later, Schindler opened his eyes, saw white and felt wary. He moved his hand to his stomach, but it was hard work and several times the purple ring returned. Finally, he was able to rest his hand on his stomach. When he tried to pinch himself he was too weak to close his fingers. From this, he surmised he wasn't dead. Then a blurred head moved into his field of vision.

"Are you awake?" a soft, feminine voice asked.

"Lise?" His mouth was very dry.

"No, I'm Karin. I'll get the doctor."

Tears of joy trickled down his face. He was alive. Then he could see another head. It was bald.

"How do you feel?" the head asked.

"Fine, I think. Weak. Thirsty."

The head gave him a drink of water through a glass straw. "I'm Doktor Meissen, and I'm going to ask you a few questions. All right?"

"Yes, but first tell me where I am."

"You're in the naval hospital in Oslo," Doktor Meissen said.

"How did I get here?"

"I'll tell you that as soon as you answer my questions."

"All right."

"What is your name and rank?"

"Obersturmbannführer der Waffen SS Heinz Otto Schindler."

"Where were you born?"

"Berlin."

"What were you doing at the Vikmo mine?"

Schindler thought for a moment. He had gone there to destroy it. No, that was the wrong answer. "I am an inspector for the Reichsführer's headquarters. My team. What happened to my team? Commandos . . ."

The doctor laid a comforting hand on his arm. "I was checking first to see if you had brain damage and second to see if you were who your identity disc said. Now get your rest and tomorrow I'll tell you about your comrades and how you got here."

Schindler wanted to tell the doctor he wasn't tired, but he was falling asleep as the doctor rose to leave.

The following day, Doktor Meissen returned and told them that the meteorological station was notified by radio that commandos were attacking the mine and then the radio went dead. The first team that tried to reach Vikmo was driven back by the storm, so they were unable to reach the place until ten days after the attack. Appalled by the damage, they thought everyone was dead until they heard Schindler moaning deliriously. Although the stove had gone out, he was under several layers of blankets, which saved him from freezing to death. Unable to recover any of the bodies because of the snow, they took Schindler to the meteorological station and flew him to Oslo.

"That's it," the doctor said.

"May I ask you a question, Doktor?"

"Of course."

"It sounds crazy, but has London been destroyed? Completely, I mean."

"To the best of my knowledge, no." The doctor was slightly bemused.

"Thanks. There's one other thing. Did they find a girl, or her body?"

"No, everything was covered with snow. You were the only one taken out."

"Did they find my after-action report?

"No. The only papers you had were the copies of the orders you had in your parka."

Schindler sighed in relief.

"Do you want to rest now?" the doctor asked.

"Yes, please."

Schindler's strength returned rapidly. Four days after he regained consciousness, he could go to the latrine by himself, and he began looking for a way out. The man in the bed to his right was U-boat Leutnant zur See Klaus Arnim. They spoke a great deal about the war, which was all they had in common, and Arnim told him how bad it was in the U-boats.

"Still," he said with a sigh, "one has to do one's duty. I'll be leaving the day after tomorrow."

"Where are you going?" Schindler asked.

"Our boat is going back to Kiel to be fitted for a Schnorkel."

"A what?"

"A Schnorkel. It's a tube with valves in it that lets us breathe air from the outside and use our engines underwater. That way we can go faster and stay down without running our batteries. It gives us a fighting chance."

"Oh." Schindler really didn't understand.

"It increases the range of the boat and allows us to dive much faster," Arnim explained. "Though I doubt we'll have another patrol the way things are going."

"Take me with you, Klaus."

"What? We're leaving in a couple of days."

"I have to get to Berlin."

"You're better off waiting out the war here, Heinz. Besides, we can't take passengers."

"Not even on orders from Reichsführer Himmler?"

"If you have that kind of clout we wouldn't have any choice. But what will the doktor say?"

"Who's going to ask him?" Schindler gave him a little grin.

CHAPTER 15

VALHALLA

Kiel to Berlin
April 16, 1945

By the time the U-boat surfaced in Kiel, Schindler was about to lose his mind. He had assumed his experience in tanks had prepared him for a trip in a submarine, but he quickly learned how badly mistaken he was. Even in the worst conditions, one could usually open the hatch of a tank and grab a breath of fresh air. But since the bilge pumps could not be used, the U-boat stank like a sewer, and most of the voyage was made submerged. When at last they docked, Schindler thanked Arnim and left the pier as soon as he could.

Schindler had been gone for two months and was unprepared for the increased devastation he saw. On every wall was the slogan "Our walls may break, and our buildings crumble, but our hearts, never!" But Schindler knew the end was near and he could see that people were no longer coping.

At every road junction, military police squads were stationed to capture deserters. For those who had no papers, a firing squad or a noose on a lamppost was the penalty. His forged papers, however, went unquestioned, since he was traveling east. Nothing pointed to the coming demise of the Third Reich more than Schindler's rail connections. Trains going west were overcrowded and scrupulously checked, while those going east were nearly empty. Nevertheless, it took four days to get to Berlin, where disintegration was evident. Few offices in the High Command building on the Bendlerstrasse were still occupied, but Schindler knew that von Rittburg's would be one of them. There were no guards at the entrance, only rubble, and Schindler went directly upstairs to find Gefreiter Weiss.

"Is Major von Rittburg in, Gefreiter Weiss?" Schindler asked.

The unperturbable Weiss's jaw dropped open. "J-Just a minute, I'll get him."

"Never mind. I'll just go in. He'll see me."

Von Rittburg, standing by the fireplace in his overcoat, turned as Schindler's boots crushed the glass and plaster on the carpet.

"I've come to give you my after-action report," Schindler told him disappointedly.

Von Rittburg looked at him without surprise. "I've been waiting for you."

"I thought you might be."

"Are you the only one left?" Von Rittburg asked matter-of-factly.

"Yes."

"Would you like a drink?"

"Weiss's rocket fuel? No."

"I think there's something better. Weiss!"

"Yes, Herr Major?"

"Do we have any good stuff left?"

"Cognac."

"Bring the bottle." Weiss disappeared. "Did you succeed?"

"Not quite."

"I don't understand."

Schindler told von Rittburg the story as clearly as he could, and at the end Von Rittburg was clearly depressed.

"It really worked?" he asked a second time.

"Yes, it was terrifying. A single bomb. You cannot imagine. All the destruction around us in Berlin could have been done in a few seconds."

"Well, I have some news that will make you feel a lot better."

"What's that?"

"We have a report that Lamm's plane crashed outside of Oldenburg. It burned and there were no survivors."

"What happened to LOKI?"

"You said it contained high explosive."

"It did."

"Then it must have gone off, because there was nothing left of the plane."

Schindler looked at von Rittburg. "I hope to God you're right."

Von Rittburg changed the subject. "It can't last much longer, you know. The Allies are across the Rhine, Field Marshal Model is bottled up in the Ruhr, and the Russians are only a few kilometers from here."

"I'm resigning," Schindler said, flatly.

"In that case I have one more assignment for you."

"I'm not doing anyone's dirty work any more."

"It's not dirty work. I want you to get Lise Elbing out of Berlin."

Schindler was stunned. "Lise, here? Why?"

"She had some work to do for us and now doesn't have a way out. She's in the safe house in the Lausitzerstrasse. Will you do it?"

"Of course."

"Good. I knew you wouldn't fail me," von Rittburg said, without emotion. "Take Weiss with you."

"What about you?"

"I still have much to do. Let's hope we'll meet again in better times." He smiled weakly and they shook hands. "Weiss!"

"Yes, Herr Major."

"You are leaving with Obersturmbannführer Schindler."

"Is that an order, Herr Major?"

"Yes, that's an order, Weiss."

Weiss said nothing, but Schindler saw tears in the Gefreiter's eyes.

"We have to have a plan," Schindler declared. "There are Gestapo and SS military police ready to hang or shoot anyone they think is a deserter. If we don't have a reason to head west, they'll stop us."

Von Rittburg thought for a moment. "I have it." He went to his desk and pulled out a sheaf of papers. "Weiss, I need a locking briefcase."

"Yes, sir." Weiss went into the next room and returned with a brown leather briefcase with a brass lock and a pair of handcuffs.

Von Rittburg stuffed the papers into the briefcase and locked it, then handed it, the keys, and the handcuffs to Schindler. "These are all the secret papers we had on OPERATION NORD. A lot of it is scientific material, so it will look important to the casual observer.

Hitler is in the bunker and will probably die there. As a result Himmler and Göring are each trying to arrange a surrender to the Allies in order to be recognized as Germany's leader after the war. Personally, I think they're kidding themselves. The Russians will shoot the lot if they have their way. There is a rumor that a government will be set up in Flensburg, near the Danish border. I will have Weiss cut orders sending you both to Himmler at Flensburg."

"What can we do for transportation?"

Von Rittburg thought a moment. "There are two official trains leaving from the Lehrter Rail Station at two in the morning. Supposedly one is for army plans and records and the other is valuable material being shipped west to a new headquarters. The real reason is for high Party officials and their families to get out of Berlin. Weiss's orders will allow the three of you to get on that train. Once you're away from Berlin, you can get off anywhere you choose. It's the best we can do on such short notice." He turned to the Gefreiter. "Weiss, type up the orders."

"Yes, sir."

"And Weiss, can you get a SS uniform?"

"Yes, sir. Several have been left in abandoned offices in the building."

"Make yourself an officer."

"Yes, sir."

"But he doesn't have a tattoo," Schindler interjected.

Von Rittburg gave Schindler a sardonic grin. "If they ask you to take your clothes off, you're dead anyway."

Schindler shrugged in agreement. It was true.

Weiss returned with the documents, to which von Rittburg skillfully forged several signatures, including Himmler's, and predated them. Before Schindler could remark on the Major's unique talent, von Rittburg said. "Now get going and God bless you."

"You too, von Rittburg."

"There is another bottle of whiskey and a little coffee in my desk, Herr Major." Weiss clicked his heels and von Rittburg returned the salute. Weiss and Schindler left without another word. They stopped at an office where there was a tunic of a Waffen SS sturmführer that was a little large for Weiss, but it was believable.

"I never thought I'd wear one of these," the Gefreiter said in distaste.

A few weeks before, Schindler would have roundly reprimanded him for that kind of remark. Now all he said was, "Hurry up, Weiss."

Weiss finished dressing and grabbed two haversacks.

"What are those for?"

"Just in case, Herr Obersturmbannführer," Weiss answered with a smile.

To the east there was the rumble of the Russian guns, which by now had become constant. Still, the battered capital of the Reich tried to maintain some sort of normality. Some streetcars still ran and shops sold a little bread while columns of troops in camouflaged smocks carrying Panzerfaust antitank rocket launchers marched eastward between rows of bombed-out buildings. Many of the troops were only thirteen or fourteen years old. Groups of civilians carrying picks and shovels to dig antitank ditches accompanied them, even though it was far too late for that sort of thing.

Schindler and Weiss managed to catch a streetcar for part of the way, and then they hitched a ride on a SS truck for another bit. Most of the time they walked. Like the rest of Berlin, Lausitzerstrasse was a series of partially and totally destroyed buildings. The safe house had lost the top two stories.

"Fräulein Elbing? Lise?" Schindler called. "Are you in there?"

Cautiously, Lise emerged from the side of the building holding a pistol. When she saw who it was she was deliriously happy. Her face erupted in a smile and she threw her arms around Schindler's neck. "Oh, Heinz, you survived."

He held her close, loving the feel of her in his arms. "Yes, for now. Pack something you can carry over your shoulder. We have a train to catch at the Lehrter Rail Station in just a few hours."

"This way," she said.

They followed her to the back of the building and down the steps into the basement. Lise had created a small living area with a washstand and a sofa that doubled as a bed. She cooked on the small stove she used to heat the room. On a shelf was some canned food. Ever practical, Weiss put several of the cans into his haversack.

"We must be very careful, Heinz," she said fearfully as she packed a small knapsack. "After dark, Berlin is full of marauders. They'll kill you for a pair of boots. The police only patrol where there are Nazi Party officials—and food."

"All right, we'll be careful, but we have to leave now." Schindler insisted. "I don't want to get caught in Berlin by a bunch of Russian troops thirsting for revenge. Worse, I don't want them to catch you." He took her hands in his and they looked at each other for a moment.

Paying no attention to their longing gazes, Weiss told them, "Take the food. It's worth more than money."

Schindler and Lise separated. "He's right," Lise agreed.

Schindler began putting as many cans as he could in a haversack. Then they moved out into the street and Schindler turned to his two companions. "Lise, can you handle a machine pistol?"

"Of course."

Schindler handed her his MP 42. "I'll go first. Lise will be in the middle and Weiss will bring up the rear." Lise and Weiss nodded. "We will stay in the center of the street whenever possible. That way anyone who comes after us will have to move out to meet us instead of coming out of an alley. I don't think they want to shoot and attract attention, especially if they're deserters. Let's go."

With the city blacked out and the streets deserted, Berlin had assumed a macabre countenance. The flashes of the Russian guns in the distance provided some illumination, but it only made the scene more eerie, with grotesque shadows of bombed-out buildings thrust into relief only to disappear into the void a second later. Unlike the daytime, there were no streetcars or trucks. The only signs of life were some soldiers around the entrance of a subway station, smoking cigarettes and talking in hushed tones. Most of the population of Berlin lived in the subways, especially at night. The men looked their way for a moment, then returned to their conversation. No one was curious about anything any more.

Schindler, Lise, and Weiss walked directly down the center of the street, and soon the men and the subway station were swallowed by the darkness. Wordlessly, they progressed through what had once been thriving neighborhoods. Schindler couldn't shake the feeling that they were being watched every step of the way.

"Halt!"

All three froze as a dimmed flashlight glowed in the dark and first one figure then five loomed out of the pitch-black night. They were SS troops wearing silver gorgets—military police.

"Heil Hitler," Schindler shouted as he gave them a straight-arm salute.

"Heil Hitler." The voice sounded bored and already disbelieving. "Let me see your papers." An SS Hauptsturmführer stepped close enough to be recognized and Schindler handed him the orders. He read them carefully. "These look genuine enough," he muttered. "Let me look in the briefcase."

"No!" Schindler insisted. "These papers are for the Reichsführer, not you."

The SS officer was taken slightly aback, but he was a man accustomed to getting his way. His patrol did not yet have the authority to shoot someone on sight, but he could turn him over to a checkpoint that did.

"I insist," he snapped at Schindler.

"You neither have the authority nor the rank, Hauptsturmführer, so step aside."

The man hesitated for a moment, then decided that no Obersturmbannführer with a briefcase was going to tell him what to do. He started to draw his pistol and his men brought their weapons up. Unlike experienced combat troops, they were all concentrating on Schindler.

"Give me the briefcase and your weapons!" he demanded.

Lise tensed. An avalanche of fear coursed through her. She was afraid for herself and for Heinz. If these men had their way, she would never know if she and Schindler had a chance for the future. The SS men were so intent on Schindler and Weiss, they hardly noticed her. Lise moved slowly to the side and lifted the MP 42 from her side. "Drop your guns," she shouted.

The Hauptsturmführer continued to draw his pistol, but turned toward her. "Stupid tramp—"

In her years in the Resistance, Lise Elbing had never fired a shot, but as soon as the Hauptsturmführer turned, her finger tightened on the trigger. The first burst killed him and another man while Weiss shot the others.

"What a mess," Schindler sighed. "Thanks. We'd better get going."

"Take their gorgets," Weiss suggested. "We may get farther if they think we're military police."

"Good idea."

When Weiss leaned over one of the men he moaned. "Help me."

"Help yourself," Weiss muttered.

"Let's go," Schindler insisted. "Someone may get curious and I don't want to be here when they do."

Weiss removed all the gorgets but the two he and Schindler were to wear and threw the others into the rubble. Another of the SS men groaned. Two were still alive. "Do we finish them?" the Gefreiter wanted to know.

"No, " Schindler replied. "I'm sick of killing. Let them be."

"I feel like there's someone watching me," Lise said.

"I know, Fräulein," Weiss agreed. "I've felt that way since we started."

"Let's get going," Schindler insisted.

The three of them moved quickly away from the dead and wounded SS military policemen and were only half a block away when they heard scuffling behind them. Then someone screamed "Please, no!"

"Marauders," Lise whispered.

For a long time they walked through streets that were in complete ruin and totally deserted. Signs warning of unexploded bombs were everywhere. Every so often they stopped and sat on a curbstone to rest. Sometimes Lise rested with her head against Schindler's shoulder while Weiss stood guard. Most of the time they were silent. As they neared the railroad station, more and more people were in evidence. Mercedes sedans were parked on the streets near the wrecked station. There were a few men in field-gray SS combat uniforms, but they were in a distinct minority. By far the overwhelming majority wore the brown uniforms of high Party officials. Loitering around the cars were large numbers of elegantly dressed young women.

"Mistresses," Lise whispered to Schindler.

"How do you know?" he asked.

"See any older women or children?"

"I see what you mean."

"Most of the Party men that could afford it sent their families to the country for safety, but remained in Berlin to do their duty and fool around on their wives."

"What do we do now?" Weiss asked.

"We walk right in as if we're supposed to be here." Schindler replied. "What else can we do?"

"We'd better get rid of the military police insignia," Weiss told him. They straightened their uniforms, tossed the gorgets far into the rubble of a bombed-out building, and marched into the remains of the station. The facade was crumbled and the doors were boarded up, but it had part of a functional lobby where a brown-uniformed man at a table was checking passes and orders. There were no tickets for these trains. He took one look at Schindler's orders and shook his head.

"I'm sorry, there isn't enough room. You'll have to take another train."

Schindler would gladly have shot him, but he knew no amount of logic or military orders would do any good.

"Thank you." He took his orders from the man's hand and walked away.

"Aren't you even going to try to reason with him?" Lise asked.

"No good. Watch the next ticket holder."

They watched as the next in line, a large man in a kreisleiter's uniform, gave the man at the table a huge wad of bills.

"We don't have that kind of money, not that it's worth anything." Schindler explained.

"What are we going to do, Heinz?" Lise clung to his arm.

"I don't know."

"Why don't we just go out on the platform," Weiss suggested. "Since there are no tickets, who's going to know?"

Schindler looked at him. "Good idea."

They left the station, went half a block north, then cut back through the rail yard, which was a twisted mass of steel from tracks and rolling stock. One pair of tracks was intact and as they got closer to the station, they could see hundreds of slave laborers working to finish it for the train.

"My God," Weiss whispered as they passed rows of moving skeletons that seemed to part and look through them. The stench was terrible. "Who are they?"

"Political prisoners, Jews, Gypsies, and all the rest of humanity the Third Reich said were subhuman, Weiss." Lise said.

Weiss said nothing as a blacked-out train pulled into the station. The crowd of men and women on the platform swarmed toward the cars as it came to a halt. Schindler, Lise, and Weiss joined the throng and moved toward one of the passenger cars in the middle of the train.

"You! You don't belong here!" someone shouted. "Grab them!"

They turned to see the man from the desk directing four SS military policemen toward them. The crowd prevented them from running anywhere and there was no way to use their weapons in the mob.

Schindler cursed as the military police disarmed him and Weiss and pushed them away from the train.

"You'll be shot for this," the man in the brown uniform assured them.

"For what, not giving you a bribe?" Lise was indignant.

"Shut up!" The man ordered. "The Gestapo will deal with you."

They pushed them toward a group of SS men near a corner of the building. One of them was a one-armed Standartenführer with a patch over one eye, smoking a cigarette. "Yes, Schneider, what is it?" He was obviously bored with the whole proceeding.

"Herr Standartenführer," Schneider said, "these three were trying to board the train illegally."

"He means we didn't give him a bribe," Lise snapped.

The Standartenführer dropped his cigarette and crushed it with his boot before turning to look at the three. His face was terribly scarred and when he looked at the three of them, his mouth turned up in a crooked smile. "Heinz Schindler! What hole did you crawl out of?"

Schindler blinked, not recognizing the man for a second. "Franz? Franz Degenbach? What happened to you?"

"You missed the party in Belgium, Heinz. It was fun until the weather cleared. The American planes shot us to bits. They caught my tank with rockets. That's why I'm now a one-armed military policeman. What are you doing here? Are you still in the spy business?"

Schindler reached into his tunic and the guards pulled their guns.

"Put those things away," Degenbach ordered, waving his hand. He reached for the orders and turned on a flashlight to read them. He whistled when he saw the signatures. "I didn't know you ran in such exclusive circles."

"I don't. My boss does."

"What's in the briefcase?"

Schindler unlocked his handcuff, opened the case, then handed it to Degenbach.

"Hold the light," the Standartenführer ordered, and then one Scharführer held a flashlight while another flipped through the pages of formulae for him. He looked dismayed. "Do you understand this stuff, Heinz?"

Schindler laughed heartily, partially due to the release of pent-up tension and partially because it was funny. "No, I'm just the errand boy."

Degenbach laughed too, and nodded to the Scharführer, who stuffed the papers back into the case.

"Let them on the train," he ordered Schneider.

"But, Herr Standartenführer—"

Degenbach cut him off with a look. "See you after the war, Heinz."

"Be careful, Franz."

"Who, me?"

"But . . ." Schneider protested.

"How much did you get, Schneider?"

"Nothing, Herr Standartenführer, honestly."

They didn't hear the rest of the conversation. The SS guards gave them back their weapons and they boarded the train. It was pitch-black inside, and they couldn't move around without bumping into people. The train lurched and eventually began to move.

"Are the blackout shades in place?" someone asked.

"Yes."

The lights went on and Schindler, Lise, and Weiss were dazzled. People were sitting and standing around with hampers of food and bottles of champagne. As soon as the lights went on the bottles were opened and the food was passed around.

"This is most bizarre thing I've ever seen," Lise whispered.

Schindler shrugged. "I know. The country is in ruins and the Russians are about to capture Berlin and these people are eating, drinking, and laughing as if it were the Party Congress in 1936."

"I know they're all crazy," she whispered, "but would it hurt if we got something to eat?"

"No, I guess not."

They passed around some of the canned food they had and ate sandwiches, drank champagne, and finally slept sitting in the aisle. All along the line, passengers got off to make their way to some place they though might be safe. Schindler, Lise, and Weiss left the train before Hanover and made their way north to Celle, where Lise's parents were. Shortly after they arrived, Schindler and Weiss burned the papers in the briefcase, as well as their uniforms. Schindler and Lise watched the flames.

"What kind of world do you think it will be without Hitler and his Nazis?" he asked.

"I don't know," Lise replied. "But it has to be better without places like Auschwitz and Belsen."

Schindler nodded but didn't look at her. He continued staring into the flames.

"You're thinking about LOKI, aren't you?" she asked. She secretly wished she could make him forget everything that had occurred in his life until now. Lise put a comforting hand on his arm. "If Lamm is dead and LOKI destroyed, we don't have anything to worry about."

This time he turned to look at her. "LOKI is not the problem. Bombs like it are. Levinsky said that LOKI was only the beginning."

"Do you think he was right?"

"Yes, but no one should have the right to have that kind of power. No one."

Lise squeezed his hand. "Let's go inside."

The High Command Building, Berlin
Late April 1945

Von Rittburg stared at the thick folder before him. On the cover he had scrawled "The Loki File." It was an appropriate name. He had thought of destroying it by burning it in the fireplace as soon as Schindler and Weiss had gone, but he couldn't bring himself to do it. Someone had to know the truth. Who would find it? Outside, the Russians were grinding what was left of Berlin into dust. For the last time he opened the false bottom of the drawer and slipped the file into it. As soon as the drawer was closed he heard the boots on the staircase. So, they had finally gotten around to it. Von Rittburg drained the last of the whiskey from his glass, put on his overcoat and walked over to the fireplace. Looking around the room he still did not understand how he could so hate and so love the same thing at the same time.

The boots reached the top of the stairs and came down the hall. From the sound there were three of them. A Gestapo agent in a brown leather overcoat and two SS men in their black uniforms and helmets strode into the room. They looked very neat to be living in a city as full of dust and rubble as Berlin.

"Major Hans Meiler Freiherr von Rittburg?" the Gestapo agent asked.

"Yes?"

"I arrest you in the name of the Führer."

"Oh? On what charge?"

"High treason," the man said, pulling a paper from his pocket. "You are charged with consorting with the criminal Canaris and being involved in the attempt to assassinate the Führer on the twentieth of July, 1944."

"Is that all?" von Rittburg asked.

"This is no laughing matter, Herr Major," the man said sternly. "You will come with us."

"I don't think so," von Rittburg replied.

The Gestapo man's mouth opened in surprise. In his entire career no one had ever refused an order from him. He stood frozen in that position as the Major lifted the machine pistol from beneath his coat and pulled the trigger. The three men jerked in the hail of the bullets and fell to the floor. The Gestapo man lay on his back staring at the ceiling with the surprised expression still on his face. Major von Rittburg put on his hat, fixed his monocle, and picked up the two Panzerfaust anti-tank rockets leaning in the corner. Putting them over his shoulder, he walked to the door, pausing to look at the three dead Nazis.

"I hope you will excuse me for being rude," he said. "But I have a previous engagement with some Russian gentlemen." Von Rittburg stepped over their bodies and walked down the hall.

Here is an excerpt from

The Loki File

By Benjamin King

The intrigue and action surrounding Germany's development of atomic weapons begun in *The Loki Project* will continue in his forthcoming novel, *The Loki File*.

IT WAS EMIL JÜRGEN'S TURN TO WATCH the Americans and Norwegians at the old Vikmo coal mine. The young terrorist couldn't see much at this distance, even with powerful Russian binoculars. Suddenly he was aware of sounds coming across the snow, and he turned while he focused the field glasses. Snowmobiles. They were coming closer. Quickly, he ducked below the ridge and slid down to his companions. "Troops," he said in a whisper. "They're headed this way."

Susan Rollins remained silent, and Craig Filmore, the team leader, reached out his hand for Jürgen's binoculars. Stealthily, the tall American moved up to the ridge and focused the glasses. The troops on snowmobiles were headed their way all right. Then his eye caught something around the big pneumatic shelters standing above the snow. *Body bags! They must hold the bodies of the Germans killed at Vikmo. The Loki File was right. There was a bomb project here, and somewhere in Germany was LOKI, a functional atomic bomb.* Excited, he slid down the ridge.

"Let's go, quickly. Leave everything."

The three terrorists donned their skis and left the ridge in a hurry. Their rendezvous with the light plane was hours away. Buying time, Filmore led them into the thick scrub. Kicking off their skis, they used jackets to obscure their tracks and then lay down in deep snow among the scrub.

The patrol radioed Martin Grove and Colonel Nielsen. "We found the campsite."

"Stay there and touch nothing," ordered the Norwegian officer.

"Definitely not campers," Nielsen observed.

"How do you know?"

"These people left in a hurry and abandoned their equipment. Campers wouldn't do that."

Grove climbed to the top of the ridge. "They had a complete view of us."

"They couldn't have learned much."

Grove raised his binoculars to his eyes. "No!"

"What's wrong?" Nielsen asked.

"They saw the body bags. They must know LOKI is real."

Quietly, the three terrorists hunched deeper as the sound of the snowmobiles grew closer. Filmore motioned for attention. "Our only chance to make the plane is to capture a couple of snowmobiles," he whispered. "The troops approached in threes. We take them by surprise and get all three machines. Okay?"

The others nodded in agreement.

"Keep your heads down and let them pass," Filmore said very softly, "then fire high. We don't want to damage the machines. Wait for my signal."

They watched wordlessly as three Norwegian soldiers moved slowly by on their machines. Silently, Filmore indicated which terrorist was to attack which driver and then shouted, "Now!"

The three rose, spraying the area with bullets. One of the snowmobiles went over, its driver sprawling in the snow. The second slowed, then moved on a little way and stopped, its driver slumping over the handlebars. The third sped off, leaving a trail of blood in the snow. Rollins cursed and fired again.

"Forget it," Filmore ordered. "He won't get far the way he's bleeding. The shots have already warned the others. Let's get out of here."

While Filmore and Jürgen righted the snowmobile that had tipped over, Rollins found the driver of the second machine alive. Grinning, she cut his throat.

"I'll drive one. Susan, you drive the other while Emil rides shotgun." Filmore checked his compass bearing. "Let's go!"

The two machines sputtered, then roared to life, and the three sped off in the direction of their rendezvous with Hamsen's plane. *Yes,* Filmore thought, *we're in the clear.* Then he saw the ski patrol directly across their path.

"Bull your way through," Filmore shouted, unslinging his assault rifle.

The soldiers, caught by surprise, turned, and one went down immediately as Filmore began shooting. They dove to one side as Filmore's snowmobile sped past them, with Rollins close behind. Rollins felt Jürgen jerk, and then his arms left her waist. She gunned the snowmobile as he fell off. With bullets kicking up the snow and buzzing around her head, she didn't turn around.

Of the five-man ski patrol, one was killed and another wounded. While one of the uninjured soldiers gave his wounded comrade first aid, the other two cautiously approached the fallen terrorist. Carefully, one soldier held his rifle at the ready, while the other kicked him over. Jürgen groaned.

"Hey, he's alive. Call the colonel."

Grove and Nielsen were angry at the escape of the two terrorists, but the capture of a live one was a rare piece of luck.

"Maybe now we'll find out whom we're up against," Grove said grimly.